# The Secret of Hades' Eden

## by

## Graham J Thomson

This novel is a work of fiction. All characters, names, organisations, events and places are conjured from the author's imagination and any resemblance to real persons, living or dead, actual events, or organisations is purely coincidental.

-1101101010111011-

Graham J Thomson was brought up in the picturesque Scottish coastal town of Kirkcudbright – known as The Artists' Town. After reading Genetics at the University of Glasgow he joined the British Army and served in the Intelligence Corps. Since leaving military service he has worked in international corporate crime investigations and information security. He lives with his wife near Cambridge.

For Annabel and Libby, for their love and the memories that make it all worthwhile.

And for Margaret, who will never be forgotten.

"See how the god hurls his bolts at the greatest houses and the tallest trees. For he is wont to thwart whatever is greater than the rest."
Herodotus of Halicarnassus, 484-425 BC.

# Monday

*Hemera Selenes* 'day of the moon'

# Chapter 1

*0627hrs – Glenancross, Scottish Highlands*

A NEW DAY began on a remote highland beach in the far northwest coast of Scotland. The pale orange glow of the dawn sun pushed away the darkness of the dying night as it rose slowly over a damp green hillside. Morning dew sparkled in the short grass, a thin layer of mist hovered just above the ground. Down the hill and over the beach, the fresh sunlight spilled out onto the calm sea that stretched all the way to the horizon, while seawater lapped calmly at the shore's edge.

A light onshore wind blew gently up the beach, over the rocks and onto the narrow country road where several sombre men dressed all in black waited impatiently by their vehicles. They fidgeted and shuffled to keep warm, it had been a long wait. One of them, a colossal hulk of a man with a shaved head, scanned the horizon with a large set of binoculars.

Further down the beach two men stood side by side, arms folded, and stared out to sea. Cold salty air filled their nostrils with a heavy scent of the ocean.

'They're late,' one said to the other in a broad Scottish accent.

'Don't worry, they will be here,' was the stern reply. The man's voice was deep, the accent Russian. 'Just be sure your men are ready. And stick to the plan, whatever happens.'

'I don't like this,' the first man added. He blew into his hands and rubbed them together vigorously. 'It's too light. We can be seen for miles around. And this terrain carries sound for a great distance.'

'Then shut up,' barked the Russian. Impatiently he checked his phone; there were no messages. 'Come on. Idiots.'

The man with the binoculars waved frantically down to the two men on the beach. The Russian narrowed his eyes and nodded to him. The rest of the men reacted to the silent order immediately. They scurried away and took up their positions.

Slowly, from the distance the vessel approached. The jug-jug of its engine grew louder as it neared, breaking the calmness of the morning. It was a mid-sized fishing boat painted blue and white. Lines of red-brown rust ran down its sides from the gunwales all the way to the water's edge like tears of blood. Up on the bow was the silhouette of a man. He stood motionless, like a hunter stalking his quarry, and carefully scanned the coastline through binoculars.

When the vessel was only a few hundred metres from the shore the man on the bow adjusted his skipper's cap and made his move. He raised both his arms out and held the position for a few seconds. Back on the beach the Russian in response raised his arms out in a similar fashion, but then moved them up over his head and down again. He repeated this movement twice. Seeing the corresponding response the skipper disappeared into the cabin.

Moments later the low rumble of the engine stopped with a grunt. Once again there was only the eerie sound of waves breaking on the sand and rocks.

The skipper reappeared, another dark figure joined him and they walked to the bow. The skipper threw an anchor overboard, while his first mate threw a rope ladder over. Together they lowered a small rubber dinghy into the sea and one by one climbed down into it. They rowed around to the stern of the vessel where the skipper precariously leant over the edge and untied a rope that was hidden somewhere below the water line. With the end of the rope secured, they turned and rowed towards the shore.

Once they had beached, the sailors jumped out. The skipper walked up the beach with the sodden rope dragging behind him, while the first mate pulled the dinghy up onto the sand. As he approached the skipper grinned and held out his arms to the side.

'Your delivery is here,' said the skipper. Jamaican in appearance and accent, he smiled widely as he spoke. His gold encrusted teeth sparkled in the sunlight.

The Scottish man took the wet rope without a word and dragged it further up the beach to a green Range Rover. He bent down and attached it to the winch at the rear of the vehicle. Another of the men then jumped into the driver's seat and started the engine. The winch turned and began to reel the rope in. At first it groaned and struggled with the weight. The vehicle was pulled a few inches down the beach until its wheels dug into the moist sand and held firm. Slowly two large black streamlined objects emerged from the sea. At the same time two other Range Rovers each fitted with a trailer were reversed down the beach.

As the objects were pulled further out of the sea they began to resemble mini submarines. Once they had been dragged a few metres up onto the sand, the rest of the team set about securing them onto the trailers.

'Is it all in there?' the Russian asked the skipper.

'Yeah-man. Six tonnes of pure white,' he said, still grinning. 'Now where is my . . .' he held his hand out and rubbed his fingers, '. . . money?'

The Russian turned and nodded for the skipper to follow him. They walked up the beach and on to the road where there was a black BMW parked. The Russian opened the back door and leaned into the seat. The rest of the men stopped their work momentarily and turned to watch. Taking a few seconds to rummage around, the Russian then took hold of something, withdrew and turned to face the skipper.

The skipper's eyes widened in confusion as they focussed on the short black silenced MP5 submachine gun that was held firmly in the Russian's hands. Before the skipper's brain had time to tell his legs to run like hell, the Russian fired from the hip. Almost soundlessly a quick burst of three rounds penetrated him in the chest at point blank range.

Falling instantly to the ground he looked up, his mouth soundlessly opened and closed as he crumpled onto the sand. Callously, the Russian aimed the muzzle at the man's head and pulled the trigger once more. A single silenced shot was sneezed out. The skipper's life expired where he lay.

Seeing his skipper fall, the first mate staggered backwards, turned, and ran back towards the dinghy by the shore edge. In his rush his petrified legs failed him and he tripped and fell. Quickly, he picked himself up and ran at speed towards the sea.

The Russian calmly took aim and fired off several short bursts. Despite the distance most of the shots found their target. The first mate was thrown forward onto the shoreline by the force of the rounds that perforated his back. Struggling to hold on to his life he crawled away with all his might. Sand and water exploded around him as more rounds rained down. His struggle ended abruptly when a round rammed into his spine. Waves broke over his lifeless body; the water pulled at it trying to claim it for the sea.

The show over, the men went back to work. The Russian congratulated them for a job well done.

'Get the goods to the plant exactly as planned,' he said. 'You have one hour. Drive carefully. We cannot risk a crash now. Remember, your reward awaits you at the island.'

When the men had driven off with the cocaine covered and secured, the Russian took out his phone and called his boss to update him on the good news.

'It rose in the east,' he said and waited for the reply to his code-phrase. 'Yes, boss, they were there just as you said. We were successful . . . It is on its way now . . . Yes, of course, there are no witnesses . . . Thank you boss, that is very generous.'

He hung up, pocketed the phone, and sat back settling into the warmed leather seat. He ran his thick fingers through his short blond hair, rubbed his scarred face, and slowly breathed out. The huge weight that he had carried for months had now lifted. The plan had worked, as he knew it would – his KGB covert operations training had never failed him, skills for life. The difficult part of the mission was over. It was only a matter of time now. The rest of the plan would fall neatly into place. It was all downhill from here.

He smiled to himself. The world wouldn't know what had hit it.

# Chapter 2

*1918hrs – Cambridge*
SITTING IN FRONT of a computer screen in the Cambridge University Library, Ella Moore stared out of the small leaded window lost in her thoughts. Scattered across the old scarred wooden desk in front of her were several books on Egyptology, astronomy, and ancient Greek mythology. She held one open, its spine rested on her lap. She hadn't read more than a page of it before drifting off. She stared into space lost in her thoughts and daydreams. She twirled her long auburn hair in her fingers.

Ella found the sanctuary of the library peaceful and comforting. Quiet and hidden away, she could lose herself in her books, and reflect on her studies. And, it being summer, there were few other students around to bother her. She had the place almost to herself most evenings.

The University Library, or the UL as it was known, was one of the great libraries of the world. Its vast, and often rare, collections boasted everything from a three-thousand year old text written on bone, to a colossal electronic archive of the world's literature. Over the centuries its labyrinth of one-hundred miles of shelves had hoarded a countless number of books including some dangerous and controversial works. Like the Codex Bezae Cantabrigiensis, one of the earliest copies of the original four Gospels. When it was first given to the library in 1581 it had to be concealed from the religious zealots who sought its destruction. Its Greek and Latin text differed significantly from the official version of events, and as such it was considered dangerous and heretical. It was an old story, the suppression of knowledge, and one very familiar to Ella. Learning about, and uncovering, historical secrets was a personal obsession of hers.

Ella had gained a first in History and had gone on, despite her mother's protestations, to do a post graduate degree at the university in Egyptology. Ever since she could remember she had been fascinated by the pyramids of Giza. She found them truly amazing; there was something almost magical about them, their sheer size, their mystery, the secrets they held that were yet to be discovered. She was thinking of them again now, dreaming, wondering what purpose they really served, fantasising about the—

From nowhere a large black hand landed firmly on her shoulder and gripped her tightly. Ella gasped and almost jumped out of her seat. Her book fell to the floor. Her head snapped around and her wide eyes set on the culprit. Quickly recognising the man's face, she let out a nervous laugh and elbowed her friend lightly in the stomach.

'You frightened me!' she scolded, sitting up.

'Ow. That hurt,' the man said from above her. His voice was deep with a mild east London accent. 'Thought I'd find you here. Don't you have a life to be getting on with? No, of course not, I forgot, you need to find one first.' The young man who beamed down at her had a huge smile that was infectious; the gaps between his teeth seemed to enhance the effect. His closely shaved head sat on a thick neck, under his jumper his torso bulged with toned muscles, the result of years of rigorous rugby training.

Ella had known Darren Winters ever since freshers' week when they had first arrived at Cambridge. He was a bright guy from an underprivileged background and who, like Ella, had won a scholarship to the university. Darren's chosen subject was the History of Art. Cambridge had been an ideal place to study this craft. His department was located in a row of historic buildings on Trumpington Street, close to the architecturally impressive Fitzwilliam Museum. The art museum held one of the finest collections in the world, from ancient Egyptian to modern masterpieces. It also boasted a modern laboratory where paintings were carefully analysed with state-of-the-art tools and techniques and works were professionally restored by the students, even after decades of shameless neglect.

'What are you after?' she asked, smiling up at his kind face.

Darren noticed that her smile was somewhat strained. 'I'm after you,' he said. 'Everything okay? You look pensive.'

As beautiful as she was bright, Darren despaired of her for wasting her God-given talents. Despite being at the top of her classes, Ella lacked both motivation and confidence. She was a dreamer. He knew it, and she knew it too. Modest and shy, she never flaunted her looks, nor showed off her figure. She dressed plainly and wore little in the way of make-up. Only once since Darren had known her had she gone all out on dressing up. It was for one the May Balls, he recalled. She had rented a revealing silky black ball gown, had a friend do her makeup, and her hair was professionally styled. Her friends barely recognised her, and Darren, her platonic date, didn't know where to look.

Ella picked up her book from the floor and placed it on the desk. She paused in thought for a moment, and then said, 'I called the lawyer's office. They said I need to go and see them as soon as possible. It's about my dad.'

'Sorry to hear about that. I know you weren't close, but still, it must be hard,' Darren said sympathetically.

She made it no secret that her father had walked out many years ago – or abandoned them, as her mother regularly described it – and had never stayed in touch. Ella remembered little about the man and had learned virtually nothing about him since his departure. Only that he was selfish and penniless to boot. At least that was she was told whenever she asked. But, despite her intrigue, she believed what she had been told; there was no evidence to the contrary. He never sent her as much as a birthday card and had shown no interest in her upbringing. It had been a struggle for her mother, Ella knew, but they had managed somehow despite the hardship. She had long ago stopped worrying about her father. She had written him off convinced he would never play a part in her life.

But that had all changed now.

A few days previously, on a dull, wet evening, a police officer turned up at her flat unannounced. On opening the door Ella saw that he had the demeanour of someone bearing bad news. When he took his hat off, Ella went weak at the knees and panicked thinking something had happened to her mother. But the policeman calmly explained that a man had been killed by a burglar. The victim had no wife, no family, he lived alone. The police found that Ella was registered on his passport as next of kin. The victim was her father. The policeman gave her the details of the law firm that were dealing with his estate. Much to her surprise her father had left a will. Ella was his one and only heir.

'It's just so weird,' she said. 'Don't you think?'

'Why? He left a will, nothing weird about that.'

'Well, for one thing the lawyer's office is here in Cambridge. I often wondered where my father was, but it sent a shiver up my spine to think that he could have been so close to me all of this time.' She couldn't help thinking what an odd twist of fate it was. 'We might have passed each other in the street, or eaten in the same restaurant.'

'Maybe he's been secretly watching you,' Darren teased.

Ella didn't see the funny side. 'They want me to drop in to see them tomorrow. They said it's urgent.'

Darren changed his tact to try to cheer her. 'I'll bet he's left his secret millions to you. Lend me a tenner?' He laughed a deep, hearty chuckle.

'Yeah, as if that kind of thing would happen to me,' she sneered back. She looked down and went quiet for a moment.

'You know you can talk about it if you want to. He was your dad after all,' Darren said breaking the silence.

'He was a selfish idiot,' she snapped, her eyes wide. 'Sorry. You didn't deserve that.' She reached for Darren's hand and squeezed it gently.

Darren winked at her: forgiven.

'It's just that I never knew him, I can't even remember him. Really, he meant nothing to me.' Ella believed what she said, but there was a sad tone to her voice that betrayed her.

'Come on, let's go get a drink. It's happy hour at the White Horse.'

Ella collected her books together. She was about to get up when Darren noticed something on the computer monitor.

'Is that marker pen on the screen?' he quizzed. 'What the hell have you been doing?'

'It'll wipe off,' she said guiltily. 'I was just doing something for my thesis.' As part of her PhD she was writing an exploratory piece on an alternative history of the pyramids and the Sphinx. It wasn't the first time she had gone against the grain of academia. It pleased her to challenge the established theories.

'What's it about, graffiti?'

'No.' She paused and pondered whether to explain further. She looked up into his inquisitive eyes which gleamed in the low light. She sighed and shook her head. 'It's the position of the pyramids. I was matching them up with the stars in a constellation. I just wanted to check something, silly really. Come on, let's go.'

'Hold on a second. You've never mentioned that one before. Is this some new conspiracy theory of yours?'

Ella brightened up and enthusiastically said, 'No, it's fairly old. But it's amazing. The three pyramids of Giza map exactly onto three stars on Orion's belt.'

'Really? I gotta see this one.'

'Okay, watch.' The worries of her day were momentarily forgotten. On the computer Ella opened a planetarium program that showed the night sky with the names of the constellations. She spun the sky around to the correct position and angle, and then zoomed in on Orion's Belt.

'These stars are called Alnitak, Alnilam and Mintaka,' she explained. Then she aligned the star map so that the three stars fitted onto the three black dots she had drawn on the monitor with the marker pen. 'Okay, so that shows the relative positions of the three stars of Orion's Belt,' she went on. 'Now watch this. I'll arrange the map of the pyramids in the same way.' Using Google Earth she zoomed in on the satellite map of Giza, it was like dive-bombing onto it from space at a dizzying speed. Once fully zoomed in the diamond shapes of the three pyramids were clearly visible against the sandy desert. Again, she spun the image around until the three pyramids were at the correct angle and lined up their peaks onto the three black dots on the monitor.

'See. They fit,' Ella said pointing to the screen. The three dots were aligned diagonally with one deviating offside slightly to the left. 'The relative positions of the stars and pyramids match each other almost perfectly.'

'But there must be billions of stars to choose from. Surely there's a high chance that three stars somewhere in the sky just happen to match up like this?' Darren challenged. 'It's just coincidence, surely.'

Ella took the bait as Darren knew she would. Her ears and lower neck reddened, her voice rose as she replied. 'There's more to it than that.' But she quickly caught herself, and her eyes narrowed. She knew her rage only seemed to fuel Darren's enjoyment. 'The relative brightness of the stars and the size of the pyramids also match up. The offset star at the top of the three, Mintaka, is the least bright one. Corresponding with this, the offset pyramid, which is called the Pyramid of Menkaure, is the smallest of the three pyramids.'

Darren frowned and leaned into the screen. 'I want to believe you, but I'm just not convinced, babes.'

'Well, let's zoom out a little on both the satellite image of Giza and the constellation map.' She switched back and forth between the two programs showing the night sky and the surface of the Earth and waited to see if Darren could figure it out for himself.

Dutifully, he studied each image. 'I don't see anything,' he complained after a few seconds.

'Look, see the river Nile?' She pointed to the features on the screen. 'And here, in the sky, is the Milky Way. Well, they too are in similar positions relative to Orion and the pyramids. Watch. . .' To the left of the constellation Orion was the Milky Way, a long pale cloud-like line that was made up of more than a hundred-billion stars – our spiral Galaxy as seen side on from Earth. Ella switched to the zoomed-out satellite image of Giza and ran her finger along the river Nile. 'See how the river runs in a long line to the left of the pyramids at precisely the same angle as the Milky Way was to Orion?'

Darren raised his eyebrows and whistled.

'And you'd never guess what the Egyptians called the Milky Way.'

He shrugged his broad shoulders.

'The Nile of Heaven.'

'Can we have that drink now? My brain hurts.'

'Nearly done. Now, here's the really freaky part of the story.'

'Oh, this is the freaky bit is it? I was wondering when we'd get to that bit. Great.'

Ella ignored his sarcasm and clicked back to the constellation chart. She navigated to the settings and set the program to show the shapes as well as the names of the constellations. 'See the constellation that's slightly further over from Orion?' she said. 'That's Leo.'

'Leo the Lion?' Darren could just make out its lion like form in the stars.

'Yes, exactly. Now look at the angle from the three stars of Orion's Belt to Leo.'

Darren did as instructed.

'Now watch this.'

Ella drew a line on the monitor with the marker pen from Orion's Belt, past the misty line of the Milky Way, through Cancer, to Leo. Then she flicked over to the satellite image of the pyramids and lined them up with the three dots once more.

'What am I looking for now?' Darren leaned into the monitor, genuinely fascinated now.

'The Sphinx.' Ella pointed to the rectangular object on the screen. 'See it? See which way it's facing?'

'East, it faces east. Isn't that to watch the sunrise? Wait, it's also in line with your line.' Darren paused a moment to think. 'The Sphinx is looking towards Leo!'

'Yes. The Sphinx, which is clearly a statue of a Lion – King Cheops chiselled over the original Lion's face – is looking in the direction of the constellation Leo.'

'I still don't get the significance,' he conceded, frowning. 'So what, the Sphinx points to Leo. Okay, it's a Lion and not whatever they said it was. Big deal.'

'Big deal! Here's the big deal, Darren. When the stars and constellations rise over the Sphinx tonight it won't be Leo that the Sphinx looks towards. The Sphinx doesn't look towards Leo, not any more anyway.' She smiled at Darren with that I-know-something-you-don't look.

Darren looked into her bright eyes, he thought she looked beautiful.

He felt his pulse rise as he lost himself in her wide gaze. 'Come on then Ella, tell me the big secret.'

'Stellar precession.'

'Come again?'

'The stars aren't fixed. Well, I mean their position when they move over the Earth isn't fixed, they shift very, very slowly.'

Darren frowned.

Ella shook her head. 'The Earth spins on its axis every twenty-four hours and we get day and night, yes? And the axis is at an angle to the sun, that's why we get the seasons?'

'I think I learned that in primary school. So what's new?'

'What they probably didn't tell you at school was that the Earth's spin wobbles too, a bit like a spinning top. The end result is that the sky, the stars, the sun and the moon appear to shift position over time. We'd never notice the difference in our lifetime, they only move about one degree every seventy-odd years, but over tens of thousands of years the change is dramatic. Where the sun now sets over a particular hill, will, in thousands of year's time, set over a different place. Then, eventually, it will come back to set over the original hill again.'

'So how long does each wobble take?'

'A full cycle is around 26,000 years.'

Darren whistled.

'So, what is the obvious question?'

'Let me think.' He put his hand to his chin and stroked it theatrically. Then he raised his finger in the air and asked, 'When was Leo last in the right place for the Sphinx to be looking right at it?'

'Well done, *that* is the right question.'

'Come on then, put me out my misery. When was it?'

'About 10,000 years BC.'

'Whoa! Hold on lady,' Darren roared. 'That's just after the last ice age. Weren't we just a bunch of cavemen then?'

'No,' she laughed. 'We were anatomically no different back then than we are now, same brain size, same physical look. If you transported a baby from back then to now you wouldn't know the difference when she grew up. She'd have every chance in life as any of us would.'

Darren raised his eyebrows, Ella mistook it for disbelief.

'There's a lot of evidence that there were advanced civilisations around then. A Greek scientist called Herodotus visited Egypt around 500 BC and recorded that the locals claimed to have been there for 341 generations. That works out at 9,000 years before his time and over 11,000 years before ours. He also recorded that the locals said

11

that the sun once set where it now rose. It didn't make any sense to Herodotus, but we know now that it was because of precession. The Earth's little wobble.'

'All right, so maybe it's true. But what does it mean? We've been lied to about the age of the pyramids? Does it matter?'

'I don't know what it means,' she conceded quietly. 'But it does matter, the truth matters. I just don't think that the pyramids are simply tombs. It's never made any sense to me that they were built just to put a few dead kings in; most of the Pharaohs were buried in the Valley of the Kings in any case. I think that whoever built the pyramids wanted to tell the world something, not just about who they were, but *when* they were there too. It's important for some reason.'

'I don't want to rain on your parade, but there's strong evidence that the pyramids were indeed built in 2,500 BC.'

'True, but there's evidence that the Sphinx is significantly older than the pyramids.'

'So, someone built the Sphinx, and then much later they built the pyramids?'

'Possibly, but they all match up with Orion *together*. The site must have been built at the same time to some kind of plan. Maybe the pyramids were built on the site of something else, something that was built long ago by a forgotten civilisation. And then, thousands of years later, the Egyptians came along and built the pyramids over whatever was already there.'

'A restoration project?' Darren smiled cheekily.

'It's happened since then, many times over. The Roman Pantheon was originally a temple to all their pagan gods. Then, in 609 AD the Christians took it over after the Byzantine emperor Phocas gave it to the pope.'

'Okay, so an old site was taken over by later invaders. I can believe that. But why would the original builders have them in line with the stars? And who were they anyway?'

'I don't know. But it must mean something.' Ella paused for a moment and stared at the images on the screen. 'But why make a map of the stars on Earth? What are they telling us?'

They regarded the mysterious images. They weren't the first and would not be the last people to stare in wonder at the ancient structures.

'Come on,' Darren prompted. 'You're about to get in trouble.' He pointed towards to the drab librarian who was heading in their direction.

'That old bat.' Hurriedly, Ella wiped off the marker pen and gathered up her books. Together they left the tranquillity of the UL and exited onto the street.

'Come on. Let's get drunk,' Darren said.

'I'll meet you in the pub in thirty minutes. I need to drop these off at home.'

'Okay. See you later.'

'In this world or the next.' She waved and walked off down the street.

Darren gazed after her as she went.

# Chapter 3

*1957hrs – Vienna*

AGENT WILLIAM TEMPLE sat on the end of his double bed in the Hotel Ambassador, Vienna. The small but modern room seemed much bigger due to the long floor to ceiling mirrors on the doors of the cupboards by the side of the bed. In one corner a muted news channel silently flashed images of the latest disaster on the flat-screen TV. Above the drinks cabinet were three empty mini-bottles of whisky.

William stared down at the small black pistol he held in one hand. A generous glass of whisky – a decent blended malt, but not his usual brand – hung loosely in the other. He took another sip while the tears ran down his cheeks. Mindlessly, he tapped the end of the barrel on the rim of the glass while he stared at the floor. Held at a precarious angle, the yellow liquid threatened to spill onto the carpet.

He turned and caught his reflection in the mirror. Thirty years old, tall, well built and athletic, he was the type of confident handsome man that men envied and women desired. But at that moment all he saw, through watery eyes, was a sad lost soul, an empty shell of his former self, devoid of the lust for life that once raged like a fire through his highly trained body. Alone. Empty.

It would be so easy, he thought, just one bullet, one bullet was all it would take. One gentle squeeze of the trigger, a few pounds of pressure on cold metal, and all the pain would be gone forever. No more hate, no more guilt, no more regret. No more nightmares. The survivor guilt that overwhelmed him day and night would be vanquished forever.

But he knew it would be stupid, selfish and cowardly. He cursed at himself for even thinking about it. His strength of mind had weakened; his direction in life had been derailed. He had to get a grip of himself before he totally lost it. After all, there were new opportunities for him now, a new chance at life.

"A fresh start," was what his former commanding officer had said to him with a sickly, patronising smile. He had listened, like the good soldier he was, and had hid his anger well. What did they know of his suffering, his pain; nothing.

Without her he knew that life would never be the same again. He could still see her warm smile, her loving eyes; he could still feel the softness of her hair and smell the delicate sweet aroma that had radiated from her. It was impossible to believe that he would never again touch her soft skin, never share a moment of joy with her, never make love to her. And then there was the other one, the one that never was. Fate had stabbed him in the heart, and then twisted the blackened blade.

Clenching his eyes shut, he fought back the tears. His face tightened, his nostrils flared. He quickly stood up and threw the whisky glass away. The glass bounced on the floor, its contents exploded all over the carpet. He turned sharply to face himself in the mirror. In a swift, well versed move, he clasped the weapon with both hands and pointed it at his reflection. His aim was firm, his hold steady.

'You can do this,' he said through gritted teeth as he squinted down the barrel. Then he put the weapon to his temple, and pushed it hard against himself. Slowly, he squeezed the trigger. The hammer released and surged forward onto the pin.

Click.

'Life goes on regardless,' he said, recalling something his old CO had said to him. He sat back down on the bed. And then he cried. Head down, his whole body shook. He cried for her, he cried for himself, he mourned what was and what would never be. He knew that he would never love again.

Wiping the tears away, he calmed himself down and decided to clean his weapon. It would pass the time and would hopefully take his mind off things. The sleek weapon was a SIG-Sauer P230. Smaller and less powerful than the P229 that he was used to, it was all that the embassy had provided him with in their live drop earlier in the hotel lift. He had always felt that the small Walther PPK lookalike was something that should be kept in a ladies handbag. But there was some consolation; with a barrel length of only three-and-a-half inches it was ideal for concealment. For his current assignment, it would do the job nicely.

Poised on the end of the bed he stripped it, cleaned it and oiled it lightly to prevent jams. Once he had put it together he pushed eight nine-millimetre rounds into the tiny magazine. He then placed one further round in the breach ready for action. He gently slid the magazine into place with a click and secured the weapon in the concealed holster in the small of his back.

The ritual had settled his mind. He was ready to face the world, ready to do his job. A good soldier.

During his ten years as a Military Intelligence officer in the British Army, William had more than adequately demonstrated that he was talented in his craft, and had suitably impressed the right people. So when his military career had come to an abrupt, and unfortunate, end, his commanders, not wanting to see someone of William's calibre go to waste, recommended that he be recruited into a specialist operational arm of MI6 known as F-Branch.

This was his first mission.

F-Branch was a highly covert unit tasked with gathering intelligence from hostile groups suspected of posing a threat to national security. The hand-picked agents were usually former special forces personnel who had shown a flair for intelligence gathering, and were impeccably trustworthy. Also on the team were talented intelligence analysts seconded from MI5 and MI6 who specialised in covert research projects. Various technical specialists were recruited from the super-bright ranks of GCHQ: electronic engineers, mathematicians, computer programmers, hackers and the like.

Stood facing himself in the full length mirror, William clipped on his bow-tie and checked his appearance one final time. The black dinner jacket was not his normal attire, but, he conceded, in the area of Vienna he was in, black ties and ball gowns were a common sight.

'Come on. Let's do this,' he said. He looked himself in the eye for a moment. Then, to psych himself up he said, 'You can do it. Do it. Do it. Do it!'

His mission was simple, the usual set up for this sort of thing, and no different, in principle, from the work he'd done in the middle-east and other war zones around the world. He was to meet up with a new informant, build rapport, probe for information, although not too deep on this first occasion; he didn't want to scare him off. At some point during the meeting he would give the informant a small task to carry out before their next meeting. The task would be a minor one but, once done, would mean there was no going back. It was a kind of loyalty test, although some would call it entrapment.

Choosing to walk to the informant's choice of meeting location, William mulled over the details of the ops briefing he had had in London the day before. A call had been made to a UK whistle-blowing number. The caller claimed to have information on a terrorist group and said he would only talk to MI6, not to the police or any other security agency. Unwilling to give his name or any contact details, he simply stated that he had been approached by some people unknown to him who tried to coerce him into doing some work, work that involved a weapon of mass destruction. The call had been passed straight to the MI6 duty analyst and a meeting was promptly arranged. Wanting to make contact on neutral ground at a busy location, the informant insisted on the Viennese Opera House, the Wiener Staatsoper. He was an opera fan; no one would question his presence there. Confirmation of the seating arrangements were made using a coded posting in the *Times* personal column the following Friday, the codename *Asclepius* was used at the informant's insistence. William's seat was booked next to the informant in a cover name. After exchanging the code-phrases that had been agreed during the call, William was to conduct the debrief in the best way he saw fit.

A standard set up, simple.

'Any deviation from this plan,' William had heard the informant say during the recorded call, 'and I will have no choice but to disappear for good. The consequences will be so grave for all of us that it does not bear thinking about.'

Research by F-Branch technical specialists revealed that the call was made from a phone-box in Moscow. It was unlikely he was a local as the man's accent was English. Voice analysts assessed that it was his genuine accent, neither put on nor digitally altered, and a scan of the voice pattern on known terrorist suspects drew a blank. *Asclepius*, William was told, was the name of the ancient Greek god of medicine. He wondered if his informant was a doctor, or some sort of medical professional.

William reached his target in central Vienna in good time. From the road he looked up at the Wiener Staatsoper, it was an impressive building. It radiated with a golden yellow colour from the night-lights that were focused on its stone façade. William made his way to the busy main entrance and stood outside for a few minutes pretending to wait for someone. He checked his watch and phone occasionally to keep up the ruse. Groups of men in dinner jackets and women dressed in elegant ball gowns poured out of sleek executive taxis and polished chauffeur driven cars into the building. Passersby talked loudly and cheerily as they went, he heard a half-dozen different languages being spoken. Wealthy looking men went arm in arm with attractive younger women who were barely wearing their tiny designer dresses. Some of the girls regarded William with interest as they passed him. One, a tall slender blonde of eastern European appearance, held his steely gaze for a moment until she disappeared into the building.

William never forgot a face, a talent that had come in useful many times in his military career – twice it had probably saved his life. Despite being highly trained in both armed and unarmed combat, the best and first option was always to avoid it. A few people he recognised from the hotel had entered the building and two or three he recognised from the airport too. But he judged that there was nothing suspicious about any of them. It dawned on him that he had no idea what the informant looked like, he knew nothing of his age or race. He looked at his watch one final time and then walked into the main reception hall.

Seated in the upper slips, William was pleased to be close enough to the stage to see without requiring the world's most powerful binoculars. His chair was comfortable too. A glass of champagne was brought to him by an attractive waitress, a cheerful brunette who wore tight black leggings and a white blouse that hung loosely just below her tiny waist. William read her name tag and guessed that she was either Austrian or German. He thanked her in German; she smiled back but said nothing. William settled into his seat and sipped from his champagne flute.

The great hall was almost full, everyone was seated save for a few stragglers who bustled past all hot, flustered and embarrassed. But the seat to William's immediate right remained resolutely empty.

The lights dimmed, the audience settled down. The low rumble of two-thousand excited voices vanished as the orchestra began the composition with a low base that gained in volume to a dramatic crescendo. Huge curtains rose to reveal an elaborately dressed stage. Act 1 of *Don Giovanni* by Wolfgang Amadeus Mozart began with *The Garden of the Commendatore*. The seat to his right was still empty. He shook his head. What a waste of time, he thought.

Almost an hour into the performance, William was considering leaving when a balding, short, overweight man, sweating and out of breath, squeezed his way noisily along the row. He took his seat next to William.

William rolled his eyes. 'So much for a discreet entrance,' he said quietly under his breath.

'Sorry I'm late,' the man whispered to William. With a sausage like finger, he pushed his round glasses into place on his nose and settled himself into the seat.

William said nothing and looked straight ahead at the stage.

The fat man's head recoiled back and he cursed under his breath. He tilted his head to William. 'Is your mother here or is she still at home with Asclepius,' he said without even attempting to make the code-phrase sound like a question.

'Neither. She is in London with my niece,' was the whispered reply. 'Is everything okay?'

'Yes, just a bit late in getting ready,' the informant said with a sheepish smile. He wiped the sweat off his reddened, chubby cheeks and forehead with a crumpled white handkerchief.

From the corner of his eye, William regarded the little man. He suspected he was in his late fifties, married as he wore a thin gold wedding band, and, interestingly, he had a gold signet ring on his right pinky. His glasses were the little round type that reminded William of an overly camp university lecturer he once knew. His dinner jacket was old and ill fitting; the man was bursting out of it. The bow-tie looked like a real one and it sat loose around his wide, flabby neck – an ordinary looking person in every way, an academic most likely. He looked harmless.

'I'm William. Here's a contact number for you,' William whispered, 'it's manned permanently and untraceable. There's also a Web site on there, you can contact us from the site's feedback page or the instant messaging tool.' William knew that when he logged on to the site his computer would be scanned and bugged using techniques that would make a hacker weep with joy; but he thought it best not mention that. He handed over the plain white business card. 'Please make sure you contact us somehow when you return home, just to check in. Let us know you are safe. You did the right thing, you're with us now.' William offered his hand to the informant, who accepted it.

'I'm in grave danger, William. We all are. I have done something terrible, something unforgivable. But I'm here to make amends.' The informant shook his head; tears welled up in his beady little eyes. He dabbed at his face with the handkerchief.

'Don't worry. Help us and we'll help you,' William reassured him. He knocked back the remainder of his champagne. It was a good one, he thought, but not quite as good as the vintage bottle that he had acquired from a drugs baron in Colombia a couple of years previously. Nothing would ever beat the sweet taste of that one, he mused to himself. He looked around for the waitress and motioned for two glasses to be brought over.

'You didn't say your name,' William asked.

The informant hesitated for a moment. 'Can you really protect me, if I help you?'

'Of course we can. That's what we do.'

The informant sighed; he sat back in his chair, closed his eyes and breathed out slowly. 'My name is Professor John Barry,' he said after a long pause. There was no going back now, he knew. 'I'm Head of Viral Research, at the University of Strasbourg.'

Rapport building mission successful, thought William. 'Relax. You've done the right thing.'

Act 1 ended with a rapturous applause. The curtains lowered. When the lights came on, two-thousand excited voices erupted into a roar as if a switch on their voice boxes had been flicked on all at once.

'So, John, just what kind of trouble are you in?' William probed.

'It's a long story.'

'I'm in no hurry.'

The informant took out his handkerchief and cleaned his glasses. 'For the last twelve years I've been a leading figure in the gene mapping of various Level 4 viruses. Namely Ebola and Influenza strain H5N1, better known as Bird Flu. I also worked on a Level 2 virus, Human Immunodeficiency Virus – HIV as it is better known. The objective of my research was to sequence their entire genomes and identify the genes that made up each virus. Each gene was then analysed to see how it worked and what it did. My results were published online periodically so that the international virology community could conduct further research into cures and vaccines.'

'Sounds like rewarding work.'

'Yes, it was.' The professor drifted off in thought before getting back on track. 'Despite the challenges, I made significant headway and published several papers, all of which were widely praised.' He smiled as he recalled the successes, but the smile quickly faded. 'That's probably what got them interested in me in the first place. The papers I published.'

'Them? Who?'

'A man and a woman approached me one evening after an industry charity event that I was speaking at. They took me aside and asked me if I'd like to join a very private club of theirs. They said it would help me further my career, network, I'd have close contact with various people of influence in my field.' The informant held out his hand and pleaded with William. 'Look, I never knew what it was all about to begin with. If I had done, none of this would have happened. Anyway, it is of no concern now, too late for regrets. Once they had what they wanted on me, what they had clearly planned from the beginning, they blackmailed me into working for them.'

'Blackmail? What with?'

The professor smiled and shook his head. 'What makes the world go round William?' he asked.

'Money?'

The professor laughed. 'No, William. It's what makes every human tick, every animal, every living thing on the planet. You know what I mean.'

With a wry smile, William nodded his understanding.

'What's important,' the professor continued, 'is what I found out about these people much later on.' He looked around suspiciously, and then shifted in his seat to face William. He leaned in close to William's ear and spoke quietly.

'It is an organisation . . . no, they are more like a secret society. One so old and so powerful it defies belief. They have people in very high places all around the world. Governments, intelligence agencies, you name it.' The professor sat back and studied William's face for a reaction.

William looked into his eyes, the windows to the soul.

'I'm not paranoid, if that's what you think,' the professor said defensively. 'I have substantial proof.'

Their conversation was interrupted when a slender and elegant woman of East Asian appearance, Chinese perhaps, brought over their champagne flutes on a silver tray. She bent down and smiled as she served them showing a row of perfect white teeth. William looked for her name badge, but didn't find one. He thanked her in English and took the drinks from the tray.

'Thank you, William. Boy do I need this,' the professor said. He guzzled half of the glass in one. He sighed and reached into his jacket pocket. He pulled out an opera programme and placed it on the arm of William's seat.

'Perhaps the gods will see to forgive me.' He tapped the programme. 'This is my salvation. Take it back with you, inside is a micro memory card. Give it to your defence laboratories. I knew some of the scientists there a few years ago. They'll know what to do with it. But they must act quickly. *You* must act quickly too. Time is of the essence.'

'Why?'

The professor once again looked over his shoulder. He leaned into William and whispered. 'You don't have long, a week maybe, possibly only days.'

Flicking to the centre pages of the programme, William saw a tiny black memory chip taped to the middle of the page. It was so small that it was barely noticeable.

'Impressive, well done,' he said sliding the guide into his own inside jacket pocket.

The professor coughed hoarsely into his hand a few times. He downed the rest of his champagne to clear his throat. 'The files are protected. To open them you need . . .' Another wheezy cough. '. . . the password which is the name of this . . .' The professor wheezed, his face reddened. He struggled to take a breath. 'This . . .' He tried to speak again, but his voice was a mere hiss.

William frowned and grabbed the man's shoulder. 'Professor? *Professor?*'

But there was no answer; he appeared to have fallen asleep – with his eyes and mouth wide open. White bubbles of champagne and saliva dribbled out from his mouth over his fat chins and onto his shirt.

Crowds of people started to return to their seats, Act 2 was about to begin.

'*Professor,*' William prompted one final time. He shook the man's arm. The champagne flute slipped through his fingers and rolled onto the floor where it smashed. He clasped the man's wrist. There was no pulse.

William sat back and tried to remain cool as the theatre lights dimmed. He wondered if the champagne had been poisoned. He picked up his own glass from the floor and was thankful he hadn't drunk any of it. Whoever was watching the professor would likely be watching him. Calmly, he looked around the seating area. Most people had returned to their places. The waitresses were stood by the doors chatting, but he noted that the Chinese girl was nowhere to be seen.

Time to leave, he thought.

As the curtains opened for Act 2, William calmly slid out of his chair and, still holding his full champagne glass, headed for the nearest exit. Swiftly making his way down the marble stairs and through the reception hall, he hastily left the Wiener Staatsoper and walked into the night.

\*

After pouring most of the contents of the champagne glass out onto the pavement, William pushed his handkerchief down the flute to soak up the remaining liquid. He hid the glass away carefully in his inside jacket pocket; a gift for the forensics team back in London.

Headed for his hotel, William took a circuitous route. After a few hundred metres he stopped and looked innocently into a jeweller's shop that had large, conveniently reflective windows. With a quick glance up the street he memorised who was walking behind him. He noted their hair, their type of clothes, and particularly their shoes. Shoes were often overlooked by amateurs following a target – while the untrained follower might change their wig, hat, or jacket, their shoes usually went forgotten.

He continued up the road to the next junction and turned the corner. Abruptly, he about-turned and walked back the same way he came. Again, he kept a sharp look out for anyone behaving oddly on the street, and for anyone he recognised from earlier.

It all looked clear.

After repeating this manoeuvre several times, he felt that the road was clear of any unwanted attention. He was just about to take a shortcut back to the hotel, when . . .

Someone coughed from close behind him. It was a dry cough with a distinct sound to it and was immediately followed by a loud sniff. Immediately it grabbed his attention, he was sure he had heard it before, and very recently. Or was that just his imagination? He feared the pressure of the day was playing tricks with his mind.

On the main road there was a gap in the traffic, he turned sharply and crossed over the road. While looking out for the traffic as he crossed, he used the opportunity to look behind him down the street he had come from. A red haired woman and a short fat man in a grey suit walked arm in arm, a young man in blue jeans stood outside a shop smoking, a group of youths staggered along pushing each other and laughing.

Nothing out of place.

At the next crossroads he turned the corner and waited with his back to the wall. He cursed that he no longer smoked, it made anti-surveillance look so much more natural. Turning around, he walked back up the street he had come from, all the while carefully observing every pedestrian he passed.

It came to him in a flash; he'd figured out where he'd heard the distinctive cough before. It was in the queue for his seat on the upper floor at the Wiener Staatsoper. It belonged to a man who must have been seated somewhere behind him, but he couldn't picture his face. Maybe he'd also had enough of the opera and was going back to the same hotel. Coincidence? Probably not, he feared.

Chancing a quick glimpse behind, he looked around . . .

As quick as a thought, the blow to the back of his neck came from nowhere and sent William stumbling forward in a daze. Before he could steady himself a pair of gloved hands grabbed him by his jacket and pulled him with frightening strength into a back alley.

A quick and hard punch to William's solar plexus forced the air out of his lungs. Winded and dazed, William lost his balance and fell over on to the filthy ground. Instantly his assailant was on top of him, punching and kicking without mercy.

Blindly, and acting on instinct, William defended himself by curling up into a ball. His attacker leaned down closer and threw punch after punch at his face. Swiftly, William grabbed the man's wrist and tried to pull his attacker into an arm lock, but he only succeeded in pulling the man to the ground. They rolled around together exchanging blows and grappling with each other. Then, in a move that was more luck than skill, William soundly elbowed the man in the ear. The attacker recoiled and stalled his assault momentarily. It was just long enough for William to roll away and spring to his feet.

But the attacker was nimble and he quickly stood to face William. The man wasted no time and launched himself at William.

Standing defensively, William blocked a series of punches using moves that were second nature to him. Frustrated by his lack of progress, the man leapt onto William and wrapped his arms around him. William tried to shake him free. The man's rough hands quickly found their way around William's neck. They grappled with each other for a second, and then William head-butted his aggressor in the face. There was a satisfying crunch and a sharp intake of breath from him. The moment of shock was enough for William to get a small advantage. He took a swing, a powerful right hook, in the direction of the man's head.

But his target had seen it coming. He ducked and grabbed William's arm as it swung past, then twisted it around William's back. The force spun him on his unsteady feet and his assailant pushed him up against the alley wall in a firm, painful arm lock. His face was pushed hard against the rough sandstone; he tasted the grainy material as it mixed with the blood in his mouth.

Metal collided with tarmac. William's P230 had fallen out from his belt. He cursed inwardly at the ineffective holster and hoped the man hadn't heard it.

A glint of reflected light flashed in the air above William. Cold metal was pressed against his hot skin. He froze. The blade of the short combat knife was pushed hard onto his throat.

'Good. That's it, stay calm. Shhh,' said the man between sharp breaths, the accent was middle-eastern. He kept the pressure on William's twisted arm, pushing him uncomfortably into the wall. His face was right up against William's ear.

The honed knife edge dug into William's skin close to his carotid artery. One swift move and he knew that it was lights out.

'Who are you? Why are you here?' the man demanded.

Anger and frustration surged through William. He recalled his close quarter training sessions with special forces instructors. It had been drilled into him that a fight was won or lost in the first minute. Confidently, he assessed that he was still in that window of opportunity.

'My name is Christophe Dupart. I am a virologist,' William said slowly in a poor French accent hoping to buy some time. A few seconds was all he needed. With his free arm he carefully reached into his jacket pocket. Most of the glass was broken, sharp fragments jabbed at his fingers, but mercifully he felt the long solid stem of the champagne glass.

'Bullshit,' spat the attacker. The knife pressed further into William's skin. 'One more chance, then I'll gut you like a fucking fish.'

William gripped his improvised weapon. Boiling with fury he withdrew the shard at lightning speed and stabbed behind him at face level. A loud yelp in his ear let him know he had successfully hit his target. The pressure on William's arm was released. The knife was gone.

Without hesitation, William threw himself backwards as hard as he could. He hit the attacker's already bloody face with the back of his head. Another yelp. William twisted around to face his opponent.

Staggering backwards, and clutching his bleeding eye with one hand, the attacker waved the combat knife around in the half-light.

Resolute, and without hesitation, William picked up his pistol.

He took aim.

And fired.

Instantly the man crumpled to the ground. His arms and legs twitched violently as the nervous system shut down. William kept the pistol aimed at the body until it stopped moving. Motionless and twisted it lay, blood oozed from the punctured eyeball. In the middle of the man's forehead was a tiny black hole.

William frantically looked up and down the dark alley to make sure there was no one around, and then he quickly searched the corpse. Like a common thief he took the man's phone and wallet. Satisfied there was nothing left of intelligence interest, he checked that the end of the alley was clear and collectedly strode away onto the main street.

*

Pedestrians stared at William and pulled away fearful of his ragged and bloody appearance as he staggered past in ripped and filthy clothes. Bruised and exhausted, he knew there was little point in trying to look respectable. It was too dangerous for him to return to his hotel now, but he knew exactly where to go.

From the road side he waved his arm and hailed the first taxi that came by. The driver stopped and eyed William with suspicion; he climbed into the back and pulled the door shut.

'*Stronhgasse street please*,' he said in German with a Berlin accent. A little trick he had learned whilst posted in Germany some years previously. After catching a glimpse of himself in the rear view mirror he felt an explanation was required.

'*Kids these days. No respect*,' he said and wiped the blood off his face with a handkerchief.

With a dismissive wave, the driver nodded in agreement and drove on. He'd seen worse.

At Stronhgasse street, William tipped the driver generously and climbed out into the cool night. He was close enough to the British Embassy to walk; being driven to the door would have been too obvious. At the embassy entrance he flashed his ID to the suspicious guard. He looked him up and down, scrutinised his ID, then nodded in acknowledgment and allowed him in.

William freshened up, ate, and then wrote a quick situation report on his phone and emailed it to his boss. He had a dozen lines of enquiry to follow up on his return to London, his mind buzzed with questions. But one thing in particular bothered him: he had been so careful, he had followed protocol to the letter, yet he had been found so easily – way too easily.

# Tuesday

*Hemera Areos* 'day of Ares'

# Chapter 4

*0728hrs – Cambridge*

ELLA AWOKE. Rays of the early morning sun radiated through the window. Her bedroom was already too hot. She kicked the duvet back and tried to cool down. Her head pounded, she reached for the glass of water by her bedside and gulped it down. She sat up, bleary eyed, put her head in her hands and rubbed her face.

It had been a good night, she recalled. After the pub she and Darren had met up with some friends in a nightclub and they had danced and drank until it closed in the early hours. She racked her mind to ensure that nothing too embarrassing had occurred; she was sure nothing had. She threw herself out of bed and headed for the bathroom.

After a long shower, she stood in front of the sink wrapped in a long white towel. She wiped the steam off the mirror and stared at the reflection of herself thoughtfully. Most of her friends had jobs now, serious partners, some were even married. What did she have to show for her years? She wondered where life was taking her, what journey her seemingly rudderless life was on.

After a light breakfast of cereal and low fat milk, she paced around her flat and debated what she should do with the day. Her thesis beckoned to her. Settling down in front of her laptop, she opened up the file that contained her thesis and stared blankly at the lines of text. After a few minutes of fruitless key-bashing she cursed, closed the lid, and stood up. Her mind was elsewhere.

She had to tackle it now. It was eating her up. 'Now or never,' she said. She grabbed her handbag, took out her phone, and dialled the lawyer's office.

\*

The offices of Bingly-Hilary-Newman were modern and spacious. In the reception area several highly colourful abstract paintings decorated the walls. Bright colours mingled on the canvases thick with texture. Elsewhere, obscure stone sculptures sat proudly on smoked glass desks. When Ella entered she thought the place looked more like an art gallery than a solicitor's office.

At the reception desk she was greeted by a heavily made up blonde girl whom she felt was no more than eighteen years old, a strong scent of perfume emanated from her. She took Ella's name and told her to take a seat, she pointed to a soft black leather sofa by the window. Ella sat and watched as the receptionist spoke quietly into the phone, occasionally she glanced over at Ella as she spoke. Ella picked up a fashion magazine from the glass table and pretended to read it.

A few minutes later a smartly dressed man, who looked to be in his late forties, appeared at the reception desk. After a quick word with the girl he headed straight towards Ella.

'Well, hello at last, Ms Moore. *Very* pleased to meet you. I am Winton Newman, senior partner,' he said in a very posh accent, the kind reserved for the genuine English upper classes. Ella had seen his type many times before at the university, both students and staff. Well educated, well presented, polite beyond the pale, he was most likely a man from a family of good breeding, Ella thought. Old money, as they say. She guessed he would have come from a long line of well-to-do ancestors and probably knew exactly who his great-great grandfather was. Winton Newman had been born with a large, solid silver spoon surgically attached.

'Nice to meet you too. Please, call me Ella.' She shook his hand. His skin was soft, his grip gentle.

Feeling slightly nervous, she followed him into his office. He took a chair behind his cluttered desk and sat down. Ella sat on a green antique club leather chair that was in front of the desk. The office was decorated in oak furnishings, old oil paintings hung on the walls. It was in stark contrast to the modern reception hall. One of the paintings depicted an impressive looking man dressed in an old red and white military uniform. Medals and jewels hung from his red tunic. Two sleek brown hounds sat obediently beside him. Ella scrutinised it, there was something familiar about the man's face . . .

'My great-great grandfather, an outstanding character.' Winton looked up at the picture and grinned proudly.

Ella bit her lip; it was all she could do to stop herself from sniggering. Winton turned back to her; Ella composed herself.

'He started the company with his war pension after the Boer war,' he went on. 'Mainly looked after the wills and legal affairs of fellow commanders and friends. We've expanded somewhat since then though. Employment law, family law, civil litigation, you name it. But more to the point, we also look after wills and probates.'

Ella's stomach jumped, her heart raced, she feared Winton could hear it beating hard in her chest. Embarrassed by her lack of control of her own emotions, she blushed and shifted in her seat.

'A very odd one this, I must admit,' Winton continued peering down at his desk and fingering his way though some papers.

'Odd? What do you mean?' Ella asked with a slightly worried tone.

'Well, your father . . . Sorry, but I must ask. James Davidson was your biological father?'

'Yes. He left us a long time ago. I never knew him. After the divorce my mother reverted to her maiden name, she never remarried.'

Winton gave her a look that she interpreted as pity. 'James Davidson came to this office two months ago to make a will. As he had no close family to take care of things, he made specific instructions as to what was to be done in the event of his death. He wanted to be cremated without fuss or interference and even paid for the proceedings in advance.'

'That's weird. He made a will barely a month before he died. Did you know he was murdered by a burglar?' she asked. Ella had never cared about her father before, now she couldn't help but wonder about his last moments on Earth.

Winton frowned at her lack of emotion. 'I did, yes, a terrible thing, just terrible. James also asked us to secure some items for him, a letter and a small box.' He leaned over the desk and lowered his voice. 'He was quite specific that one of the letters must be read on the event of his death to you and you only.'

'But why? He never knew me,' Ella said. 'Was there really no one else in his life?'

'I have not the slightest idea, I'm afraid.' Winton walked over to one of the oil paintings on the wall. It was that of a hunter mounted on his huge dark brown steed, he loosely held a silver shotgun in one hand; the black reins were in the other. He pushed the painting aside, hidden behind was a small safe. After tapping the code into the keypad he took out a flat wooden box and a white envelope.

'These are the items he has left in our trust,' Winton said, he returned to his desk and placed the wooden box on the table in front of Ella.

'What is it?'

'Again, I've no idea. I am as captivated as you are.' Winton searched in his desk for something. He eventually found his antique letter opener, it was in the shape of a sword. He sliced through the envelope and pulled out a single page of typed script and two other smaller envelopes. One envelope was red, the other was blue. Donning a pair of reading glasses, Winton held the typed page out and began to read:

'*My darling Ella. If this is being read to you, then my worst nightmare has become a cruel reality. I have passed away without getting to know you as I had planned to do so one day. My own fault, I know, I left it too late. Please find a place in your heart to forgive me. If only I could have spent time with you, you would have understood what happened and why I had no choice. We all had no choice. But you now have a chance to learn the truth. I have left you all that are important. If you accept the red letter, all I ask is that you do as described. But if you would rather forget me – and I wouldn't blame you if you did – then there is only one other who may help. Do what you feel is right, Ella. All my love, James.*'

A single tear ran down Ella's face. She quickly wiped it away and composed herself.

Winton gave her a moment and then concluded the process in a sympathetic tone. 'It appears the inheritance is conditional. If you accept, you must take this red letter and follow its instructions. I presume you will want his ashes; I'll leave you the details of the crematorium.'

'Who is the other person he refers to?'

'I don't know. I assume it is detailed in this blue letter. But if you take the red letter I am to burn the blue letter unopened right now. Conversely, if you don't accept his request then you must leave now empty handed. I will burn the red letter unopened. The blue letter holds further instructions for me alone. That is the last will and testament of James Davidson.'

Winton held out the coloured envelopes, one in each hand. He leaned towards her.

'So Ella. What's it to be?'

# Chapter 5

*1017hrs – Oxfordshire*

IT HAD BEEN a relatively comfortable flight from Vienna; William had slept most of the way. The RAF Hercules touched down gently on the runway of Brize Norton and braked hard. It taxied to its bay and the engines powered down. The few occupants, mostly soldiers, gathered their bags and Bergens, and disembarked down the rear ramp. William was rapidly cleared through the military terminal and was met outside by a military driver, a skinny young dark haired woman from the Royal Logistic Corps. Dressed in jeans and a T-shirt, she barely looked old enough to drive, he thought. He followed her to an unmarked Army car, an indistinct Ford Mondeo, and in silence he was taken straight to central London.

Few people, even those who worked in intelligence circles, knew of F-Branch's existence. Even fewer knew where the F-Branch office was located. To maintain security, William was dropped off close to an MOD building. From there he made his way on foot through the busy streets to the closest underground station and took the tube to a station that was second closest to the office. He walked a short but effective anti-surveillance route along the bustling streets of London before completing his journey to his final destination.

Since its formation during the cold war, F-Branch had been located in a Victorian Grade II listed building in an exclusive part of central London. Various shell companies had owned the premises, names changed regularly. The discreet branding on the brass plaque outside matched whatever company was in use at the time. Presently it was called Ajax Security, a private security and investigations firm registered in the British Virgin Islands. To maintain an effective cover-story they even had a few retired operators who were available for such consultancy work, albeit at an obscenely high price.

The old building was architecturally impressive, spacious, fitted out with the latest in IT equipment, and, to William's pleasant surprise, it even boasted its own bar. The *Greenfly*, as it was known, was a mid-sized room with a small bar area at one end and had the look of a private club. The walls were clad in natural wood panelling and the club leather chairs were comfortable. In addition to the canned and bottled drinks, it had a small selection of sandwiches and ready-meals to sustain those who worked through the night and beyond. There was a large flatscreen TV on one wall that was almost permanently on a twenty-four hour news channel. All in all, the bar was a very decent, convenient and, importantly, secure place to relax and socialise with the rest of the staff.

Confidently striding through the revolving doors into the main building, William showed his ID card to the security guard. Although the guards were dressed like any other contract civilian guards, they were in fact serving marines on attachment to the unit. The guard nodded to William and waved him through. After he swiped through the security turnstile, William headed for the lifts. He pressed for the second floor and the lift accelerated upwards. Once on his floor, before he could get past the steel security door to his office, he was required to authenticate via a retinal scan. He placed his left eye to a small dark hole in the silver control panel by the door. Instantly the machine verified his identity and the door unlocked with a dull click. Beyond, the office looked like any ordinary open plan office. It had wooden desks and flatscreen computers and staff that buzzed from room to room carrying papers and coffee cups. Heads turned towards William as he headed straight for his boss's office. He was still seen as the new boy, an object of quiet interest. A couple of women who stood talking to each other by a desk flashed him a glance as he walked past. They looked back to each other, said something, and giggled quietly.

Adjusting his tie unnecessarily, William paused for a moment outside his boss's door. Refreshed, clean shaven and dressed in a new suit that had been kindly provided by the embassy back in Vienna, William was ready to fight the next battle. Although he had considered the mission a success – he'd made contact with the agent, obtained information, and survived an attack on his life – he feared his new boss may view it differently: two deaths, a police enquiry and no actionable intelligence to speak of. He knocked three times on the solid oak door and walked in with a confident smile on his face.

'What the bloody hell were you bloody playing at?' shouted Albert Pinkerton from behind his desk before William even made it across the threshold. 'Are you trying to start some kind of diplomatic incident? A dead body in the streets, a dead informant in the bloody Wiener Staatsoper! And, by Jingo, no actionable intelligence!'

Pinkerton slammed his fist on his desk, pencils and pen jumped into the air and rolled across the desk onto the floor. 'You're worse than the bloody terrorists, Agent Temple. You're still on probation here you know. Mark my words; you are walking on thin ice. Thin ice!'

Pinkerton had clearly read William's short email report. Sitting behind his desk perched on an old green leather chair, he stared at William across the small office and shook his head. In his late fifties, Pinkerton was tall and thin, he had short grey hair. From obvious good breeding and good schooling – Eton, then on to Cambridge, Trinity college, of course – he had the look of an academic and dressed like an aristocrat. Originally a linguist for the Secret Intelligence Service, he had quickly moved up the ranks and had been in a comfortable senior position at F-Branch for some years.

'Sir, I . . .' William began, feeling like a naughty child for the first time in a long while.

'Just sit down, Agent Temple,' Pinkerton commanded.

William had seen many like Pinkerton in the Army; he readily believed that there was a factory churning them out somewhere in Wiltshire. Bright and articulate, they climbed the ladder fast and strutted around like they owned the place. Spoilt blue-blooded types, they were the kind of chinless wonders who went straight from a leading university into the service and reached the top jobs without ever having done a real day's work, or having taken a real risk themselves. William doubted they would last five minutes on their own in the real world.

'I was attacked, sir, totally unprovoked. Probably by one of the terrorists,' William replied calmly.

'Oh, they're terrorists are they? Well, that's all right then. But we'll never know now, will we, because of your damned trigger happy finger.' Pinkerton shut his eyes and took a deep breath; he let the air out slowly. 'I do you hope your little incident in the Army has not affected your judgement. Post Traumatic Stress Disorder can affect people in many different ways. Believe me, I know. I've seen my fair share of physiologically damaged operators in my time.'

If Pinkerton had been closer to William he would have seen his pupils dilate and the veins in his neck throb. He may even have received a firm punch in the face. But William put his emotions in check before he answered.

'I can assure you that there is nothing wrong with my judgement, sir,' he managed to say calmly. William's eyes bored into Pinkerton's as if he was trying to read the man's mind. 'I've been . . . how do they put it

. . . *assessed,* by a service physiologist.'

Pinkerton eyed him carefully before responding. He sat back and clasped his hands together. 'All I'm saying is be careful in future. You're new here, it's only natural that you will be watched and judged more than the rest. If there are any problems – drink, drugs, women – I want to know about them before someone else tells me about them.'

'There are none,' William said firmly holding Pinkerton's gaze. 'Shall I update you on the job at hand?'

Pinkerton nodded. William reached into his jacket and took out the phone and wallet that he had taken from the corpse and laid them on the desk.

'I relieved the suspect of these.'

Pinkerton peered over his glasses and eyed the objects with suspicion. He stroked his chin. 'Well at least it's something,' he said. 'But I don't recall you mentioning this in your CX report. Which, by the way, was full of grammatical errors. Attention to detail Agent Temple, attention to detail. The way a report is written is as important as its content. Nothing should be left out, and nothing should be left open to interpretation.'

'I was pushed for time, sir. And I was a little . . . perturbed.'

'No excuse, you've seen plenty of action before, I've read your career history,' Pinkerton stated coldly. 'Anyway, as I was saying, don't underestimate the importance of accurate grammar. Just remember the Jameson Raid of 1896.'

'Noted, sir,' William said, although he hadn't a clue what the Jameson Raid was and had no intention of taking any English courses to brush up on his grammar either. 'There was a lot of cash in the wallet, but no credit cards or IDs. There may be some fingerprints, but my money is on the phone. There's bound to be something interesting in there once our techies get their hands on it.'

'I hope you took the battery out of it,' Pinkerton said, nodding to the sleek black device on the table.

'Afraid you can't with these ones, sir. But I did power it down, it's been made safe. I'll never forget a little job in Afghanistan I did with the Americans.' William recalled the hunt for a prominent al-Qaeda commander. After much difficulty, and at great cost to the tax payer, he had managed to get the target's mobile phone number from an informant. The CIA tracked the phone by triangulation of its signal, and then followed it with an unmanned spy plane fitted with a single Hellfire missile. With great hilarity the CIA officer, a thuggish former US Marine, phoned the terrorist to say goodbye just seconds before the missile struck.

'I also found this.' William held out a tiny white pill. 'It was hidden in the wallet. I doubt it's a fresh mint, but best not to taste it to find out.'

'A suicide pill? I'll be damned.' Pinkerton said with a frown and inspected the deceptively innocent looking item. 'Cyanide would explain the rapid demise of our informant.'

'It looks that way. The lab will analyse it, we'll know for sure soon enough. And with any luck they may be able to extract a sample of the contaminated champagne from my handkerchief too for a comparison.'

'And the micro-chip?'

William produced the tiny black memory chip and placed it on the desk. 'It's a micro memory chip, the kind used in phones.'

'Hmm. So our virology professor was coerced into doing some unknown work for an unknown group who blackmailed him. He was silenced by poison and they tried to silence you.'

William regarded Pinkerton, unable to read him. 'Yes, it looks that way, sir. But if he is right, then something unpleasant is going to happen soon, maybe in the next few days.'

Pinkerton sat back in his chair and threw his arms back and rested them on his head. 'Get the phone and the chip to the duty TSU and get back to me as soon as you know something useful. In the meantime, I'll see what I can dig up on the professor. I'll also have a sniff around for any chatter in the community about virus plots.'

Pinkerton replaced his reading glasses and placed his hand on his mouse, an indication that the meeting was over. Without further ado, William stood up and strode over to the door.

'One more thing,' Pinkerton added as William reached the exit. 'This investigation will remain F-Branch eyes only for the time being. Nothing must leave these walls without my authorisation.'

'Understood, sir.'

'And William?'

'Sir?'

'Well done.'

*

In the basement lab, two floors under the main building, William strolled through the cellar-like corridors and found the man he was looking for in one of the state-of-the-art computer rooms.

Ollie Slack was a long haired, sandal wearing techie that William had met during one of his induction briefings. In his early twenties, he was a particularly talented hacker who had been seconded to F-Branch from GCHQ. Several members of the Technical Support Unit were drawn from the ranks of GCHQ where the country's leading code-breakers, hackers and forensic computing specialists, quietly protected the nation's secrets – and broke into everyone else's. A few of their best in each discipline were periodically hand-picked for F-Branch service, and between them there was no end to their technical wizardry. If it had a micro-chip they could hack it, crack it, and uncover its secrets.

'Ollie! Just the man. How are you?' William said thrusting his hand outwards.

'Hi. William, isn't it?' Ollie took the proffered hand and shook it vigorously. 'Settling in I hear, making your mark.'

'News travels fast,' he said with a wry smile. 'I need a favour.'

'Always happy to help.'

William produced the phone and the tiny memory chip and held them out to Ollie. 'I need these looked at.'

'Wonderful,' Ollie exclaimed and keenly took possession of them. 'You've come to the right place. Follow me.'

They headed straight for the Faraday room, a specially sealed room protected from any incoming or outgoing radio signals. Phones and other communication equipment could be switched on safely without fear of any unwanted signals being sent to or from the devices. Ollie hooked the phone up to a computer and switched it on. He was met with a passcode.

'Not a problem,' he said. 'I have a way around that.'

Using forensic software specially designed for modern phones, he copied all the data stored on its hard drive, internal memory and SIM card. Once done, he switched the phone off again, and bagged and tagged it. After, they returned to Ollie's workstation in the lab.

There wasn't much Ollie Slack couldn't do with a computer. His fascination in computing had started in his teenage years and he quickly earned himself a reputation. The first incident happened after he took a dislike to an arrogant teacher at his secondary school. When taking attendance at class the teacher would sarcastically call out, "Slack by name". Taking quiet revenge, Ollie hacked into the teacher's school email account and caused him a near nervous breakdown by faking an erotic email to the headmistress. By the time he had started at university, Ollie had become an accomplished cyber-warrior. It always amazed and surprised him how many things had IP addresses – the computer equivalent of a phone number that allowed communication over the Internet. Phones, fridges, TVs, planes, cruise missiles, submarines; the list was dangerously endless. And if it had an IP address, it was a good bet that Ollie could hack into it. During an anti-war protest when Ollie was at university he 'did his bit' by hacking into a defence satellite and caused a major national security alert. After a highly embarrassing, and hushed up, MI5 investigation, GCHQ offered him a job. That kind of talent, in their opinion, should be put to good use. With little real choice, Ollie accepted. He convinced himself that he would be able to prevent further conflicts and unnecessary deaths. It was also a great wage and it kept him out of jail. In his few years in the job he had hacked into foreign governments and stolen sensitive information, tricked enemy radar systems and had even planted an untraceable spying Trojan within a rogue state's nuclear development programme. He was in his element.

'Right, let's see what we have here,' Ollie said getting to work with the forensic software. He worked his way rapidly around the program, it was like second nature. Most of the searches were standardised and all he had to do was tick the boxes and click on run. It scanned the data in seconds and the results were presented on a tab within the program.

'It has a British phone number,' he said. 'I'll just check it on the subscribers' database . . .' He opened another database and searched for the number, when the result came up he tutted. 'Unregistered pre-pay, totally anonymous. Always a favourite.'

'Is there a call history?' William asked.

Using a database that collated call data from all the phone companies, Ollie clicked away. He frowned at the results. 'That's odd, there's nothing, no calls at all, not incoming nor outgoing.'

'That's disappointing. Is there anything else that we can use?'

'Let me go back to the phone data. I think I know what's going on.' Ollie navigated to the forensic results and scanned through them.

'Bingo!' he said.

'What is it?' William leaned in towards the screen.

'Smart-phones are more like tiny laptops than phones,' Ollie explained. 'Look, see that? He's got the Skype application on there, an Internet phone application. He's been making secure, Internet calls instead of normal phone calls.'

William nodded, he recognised the icon. 'I've come across that one before, it's popular with the terrorists.'

'Secure communications free for all to use across the globe. Sheer genius,' Ollie moaned sarcastically. 'Data, voice and video is sent over the Internet using strong encryption. Even if you could tap the line, which you can't – not in the usual way anyway – you wouldn't be able to listen in. It's very clever stuff, a well written program.'

'But you have a way in?' William inquired, always hopeful. 'A government back door?'

Ollie laughed. 'Ha. No, oh no. If there were any back doors in public encryption algorithms the hackers would find them, publish the fact, and no one would ever use the product. No, there really aren't such things these days.'

'Pity.'

Ollie looked over his shoulder, then leaned towards William and quietly said, 'But there may be something I can do, although officially we'll need Home Office approval.'

'Officially?'

Ollie smiled. 'There will be a list of the suspect's Skype contacts in there. Let's have a closer look.' After Ollie extracted the data a list of names and email addresses came up on the screen.

'Hades, Asclepius, Erebus and Nike,' William said reading the names out.

'Unusual names. And the owner of the phone used the name Morpheus to log in. Codenames?' Ollie proposed.

'Probably. The informant asked us to use the codename Asclepius to contact him. Evidently he's the Greek god of medicine.' William wondered why this name would be on the terrorist's phone.

'The King of the dead,' Ollie said.

'Come again?'

'Hades was the brother of Zeus, gods of ancient Greece. He was lord of the underworld and ruled over the dead. He was also the god of wealth, greedy and unpitying.'

'Can you trace the other contacts? Find the owners real names or numbers?'

'Probably not,' Ollie shook his head and screwed his face up. 'I'll try my luck with the email addresses, but these accounts can be set up without any proper identification – totally anonymous.'

'So what can you do then?' William asked, hopeful that Ollie had some technical wizardry up his sleeve. 'There must be something.'

'There may well be something, my friend,' he said grinning. 'If all the contacts are using a smartphone then it should be easy to hack the actual phones themselves. There's usually no additional security on smart-phones, it should be child's play with tools I have. Even if they're using PCs instead of phones I shouldn't have any major problems, I get advanced access to all sorts of exploitable vulnerabilities. There's also something else I can do to trace the IP addresses from the Skype calls he's made.'

'Do it.' William encouraged. He had no doubt Ollie had the skills, and importantly, the drive to do a thorough job. 'But first, I want to see what's on that memory chip.'

After making an exact copy of all the data on the chip, Ollie analysed the contents of the copy using another forensic tool. He opened the data viewer on the screen and sifted through the contents of the chip.

'It's just a jumble of random characters, William. I recognise what it is though. All the files are encrypted,' Ollie said. 'We'll need to crack the passwords. It may take a while, but I have access to a pretty powerful supercomputer.'

'I think the agent was about to explain what the password was before he was silenced,' William said.

Ollie regarded William and wondered what it would be like to be on the front line in the thick of the action. Dangerous, was his main thought, frightening, was another. He was more than happy to be safely hidden away in the depths of his high-tech fortress.

'I'm sure he said something like, *"it's the name of this . . ."*, before it was lights out.'

'The name of this what?' Ollie picked up a pencil and chewed on the end of it.

'This *city*, this *country*, this *building?*'

Working fast, Ollie typed away on his keyboard trying out various combinations of the most commonly used passwords. It always amazed, and frightened him how often they worked. Governments spent millions developing strong, uncrackable encryption algorithms, only for their dozy staff to choose ridiculously simple passwords. But the professor had been more careful. Ollie tried *Vienna*, *Austria* and *Wiener Staatsoper*.

'No luck,' he said after exhausting his mental list. 'It could be anything. Let me crack it, it won't take long, trust me. I can extract the hashed key and use our terabytes of rainbow tables to find the corresponding password.' There was little Ollie enjoyed more than the challenge of password cracking. Not that it was too much of a challenge with the computing power he had available to him. Encryption worked like a lock and key, to open the lock you had to have the correct key: the password. And with the kind of supercomputers F-Branch had, passwords that would previously have taken years to crack could now be found in days or even hours.

But William's very own supercomputer was processing the possibilities. People were predictable, he knew, and he was confident that the professor, the opera loving virologist . . .

'Try *Don Giovanni*,' William suggested.

After a few tries of the words with and without spaces and capitals, one of the files opened up on the screen. Ollie beamed. 'Nice one,' he said.

'*The name of this Opera*,' William said thoughtfully. 'That's what he was going to say.'

After decrypting all the files, Ollie scanned through the forensic program and tried to make sense of it all. He tapped away harshly at the keyboard, frowning and cursing under his breath as he did so.

'Is there a problem?' William asked.

After a barrage of more curses, Ollie threw his chewed pencil at the screen. 'Damn it! It doesn't make sense. There must be another level of encryption. They're data files all right, but the entire data is just a series of letters. There's thousands of lines of them all consisting of the same four letters, G, C, A and U. Sorry, but this is going to take a while to figure out. I've never seen anything like it. Well, except for Enigma, but that used all the letters of the alphabet, not just four of them.'

'Wait a minute, Ollie. The professor's work involved gene sequences,' William said. In his mind the pieces were falling into place. 'He dissected the genetic codes of lethal viruses.'

Ollie brightened up, he was following William's train of thought.

'The files are full of code all right,' William said. 'But it's not encryption, it's genetic code, gene sequences. The letters represent the four amino acids that make up RNA, the genetic code of certain types of virus. Best we get them to the Defence Labs as soon as. They should be able to make some sense of them.'

'As good as done. Then I'll get cracking with that other thing for you.' Ollie smiled to himself, but the pun was wasted.

'Good. Let me know as soon you have something.' William thanked Ollie and headed for the exit.

At the door, William thought of something else, he stopped and turned. 'What do you make of Pinkerton?' he asked.

'Pinkerton? The old man? He's all right I suppose. I never really have much to do with those at his level. Keeps himself to himself, very strategic, not really a hands on kind of guy. But he is a bit, what's the word, status conscious. Been here forever it seems. Supposedly he's turned down many a cushy little number in the private sector. Loves it I guess, or maybe he's waiting for his knighthood before he moves on.'

William thanked his new friend again and returned to his office.

\*

When William entered the briefing room on his floor, Pinkerton and a young woman were in the midst of a meeting. They sat opposite each other at a long wooden table in the middle of the room. The woman had short auburn hair, and her freckled face, though not beautiful, was noble. Pinkerton sucked on the end of his reading glasses while the woman sifted through some documents that were spread across the table. A presentation was projected onto a white screen on the wall.

'May I join you?' William asked.

They both looked up at him. The woman smiled welcomingly at him.

'Agent Temple. Come in, please take a seat,' Pinkerton said holding out his hand and gesturing to the seat opposite him. 'We have just been doing a bit of research on your friend, the professor. This is Sarah Jackman, one of our top analysts.'

William recognised Sarah from his orientation day. She was a civilian intelligence analyst who worked in the operations support office. Her role was to run around for the field agents doing the valuable research work that supported their investigations.

'We've found out rather a lot about the man, but nothing that takes us anywhere,' Pinkerton added.

'I've just been with TSU, sir. The chip contains files of genetic code. It's Greek to me but it's on its way to the Defence Labs as we speak,' William explained. He frowned when he noticed a flicker of anger in Pinkerton's eyes.

Pinkerton slammed his fist on the table. 'What did I say about information leaving these walls?'

'Sorry sir, but I thought it was best to get it across as quickly as possible given the circumstances.'

'What circumstances?' Pinkerton held out the palms of his hands and frowned questioningly at William. 'Look, from now on everything goes through me. Do you understand what that means? You get the information, I process it into intelligence and disseminate it accordingly.'

'Of course, sir. It won't happen again.'

Sarah remained silent and kept her head down, she pretended to read one of the documents that lay on the table.

William tried to recover the situation. He was beginning to tire of Pinkerton's outbursts. 'The phone I recovered from the assassin in Vienna may well provide some actionable intelligence, sir,' he reassured. 'TSU will call me as soon as they have something, they're working on it as a priority.'

'Good, let's hope it produces something useful. The police in Vienna are investigating the deaths, but I won't hold my breath for any quick resolution. By the time they complete their paperwork this will be old news.'

Neither William nor Pinkerton were great fans of the justice system in any country. Bureaucratic judicial processes generally required black and white facts: evidence. It was far too slow a process for the intelligence game. Pinkerton had made some hard decisions based on the loosest of information. He never assumed that he always got it right.

'Agreed,' William added.

Pinkerton turned to Sarah. 'Show Agent Temple the research so far,' he ordered.

Sarah clicked the mouse a few times and her briefing slides appeared on the projector. Her work was thorough and highly detailed. After all, she had access to virtually every database that was of any intelligence use: all government owned records; banking data; flight bookings; phone records – the list was huge. The information that could be gathered on a person, literally at the touch of a button, was staggering.

'Professor John Barry, codenamed *Asclepius*, was a British citizen who worked as Head of Viral Research at the University of Strasbourg in France.' Sarah's voice was soft, but she spoke with confidence directly and clearly to her small audience. 'According to their Dean he's been missing for about three months. They never reported it though, thought it was due to the pressure of his recent divorce, and compounded by his lack of progress on his research. It seemed he was on the verge of losing his funding and with it his reputation.'

'He said the research was going well,' William interjected.

'So much for your debriefing skills,' Pinkerton chided shaking his head.

William opened his mouth to fight back. He was beginning to despise the man. But Sarah quickly resumed her briefing.

'No criminal records, no known criminal or terrorist associates. Finances appeared to be fine, no obvious debts other than a modest mortgage, but he stood to lose a lot in the divorce and even more if he lost funding for his work. More interestingly, he has travelled a lot recently. Especially so in the last three months. To the UK, France, South Africa, Croatia, Egypt and Moscow.'

'Moscow, where he made the call?' William asked.

Sarah rarely left any stone unturned. She smiled knowingly. 'Yes, the dates match up.'

'Have you cross-referenced the flights?' William stopped and smiled appreciatively when he saw Sarah's face light up again. He knew she was a step ahead. Another talented asset.

From under a pile of papers on the table Sarah picked up a printout and handed it William. 'A man called, Abdul Haqq, was on five of the same flights as our professor. The final one was from Paris International to Vienna.'

'Unlikely to be a coincidence,' William stated looking over the document. 'Anything on him?'

Sarah picked up another printout, a photo from CCTV at Paris Charles de Gaulle International airport. It was a good quality shot from passport control, a close up of the man's face. 'This is him,' she said and slid the photo over to William.

William scrutinised the image. He'd never forget the man's desperate look of disbelief in the brief moment just before he squeezed the trigger. 'It's him, I'm pretty sure,' he said.

'Pretty sure?' Pinkerton challenged.

'It's him,' William affirmed looking Pinkerton in the eye. 'So, who is he?'

Sarah held her tongue and looked to Pinkerton.

'Servant of the Truth,' Pinkerton said. He looked at William and narrowed his eyes.

William shrugged his shoulders.

'That's what the man's name means in Arabic,' Pinkerton explained. 'And he's dead.'

'I'm aware of that, sir. I was there when I shot him,' William said with little regard for his obvious flippancy. He noticed Sarah suppress a smile.

Pinkerton was less than amused. He leaned forward and sneered. 'What I mean, Agent Temple,' he said sternly, 'is that the original Abdul Haqq is dead and has been for some time. Whoever that man is,' he pointed to the photo, 'had stolen the dead man's identity. So we're none the wiser of who he really is, are we? A great job this is turning out to be.' Forcefully, he sat back in his chair and sucked on the arm of his glasses.

'Do you have the passport pictures of everyone on the same flight as the professor and Haqq?' William asked Sarah.

'I can get them,' she replied and held William's gaze for a moment. 'You think the waitress who served you will be there too?' Sarah smiled; it pleased her to work with such exceptionally bright field operators. It was a rare thing in her experience.

'That's what I'm hoping for.'

To finish off her briefing, Sarah projected an intelligence map of the case onto the wall. She walked over to it with a laser pointer in one hand. The projection showed little icons that represented all the known people involved so far, thin lines connected them to all the relevant information she had found. She had added the contacts from the suspect's Skype application. Bit by bit an intelligence picture was built up.

Cases often acquired literally thousands of pieces of information: suspects, addresses, phone calls, money transfers, bank accounts and credit cards, flights, associates, computers. Every piece of information available was researched and logged. An electronic mind map showed all the data and all the links between them making it easy to see connections that would have been impossible to find in paper records that were feet thick.

Sarah spotted something that she hadn't seen before and pointed to the map with the laser. 'See the codenames from the phone contacts? Morpheus, Hades, Asclepius, Nike and Erebus,' she said.

'Yes. We know who Asclepius was,' Pinkerton pointlessly pointed out. 'And Morpheus, we assume, was William's sparring partner.'

'No, I mean the *names*, sir. Aren't they all Greek?'

'Greek gods to be precise,' William interjected seeing the link. 'Hades was the King of the dead. Asclepius was the god of medicine and healing.'

'Morpheus was the god of dreams,' Pinkerton added to William's surprise. 'A black winged demon. And Nike was the goddess of victory.'

'And Erebus?' William asked, feeling somehow that Pinkerton would know the answer.

'Erebus was the god of darkness and shadow, the son of Khaos. Where we get our word *chaos* from. In fact about a fifth of English words still in use today originally came from ancient Greek.'

'Fascinating, sir. Isn't it Sarah?' William said sarcastically trying to get a rise from her.

Sarah smiled at William and raised an eyebrow.

Oblivious to the subtle teasing, Pinkerton continued. 'Asclepius and

Erebus were primordial deities, gods that ruled over the workings of nature. Whereas Hades was one of the twelve Olympian gods, the gods that ruled over the people. They controlled love, marriage, war, all the affairs and journeys of human life.'

'So there's a pattern. The codenames are Greek gods. And where there's a pattern there's a key,' Sarah said. 'An old codebreakers saying.'

'I prefer, where there's a pattern there's a *reason*,' Pinkerton added. 'We need to find that reason.'

They all looked towards the mind map hoping the reason would jump out at them. William's phone vibrated on the table, he looked at the caller name before answering it.

'I'd better take this, sir,' he said and pressed to answer.

Pinkerton glared at him disapprovingly, William pretended not to notice.

'Yes, good. Well done Ollie, great work. Call me when he moves.' He replaced the phone then picked up the photograph of his attacker and examined it.

'And who was that?' Pinkerton demanded irritably.

William looked up innocently. 'TSU, sir. They've hacked the phone belonging to the contact called Hades.' He over emphasised the Greek pronunciation for Pinkerton's benefit. 'No subscriber details, it's a pay-as-you-go SIM, and the payment method can't be traced either. Nothing to identify the owner of the phone. But they have the IMEI number and have already geo-located it from the masts.' William paused for effect before delivering the shocking news. 'It's here in London, sir. Somewhere in the financial district.'

'By Jingo!' Pinkerton exclaimed, he pulled the arm of his glasses out of his mouth and sat bolt upright. 'We need to find him, urgently, and identify who he is. Exactly what part of the city is he in?'

'The phone has been located down to fifty square metres. It's in or around the Gherkin at St Mary's Axe. But that's still too wide an area to search, there are literally tens of thousands of people there at this time, and he could of course just be visiting or passing through. But when it moves they'll track it and call me with updates.'

'Good. Follow it, but do not engage. Got that? Just house him, that's all. We'll do the research on everything about him and then plan our next move carefully,' Pinkerton ordered.

'Any chance of a surveillance team? Maybe a bike and a chopper?' William asked, but he already knew the answer. Pinkerton just shook his head. Resources were sparse and a short notice job had no chance unless an immediate threat was known. 'Or how about letting Sarah out to help me? She seems like a talented girl. I could use someone to watch my back.'

Sarah blushed slightly at the compliment, and couldn't help feeling a little excited at the thought of going out on an operation. But when Pinkerton laughed heartily, Sarah's smile vanished.

'She has a job to do here, and an important one at that. I need her in the office.'

'Do you want a report for the IMS?' Sarah asked collecting her things together. The Intelligence Management System was a secure global network used to disseminate and collaborate on intelligence material. It was a key tool used by all of the major NATO intelligence and security agencies.

'No,' Pinkerton said. 'I'll handle that. Right, let's not waste any time. Get to it everyone!'

Sarah picked up her things and left the room. William was about to follow her out.

'Wait here a moment, Agent Temple,' Pinkerton said. He waited until Sarah had left before continuing. 'Something worries me about this. Assassins, suicide pills, Greek gods.' He shook his head and released a long sigh. 'There are no reports whatsoever on the IMS about a virus plot. I've checked with the Company, the Mossad too, even the Pakistanis. There is nothing like this on the radar anywhere else.'

'Do you think we may have a new terrorist group? One that's right here under our noses?'

'Terrorist group, doomsday cult, organised crime gang. Who knows these days,' Pinkerton shrugged.

This raised William's eyebrows. 'Doomsday cult?' he questioned. 'Our very own Aum Shinrikyo?'

'I'm keeping an open mind at this stage.' The arm of Pinkerton's glasses was, once again, inserted into his mouth. 'I'll keep my ear to the ground. In the meantime just find who exactly this Hades is, our lord of the underworld. And William?'

'Yes, sir?'

'Don't kill any more suspects. That's an order.'

'Yes, sir.'

But William didn't like to make promises he couldn't keep.

# Chapter 6

*1232hrs – Cambridge*

CURLED UP ON her bed with a large furry teddy bear, a young Ella clasped her hands tightly over her ears. Tears ran down her pale face. The arguing had gone on for what seemed like all evening, it had started long before dinner. For weeks the shouting had been getting worse. Every day there had been an argument between her mother and father. Plates had been broken, doors slammed. Ella wondered if it was because of her, maybe she had caused it. They must have been happy before she came along. She wished it would stop. Anything to make it stop.

A door slammed shut, and then her wish came true. Finally, there was silence.

Stairs creaked, someone slowly climbed them. They paused occasionally. Ella heard sobs and sniffs. Her bedroom door opened and her mother stood in the doorway with her head down. She was crying.

Confused and worried, Ella ran over into her mother's open arms. She pulled Ella tightly into her chest.

'He's gone,' her mother snivelled between breaths. 'He's left us for good.'

Ella held on so tightly that her arms hurt. And then she cried, and cried, and cried.

*

Ella awoke on her sofa in the lounge of her flat. She had only lain down for a moment, and must have drifted off. She sat up and rubbed her heavy, wet eyes. It had been a long time since she had dreamt about the day her father left.

In the kitchen, she made herself a cup of tea and sat down at the table. The radio played quietly in the background. In front of her was the red letter from the lawyer. She found herself staring at it, it pulled her in. It would be so easy to just rip it up and burn it, she thought. It would certainly end the worry that consumed her. But she was curious.

She took out her phone and called Darren.

'It's in front of me,' she said, bursting into conversation before Darren could even say hello. 'I'm tempted to burn the damn thing.'

'Calm down,' Darren said, he recognised the tension in her tone. 'Think it through, there's no rush. Shall I come round?'

'How dare he do this to me,' she spat. 'And after all this time. To just assume that I would care. I don't care. Who the hell was this man anyway?'

'Ella, he was your father. You can't blame him for putting you in his will. He might have left some answers. Look, you know that you've only ever heard one side of the story. It's not for me to say, but there are always two sides.'

Wiping the tears from her face, she reached for the letter. Her hand shook slightly as she held it up. 'Sorry to vent off on you, Darren,' she said apologetically. 'But I know exactly what I'm going to do.'

She hung up and walked over to the cooker with the letter. She turned on one of the hobs; there was a brief smell of gas before it exploded into a crisp blue flame. She lowered the letter towards it, slowly. The corner blackened and gave off a white smoke, and then it burst into a yellow flame.

A moment later she whipped it away and blew the flame out. Wisps of sweet smelling smoke dissipated around the kitchen. She turned off the gas and quickly ripped open the letter.

Inside was a single handwritten note written in blue ink. The handwriting was messy, and there were smudges all over it. But it was readable. She read it out to herself:

*Find my mother's final place*
*Where there is a headstone to trace*
*This is the place where my soul must rest*
*Saint Mary the Virgin, where we were blessed*
*Her code of honour was always true*
*That courage now must pass to you*
*In the silence I'll find peace at last*
*The Biblos Aletheia, the key to the past*
*It's yours to decide*
*Whether to follow this ancient guide*
*But in secret I ask*
*That you undertake this task*
*Forgive me my dear*
*All will soon become clear*

She frowned. Her face reddened, she regretted not burning the note there and then. She scrunched the paper up and threw it onto the table.

'What the hell was *that* all about?' she shouted.

She picked up her phone and called Darren again.

'It's a bloody poem!' she snorted. 'All that worry, and it's just a bloody stupid damned poem.'

\*

After a while, Ella calmed herself down and read the poem again. It made no sense to her. *My mother's final place.* She guessed her father wanted his ashes scattered close to his mother's grave. But she never knew her grandmother on her father's side, and had no idea where she was buried. She considered just pouring his ashes down the sink. But the words nagged at her, called to her. There was something about them. *But in secret I ask that you undertake this task.*

It was too much for her to think about. She put the note away and made herself another cup of tea. She sat at the table and tried to get her mind off it by reading one of her books from the UL.

Bright sun beams shone through the window blinds. They moved slowly across the kitchen table as the minutes passed until they illuminated the wooden box that lay there. Ella had forgotten all about it.

'You're a handsome devil,' she said and picked it up.

It was sealed by brass screws. She found a screwdriver in a drawer and went to work opening the box. When the last screw was undone she carefully pulled the lid off. Inside was something large and flat, it was wrapped in shiny brown paper. She peeled the wrapping back and found a small painting, about the size of a magazine.

It was an oil painting set in an elaborate gold coloured frame. The painting itself was a highly detailed and realistic portrait of a man, almost like a photograph. The man had long grey hair and a grey beard; his aged, wrinkly face had a serious, almost sombre look. But there was something warm and fatherly about him too. Dressed in black, the outfit he wore looked like something from medieval times. Circles of white frilly lace poked out of his sleeves and he wore a large intricate white collar that stuck far out from his neck. In both of his hands he held what looked like a box. No, it was a book, a book with a gold cover she realised, and on the cover was a large embossed triangle with dozens of other smaller symbols within it. Ella leaned in for a closer look and realised that they weren't symbols at all but numbers in an unusual artistic font. In the background, to the right of the man, were dark grey stone castle turrets. To the left was a dark green landscape, a forest, and a meandering grey-black river. There was a small stone bridge over the river.

Ella sat back and contemplated her inheritance, she was feeling better now. She hoped the painting was worth something. It certainly looked old. Maybe it was by an old master, she wondered, or maybe the man in it was someone famous.

Maybe it was stolen.

She noticed something on the frame: a discoloured brass plate. After digging out some brass cleaner, she polished the plaque. In no time at all it gleamed like new. As she suspected there was a name on it. It read, *Francis Perryvall*. There was a number below the name, *1517*.

Curiosity getting the better of her, she sat by her laptop in the lounge and powered it up. Firstly she Googled the words *Francis* and *Perryvall*. There were a few meaningless hits so she narrowed the search by putting the two words in quotes. Disappointingly there were no results at all. After a number of different searches involving *Perryvall* and *surname*, *Perryvall* and *painting*, *Perryvall* and *famous*, and so on, Ella concluded that although the name was popular in the 1500s in England, there were few people with it any more. And Francis Perryvall wasn't anyone famous in any case.

Clinging to the hope that the artist was well known, and eager to learn if the painting was actually worth anything, she made a mental note to take it to Darren to research it further. Hopefully he could do something with it in his lab. Maybe they could x-ray it to find hidden details, or date it somehow. She hadn't given up hope of a windfall just yet.

Still curious about the poem, she went back to the kitchen and read it over again. Other than the cryptic request itself, there was something else she didn't understand: the strange words. She knew their Greek meaning, she had seen them before, but separately. A thought occurred to her.

Back at her laptop she typed the words into the search engine one at a time. First she tried *Biblos*, there were thousands of hits, they confirmed to her that the word was ancient Greek for *book*. Then she tried *Aletheia*. Another thousand-odd hits confirmed it meant *truth*. The Book of the Truth, she wondered.

*The Biblos Aletheia the key to the past.*

Something else occurred to her: the two words were capitalised. In the search box she typed *Biblos Aletheia* and put the words in quotes to narrow the search to that specific phrase. She punched the return button and a nano-second later she frowned at the result. There was only one direct hit with both the words together. She clicked on the link and a Web site opened up on the screen. It only contained four words, they were written in large bold black letters: The Truth is Coming. Beneath the text was a symbol: a large triangle with a large pentagram in the middle, in the centre of the pentagram was an eye. Ella recognised the eye, it was an Egyptian hieroglyph, The Eye of Horus, a symbol of power and protection. Surprised and a little confused by what she saw, she scrolled to the bottom of the page. There was no more text, no links, and no flashy graphics.

Having reached a dead end with the internet she went back to the painting that lay on her kitchen table. She flipped it over and inspected the back looking for any useful information. There was some old brown masking tape on one of the corners that stuck out further than the rest. She ran her fingers over it and felt a small hard object hidden behind. Carefully, she peeled off the tape to reveal the hidden object. It was a gold ring. Dulled from age, she turned it over in the sunlight. It looked like a signet ring, the face was flat and had a symbol on it. She examined it closely, it was a triangle with a star in the middle – no, it was a small pentagram. And at its centre was a tiny eye. A cold shiver ran up her spine. The Eye of Horus, she knew, was not the organ of sight, but an instrument of action.

*In secret I ask. All will soon become clear.*

She twisted the ring around in her hand and wondered what to do. Secrets had been kept from her; she had no doubt about it. But it was time to change that.

Time to find the truth; she knew exactly where she would start.

The truth *is* coming, she thought.

# Chapter 7

TEMPESTINVEST WAS a highly successful global private investment company. Their plush, modern head office was located on the top floor of the Gherkin in central London, an iconic skyscraper which looked much like a huge tapered bullet, or perhaps a rocket from an old B-movie. The chief executive's office was large and lavishly furnished; it boasted outstanding panoramic views of the southern part of the city. The Tower of London could be seen to the left, and the tip of Big Ben and Parliament could just be made out on the far right. Connecting them was the meandering River Thames. Small ships and ferryboats navigated slowly along the river, while larger vessels waited patiently for Tower Bridge to lift its huge iron arms and free their path.

Sir Arthur Anthony Tempest relaxed on his large, soft leather sofa by the window and watched the world go by. Cradled in his hand was a crystal glass that contained one of the finest – and most expensive – Scotch whisky's ever made. He raised the glass to his nose, swilled and tilted it, and smelled the sweet, peaty aroma of the *uisge beatha* – the *water of life*, as known by its Gaelic creators.

The cost of such things was rarely a concern to Sir Arthur. He had no idea what he was worth, he had stopped caring. Some said it was £200 million, but others put his wealth at a cool half-billion. It was just numbers to him. His trust fund had made him a millionaire before he left education and after that it just seemed unimportant.

Handsome and charismatic, Sir Arthur was seen as a dream catch by the many beau monde beauties he knew and socialised with. But he was not known to have any interest in settling down with just the one woman – quite the opposite. His thirst for the pursuit of beauty was like an addiction, a drug more powerful than any narcotic. But he kept his vices well hidden from all but his closest of friends. A clever and cunning man, Sir Arthur presented his public self as a kind and charitable character. He was highly respected by the high society that he mingled with.

He was also, it seemed to some, a genius in the world of finance. When it came to making investments he had the Midas touch. Over the years he had seamlessly navigated from one success to another, making fortunes as he went. In the quiet confines of the city's private members clubs and societies many of his peers wondered what his secret was.

If only they knew.

Tenderly, he stroked the long soft red hair of the girl who had her head in his lap. Amber was her name. She was a new recruit from his modelling agency and he was showing her the ropes. He found her to be an enthusiastic learner. He would reward her well.

Of the many companies that Sir Arthur ran, his modelling agency was by far his favourite. It was also his most useful source of recruitment for his more duplicitous endeavours. Unbeknown to anyone other than his closest confides, he ran a highly secretive, and highly selective, private club. Prospective members were approached and given a brief taste of what they could expect. It was rare for anyone to refuse the offer of lifetime membership; those who did though, didn't live long enough to tell the tale. Within the highly private and luxurious confines of the clubs, which were located in several major cities, members found themselves surrounded by every indulgence. It didn't take long before new members became hooked on the pleasures of the flesh and whatever else was on offer. Members ranged from wealthy business-people to politicians, there were military commanders and spy masters alike, leading research scientists and journalists. Also on the books were international criminals, hit-men, hackers and underground rebels. The post-coital chatter would have been the envy of the CIA, had they any idea of its existence that is. But the cost of membership was high. For each member, willing or otherwise, became an asset, a tool of Sir Arthur's to call upon in whichever way he saw fit. Assets were frequently reminded that there was only one way to leave his service.

Drunk with intense pleasure, Sir Arthur shut his eyes and rolled his head back in ecstasy as Amber busied herself on him. She was delightful, perfect in every way. Just the type that Sir Arthur wanted on his island.

A mobile phone rang, its impatient ringing tone demanded attention. Sir Arthur snatched it from his trouser pocket, irritated, and looked at the screen. There was no caller number, only a single name, but one he instantly recognised. The call was not coming over the phone lines but instead over the Internet. Anonymous and encrypted, it was secure from any eavesdropping. Reluctantly, Sir Arthur withdrew himself from his playmate and stood up.

'Amber, my beauty, can you give me some privacy for a moment? Business calls.' He fumbled to make himself decent as if the caller could somehow see him. He walked over to the window and stared out across the city.

Behind him, Amber tilted her pretty head to the side and pouted. Unable to get Sir Arthur's attention she glided over to the private bathroom in the corner of the office. At the door she stopped and turned to face him once more, this time he looked over at her. Leaning on the frame provocatively, she teasingly exposed part of her curvy, smooth figure from under her red silk dressing gown.

'I'll be waiting for you,' she said in her sultry French accent. She blew him a kiss and disappeared into the bathroom.

Fighting lustful instincts, Sir Arthur almost acquiesced to his urges. But the call was from a key asset. Pained, he answered it.

'Hello my friend, thanks for me calling back,' he said. The code-phrase let the caller know he was alone and that is was safe to take the call.

'I died of laughter,' the male caller replied with the corresponding code-phrase.

'My boy, Calchas. Is all well?'

Calchas, the asset's codename, came from the name of a clairvoyant from ancient Greece who had made various seemingly accurate predictions about the Trojan war. According to the myth, a rival soothsayer had predicted the very day that Calchas would die. But when that day arrived the prediction failed to materialise, and Calchas, mocking his rival, had a fit of uncontrollable laughter. He choked on his wine and died on the spot.

'All is well indeed. Very well in fact. I have good news for you.' The voice sounded calm but Calchas was straining to contain his excitement. 'The trap has been sprung.'

'Go on,' Sir Arthur prompted. 'Enlighten me.'

'The Web site has had a visitor.'

'Which one?'

'The one with the symbol.'

'A chance find?' Sir Arthur asked, his hopes had been dashed before.

'No. The visitor was directed to the page after a very specific Google search,' Calchas said hurriedly. 'The user was on a computer based somewhere here in England.'

'What was the search phrase?' asked Sir Arthur, hopeful but not wanting to jump ahead of himself.

'*Biblos Aletheia.*'

The words hit him like a sledge hammer. For a moment time seemed to stop. Sir Arthur's stomach jumped into his mouth, blood rushed to his head. Dizzy, he swayed on his jelly-like legs. Then his brain exploded into a million thoughts all at once. He clutched the window ledge to steady himself. Adrenaline rushed around his body, he felt giddy, elated. He felt like laughing.

'It worked,' he said and threw his fist in the air. 'Well done, good work. Do you know who the visitor was or where they live?'

'I have the IP address, I'll be able to get the owner's address but it will take a few days.'

'No, you must work faster,' Sir Arthur demanded.

'It will cost some. I know a guy who can get it discreetly, keen as mustard. But he'll need a fat brown envelope, if you know what I mean.'

'I will cover it, whatever it takes. Just get me that address.' When he ended the call his hand was shaking. Someone *was* looking for it. He knew it would work, he knew someone would look for it. His prey had wandered into the trap. Now all he had to do was find them. They would lead him to the prize, he would reclaim what was rightfully his.

Dry mouthed he wandered over to the drinks cabinet and poured himself a generous dram of a 1926 scotch. A Dalmore 62 single Highland malt; the only remaining bottle of its kind. A privilege and a joy to drink, he swirled the yellow liquid around in the crystal tumbler and inhaled the sweet fumes.

'*Ipsa scientia potestas est,*' he said in toast to his own brilliance and raised his glass. Knowledge itself is power.

Returning to the long curved window of his office he gazed down onto the sprawling streets far below and beyond as far as the eye could see. Cars and taxis queued impatiently at traffic lights, there were buses and trains bursting full with commuters and tourists. The streets buzzed with thousands upon thousands of people of all colours and creeds, all shapes and sizes. The tall and the short, the pretty, the ugly, the rich and the poor.

'Look at them,' he sneered. 'They scurry like rats. Selfish capitalists. Greedy and pathetic. Godless pests that must be culled.'

Sir Arthur despaired at the state of things. The world had become corrupted, rotten even. Faith had been replaced by greed; politicians were inept and self serving. No one worked for the greater good any more; it was every man and woman for themselves. Everyone just wanted more; more money, bigger houses, better partners, more material things to make them feel better and successful. To have more was to be happier. But long, long ago he knew that it had been so different. So much *better*. And he knew he could restore it to the way it was. The way it should be.

'Our time has come.' He raised his glass once more towards the city and then downed the sweet liquid in one. 'To my destiny.'

After wiping his lips, he snatched up his phone, opened the Skype application and tapped on a contact. It was time for action. 'Hestia, something has happened,' he said. 'Something wonderful. We all need to meet, face to face. Get everyone together, we'll meet at the hall. The time has finally come.'

Overjoyed with the news he almost forgot about Amber. He wandered over to the bathroom and found her relaxing patiently in the Jacuzzi. White bubbles frothed around her pert breasts in the candlelit room. She raised her flute of champagne and beckoned him over. He knelt by her side and cupped her soft face in his hand. He ran his thumb over her cheek and lips and then plunged it into her mouth. She sucked on it eagerly and smiled. Golden light reflected off his signet ring onto her cheek. He withdrew his thumb and, with both hands, pulled her soft, pretty face towards him. Greedily, he explored her mouth with his tongue. She was warm, moist and willing.

He liked this one. She was as perfect a specimen. She would become one of the *chosen*. One of the few who would be invited to the island. To Sir Arthur, it was all about the genes, a simple arms race, survival of the fittest. Soon the weak would be eliminated. Only the chosen would survive. And the true Gods would rule once more.

# Chapter 8

*1345hrs – London*

'You've been a naughty boy,' Sarah tutted at William, waving her finger. 'Albert is not pleased, not pleased at all. Not a great first impression I'm afraid.'

'For me or him?' William asked sarcastically.

Sarah laughed and took a drink of her frothy latte. 'He can really hold a grudge you know,' she said. 'When he doesn't like someone they'll sure as hell know about it.'

'He'll get used to me.'

They were seated at a table in the near empty *Greenfly*. William had a double espresso, black with sugar. The caffeine injection helped him stay alert.

Unable to switch off from the job for too long, Sarah pulled out a large fat manila envelope and poured the contents onto the table. 'The copies of the passport scans from Paris airport,' she stated.

'Who's the lone drinker?' William asked looking over his shoulder.

Sarah followed his gaze. By a window in the corner of the room a man with yellowy-white hair sat reading a pile of newspapers. Reading glasses were perched on his nose, he looked like he was in his seventies, there was an orange bow-tie around his neck and he wore a tweed blazer. Occasionally he sipped from a glass of whisky that was by his side.

'That's Sir Robert Mansfield, OBE,' Sarah said. 'Retired now. Spent most of his working life in these offices and, it seems, intends to spend his retirement here too. Treats the place like a private club, no one really minds though. He has some stories to tell, buy him a shot of whisky and I'm sure he'll tell you some of them.'

William regarded the man, he looked frail and unsteady. He may have been battered by the years, but he refused to be beaten by them. William wondered if he would one day end up like that. Alone, unimportant and unwilling to leave the past behind.

Turning his attention to the photos, he picked up a handful and flicked through them one by one. The faces of strangers, how different they all looked, he thought. Yet, he believed, fundamentally everyone, regardless of religion or race, were much the same. They desired the same things, they had the same basic fears. The same weaknesses. Everyone was exploitable at some level. Everyone had their price.

When Sarah took a sip of her latte some froth stuck to the end of her small nose. William noted her pleasant and youthful face. Freckles surrounded her button nose. Her auburn hair was cut short in a bob. Plain, but not unattractive, she was undoubtedly very bright. William subtly motioned to her nose, she quickly wiped the froth off with a serviette.

'What is it with you opo's?' she asked. 'A law unto yourselves?'

'The man in Vienna? Just doing my job,' William said. 'It was his choice, his path in life that led to that outcome.' There was never any doubt in William's mind that his actions were fully justified. There were good guys and bad guys, plain and simple. He was one of the good guys.

'So, Sarah, tell me about you. You seem like an intelligent girl. How did you end up in this place and not earning a fortune as an international bond trader in the city?'

Sarah screwed her face up and laughed. 'Bond trader? I don't think so,' she said. 'I graduated from Edinburgh – politics and psychology – then, after applying to MI5 and sitting a few of their tests, I was offered a job here. I'd never heard of F-Branch before but the brief sounded interesting so I jumped at it. I like to think I'm making a real difference here, that's what motivates me. Anyway, I've been here three years now and loved every minute of it. Well, almost every minute. Nothing is perfect, it's had its moments now and again.'

'The lovely Mr Pinkerton perchance?'

Never one to let her tongue get the better of her, Sarah smiled but didn't say anything.

William nodded. 'There's more than a few like that in the Army,' he said. 'Although they're often called Rupert for some reason.'

Sarah laughed into her latte. 'Have you been in his office yet?'

'Pinkerton's? Yes. Why?'

'Did he show you his prize possession?'

'No,' William said perking up. 'Does he do that to all the boys?'

'Stop it! No. This is something he keeps in his cabinet. It's a Louis XIII Cognac. Very, very expensive. He'll tell you the story himself eventually, but it was given to him by the Sultan of Brunei.'

William raised his eyebrows. 'A very wealthy guy. Why?'

'Well,' Sarah said, adopting a quiet tone, 'many years ago, long before my time when Albert was a junior officer, the Sultan asked for our help. He suspected he had a mole in the higher echelons of his office, someone who was working for the Russians. Albert was known for his knack of sniffing out Russian moles, but that's another story. So Albert was sent out, on his own, to run the mole-out operation. After only a month he had found the problem. It was a textbook job. The Sultan was clearly impressed with him.'

William frowned. 'A textbook operation? Is there such a thing?' He saw a twinkle in Sarah's eye and smiled. 'So what really happened?'

'Cynic,' she chuckled. 'Apparently, the suspected mole vanished before the operation was complete. But Albert won't tell you that bit.'

'So what happened to the mole? He didn't whack him, did he?' William sounded surprised.

Sarah shook her head. '*Her*,' she corrected. 'But no, although that was what he wanted the Sultan to believe. The so-called mole, a very attractive young Czech woman, resurfaced some years later during another operation. Turns out she was spying on the Russian GRU for, you guessed it, Albert.'

'The old devil,' William spurted with a wry smile. 'He used the Brunei operation to recruit her.'

'Anyway, enough about all that. What's your story?' Sarah asked.

Talking about his past was something William generally avoided. He shifted uncomfortably in his chair and fidgeted. 'I joined the Army straight from university,' he began.

'What did you study?' Sarah asked looking strangely surprised.

'Molecular Biology,' he replied.

Sarah raised her eyebrows. 'You don't seem the academic type.'

'I'm not. Working in academia never did it for me, so I joined the Army, something I'd always wanted to do. During the initial aptitude tests I did surprisingly well in modern languages. As a result, I ended up at the Defence Intelligence School learning Russian and then a bit of Arabic and some others immediately afterwards. Odd really, I never did well at languages when I was at school. Anyway, that led to some work with special forces and, voila, I end up here.'

'Lucky for you,' Sarah said, having noted the ridiculous simplicity of the story. She considered probing further, but knew how cagey many of the field operators were about their past. She opted for a softer approach. 'Any women in your life, or men?'

'No, on both fronts,' he said in a tone that let Sarah know she was close to the line.

'That surprises me,' Sarah said. Instantly she realised she had to explain further. 'I mean for a handsome man like you. You must have broken a few hearts.'

William looked beyond Sarah at nothing in particular, and seemed to drift off in thought for a moment. He looked down, and said, 'There was someone . . .' He stopped when something vibrated in his pocket; he took out his phone and answered it.

'Saved by the bell,' Sarah murmured into her latte.

'Hades is on the move,' William said to Sarah after ending the call. In one gulp he finished his coffee.

'Got to go, gorgeous. Oh, by the way.' He picked out one of the photos he'd been scrutinising and passed it to Sarah. 'That's the waitress, the Chinese girl.' He winked at her and left.

Sarah watched him as he strode out of the room. 'Be careful,' she said quietly to an empty chair.

*

As William sped out of the bar, he almost careered straight into another field agent, Patrick 'Paddy' Howard. He side stepped, and continued on his way.

'No fraternising with the scutters, Willy Wanka,' Paddy mocked in his strong Geordie accent as William went past.

During his induction week at F-Branch, William had received a briefing from Paddy. Short and stocky with a thick neck, Paddy had a strained look, as if he constantly struggled to breathe under the weight of his barrel chest. He learned that Paddy had spent ten harsh years as a special forces trooper before he had been recruited into F-Branch as an operational officer. He was barely recognisable from the young, nine-stone weakling who had joined the Parachute Regiment all those years ago. He'd seen action in a dozen countries and had been involved in a plethora of anti-terrorist operations, hostage rescues, surveillance missions, and even a few covert kill-ops. Impulsive and rude, his experience of planning covert operations in hostile environments was second to none.

Noting the petulant remark, William smiled and walked on. He suspected that because he had held the rank of Captain, Paddy, who had never risen above Sergeant, felt it his right and duty to verbally abuse him at every opportunity. 'Fuckwit,' he responded rather too loudly.

Instantly enraged, Paddy rounded on him. 'What was that you said, Wanka?' he demanded, his reddened face inches from William's.

61

Squaring up to him, William stood his ground and looked directly into Paddy's eyes. 'Fuck. Wit. It's a noun. It means selfish, insensitive and otherwise useless prick.'

They eyeballed each other for a few more seconds. William felt the adrenaline rush through his body and tensed himself ready for a fight. Paddy, his face strained, stared for more than a moment too long, then he laughed out loud and stepped back. He slapped William on the shoulder and disappeared into the bar without a further word.

Unfazed by the altercation – William had dealt with such gorillas many times before – he headed out of the building to the underground tunnel and emerged into a secure back street car park where his new souped-up BMW was waiting for him.

There was a hare on the run and the clock was ticking

# Chapter 9

ELLA, SITTING ALONE in her kitchen, stared down at the piece of paper in front of her. From the corner of the room a quiet voice from the little radio announced the news headlines. She raised her head and listened to the report. Several Islamic terrorists had been arrested, they had been in the latter stages of an attack on London. More were thought to have escaped the net, the police were hunting for them, the public were told to be vigilant. Ella wondered what that really meant. The report was immediately followed by news that a celebrity model had been photographed entering her million pound Chelsea flat in the early hours with a married film star who was supposed to be in rehab. Ella shook her head and returned to the matter at hand.

*Find my mother's final place. It's yours, to decide. Whether to follow this ancient guide.*

Over and over the words echoed uneasily in her mind. If she was going to make any sense of the cryptic poem she had to start somewhere. At speed, she headed for the phone.

'Hello mum,' she said when the call was answered.

'Hello darling,' her mother replied in a low, soft voice. 'Nice to hear from you.' A deliberate reference to Ella's lack of regular contact.

Ignoring the dig, Ella ploughed on with her plan. 'I've been helping a colleague in the Medical Genetics department. They've taken DNA samples from me for a project. I'll get a bit of cash for it, it all helps, you know how it is.' Ella shut her eyes and took a deep breath. Deception was not her forte, especially with her mother who usually saw straight through her.

'Good for you, but isn't it time for a proper job now? Time to settle down and get ready for a family?'

Ella wasn't going to be dragged into *that* conversation again. 'Well, you see, they need to a know a little bit about my grandparents to help with the analysis,' she lied. Her heart beat hard in her throat. There was pause on the line, Ella wondered if she'd pushed it too far. She regretted making the call instantly.

'Oh. Well, they died a long time ago you know,' her mother answered in a frosty tone. 'What do they need to know about them?'

'How they died, how old they were. Just roughly, the nearest decade will do.' She felt awful but there was no other way, she reassured herself.

'My mother died not long after you were born. She was in her 60s, it was a stroke that started it. She never really recovered, poor soul. It was terrible to watch. But at least she died peacefully in her sleep, eventually. They say it's hereditary, you know.'

Ella winced. 'Ah, yes. I remember you telling me now.'

'Your granddad, well he died a few years later from a heart attack. But he was much older than my mother. He was in his 80s when he died, a very strong man, still the full shilling right up to the end. A real fighter your granddad was.' She paused for a moment. 'So when are you coming up for a weekend?'

'Soon mum. What about my other grandparents?' Ella asked with bated breath.

There was a much longer pause this time. Ella realised that she was holding her breath.

'Why do they need that dear? It was such a long time ago.'

There was something else in the tone of her voice now, Ella detected. A kind of defensiveness.

'It's important for the research mum, they need both sides of the family.' Guiltily, Ella wondered if an honest approach would have been better.

'Well, the father died during the war,' she said as a matter of fact as if it pained her to talk about it. 'Executed in France by the Nazis.'

'Oh, my God,' exclaimed Ella. There were so many more questions she wanted to ask, but she held back.

'And the mother, Elizabeth, she never remarried. Actually I'm not sure if she was ever married in the first place. Probably a disaster, just like your father.'

Here we go, thought Ella. She desperately wanted to avoid any discussion about her father. 'So how and where did she die, mum?' she added quickly.

'Died in the 1960s, I believe,' she stated a little too firmly. 'Very sudden anyway.'

'Oh. Did she live close to us?'

'Lived in Bedfordshire, a little village somewhere. Everton, that was it. I remember because it's the same name as the football team, but not the same place.' The words were delivered quickly without emotion.

'Oh. Was she buried there too?' Ella held her breath; this was the only question that mattered.

Her mother sighed deeply down the line. 'Yes, I believe she was. In the same church I married your father in, in fact.' Her voice was softer now and slower, like she was recalling the past. 'He was very insistent that we were married there. Said it was a family thing. Lovely old church, St Mary the Virgin.'

'Thanks mum. Bye.' Ella breathed out.

'Ella.'

'Yes?'

'Be careful.'

'I will,' she said with a frown and put the phone down.

Suspicious that there was more to know, Ella put the million other questions in her mind to the side. She had what she needed for now.

In any case, there was another mystery to be solved. She picked up the phone again and dialled another number. 'Hi Darren, it's me.'

'Babes, everything okay?' Darren asked.

'Yes, great. Are you in the museum lab tomorrow morning?'

'Yes.'

'Good. I have something for you to look at, if that's okay?'

'Sure, what is it?'

'You'll see,' she teased. 'See you tomorrow.'

Ella replaced the receiver and smiled to herself. She had a strange feeling that somehow her dull, monotonous life was going to change.

Some say be careful of what you wish for.

# Chapter 10

WILLIAM SEARCHED UP and down the car park for his vehicle. He eventually found it hidden between a dirty white transit van and a motorbike. The sporty BMW was dark metallic blue in colour and had silver alloy wheels. The tyres were run-flats and the doors and windows were bullet proof. The underside of the car had been made with a special alloy that was moulded to ensure that improvised explosive devices could not be stuck to it with magnets.

When he pressed the button on his key fob to open the car the encrypted wireless code was automatically changed, it prevented anyone who may have intercepted the signal from being able to copy and use it. He climbed in and settled into the black leather seat. He was impressed, it was clean and comfortable. He turned on the ignition, the powerful engine roared into life and put a satisfied, if not a little boyish, grin on his face. After switching on the sat-nav system, he pushed a tiny covert ear piece into his left ear and linked up his phone with it. It created a secure open line back to the support staff at F-Branch. Compared to the Army, William learned, F-Branch technology was light years ahead.

Gently, he slid the car into gear and accelerated past the barriers out onto the busy streets of central London. He was looking forward to feeling the power of the machine on the open road, he cursed when he turned the corner and instantly came to a halt behind an ocean of traffic. It was rush hour; rush *period* was a more accurate description, a three hour slot of nightmarish traffic that brought London to a virtual standstill twice a day, five days a week. It wasn't going to be easy catching up with the target in the centre of town, William hoped his hare would take him far out of the city and on to the motorways.

'Okay, Ollie. Where am I going?' he asked over the secure link.

Ollie was sitting alone in the TSU lab surrounded by screens. Eagerly, he watched the digital map that showed where Hades' mobile phone currently was. He looked at the data from his hack-tool and shook his head, something was worrying him. 'William, I'm sorry, but

I'm going to switch over to passive triangulation. Using the GPS module is hard on the battery and he's already pretty low.'

Triangulation of the phone masts would locate the phone to within a radius of ten or twenty metres in the city, but only to one or two kilometres in more rural areas. Ollie logged out of the target phone, closed his hacking program and switched to the cell-site triangulation tool that he already had open. A small red circle on a map showed the area that the phone was presently in. The program also showed the roughly estimated speed of the device that was being tracked.

'Do what you can, Ollie. I've every confidence in you. Where is he now?' William asked.

'He's already gone up Goswell Road, through Islington and is now heading northwest. Speed is about forty, that's four-zero. Probably on the A1 motorway heading towards the A406 ring road. It's not that clear, but that's my guess, for what it's worth.'

'Got that. I've got some time to make up then.' William feared that his prey would be quickly lost in the crowd if he headed for somewhere in the London area. But if he headed out of town would William have a chance at getting his eyes on the target. Frustratingly, his options for catching up at this stage were limited. The average speed in central London was eleven miles per hour – the same speed as it was in the nineteenth-century when travelling by horse and carriage.

'Right, he's just gone past Highgate golf club.' Ollie slurped from a large Starbucks coffee cup. Snacks, sweets and canned energy drinks were strewn all over his cluttered desk. He had prepared for a long evening.

In the car, the in-built sat-nav system set in the centre of the dashboard showed William's current location on a map. He was nowhere near his prey, but at least he could see the shortcuts that would lead him out of town. It was also updated with live traffic speeds for many of the major roads. William easily picked the quickest routes.

'Onto the A406. Wait out.' Ollie waited and keenly watched his screen until he could clearly determine which road the target had taken. 'A1 north, repeat, A1 north.'

William pressed his foot down on the accelerator, only to be stopped moments later at another set of traffic lights. Damn it, he cursed. He could have done with a surveillance team and a motorbike, but as Pinkerton ardently pointed out, such a last minute job left him with no option but to do it all himself. A high risk approach, but there was no choice.

At Mill Hill the M1 and A1 motorways converged, William's hare could easily run up either one. The former led north to Birmingham then on to the M6 and Manchester, the latter to Newcastle and, eventually, Edinburgh. Ollie watched the screen closely and prayed that the battery would last and that the phone would remain switched on. On the screen the red circle moved northwards, it remained closer to one of the roads than the other. Ollie took a best guess.

'He's still on the A1. Definitely heading north,' Ollie said as clearly as he could with a mouth full of blueberry muffin.

William had finally made it onto the A1, but he was still some way behind his target. To close the gap he weaved in and out of the traffic and raced up the track at a dangerous speed. Horns were blown, fists and insults were thrown at him. He ignored them, but kept a close look out for traffic police. Although he had a get-out-of-jail ID, he didn't want to waste any time having to stop and explain the situation to a fresh faced, twelve year old copper who was pumped up with adrenaline and full of self importance.

Eventually, after a few miles, the road led out of the city and onwards into the Hertfordshire countryside. Ollie kept William updated with the general location of his target every thirty seconds.

*

After about three quarters of an hour, William and his target remained on the A1 and headed north. William was confident that he could catch up with and identify his target. They were well away from the city and the longer he spent on the motorway the better chance he had at getting a visual on his hare.

'He's just past the Hitchin turn-off, speed is seventy-five, that's seven-five,' Ollie observed.

William was gaining on him fast, he was only a mile or so behind. Ollie, getting a little bored, had worked out the time it would take William to close the gap based on the average speed of the two vehicles.

'You know if you go five miles an hour faster, you'll catch him in three minutes,' Ollie keenly pointed out having scribbled the maths on his notepad.

Enjoying the power of the acceleration, William floored the pedal and quickly reached over one-hundred-thirty miles-per-hour. The road was full of vehicles. He sped past cars, HGVs and motorbikes alike. Woefully, his hare could be any one of them. There was no way of knowing.

'You're too close now, William,' Ollie said, noticing that the dot on the screen that showed William's own GPS location was almost at the centre of the target's much wider circle. 'Hang back. If he comes off the main, I'll let you know in time. Trust me.'

'Roger that, Ollie.' He slowed as ordered to create a little distance and then matched the average speed of his target.

'He's approaching a roundabout. It's almost a mile ahead of your location. He's gone straight over, still on the A1, but there's another roundabout a further mile ahead. You may want to close the gap a little, just in case.' William accelerated.

'He's at the roundabout, wait out. Left, left, left. He's off the A1 onto a minor road. You better catch up, it's pretty rural out there.'

'Game on,' William said and accelerated. He weaved in and out of the traffic aggressively then screeched round to the left and drove down the minor road. Annoyingly, he immediately found himself stuck behind a white van. The road curved round to the left making it impossible to overtake.

'How's that signal Ollie?' he asked. For a short distance the road straightened. William floored it and overtook the van with fearsome acceleration.

'The circumference is widening but it's still manageable. You're about five-hundred metres behind. Speed is forty, that's four-zero. Another roundabout ahead, go straight over. Try to get eyes on. We may lose it soon.'

The road narrowed, it was surrounded by woods on either side. Five hundred metres was a long way on a country road. William couldn't see much further than a hundred metres or so ahead. Traffic was light, but not a clear road by any means.

At a junction up ahead, William saw an old, battered car pull out and travel up the road in the same direction as William – very slowly. William was stuck behind the old man and there were no immediate overtaking opportunities. Impatiently, and rudely, William moved closer up behind the car and tried to bully him into pulling over. He could see the unhappy driver in his mirror. Eventually the old man took the hint and pulled over. As William shot past he gave a thankful wave.

'Approaching a crossroads,' Ollie reported. 'The circle is widening, it will take me a bit longer to figure out which direction he's going in.'

'I'm going in close, Ollie. I can't risk losing him now.'

Risking being burned by the target, William sped ahead regardless trying to get to the target before the next junction. He saw only two cars up ahead, one was red, one silver. The red one looked like an ordinary family car, the silver one was much smaller, a soft-top sports car of some kind. At the junction the red car turned left while the sports car headed straight over. William strained to see the number plates but they were too far away. He had no choice but to stay at the junction and wait for Ollie's word.

'Where now Ollie?'

'Wait out.'

Another car pulled up behind William, an overweight woman sat behind the wheel. Another car pulled behind her. One of them was on their horn.

'Come on Ollie,' William said.

'Just a few seconds more.' Ollie scrutinised the map, anxious for the large circle to move somewhere so he could work out the route. 'Got it. Straight over, William, he's gone straight ahead.'

Wheels screeching and spinning, William shot out across the junction leaving a trail of white smoke and the smell of burnt tyres, he narrowly missed another car and drove like a madman along the tiny farm road to catch up. On each side were fields and farms, he passed a thatched house, then a barn, a farmhouse, more fields. At least the winding road was empty, only occasionally did a car pass him on the other side. Tyres burned as he raced round the corners at dizzying speeds.

After a mile or so the road straightened out and he saw the silver sports car only a few hundred metres ahead of him. But as quickly as it appeared, it disappeared over the brow of a hill. William was confident this was his hare. He slowed down slightly, not wanting to get too close. If the target was surveillance aware, William feared that he may try an anti-surveillance route at some point. It was easy to do in rural terrain, and if he did do one William's car would be burned and the operation would be over.

'I have eyes on, Ollie,' William said. 'The target is a silver sports car of some sort, but no details of the plate yet.'

'Good, well done. The circle is about a mile in diameter now. Better keep your eyes on the ball from now on, the triangulation is not going to be much use. If you do lose him I'll try to hack the GPS again, there should be enough battery life for a quick check.'

In the distance the silver car's brake lights burned crimson for a few seconds. To the right of the road was a vast expanse of farmland and forest. Half way up the hill was what looked like an old mansion, some kind of stately hall, William guessed, or perhaps a boutique hotel.

'Ollie, he's slowing down, possibly about to take a turn, but it could be anti-surveillance.'

William had seen targets drive for dozens of miles on an anti-surveillance route before turning back on themselves and then driving miles to another location only to do the same thing again.

'It's a tiny road, Ollie. What's on the map?'

Ahead of William the target took the right turn and sped off up the long private road that led to the mansion. Pulling up onto the grass verge a few hundred metres beyond the turn off, William stopped and watched. The sports car drove up the track road all the way to the building and stopped in front of it. A man dressed in a dark suit stepped out of the car with a briefcase and headed straight to the front door. He opened the door and vanished inside.

'It's not named on the map, but looks like a private estate from the satellite images. Pretty big place, there are several other smaller buildings behind the main one too,' Ollie replied.

'He's parked up now and gone into the house. I'm going to hang around for a while. Can you do me a favour?'

'Sure.'

'Sarah Jackman is on the ops desk. Can you show her where this mansion is and ask her to work her magic for me? I'm going to be off-line for while.'

'I'll be here all night if you need me, William.'

'Good job, Ollie. You're a star.'

\*

At his workstation, Ollie sighed and rubbed his eyes. He placed his hand on his desk phone, hesitated and withdrew it. He shut his eyes and shook his head. He glanced over his shoulder; there was no one else around – it was late. With some reluctance he picked up the phone and dialled quickly. The line barely rang twice before it was answered.

'It's me . . . Agent Temple has followed the target to an address . . . Yes, I'll send you the details when I have them . . . Of course, I understand.' He replaced the receiver and sighed deeply.

\*

Close to where he stopped, William found a farm track just off the main road. He drove up it for a short distance and stopped by a hedge. The sat-nav showed him that he was in the middle of nowhere, there was nothing but farms and a couple of small villages for miles around.

Outside he saw nothing but fields and trees.

From the glove box he pulled out a black cylindrical object that looked not unlike a digital SLR camera. The LAD-21 was a neat device that William had used many times before on covert operations, it combined a high definition digital camera with a forty-times zoom lens and a passive night sight into one. He also took out a black balaclava and his P229 which he fitted with a silencer. From the back seat he grabbed a black rucksack that contained a few more tools that he thought might come in useful, then he jumped out of the car.

Wearing the balaclava as a hat, he ran across the road onto the farmland of the private estate. He made his way towards the mansion using the trees and hedges for cover. Keeping his distance from the long private road, he crept up the side of a ditch that divided the fields. At a high point with a view onto the impressive house, he lay down in the ditch and switched on the LAD-21. He scanned the area and took some close-up pictures.

Six stone Corinthian pillars held up the grand entrance of the mansion. Four storeys high with small square turrets on each corner, the building looked much like a small castle. There were three luxury cars parked in a large gravelled space in front of the building. A black BMW sports car, a yellow Lotus, and a silver Aston Martin. William took pictures of the cars and their number plates.

A loud noise from overhead startled him. Reacting instinctively he lay still in the ditch. A white commercial helicopter flew past at low level towards the mansion. It slowed and hovered over a large space of grass before descending to the ground. The power to the engine was cut and the rotors slowed to a stop.

With the LAD-21 at full zoom, William watched as a man dressed in a dinner jacket climbed out of the cockpit. His face was hidden by some kind of a mask; it was yellow with large black spots on the cheeks and had a long beaked nose. An opera mask, William guessed. The man walked up to the main entrance and was greeted by a taller unmasked man at the door. The unmasked man was dressed in a black suit and white shirt, no tie, he looked in his early forties and had short blond hair. His looks were Slavic, or possibly Russian, William thought. He welcomed the masked guest into the house. William snapped away until the pair vanished.

The ditch, it turned out, was a good vantage point. William remained there and watched patiently while a total of four men and five women arrived separately by car. Each car was a luxury model at the higher end of the market. Each man was dressed in a dinner jacket, the women wore ball gowns. All of them wore an opera mask of some sort.

Not long after the cars arrived another helicopter landed. There were two people on board, one was masked, but the other, the pilot, wasn't. He looked to be in his mid-sixties, and had grey hair and tanned leathery skin. William thought he had the look of a wealthy playboy. William took several shots before he too put an opera mask on. The two men exited the cockpit and walked to the entrance. Again, they were welcomed in by the blond man.

Half an hour went by with no more visitors. William decided to move in for a closer look. But first, he called Ollie for an update.

'Ollie,' he said quietly. 'I'm in the grounds of the mansion, there's definitely something going on here. Some pretty wealthy looking people have turned up, all dressed for a dinner – and in masks. I'll wire you the pictures now. Get Sarah to research the number plates and the helicopter IDs.' He pressed the send button on the LAD-21, all the images would be securely emailed to the lab.

'No problem. I'll let her know. I'm with her now in the Greenfly,' Ollie replied. He had found Sarah glued to her computer screen and had dragged her away for a chat with the promise of a coffee. 'She's found some information on the mansion, by the way. It's an old stately home called Rockcliffe Hall, belongs to some aristocratic heir from a very w . . . t . . . do fam . . . Be c . . .eful . . . this one Will . . .m his fam . . . w . . . fr . . . his . . . na . . . a . . .'

The line went dead.

'Ollie? *Ollie?*' William checked his phone, there was no signal. He had experienced this type of thing before, a slow reduction in quality followed quickly by a total loss of signal. It was being jammed. But jamming devices had a fairly short range, a thousand metres or so. William guessed that by the lack of habitations around it was most likely to be emanating from somewhere inside the mansion.

Something was happening. A meeting that someone wanted kept secure. He had to get closer.

# Chapter 11

*2030hrs – Bedfordshire*

ROCKCLIFFE HALL WAS set in two-hundred acres of beautiful English countryside and was home to one of the oldest family lines in Christendom. Although the family names had changed down the centuries, two things for sure had stuck to the descendants of this noble line like a shadow: power and wealth.

The original Rockcliffe Castle had been built in the fifteenth-century to house the extended family, their guards and their army of servants. The wreck of the old castle still sat on high ground within the estate, but it was derelict and uninhabitable having been abandoned and neglected for over three-hundred years.

Rockcliffe Hall had been built in the seventeenth-century by the then heir to the family fortune. No expense had been spared on its construction and for over two centuries it had been one of the grandest aristocratic mansions in England. Across the generations the wealthy owners had filled the opulent rooms with magnificent works of art and antiques from all across the globe. Unwavering, and often unexplained, wealth had clung to the family. Even in the early twentieth-century when most of the country's stately homes were being sold or demolished due to financial hardships, war and crippling death duties, Rockcliffe Hall stood firm. A testament to the cunning of its owners.

As planned the guests arrived in the early evening. Many had travelled from abroad and chose to drive the picturesque route from the airport through the countryside in a luxury hire car. Three had come from remote parts of the UK and travelled in their own helicopter.

To conceal their faces from the nosy house staff, and to maintain the ruse for their meeting, they all wore opera masks and dressed for dinner. One man wore a pure white Phantom of the Opera mask that covered only half of his tanned face; another wore a fearsome white mask that had thin lines of reds and yellows that exploded out from a demented smile; a slender lady dressed in a revealing red ball gown wore the mask of a feminine cherub, it had long white feathers as hair; one had an extravagant mask made from long yellow and red Ostrich feathers; another wore a silver half-moon that covered the wearer's entire face, two dark eyes peered out silently from behind it.

Each guest was welcomed into the great central hall by the blond man. A young servant girl stood with a tray of champagne flutes, she tried not to stare as the new arrivals plucked their glass from her.

Once everyone had arrived, they were escorted through the building to the drawing room. For some it was their first visit to the Hall, others were regular guests. They walked past a small fortune of artwork and antiques before they reached their destination for the evening. When everyone was seated in the lavishly furnished drawing room, a total of eleven people sat around the large circular table.

Draped over the table was a huge blood-red flag with a symbol emblazoned on it: a large black triangle with a pentagram in the centre, and in the very centre of the pentagram was the Eye of Horus. Holding the flag down were two elaborate Romanesque candelabras. Above them hung an extravagant crystal chandelier that sparkled in the candlelight. Portraits of various ancestors hung on the walls, their names and titles were engraved on bronze plates below each picture. Politicians, generals, and other notable men of high attainment, could be identified amongst the exquisite works. Other personalities were less recognisable owing to their more secretive professions.

At the far end of the room was a huge marble fireplace, a freshly lit fire raged in it. The sweet musty smell of burning wood hung in the still air. At the opposite end was a huge gold statue of a seated Zeus. It was said to be over two-thousand years old; a relic from times forgotten.

The doors opened once more and their host entered. Wearing no mask, he was dressed in a black dinner jacket and bow tie. His handsome features were on full display to his familiar guests. He had short, dark, curled hair and chiselled almost perfect features. They called him Hades and he was their elected leader. He gazed upon his masked guests and took his seat in silence.

A moment later the same blond man entered carrying a black toolbox. A large man with soulless dark blue eyes, he had a wide face and rough features that were not attractive. His name was Fyodor Sergeyevich Kushnir, but he preferred to be known simply as Cossack. A former KGB agent, Cossack was no man to mess with. A trained killer with bags of experience at the sharp end, he was Hades' director of security and was responsible for all such matters within the organisation. No task was too small or too big for him, he was a loyal servant.

In silence, Cossack walked over to the table and placed the black toolbox on it. From it he took out a small hand held object which looked much like a walkie-talkie radio. When he switched it on the device beeped intermittently. He walked around the room and made a sweeping motion with it in his hand. As he passed by each guest, he swept them up and down. The beeps remained steady. Eventually, he returned to where he had started. He put the device away and took out a larger green and black object that had Cyrillic writing on it. This he positioned on a small table by the wall. He switched it on and gave a solemn nod to his boss.

'Thank you, Cossack. Excellent work as always. You may leave us now,' Hades commanded.

Cossack picked up his toolbox and glanced at the masked guests. His piercing eyes had that thousand yard stare. Scars on his face told the tale of a harsh past. He left the room without a word.

The security formalities over with, Hades stood up to address his audience. His enthusiastic voice boomed as he began the proceedings.

'Friends, brothers and sisters,' he said. 'Thank you for coming at such short notice. I know how difficult and dangerous it is to meet like this, face to face. But there are urgent matters to discuss. You may remove your masks now and please speak freely; the room is soundproof and secure. Cossack's little device here,' he pointed to the green and black device on the table, 'will block any radio and mobile phone transmissions within half a mile.'

As directed, the guests removed their masks and placed them under their chairs. Six men and five women of varying ages and races were revealed. Although each face was unique, they all had the same air of wealth and power about them, an aura of superiority.

Hades scanned his dark eyes over them all before proceeding. 'I can't say how pleased I am to see you all again, it has been far too long my friends. But soon we will be together permanently in the new world where there will be no need for the secrecy that has impeded our progress for far too long. The Brotherhood of Olympus will finally be free.'

There were the cries of approval from table, 'Hear, hear,' and, 'Bravo.'

'Much has been done since our last gathering, but not without some trouble; more of that later. First for the good news.'

Hades placed his hand firmly on the shoulder of the man sat to his left. 'Poseidon,' he boomed proudly, 'has prepared the ships for the *chosen* to set sail to our new, albeit temporary, homeland. Almost everything is ready for our arrival.'

There was a general murmur of approval. A few raised their flutes of champagne as a toast to Poseidon.

'Another victory to tell,' Hades went on. 'Our informants did well in finding such a large shipment of cocaine. As some of you already know, we successfully intercepted it and have more than we need. It is being prepared as we speak. Hephaestus, are your people still on schedule?'

Unlike the grotesque image of the lame Greek god of his namesake, the man known as Hephaestus was a well bred, handsome and charming young fellow. In his mid thirties, he had dark, shiny curly hair, dark eyes and thick black eyebrows. Originally from western Greece, he lived in a wealthy area of London from where he ran the old family sugar businesses. But his aristocratic ancestors had been more than just sugar and spice merchants, for they had also been secretly involved in smuggling. It had begun many centuries ago when the wave of Emperor Constantine's Christianity spread across the modern world and waged war on the ancient mystic religions. Under the cover of their trade they had smuggled pagan artefacts, books and treasures to safety, saving them from inevitable destruction by the new Church. Through the generations, and under the cover of a series of reputable companies, the family had smuggled everything from wine to diamonds, arms, and eventually, drugs.

'Yes, Hades,' Hephaestus hissed proudly in a low voice. 'The preparation has more than doubled its weight, much more then we need. And strangely, it has turned the powder pink.' Everyone laughed. Hephaestus looked at them in surprise, then grinned himself. 'The price will be set so low that ours will be the product of choice. I think its colour will make it very popular too. Like a fashion item perhaps, something fun for the party-goers. Our dealers are ready to distribute it in the key global locations on your orders, Hades. A good section of their market is, predictably, the middle and upper classes. Lawyers, bankers and media types, as well as the usual suspects in the entertainment industry. This way we will sell to those who travel far and wide.' Hephaestus smiled a humourless, soulless smile.

'Good,' Hades said sternly. 'The rats will carry it into the cities.'

There were general murmurs of agreement from the others. The sound level in the room rose as the guests conversed with each other. Hades drank casually from his glass before delivering the crucial news they had all come to hear.

He tapped the side of his glass and room quietened. 'I will be sending the order to distribute it on Sunday. It will only be a matter of days before it will be on the streets of every major city in the world. You must all deploy to the island before then. I will follow you there soon after.'

The atmosphere changed in an instant; there were gasps of concern from the table. Clearly not all of the guests were aware of the much accelerated plan. Instead of the rapturous applause that Hades expected, there was shocked silence. Hades frowned and looked around the table.

The silence was broken by one of the younger females. 'It's too soon, Hades. Surely we are not ready?' asked Aphrodite, her accent was upper-class English. She was the great-granddaughter of a former British Prime Minister and was infamous for speaking her mind.

One of the others, an overweight man known to them all as Apollo, shifted uncomfortably in his seat and turned to Aphrodite. 'There has been a setback,' he said weakly, he coughed and cleared his throat.

'What kind of setback?' Aphrodite asked sharply. Her delicate English rose looks were deceptive; under the skin she was as ruthless as a Mafia boss.

'We lost our professor,' replied Apollo sternly.

'Please tell me you are fucking joking?' Aphrodite laughed and looked towards Hades aghast.

'No, it is, sadly, no joke,' Hades said calmly. 'I'm afraid we had to eliminate our professor, it seemed he had second thoughts. But we were forewarned by Kerberos, our most valuable asset at this sensitive time, and took appropriate and timely action to minimise the risk. The damage is minor and we believe our plans have not been compromised to any worrying degree. The professor knew little detail of our overall objectives. In fact, I don't see it as a setback at all. If anything, it has strengthened our resolve to take action.'

'But security *has* been breached,' an older woman with grey hair said in a panicky voice. 'We must take precautions, lie low for a while, re-plan.'

'Quite the contrary, Artemis,' Hades snapped. He closed his eyes and calmed himself. 'Do not worry, I said we have taken care of the matter. And that is the end of it.'

'Don't patronise me, Hades,' Artemis barked back. 'This isn't a trip to Vegas we're organising. Any change needs careful consideration by all of us. This isn't just your mission, Hades, we're all a part of it. Our ancestors started this a long time ago in case you had forgotten. And if it wasn't for us you'd still be blindly chasing that damned mythical book.'

Hades' face remained emotionless despite the rush of blood to his head. Calmly, he replied, 'There is no going back, Artemis. Not for anyone now. If you are not happy with the arrangements then you are free to leave us.' He motioned to the door.

The others looked to Artemis, they all knew what it meant to walk out now. Artemis said nothing but her face was a picture of bitter indignation. She folded her arms and sat back in her chair, beaten down but defiant.

'That is all I have to say on the matter. And speaking of *that damned book*,' Hades said looking straight at Artemis who avoided his piercing gaze, 'it is no myth, I assure you. I have some encouraging news about it, but more of that later. Now, does anyone else have any concerns they wish to air?'

The room was silent.

'No one? Good.'

Always the sycophant, Poseidon reiterated Hades earlier point. 'You must all urgently make plans to get to the island,' he said. 'Take only what you need and you won't need much, everything is there for you. But there will be no going back to the mainland for some time.'

'Out time has come,' Hades preached. 'We will be together, all of us. Eventually we will re-colonise the mainland, rebuild the temples, teach the old ways of our ancestors. We will bring order to the new world, with better people and a better way of life.'

One of them, a young Indian man known as Hermes, stood up and raised his flute of champagne towards Hades. 'To Hades, and the new Eden. To *Hades'* Eden,' he said in toast.

The rest of the guests stood up and raised their glasses. '*Hades' Eden*,' they said in unison.

*

Outside the mansion the sun vanished over a hill behind the estate and the gentle evening breeze dropped to a mere whisper. From the shadows of the forest a dark shape stealthily appeared and disappeared, creeping ever closer to the mansion. On reaching a short wall that marked the boundary between the forest and the raised garden in front of the house, William stopped and scanned the area for any security measures.

On the top corners of the house were halogen flood lights, below each was a small dome of smoked glass or plastic. CCTV cameras, William assessed, probably infra-red, perhaps with motion detection too. He was going to get no further without being detected.

He checked his phone, it was still being jammed. He guessed that the meeting was still in progress. Deciding that he was close enough to the windows to be in range, he reached into his rucksack and took out a small black camera-like object that had a small tripod attached to it. Setting it up on the grass, he peered down the viewer and lined the device up with one of the windows of the mansion. He switched on the laser eavesdropping device and pushed the earphone into one ear.

Scanning one window at a time, he took a moment on each to listen for any voices amongst the hiss of the static. The invisible infrared laser beam picked up tiny vibrations on the glass and converted them back into sound. The quality wasn't great and it was easily defeated by curtains or by music from a radio close to the widow, but, he figured, it was his best chance at gaining intelligence given the circumstances.

In the distance, William heard the sound of gravel crunching under the weight of a vehicle. A white van had driven on to the long private road and was headed for the mansion. Peering over the wall, William watched as it stopped at the main entrance. On the side of the van was a brand name written in a curvy artistic design. William recognised it to be that of a Michelin star restaurant. He had once eaten at their New York branch, the food had been excellent and the wine list was an oenophile's dream.

The van stopped, the head lights went out. Two men, chefs dressed in white hats and black and white checked trousers, jumped out. One walked to the door of the house and rang the bell, while the other opened the rear of the van and took out some silver trays. The blond man answered the door, he spoke to the chef for a moment, then both chefs took trays and equipment from the van into the house. William's stomach rumbled. His evening meal was a standard ration pack. Boil in the bag beans and sausages, eaten cold and followed down by a tasteless energy bar and an orange drink.

In the darkness, William shuffled and crawled to various positions around the house. He directed the laser at every window in sight but with not so much as a whisper, other than the irritating hiss of static.

A shadow flashed past a small window on the ground floor. Catching William's attention, he quickly turned the laser towards it. He tweaked the squelch to get the best reception.

'... bunch of tossers,' a voice said in mid sentence.

'I've cooked for worse,' another male voice said, the accent was cockney. 'At least this lot keep themselves to themselves. I had one gig where the host kept pestering me, a real arse-hole. Wanted to taste my food before it went out! The cheek of it.'

'They're a funny bunch, this lot,' said the first man. 'The boss dropped this one on me last minute, really screwed up my routine. Anyway, looks like he's a planning a long holiday. I've been packing all sorts for him. Anyone would think he's moving the whole bloody house.'

'All ready to go,' the second man said. 'Service!' There were banging sounds, then the light in the window went out.

After a couple of hours with no more movement from the house, William began to fear that he wasn't going to gain anything useful.

The sky had cleared and the temperature had plummeted. With no street lights for miles around, the stars shone brightly above. Staring up at the sky with the night sight, William saw them in all their glory, billions of them. The long thin cloud of the milky way looked like a mysterious smoke trail that split the sky in two. A meteor streaked through the blackness silently, its silvery smoke trail was momentarily lit up before it vanished into nothing.

There was a flash of brilliant light from the front of the house. The main door of the mansion opened wide and a man, the same blond one who had welcomed the guests earlier, walked out holding two long leads. Two large lean dogs with pointed ears shot out behind him. Elegant yet muscular, they were fearsome creatures.

William recognised them, they were Doberman Pinschers. Adrenaline rushed though his veins and he considered running back to the forest while he still had a reasonable chance of being undetected. But instead he waited, crouched down behind a short wall at the end of the garden. He pulled the balaclava down over his face and withdrew his pistol.

The man spoke to the dogs in Russian. William understood it to mean, 'Hurry up and do your business, bitches.'

The dogs wandered out onto the garden still attached to the long leads. The Russian took out a pack of cigarettes and a Zippo lighter. He put a cigarette in his mouth and, using a quick and seemingly well practised move, he flicked open the lighter and ignited it. He bathed the end of the cigarette in the flame and took a long drag. He blew out a cloud of smoke which dissipated slowly across the garden in the light wind. William noted the direction of the breeze, it was going away from him.

The dogs meandered towards the walled edge of the garden

together, sniffing the grass as they went. One found its place and stopped to do its business. The other had found a scent and eagerly followed it; straight towards William. Bearing its sharp teeth, the beast growled and barked as it went.

Pushing himself close to the wall, William ducked down. He held his breath and considered his options.

'Silence!' the man snapped in English as the barking continued.

The Russian yanked the lead hard; there was a jingle of metal and a yelp from the dog. It stopped and whined; it looked pleadingly over at the Russian man and then snapped its head back towards the end of the garden. It whined with frustration and daringly pulled against the taut lead.

The man cursed at it in Russian, 'stupid dog!' With his cigarette held between his lips, he marched over to the dog, pulling in the lead as he went. When the beast saw him coming, it cowered. When he reached the dog he pulled out a large black pistol from his waist and hit the dog soundly in the body with the butt of it. The dog whined loudly and instantly lost interest in the scent. The Russian muttered more curses and sucked hard on the last draw of his cigarette. He flicked the fag end over the short wall and walked back towards the house dragging the dogs behind him.

The burning ember landed next to William, its glowing red end only an inch from his face. Foul smoke wafted up his nostrils, he felt a sneeze brewing. With all his might he held his breath to keep it in. When the dogs had been dragged back into the house, William sat up and breathed the cold air deeply. Once again he was alone in the darkness.

*

In the drawing room the meeting continued with an air of excitement. Hades had almost concluded his speech, he had loved every moment of the address. His enthusiastic, loud voice reverberated around the room.

'As I alluded to earlier, my search for the Biblos Aletheia has taken a most fascinating turn,' he said with delight. 'This may be the closest we've been to it since the Church stole it from us five hundred years ago. My plan appears to be working, but there is still much to be done, yet so little time.'

'Is it really within our reach?' Hermes asked with intrigue.

Hades nodded. 'Someone else is looking for it. Someone who knows nothing of us. Why, I ask, why do they search for something that no one knows exists?' Holding out his hands, Hades gazed in wonder around the table at their blank faces. 'The only outsider ever suspected of having knowledge of it has died. A terrible accident I must say, very unfortunate.' He acted out his disappointment. 'It would have been so much simpler if only he had chosen to talk to us. But now it seems someone else wants to know what the Biblos Aletheia is. Coincidence? No, my friends. Someone has been entrusted with the secret and we are watching her.'

Poseidon frowned. Something about the story didn't make sense. He plucked up the courage to speak. 'Someone actually has it?' he asked feigning pleasant surprise. 'But would they not have used it by now? Academia would be buzzing all over it like flies. And the Church . . .' He laughed mockingly. 'The Church would be rushing to deny its very existence.'

'Not if they didn't know what it was,' Hades replied smugly. 'A key can be inherited, but if the secret of what it opens is lost, then it is worthless. Merely an ornament.'

'You said, "watching her"?' Aphrodite asked with narrowed eyes. 'A woman has it? Who is she?'

'A young student in Cambridge.'

Aphrodite laughed condescendingly. 'So what are we waiting for?' she questioned. 'Take her in. I'm sure Cossack can make her talk.' When she referred to Cossack it was as if a foul taste had formed in her mouth.

Hades shook his head. 'No, my young friend. I need to know for sure that she has it before we take action. She may only have heard of it and may not be in actual possession of it. I have no way of knowing at this stage.' He smiled and raised a finger. 'But, be assured, I do have a plan to find out.' It was all coming together, Hades thought. After years of careful planning it was finally going to happen. The truth of the matter was that they could still carry out their plan without the book, but it would make all the difference. It was evidence that they had done the right thing, proof that they were who they said they were. And to Hades, the book was everything.

'Enough about the book for now,' Hades said, he sat down and relaxed a little. 'We have other matters to discuss. Zeus, my friend. I trust the resources we will need are ready?'

'Indeed they are, tested and in place. The energy supply will last for generations, considerably longer than we will need it for. But it has not been easy suppressing the engineering works at the island. There were a few who had to be silenced,' Zeus replied as a matter of fact.

Despite being the oldest member of the group, Zeus looked much younger than his years should have allowed. His skin was soft and tanned, his long grey hair was tied back in a pony tail. Behind his dark, unassuming eyes was the mind of a genius, a product of the best education money could buy. Although he had been born into old money, he had added to the family fortune significantly with his mining company. Having made his fortune initially in Australia, he rapidly and aggressively expanded around the globe. His empire mined everything from coal to diamonds, iron to uranium. Powerful and influential, he was a great asset to the organisation.

'Soon, none of that will matter,' Hades said callously. 'You have done well Zeus, our survival is guaranteed.'

Hades directed his attention towards an elegant and attractive blonde woman dressed in an exquisite black ball gown. 'Athena, my darling, you are as beautiful as ever,' he said with a warm smile. 'Your team has supplied us with some invaluable information. Without it we would be blind, deaf and ignorant of our enemies. None of this would be possible without you. What would we have done if the gods hadn't delivered you to me?'

'Flattery will get you everywhere,' she replied gracefully, there was the slightest hint of Russian in her accent. When she smiled her luscious lip gloss shimmered a deep red in the candlelight.

Athena was the only member of the inner circle not to have inherited her title. None of her ancestors had ever been part of the organisation, but there was no doubt that she had earned her place amongst them. For Athena was Hades' protégée. As stunning as any model and as deadly as any assassin, her natural skills in seduction and manipulation were invaluable. She directed the intelligence gathering side of the organisation and provided them with invaluable information.

Despite her apparent success, Athena had not always been so fortunate. At the tender age of fourteen, on her way home from school in Pinsk, Belarus, she was abducted by a gang of Ukrainian sex traffickers. Raped and beaten into submission, she was eventually sold to an oil-rich Arabian Sheikh. Imprisoned in his remote desert mansion, the Sheikh, a greedy overweight man, kept her as one of his harem girls. He called her his Russian ballerina and made her dance for him. Always hateful of him, but powerless to retaliate, Athena found a way to survive the misery. Like a talented actress playing a part beautifully, she quickly gained his trust as an obedient and enthusiastic servant. She soon became his favourite.

Eventually, after deciding she could be trusted, the Sheikh took her away on a business trip to a luxury hotel in eastern Europe. Whenever he was out he had her closely watched by his security team. But thoughts of escape occupied her mind. Athena formulated an escape plan. One evening, after she had shared a few glasses of champagne alone with him, she seductively tied him to the bed with the promise of a wild night. His excitement was obvious through the white sheets, but it was short lived. She gagged him tightly. His excitement turned to confusion, then panic when he realised something was seriously amiss. He pulled frantically on his bindings, his flab wobbled like a grotesque jelly while he squirmed.

Methodically, and without rush or panic, Athena gathered all the valuables she could find: cash, jewellery, watches, his laptop, and placed them in a designer travel bag. Then, when she was ready, she slowly and calmly poured a bottle of very expensive brandy over the pig. Towering above him she took out a match from its little paper book and lit it. She waited only long enough to see the look of terror and disbelief on his face as the flames licked at him before leaving the room with her things. As the fire alarms boomed, hundreds of panicked guests rushed out of the hotel into the cold night, Athena coolly walked out onto the street and breathed in the sweet smell of freedom.

Although finally free, her ordeal did not end there. After pawning the stolen valuables, she travelled back to Pinsk hoping to find her family and dreamed of a fairytale reunion. But all she found there was poverty and misery. Her mother had killed herself soon after Athena's disappearance. Her father, a heavy drinker even before she disappeared, had eventually drunk himself to the grave. There was nothing left for her. She was truly alone.

Vowing never to be a slave to any one again, but lacking in any formal education or skills, she used the only talent she had to survive. Picking a new name for herself, she quickly went to work seducing wealthy businessmen. By the end of her third marriage she was a millionaire and barely thirty years old.

One day, a few years later, her life reached a turning point. After ending her fifth marriage and assuming a new name once more, she moved to England. For her next unsuspecting victim she selected one of the country's most eligible bachelors. But the victim turned out to be, in a serendipitous twist, herself. It took her by surprise, she never knew she was capable of the emotion, but she quickly fell in love with him. The money ceased to matter and the guilt of her original intentions welled up and consumed her.

One evening, during a romantic meal in the Latin quarter of Paris, she took a huge risk and confessed everything to him. Her whole sorry life. Instead of rejecting her, as she thought he would, he admired her even more. For her lover was obsessed with the quality of a person, their sharpness of mind and, most importantly, their strength. There, right in front of him, was a perfect example of a survivor. And a beautiful one at that.

He told her that there was a reason for everything. Did she believe in fate, in a God? Taking a risk himself he told her about his secret society, not quite everything, but enough to whet her appetite. He asked her if she would join him. Without a second thought, Athena agreed. And she came to know him as Hades.

Finally, Athena had found meaning in her life. A purpose. Her devotion and loyalty were unwavering. After a position in the inner circle had become available with no obvious heir, they agreed that she was the best candidate they could ever hope for.

'Now then, enough of business, time to feast,' Hades said. 'I have arranged some entertainment that I know you will all enjoy.'

As the room exploded into excited conversation, the double doors to the drawing room opened wide and several men and women walked in. Each was dressed in a pure white silk toga. A large white hood concealed their faces. But it was clear which sex each person was from their figures. To emphasise the fact, on the front of each toga was a symbol. For the women it was a thick black triangle, and for the men, a pentagram. The men held plates of food, while the women had trays of cutlery and wine.

In single file the hooded figures walked around the room until they surrounded the table, then stopped once each person was in position. The women laid out the cutlery. Once done they stood back and waited for the next order with their heads bowed.

The room quietened with anticipation. The guests eagerly cast their eyes upon the new arrivals whose loose togas occasionally, and teasingly, exposed their tight, naked flesh beneath.

In unison, and from the right of each guest, the men leaned down and placed their plates on the table with the starters. The women servers then stepped forward and poured each guest a generous glass of Dom Perignon Oenotheque, the 1969 vintage. Once done, all silent servers retreated to the walls of the room and waited.

Hades stood up and beamed, he could barely hold in his excitement. 'You are about to embark on a culinary odyssey. There will be six delightful taster courses followed by a dessert which I know you will all thoroughly enjoy. Please begin.'

After the starter of scallops, amaranth and black corns, the servers cleared the cleaned plates and brought out four further courses in well paced succession. First, there was fresh langoustine served with foie gras and watermelon. This was followed by exquisite quail and duck dishes that listened with sweet sauces. A crisp tea sorbet cleansed their palates before they indulged in an oyster risotto. The servers ensured that a superbly complementing wine was served with each course. The penultimate course was a delicious lamb crepinette.

The table was cleared and then prepared for the dessert, trays of exotic fruit were placed down. There was rambutan from Asia, Indian jackfruit, passion fruit, and mangosteen. Once set, the servers took a step back and waited.

One of the males clapped his hands together. The obedient team responded immediately. Each of them pulled down their hoods to reveal their faces. They looked straight ahead like well trained soldiers. Another clap and they removed their togas, the silk gowns fell soundlessly to the floor.

The women were simply astonishing. They had large darkened eyes, playful lips and thick long hair of various shades. Each was dressed in designer black and red lingerie.

The men were dressed only in black shorts, their naked torsos bulged with muscles which glistened in the candlelight. Each man was as handsome as the next. Like troops on parade, they stood perfectly still and waited.

Hades rose from his seat and addressed the room. 'In the ways of our ancestors, we shall now worship the beauty of life and the beauty of the Gods. We shall join as one and together we will commune with the Gods.'

One of the girls, a tall, slim exquisite woman with long red hair, broke from the ranks and picked up a section of fruit. Seductively, she put it half in her mouth, then draped her tanned arm around Hades' neck and shoulder. Slowly, she slid down onto him, her long slender naked legs draped over his. Her firm breasts pressed up against his chest. Looking into his eyes she pulled his head towards her and offered the food to him. Hades took a bite of the manna and the embrace quickly became a passionate kiss. The room quickly erupted into applause and laughter, and the party began.

Athena enjoyed the attention of two muscular young men, while Zeus selected a delightful blonde with breasts that were bursting out of her dark red bra. Apollo tucked into the fruit and champagne with enthusiasm while an Iranian beauty satisfied him with her skills in fellatio. Bodies writhed on chairs, some took to the walls, while one girl perched on the table with her legs spread, waiting for the next communion with a partner.

After he had completed his own worship with his favourite beauty and her Malaysian friend, Hades sent the two girls to his room and dressed himself. He checked his phone for messages, grabbed Cossack's jamming device and quietly slipped out of the drawing room.

\*

Beginning to feel weary, William peered cautiously over the wall and scanned the windows with the laser once more. It had proved to be a disappointing evening. Since the chefs had left, nothing more had happened. There had been no conversations in any of the rooms he scanned. His phone was still jammed.

He was about to leave when he noticed a dim glow appear in a window on one of the ground floor corners. He pointed the laser at it and tweaked the squelch until he could make out voices.

' . . .glad I caught you . . . have an urgent job for you . . .' one man said, the voice was grainy and difficult to make out. But the accent was undoubtedly English. Posh, upper class.

'Yes boss,' a gruff, less refined voice replied.

'I have the address for you. Go there first thing tomorrow, wait until the flat is empty then have a discreet look around for the . . .' William couldn't make out the words. 'You know what to look for?'

'Yes boss.'

'It's unlikely to be there but there may be clues as to where it is. Don't follow the girl, don't intercept her, the policeman will attend to that. He'll meet you later for the transfer. Bring her to me unharmed. You can do what is required to extract the information after I've spoken to her.'

'Yes boss, of course. I'll leave at first light.' The accent could have been eastern European or Russian. It probably belonged to the blond man from earlier, William guessed.

After a couple of hours more without any movement from the house, William carefully made his way back to his car. He considered his options for the morning. He didn't have enough GPS trackers for all the cars that were parked at the mansion and it would have been too dangerous to go that close to the house anyway. There was another option, though. From the car boot he took out a small briefcase sized object. In the darkness he proceeded to the only exit road from the mansion and hid the briefcase in the undergrowth. The Portable Cell Site Emulator acted like a mobile phone mast. When any mobile phones came within its fifty meter range, they would automatically log on to it for a signal. The device would simply scoop up all the phone details that were required to track it remotely.

Back in his car, William checked his phone, he had a signal. He emailed the photos to the lab and sent Ollie and Sarah instructions for the morning. He set his alarm for sunrise and tried to sleep. It was going to be another long day.

# Wednesday

*Hemera Hermu* 'day of Hermes'

# Chapter 12

*0557hrs – Bedfordshire*

IN HIS SMALL bedroom in the house, Cossack packed his tools into a blue rucksack and slung it over his shoulder. He made his way down through the dimly lit hall to the empty drawing room. Checking that there was no one else around to see him, he entered it. The fun and games of the night before had ended, the room was empty and silent, a musty smell hung in the air. Leftovers of food and empty wine bottles were strewn all over the table. On the floor and over the chairs were some items of clothing. Cossack could only imagine what debauchery had gone on only a few hours beforehand. His employer had promised him similar rewards on the island.

Walking around the table, he ran his fingers along the edge until he felt a barely noticeable notch. At which point he reached under it to a hidden crevice. From there he retrieved a tiny black square object, about the size of a small coin. He placed it in his wallet. Cossack didn't like to be kept in the dark, a survival trait that had served him well in the past. He'd listen to the tiny digital recorder in the car. From the table he picked up an almost empty bottle of champagne and raised a toast to himself.

'Knowledge is power,' he said and downed the remaining liquid in one.

After making his way to the double garage behind the mansion, Cossack jumped into one of the two green Range Rovers, fired up the sat-nav and typed in the address of his target. He turned the ignition and set off on his new mission.

\*

The early morning motorway traffic was light and Cossack made good time. He arrived in Cambridge just before the fearsome morning rush. The sat-nav led him straight to the street he was after, a long avenue with two and three storey terraced houses on each side of the narrow road. As he drove down it slowly, he spotted the door of the flat he was looking for. Finding a suitable parking space with a good view, he pulled up and waited.

It wasn't long before the street was busy with the morning commuters. A long queue of traffic crawled past him. Cossack watched their tired and frustrated faces as they went. Cyclists whizzed along precariously close to the sides of the cars, weaving in and out. Students and professionals alike left their flats and walked towards the town with their satchels and briefcases in hand. Cossack watched them go past with an element of resentment. He hated students. But then he hated most people.

The tatty blue door of the target flat opened and a girl walked out alone. Naturally pretty, she was easy on the eye, but looked a little dull without any make up. Her clothes were the kind probably worn by a student, Cossack thought, certainly not an office worker or anyone with money. In her hand was a plastic supermarket bag that was full of what looked like books and files. An old brown handbag was slung over her shoulder. Oblivious to her watcher the girl walked down the avenue and out of sight.

Cossack waited a few minutes just to make sure the girl wasn't going to return for something forgotten. Then he left his car and walked over to the door of the flat. Hoping for no answer, he rang the bell and knocked hard on the door. There was no sign of movement. From his inside jacket pocket he took out his lock drill and started work on the simple Yale dead-bolt. Moving in close to the door to block anyone's view of what he was doing, he pushed the thin blade of the drill into the lock and squeezed the trigger. Inside the lock the blade expanded and pushed the locking bolts outwards. At the same time Cossack applied a slight torque on the device and, once the bolts were in the correct position to unlock, the blade spun around. With a satisfying click the door unlocked without complaint. Cossack pushed his way into the flat and disappeared.

After searching the living room and bedroom top to bottom it was obvious he wasn't going to find what he was looking for. The flat was small, there were few hiding places. He moved to the kitchen and started to go through the drawers.

The door bell rang.

Cossack froze. For a moment he considered hiding, but curiosity made him look towards the door. He decided to bluff it. He made his way to the front door and opened it.

At the door he found a young woman who stood alone. In her early twenties she had mousy brown hair and wore too much make-up. Her innocent eyes were dark, her skin was naturally tanned. Wearing black leggings and a raggedy checked shirt, Cossack took her for a student.

'Is Ella in?' the girl asked with a frown, uncertain of who the man in front of her was, but too polite to ask.

Cossack eyed her from her feet up to her face. When his eyes met hers he smiled. 'Yes. She is in the kitchen,' he said. 'I was just leaving. Going back to the university.' He smiled at her again and motioned for her to come in.

With an element of uncertainty the girl walked past him and headed for the kitchen. Cossack peered up and down the road before closing the door behind him.

'Ella. Ella?' she said as she walked in. Her face fell when she saw that the kitchen was empty. She stopped, snatched her phone out from her handbag and made to leave.

Cossack blocked her way.

'Ella must be upstairs.' He nodded towards the stairs behind him.

'It's okay, I'll see her later,' the girl said quickly and nervously. 'I have a class. Got to go now.' She made to walk past Cossack, but he moved to block her again.

Exaggeratedly he sniffed the air. 'Do you smell that?' he asked.

Confused and irritated the girl frowned and regarded him with a quizzical look. 'No. Smell what?'

Cossack glared at her, his eyes narrowed. He relished the moment before replying. 'The delicious aroma of fear,' he said and grinned.

The colour drained from the girl's face, her eyes widened. She staggered backwards and took a deep breath ready to scream.

Cossack lunged at her and threw a punch at her solar plexus. The air was forced out of her lungs, she curled up and fell to the floor winded. Her face reddened and her eyes bulged, she struggled to breathe. She tried to push her attacker away, but Cossack grabbed her arm and twisted it harshly around her back. Firmly, he placed his hand over her mouth and nose and held her tightly. Despite her struggles he easily pulled her head back close to his. Slowly he licked her ear. She writhed and tried to scream, but nothing other than a muffled groan came out.

'You and I are going to have a little party,' he whispered. He bit down on her ear hard, and fed off her fear.

# Chapter 13

*0832hrs – Cambridge*

THE EARLY SUN rose in an almost cloudless sky over the town. The streets came alive with the morning rush. Pedestrians walked briskly along the pavements. Cyclists whizzed past, they weaved in and out of the sea of cars that were stuck in a circus of seemingly endless traffic jams.

Ella was glad she had walked to the Fitzwilliam Museum. The fresh air had cleared her mind. By the time she reached Trumpington Street her nerves had evaporated. It was only a painting after all, what harm could it do? If it was worthless, and it probably was, then no matter, she told herself. Nothing gained, nothing lost.

She walked up the white stone steps, past the great Corinthian pillars that supported the huge triangular gable, and into the impressive Hellenistic building of the Fitzwilliam Museum. Inspired by the architects of ancient Greece and Rome, it was a temple to the arts, a monument to learning. It had been built on the principles of inspiring creative and intellectual thinking, principles first introduced by the ancient Greeks in their museums of Alexandria over two-thousand years ago.

Ella sped through the busy rooms past hordes of tourists who shuffled along admiring the works. Dashing in between the exhibits and the tourists, she headed straight for the basement labs. Darren had told her he was there working on a restoration project for the university.

'Babes,' Darren said delightedly when he saw Ella. He abandoned his desk and ran over to her.

Ella held out the supermarket bag with the painting and raised her eyebrows.

'Is that it?' he asked taking the bag. 'The masterpiece? The stolen Monet that we've been looking for?'

Ella laughed. Looking around, the lab wasn't quite what she had expected. There were no complex machines or men in white coats peering cautiously over dusty paintings. It was just a large, dated office with a few workbenches and some computers. Various pieces of technical equipment were strewn across the room. Two young students looked up from their desks for a moment and then continued with their studies in silence.

'Yeah, this is it,' Ella shrugged. 'Sorry it didn't come on a velvet cushion.'

'Okay, let's have a look at this masterpiece. Shall we?' Theatrically Darren put his white gloves on. Ella giggled. He pulled the painting out of the bag and carefully laid it on one of the tables for inspection. Poring over it, he scrutinised every little detail of its surface.

'Wow! It's a very good portrait. Decorative and highly finished. Hmm. Francis Perryvall,' Darren said looking at the bronze plaque. 'I've never heard of that name before. But I'll look through our archives, there may be other paintings of him, or by him. I take it you don't know who he was?'

'No, sorry. Can you tell how old it is?'

Darren frowned and stroked his chin. 'Well. I'd say it's not all that old babes, certainly not from 1537 anyway. The paint would have faded more and there would be a lot more crackelature on the canvas. This is in very good condition. A little dusty, but that's easily fixed. Could be early twentieth-century, maybe late nineteenth at the oldest. I can't tell who painted it from the style and there's no visible signature. X-rays might reveal something though.'

Ella looked down at the painting, she was about to say something but stopped. She sighed deeply.

'I'm gonna have to do some proper research, it could take a while. But it doesn't mean it's not worth anything,' Darren reassured.

'Doesn't matter,' Ella lied.

'Look. I'll scan it in and do some print off's, show them around on the net. And maybe the *little professors* will see something I've missed.' He nodded to the students behind him. 'You never know, it could still be a rare piece, or an early piece by a novice master. Very occasionally one surfaces out of the blue, they can be worth a fortune. Trust me, there are still plenty of clues to look for.'

Ella brightened a little. 'Thanks Darren, you're a star.'

*

Watching the world go by, Ella sat on the wall by King's College and munched hungrily on a sandwich. The town was packed with students taking advantage of the good weather. Tourists swarmed around the colleges and shops with their cameras and shopping bags. The sun was warm on her face, the sky was blue. It was a perfect day.

But Ella's thoughts were elsewhere. A line from the poem nagged at her. *In secret I ask* . . . She wondered, there *were* secrets, she was certain of it. Something occurred to her that made her stop eating. She frowned as she contemplated it. The letter was in her handbag, she reached for it.

Just as her fingers touched the letter, her phone rang. There was no caller name and she didn't recognise the number. Annoyed by the interruption, but curious all the same, she answered it. 'Hello?'

'Is this Ms Ella Moore I'm speaking to?' asked the male voice in a serious, formal manner.

Ella didn't recognise the man's voice. She hesitated, worried by his tone. 'Yes,' she replied sharply and defensively.

'My name is Detective Constable Pepper, from Cambridgeshire police. Ms Moore, do you live at 53 Kings Avenue?'

Ella's stomach jumped into her mouth. 'Yes. What's this about?' she asked quickly, her heart beat hard and fast in her chest.

'I'm afraid you have been burgled.'

# Chapter 14

*1321hrs – Cambridge*

WHEN ELLA REACHED her flat, she saw that the front door was ajar. There were no police cars on the street or officers standing by the entrance. Other than the open door everything looked normal. Cautiously, she pushed the front door open and entered straight into the small living room.

Immediately she saw the mess. She put her hand over her mouth and tears welled in her eyes. All the drawers had been pulled out. Their contents, and everything else that had been on the shelves, had been mercilessly thrown onto the floor, trodden on and crushed. Open CD cases and books were strewn all over the place, pictures of her and her friends were lying on the floor, the glass smashed.

'Hello, anyone there?' she shouted before a lump caught in her throat.

A man appeared at the kitchen door. Ella jumped and tensed up before she noticed he was holding out his police ID. In his mid fifties, he had short white hair, a red face with a bulbous nose and was considerably overweight. He wore an old, ill fitting dark navy blue suit. His tie, which was twenty years out of fashion, hung loose around the collar of his pale yellow shirt. The top button was undone.

'Ms Moore?' asked the man.

Ella nodded, the lump in her throat prevented speech.

'I'm DC Pepper, but please call me Tony.' His tone was soft and sympathetic. He moved towards her with his warrant card held out. The leather wallet was old and battered, much like its owner.

While Ella leaned forward to inspect the ID, DC Pepper looked Ella up and down. She noticed his eyes were held momentarily on her breasts. She took an instant dislike to him.

'Please, let's sit down in the kitchen. There's a few things I need to discuss with you,' DC Pepper said gesturing back to the kitchen.

Reluctantly, Ella walked through and pulled out a chair by the table. The kitchen was relativity untouched, a few drawers hung open but nothing looked seriously out of place. DC Pepper pulled out a chair next to her and sat down. A stale smell of cigarette smoke and coffee wafted into her face.

'At eleven o'clock this morning, a neighbour of yours made a call to the station to report suspicious activity at this address. I was in the area finishing another job so control asked me to drive by and a have a look. Whoever burgled the place was long gone,' DC Pepper explained. 'The front door was open, but it didn't look forced. There's no broken glass or damage. I entered the flat to check if anyone was in and found it like this. There was a mobile phone bill on the kitchen table. I assumed it was the resident's, so I called it. You answered.'

Ella blew her nose noisily into a tissue. The stench of the man was making her eyes water.

'I know it's upsetting, but please don't take it personally. These villains are usually opportunists, they're just after whatever they can find. They don't consider the victims as real people.'

Ella nodded and sniffed. She had nothing of real value anyway.

'Are you able to take a look around? I'll make a note of anything missing.'

'Yes. Fine,' Ella said, recovering from the initial shock. 'But I'm still a student, I don't have anything valuable at all.'

'It's usually drug addicts who do this. They look for things that are easily and quickly sold in the pubs. In and out as quick as possible. They're only after their next hit and they'll do anything to get it,' DC Pepper explained.

'I suppose so, poor souls.'

'Oh, one other thing. Do you have a flatmate, or a friend, or a partner who stays here?'

'No, just me. It's a one bedroom flat. Why?' Ella frowned. 'No one else has the key, other than the landlord, if that's what you're getting at.'

The detective looked lost in thought for a second. 'No, it's nothing. Just routine,' he said and wrote something on his notepad.

Together they walked around the flat and looked over the damage. The detective held his notepad in one hand, his pen at the ready. Fastidiously tidy, Ella knew where everything was. At least where it should be. A small wooden box in the bedroom held a small amount of jewellery, but it was all still there. An old phone and her cheap digital camera were still there too. In the living room the television remained intact, a small but modern flatscreen, something Ella thought would have been easy to take and sell. Her books, her CD collection, a few DVDs, all still there, albeit lying all over the place. She didn't know whether to feel happy about it or not, but nothing seemed to be missing.

'Are you sure?' DC Pepper asked surprised. 'They wouldn't go to all this trouble unless they were looking for something.'

'It all here, yes, I'm sure,' Ella said brightening up a little. 'Wait a minute. My laptop!' She rushed over the to the corner of the living room. There was an overturned coffee table where her old laptop sat. The power lead was plugged in. But the laptop was missing.

'It's gone,' she said throwing her hands in the air. 'It was definitely there this morning. Oh no.' She put her hands to her face realising her mistake. 'My thesis, it's gone. I haven't backed it up for ages.'

'And you're sure that's all that's missing, Ms Moore?'

'Is that all?' she said sarcastically and laughed. 'It was months of work, I've lost it all.' She slumped onto the sofa and put her head in her hands.

'But there's nothing else of value here?' the DC challenged.

'No. It's just as well I took the painting to the lab this morning,' she said without thinking. 'Now that would have been a disaster.'

'Sorry? What painting?'

'Oh, probably nothing really. My father died recently and I inherited a painting from him. It's probably not worth anything, but I took it to a friend this morning to get it looked at.'

DC Pepper stuck the end of his cheap Biro pen in his ear and twisted it round, then he put the end in his mouth. A disgusting habit that Ella had noticed him doing three times before. The man was foul, she thought, no wonder there was no wedding ring on his finger.

'I'm worried now, Ella. I have to admit,' DC Pepper said in a low voice. He waved his pen at her.

Ella noticed that he had dropped the 'Ms Moore' act. He sat down on a tatty old chair and looked at her like she was a child.

'Let me explain what I'm thinking,' he went on. 'There was no forced entry as is usually the case in burglaries. Assuming you really did lock up properly when you left?'

Ella nodded that she had done.

'So, let's say it was picked then and not forced. Only the laptop was taken. No jewellery or other items which would be easily sold on for drugs. Granted, laptops are also very easy to sell, but they also contain a lot of information that may be useful to the more organised criminal. Perhaps the kind of villain who has a bigger prize in mind? Like a valuable work of art that they couldn't find anywhere in the house, despite having ripped the place apart.' The detective paused and looked to Ella for a response. He let the theory sink in for a moment.

'Was there anything else you inherited that could be worth something?'

'No,' she lied. The image of the strange gold signet ring flashed in her mind. It was in her handbag. She toyed with telling the detective about it but didn't feel comfortable going into the odd details of her father's will. He might think that the whole family was mad.

Pacing around the messy living room the detective tapped the pen, clearly a critical thinking aid of his, against his sweaty forehead. 'Let's just say, for a moment, Ella, that someone knew you had a recently acquired a very expensive painting.'

'But,' Ella protested. She stopped talking when the detective raised his hand at her.

'Let's just say, for arguments sake, that it was known somehow that you had the painting here. It's not exactly high security. So they watch you. Wait until you leave, then they let themselves in quietly and have a look around. Oh no! they say, it's not here. So what do they do?'

Ella shrugged and shook her head. 'I don't know,' she conceded.

The detective snapped his fingers. 'They take the laptop to try and find out more about you, more about the painting and where it might be. But to cover their tracks they make it look like a simple burglary.' Smugly, he clasped his hands together and grinned as if he had just solved the case.

'I don't know what to think,' she said despondent. But she conceded to herself that the detective's story did make a lot of sense.

'And if they've gone to all that trouble, then we must assume that they still want it,' he said slowly and softly. 'I think you are in danger, Ella. I think that whoever has the painting now may be in danger too.'

'Darren!' Ella gasped, she looked up at the detective with her mouth open. The detective smiled wryly, then coughed and composed himself. Ella was too worried to notice.

'I recommend we pick up the painting and take it to the station for safe keeping,' DC Pepper proposed. 'Just until my team can work out what's going on. My car is outside, we should get going as soon as possible.' Expectantly the detective looked to Ella for a decision.

Despite her reservations, Ella knew she could not risk putting Darren in danger. She felt terrible already. Nodding agreement, she pulled out her mobile phone. 'Okay, let's go,' she said. 'I'll call the museum now.'

# Chapter 15

DARREN AGREED TO meet Ella and the detective at the museum immediately. Ella knew Darren had noted the poorly concealed panic in her voice. She was comforted by thought of meeting her friend, but, frustratingly, the journey took much longer than she had judged. The afternoon traffic crawled along the crammed streets of Cambridge at a frustrating pace, as they waited in queue after queue hoards of cyclists sped past them. The stench of stale smoke from the detective made Ella feel ill. The car was a mess too; old tissues and chocolate bar wrappers were strewn all over the floor and seats. Ella couldn't wait to get out into the fresh air.

'It's just up there, on the left,' Ella hurriedly pointed out as they approached.

After narrowly missing a careless cyclist, DC Pepper hauled the car onto the side of the road and parked, illegally, on the roadside by the Fitzwilliam museum. Ella undid her seatbelt and climbed out of the car as fast as she could, she noticed that the detective hadn't bothered with his own seat belt. He stayed in the car a few moments longer tapping away on his phone. Ella left him and shot up the steps. A moment later the detective followed behind, he slid his phone into his pocket.

In the reception hall, Darren was already there waiting, the painting was in his hand. When she saw him, Ella smiled for the first time that afternoon and rushed over to greet him with a hug.

'What's going on babes?' Darren asked, squeezing her tightly. 'Are you okay?'

'I'm fine now. Columbo's on the case,' she whispered quietly and sarcastically into Darren's ear. She explained everything to Darren; the burglary, the stolen laptop and DC Pepper's theory on the case.

'Is this what the copper wanted?' Darren handed Ella the framed painting.

Ella took it and frowned. It looked different somehow. Francis Perryvall was still there holding the gold book, but something wasn't right. She looked at Darren questioningly, but he just winked at her and said nothing as the detective approached.

'Is that the painting?' DC Pepper wheezed. He reached out to inspect the evidence.

'Yeah,' Darren replied coldly before Ella could answer. 'What are you going to do with it? We can secure it here no problem if that's the issue. The vaults are secure enough to store multi-million pound masterpieces. We use them all the time.' Darren directed the last sentence towards Ella.

'I'm sure you do. But best that it comes to the station along with Ms Moore, just until we can guarantee her safety,' DC Pepper explained. 'They will both be in safe hands.' He gestured to the exit, indicating to Ella that it was time to go.

'Did you manage to find anything more out about it?' Ella asked Darren, ignoring the detective's impatience.

'A bit,' he put his arm around Ella and spoke quietly so only she could hear. 'It's oil on canvas, probably painted in the late eighteenth-century. But I still don't know who the artist was. As for Mr Perryvall, I couldn't find anyone by that name. There's no other paintings or sculptures of him. But it's early days, I'll see what else I can find out in the meantime.'

The detective coughed impatiently. He raised his eyebrows at Ella.

'Thanks, Darren. I'll call you later,' Ella said reluctantly and made a move to the exit.

'I'll be waiting for your release back into the community,' Darren joked.

Ella smiled and waved. Darren stood by the entrance and watched them drive off.

\*

While they were stopped at traffic lights a few streets down, DC Pepper took out his mobile phone and made a call. Much to Ella's shock, not only did he not wear his seatbelt, but he didn't use a handsfree set either. The lights turned green and the detective accelerated away with the phone pushed to his ear. Ella shook her head and looked out of the passenger window.

'We're on our way now,' DC Pepper said into the phone. 'We have everything.' He listened for a moment and then ended the call.

'Where are we going?' asked Ella.

'To the station, it's not that far from the town.'

'Which station?'

'The CID office in Capital Park. We're not based in the main headquarters, we have an old converted house near the Fulbourn hospital. It's a lovely place to work.'

From the landmarks they passed, Ella guessed that they were headed south out of Cambridge. After a few minutes they passed Addenbrooke's hospital on their right, then took a left turn onto a minor road and headed towards Fulbourn. When they were free of the traffic lights and speed cameras, the detective sped up and they headed into the Cambridgeshire countryside.

Feeling uneasy, Ella had the urge to hear a friendly voice. She took out her phone and looked through the contacts.

'Who are you calling,' the detective asked sharply.

'My mother,' Ella replied defensively, unimpressed with his tone.

'I don't think you should do that. Best that she doesn't know anything at the moment. For her safety as much as yours.'

'That's ridiculous,' Ella said and continued to make the call.

'I said don't,' the detective shouted and snatched the phone from Ella's hand. 'It's too dangerous.'

Ella's face flushed red, her eyes widened. 'Give it back!' she demanded. 'You've no right, I'm not under arrest.'

'Sit back and keep quiet,' the detective ordered.

'I've had enough of this. Stop the car and let me out. I'll take my chances on my own thanks.'

To Ella's surprise, the car slowed. The detective pulled the car over to the left hand side of the empty rural road and onto the grass verge. He stopped and pulled on the handbrake. Ella pulled on the door handle. It was locked. She turned to the detective to speak.

In one swift move he pulled a small revolver out of his concealed shoulder holster with his right hand. With his left hand he reached over and grabbed Ella by the back of her neck. He thrust the pistol into her mouth, pushing it in hard.

It happened too quickly for Ella to do anything. Her eyes opened wide as she felt the cold metal pressed into her mouth. She tried to push him away, but he was too strong and had the upper hand. The short barrel of the pistol hit the back of her throat and made her gag. The man's firm grip around her neck was slowing blood flow. He pushed his thumb into her carotid vein. She felt faint and weak.

'Mmmf, mmm, mmff,' Ella squealed in terror. Saliva built up in her mouth, she could taste the cold metal when she swallowed.

'Shut the fuck up, bitch,' the detective shouted into her ear. Then his voice softened. 'Listen, shhh, quiet now. Stop struggling or you are fucking dead. Understand?'

Ella dropped her hands by her side and froze. She nodded and stared wide eyed into his mad eyes petrified of what he might do next.

'Do everything I tell you and you will be okay. I do not want to harm you, understand?'

Ella nodded vigorously.

The detective looked into her wide, watery eyes. Slowly, the muzzle was withdrawn from her mouth. He kept the side of the cold weapon on her cheek. Slowly, he moved it downwards along her neck, then down onto her shoulder and down further to her chest. He paused.

Ella noticed his breathing was heavy and shaky. Her pulse raced, she began to feel cold. Stay with it, she told herself. She wasn't going to allow herself to be a victim.

The detective snapped the gun back, sat back in his seat and sighed deeply. He took some deep breaths, then he picked up Ella's phone from his lap and pulled the battery out of it.

'Do exactly as you are told from now on,' he ordered. 'Do you understand? Don't fuck with me girl, or you'll regret it.'

Ella nodded and sniffed, she began to shiver. She wiped the tears from her face with her sleeve.

With the pistol still in his hand, the detective switched the radio on and drove off up the road as if nothing had happened.

After a few miles, Ella realised that they had long passed the turn-off for Fulbourn. They were travelling even further south. On each side of the quiet country road was farmland. The fields were separated by hedges and the along the road on each side ran a dry stone wall topped with barbed wire.

Ella calmed herself with controlled breaths and tried to think clearly, logically. She wondered why he had taken the battery out of her phone rather than just confiscate it. He had lied to her about the location of the CID station. Was the burglary a lie too? Was he even a policeman? It seemed unlikely now. Anger brewed up in her, she stared straight ahead. She had never been a victim of crime before and it was looking bad. Very bad. She was completely at the mercy of this psychopath. What did he want, she wondered, the painting or her? Whatever it was he had proved he was willing to do anything to get it. Her thoughts wandered to the future. What would become of her when he had finished with her? She knew what the usual result was: news reports, searches in fields, appeals by the family and friends. There was no way she was going to allow herself to become a statistic. How dare he do this to her, she had her whole life ahead of her. She couldn't allow it to happen. She wouldn't allow it to happen. Her blood boiled. She resolved to take action.

As the car sped down the narrow road, Ella lurched to the side and grabbed the steering wheel. In one swift, sharp and firm movement she pulled down on it hard.

To the shock and disbelief of the detective the car instantly turned towards the left hand side of the road and headed at speed straight for the stone wall. For a very brief moment, a second at most, the detective struggled with the wheel trying to pull the car back on the road. But it was too little too late.

With a violent jolt, the car smashed into the raised grass verge. The contents of the car were thrown upwards. There was an almighty smash and everything surged forward with neck breaking force. The air bags exploded, the windscreen smashed. The car broke through the wall and rolled over and over into the field beyond.

The vehicle came to a halt upside down in the grassy field. Covered in clumps of grass and mud, the engine whined and the front wheels spun. When the engine stopped, all was quiet save for the birds that sung in the trees.

# Chapter 16

*0612hrs – Bedfordshire*

THE MORNING AIR was still. All that could be heard was the distant chirping of birds. Keeping himself hidden in the grass and shrubs on the opposite side of the main road, William watched the house. There had been no movement for the last hour.

A green Range Rover appeared from behind the house and the morning calmness was broken by the sound of gravel crunching under wheel. William took several close-ups of the car and driver. The blond man was behind the wheel, no one else was in the vehicle. At the T-junction, the car turned left and drove down the road that William had come from the previous day.

When the coast was clear, William crept over to the Portable Cell Site device and retrieved it. He returned to his car, checked the data it had captured and called Ollie.

'I've just emailed you the IMEI number of a new target, Ollie' William said. He was feeling slightly weary having failed to sleep properly and fantasized over a strong espresso and a bacon sandwich. 'How quickly can you get it on the system?'

'Hold on . . . Done,' Ollie replied.

'Good man. I've also emailed some pictures to you and Sarah. Let me know if you find out anything interesting from them.'

'Bit early for Sarah. I'll catch up with her when she's in.'

'She emailed me the results of her research on the mansion last night,' William revealed. 'She must have worked late on it. The place is called Rockcliffe Hall, owned by Sir Arthur Anthony Tempest, a wealthy aristocrat. The house is privately owned, built in the seventeenth-century. During the Second World War it was used as a training base for the Special Operations Executive.'

'Impressive,' Ollie said. The SOE was a fascination of his.

'Police and intelligence checks on Sir Arthur himself revealed nothing other than an old allegation of insider share dealing that was unproven.'

'I assume Sarah has also mapped all his bank accounts, his

companies, phone calls and his trips abroad?'

'Of course. But other than being enviably rich, there is nothing of intelligence interest. Well, almost nothing,' William said.

'Go on,'

Well, one of his many companies, TempestInvest, is located in the Gherkin.'

'Okay, William, we're in. Your new target is headed eastwards away from Rockcliffe Hall. Probably heading back to the A1,' Ollie said. 'And look here, I've traced the number. It's a company phone registered to TempestInvest. There's no GPS module in it so we only have the triangulation to work with.'

Keeping a reasonably safe distance from his target, William followed Ollie's instructions. The target had taken the A1 south. The motorway was quiet, but would undoubtedly get increasingly busier with the morning rush. William knew that in light traffic he would be easily burned if he took any silly risks. He would only close the gap he kept when the target pulled off onto a town or city.

After half an hour it was clear the target was headed towards the city of Cambridge. The traffic levels had increased and provided decent cover for William. He followed the Range Rover closely through the busy streets.

Without performing any anti-surveillance tricks, the target navigated its way into a residential area and parked up on a quiet street. William found a suitable spot and pulled in. He sat and watched from a safe distance.

His phone buzzed, the caller ID informed him that Sarah was calling on a secure line. 'Afternoon,' he said sarcastically.

'Very funny. Some of us have a life you know.'

'So while I was up all night stuck in a mud filled, rat infested ditch, you were out on a date were you?' William teased. 'Who's the lucky geek?'

'Shut up, I don't date geeks.'

'So it *was* a date?'

'It wasn't a date,' Sarah giggled. 'And I'm sure there weren't all that many rats. I thought you were used to it, soldier-boy. Getting soft in your old age?'

'Old? Cheeky rapscallion!'

'I have some information for you.'

'Already? Did your boyfriend have to get up for school?'

Ignoring William's puerile teasing, Sarah got to the point. 'Listen, I've been researching the material you sent. It's been quite revealing.

There's some interesting stuff from the registration number of one of the helicopters. It's owned by an infamous Australian mining magnate called Carl Schoenberg.'

'Never heard of him.'

'Several of his companies have been investigated for corruption and suspected arms dealing. Worryingly, he was on an MI6 watch list for possible involvement in the smuggling of Uranium, but nothing was ever proven.'

'A pleasant guy then.'

'A notorious playboy by the looks of it, married several times. News reports say that after losing millions in divorce number one, he forced each subsequent trophy wife to sign a pre-nuptial. The most recent scandal is from one ex who sold her story to the press, she talks of wild sex parties and secret societies.'

'Sounds like fun. Can anyone join?'

'I doubt it. Schoenberg's silk-tongued lawyers had her branded as a bitter former drug addict who couldn't be believed. The negative press got the better of her and one night, after a night of partying at a London club, she took a fatal overdose of cocaine and died in her hotel.'

'So he had her killed,' William stated. He knew how easy it was to kill a drug addict and make it look like an accident, a mere self inflicted overdose.

'That would be my guess. Anyway, the owner of the mansion, Sir Arthur, is beginning to look interesting too. But I'll update you on everything when you're back in the office.'

'Fair enough. No idea when I'll be back, but everything is in good hands.'

'For now,' Sarah said then paused on the line. She debated whether she should tell him about Pinkerton.

'Still there? Something bothering you?'

'Look, William. Albert is taking a real interest in this and has demanded regular updates from me. He's reiterated the importance of the *circle of knowledge*.'

William laughed.

'He said that he will be authorising all further operations on this case and nothing is to be done without his knowledge,' Sarah explained.

'Of course. He wouldn't want to miss out on anything that might get him his knighthood,' William said cynically. 'Look, I've got to go now. Speak later.'

William used his mirrors to look up and down the street. It was getting busy. He switched his phone to silent. He had a plan.

*

When the Russian disappeared into the flat across the street, William left his car and walked casually up to the side of the Range Rover. Squatting down, he pretended to tie his shoelace. After a quick glance up and down the pavement he placed a magnetic GPS beacon under the vehicle. After double checking the number on the door of the flat, he walked back to his own car and called Sarah.

'I have an address for you,' he said.

Noting down the details, Sarah tapped away on her keyboard and, seconds later, found what she needed to know. 'Owned by a Mr Donald Brockley,' she replied. 'Buy-to-let mortgage according to the Land Registry. He owns five other buy-to-lets.'

'Any way of finding out who the tenant is?'

'Already on it, the TV licensing database. Let's see . . . Miss Ella Moore, paid this year and last.' She then cross-referenced the payment details with several other databases. 'She's a post grad student at Cambridge. No police record. No overseas travel in the last year.'

'Good one. Do some more digging on the girl will you? Wait, someone else is at the flat. Got to go.'

William watched as a young girl stood at the door and had a conversion with the blond man. She walked in and the door shut.

After about thirty minutes the man left the flat alone. He carried something in his hand, William thought it looked like a laptop. The man jumped in the Range Rover drove off. William let him go, but he switched the sat-nav on and made sure that the GPS tracker had worked. Satisfied that it had, he climbed out of his car and approached the flat.

The front door had been left ajar. William pushed it open. 'Hello,' he shouted into it. 'Police. Is there anyone there?'

There was no response.

Entering cautiously, pistol drawn, he crept from the small dark living room into the kitchen. The flat was deadly silent, there seemed to be no one home. Going from room to room he looked for the girl who he had seen enter but not leave. She wasn't there. Confused, he wondered if he had missed her leaving, or perhaps she had left through the back. Deciding she must have left somehow, he put his pistol away and went to the kitchen.

In one of the drawers he found a utility bill, the addressee was a Miss Ella Moore. Underneath the first letter was a mobile phone bill.

109

Again, the addressee was a Miss Moore. William laid the bills on the plastic worktop and took a picture of them with his phone. He emailed the pictures to Sarah who he knew would be thirsty for yet more research. He admired her keenness.

There was a noise and William turned. A car had stopped directly outside, he could see it through the lounge window and could hear the engine idling. The engine stopped and he heard a door slam shut. Someone walked past the window towards the front door. William retreated up the stairs at speed. At the top he stopped and listened.

The floorboards creaked as someone let themself in.

'I'm here,' he heard a man say, the voice was deep and gravely. A seasoned smoker, William guessed. The door was pushed shut.

'The door was still open, don't worry, she's not been back,' the man said, clearly talking to someone on the phone. 'Yes, I'll do that first then I'll call the girl. Does she have the book? Don't worry, I'll find it, she'll tell me the colour of her knickers when I'm done with her. Ha ha ha. Okay, I'll meet you there.'

William heard some loud bangs, then the sound of glass smashing. It sounded like a fight, but he realised what the man was doing. He was trashing the place. William knew he had to get out somehow. Behind him the door to the bedroom was open, he crept in. The room was tidy, but the bed covers were crumpled. By the bed was a small window which looked out onto the main road. Trying to move silently on the creaky floor, he cautiously moved over to it and lifted the locking lever. With a firm push the window opened. It was too far to jump down, but to his relief there was a black plastic drain pipe within reach that ran down to the ground.

William heard the man climbing the stairs. Working fast he grabbed the window frame and launched himself outside onto the ledge. There was no time to shut the window on his way out. Holding onto the drain pipe, he quickly lowered himself to the ground and walked off. A woman pushing a pram on the pavement looked at him with concern. Ignoring her, he turned the corner and walked out of sight.

*

A few minutes later, William returned to his car. He took out another GPS tracker and walked towards the flat once more. As he approached, he noticed that the bedroom window had been closed. When he reached the side of the car that had parked outside the flat, he stopped, squatted down and reached under it. There was a dull clunk as the magnetic device jumped firmly into place. He returned to his own car and called Sarah for an update.

'Any news?' William asked.

'Nothing of interest yet,' Sarah said. She was sitting at her desk, glued to her computer screen. 'Miss Moore has never been on the radar. No hits on her phone number either, but I've put a trace on it, if she makes or receives any calls, I'll have a listen.'

'Good. Can you check something else for me?' William asked. He gave her the vehicle registration number of the car that had parked outside the flat.

'Albert wants you back here for a briefing,' Sarah said as she typed the details into her computer.

'No chance,' William said.

'He'll be mad, he likes his huddles. He wants a full debrief on everything you've done so far.'

'Tough.' William despaired at management meetings, a lot of pointless talk as far as he was concerned. 'I'll update him when I'm ready. You can tell him I said that.'

'Anyway,' Sarah said sounding exasperated. 'That number plate belongs to a ten year old navy blue BMW. The current owner is one Anthony Pepper.'

'Anything on him?'

'Hold your horses. Ah, oh dear.'

'What do you mean, "oh dear"?'

'He's a copper. Cambridge CID. Rank of Detective Constable.'

'What the hell is going on?' William asked.

'Hold on, William. There's a call being made to the girl's phone. Wait out.' She listened to the live intercept. 'It was the detective. He's just told her that she's been burgled. She's on her way round to the flat right now.'

*

William watched as the detective left the flat with the girl. They both climbed into his car and a moment later they drove off. He glanced at his sat-nav as the car travelled past him. Satisfied that the GPS tracking device was working, he waited a few minutes and then followed from a safe distance.

*

On a narrow country road, William slowed and frowned at his sat-nav screen. There were two small car symbols on the map, one represented his own position, the other was that of the target vehicle. It appeared

111

to have stopped, he hoped the device hadn't fallen off. A sudden thought occurred to him, he had the girl's mobile phone number, so not all would be lost. Ollie could do his magic.

After a minute without further movement from the vehicle, William drove forward to try to get a look at what was going on. As he went over the brow of a hill he saw skid marks and the churned up grass verge. Then he saw the dry stone wall and a gap where the car had smashed through. He sped up. Further ahead, he saw the car lying upside down in a field. He raced forward and then screeched to a halt at the wall. He jumped out and raced to the scene.

The mangled car lay on its roof covered in mud and grass. William leaned down to the cracked window on the driver's side and peered in. 'Are you okay, can you hear me?' he shouted.

The driver was slumped beside the window. There was a lot of blood and, due to the unnatural angle of the man's head, William expected the worst. Pulling hard on the door handle was fruitless, the door was crumpled out of shape and jammed shut. William ran around to the passenger's side.

'Help,' came a muffled shout from somewhere inside.

'Are you okay?' William shouted. 'Can you move?'

'The door's stuck,' the girl cried.

'I'll try to smash the window out. Cover your eyes.' Making sure the girl was out of the way, William kicked the passenger window as hard as he could. As it was already cracked his work was easily done. In seconds he had removed most of the glass from the frame. Carefully, he reached in to help the girl.

'Wait,' she said. 'I need to get something.' She crawled to the back of the car and then appeared at the open window again with her handbag and what looked like a framed painting.

William helped her out. 'Are you hurt?' he asked. He, visually checked over the girl for any signs of serious injury. There was a bruise on the side of her head and she looked pale and shaken, but other than that, she seemed to be relatively unscathed.

'I'm okay,' she explained, calming down. 'I had my seatbelt on. Unlike that idiot.'

'Sit down, rest a moment. Let just make sure everything is okay,' William said calmly.

As the girl rested, William crawled in the window and looked for signs of life from the driver. His bloodied, motionless body lay on the roof. One of his arms was stuck through the bent steering wheel at a bizarre angle. When William grabbed the man's wrist to look for a pulse, he caught a whiff of the contents of the man's bowels.

'He's dead,' William said as he climbed out of the wreck.

'Good,' the girl snorted. 'He kidnapped me. Call the police, please.' Emotion overcame her and she started to cry.

William called Sarah and asked her to get an ambulance and the police to the scene immediately. 'Tell them of our involvement,' he said. 'But if they want to talk to Ms Moore then they'll have to go through me first. She's in our protection until we find out what the hell is going on.'

When William came off the phone, Ella was glaring at him. She looked shocked and confused. Scared even.

'Who are you,' she shrieked. Tears ran down her cheeks. 'Are you with him? Keep away from me.' She stood up and backed away from William shaking her head.

'Please. Calm down. It's okay, I'm not with him. My name is Inspector William Temple, I work for a specialist police unit. I'm here to help you,' William reassured and took out his cover ID.

Examining the ID from a distance, Ella didn't look convinced. William decided on a different tact.

'Look, I saw him trash your flat. He's after something you have, a book, I think. But I don't know why, that's what I need to find out. There's more at stake here than meets the eye, Ella. You may still be in danger.'

William walked over to the driver's side of the car and looked for the GPS tracker. It was still there stuck to the steel frame and covered in mud and grass. He yanked it off and showed it to Ella.

'This is the tracking device I put on while he was at your flat. That's how I was able to follow you,' William said flicking the mud and grass off the black device. 'We'll keep you safe, Ella. Please trust me.'

'How did you know my name?' Ella asked, wavering.

'I was in your flat just before he came. Someone else broke in first, I was following him. I entered to investigate and found your name on some bills.'

Ella sniffed and wiped her face with her sleeve. 'What's happening,' she cried.

'These are dangerous men Ella. Until I find out what's going on you're still in danger. Please trust me. Let me help you.'

Ella looked at William's face; there was something about him, something genuine and trustworthy. His eyes were kind, she thought. For some reason he had made her feel safer.

'You're a policeman?' she asked.

'Yes.'

'What unit?'

'A specialist unit. You won't have heard of us.'

Ella thought for a moment. She wondered how worse it could get. 'Okay, but I'm keeping my phone on,' she demanded. 'And I'm calling my mother.'

'Fine, whatever you want. Come on, let's get you somewhere safe. Then we can talk properly,' William said.

'If you try anything funny,' she said and pointed to the car.

William nodded that he got the message. They walked together towards his car. Ella called her mother, but didn't mention anything about her ordeal. William called Sarah to make some arrangements.

'Sarah, I need a good hotel somewhere in the Cambridge area,' William said quietly. 'An expensive one will do. Book two decent rooms in my cover name and email me the details. Oh, and Sarah, do me a favour and don't tell anyone where we are, including Pinkerton. And there is just one other thing.' He looked round at Ella, she was still on the phone. He spoke quietly and asked Sarah to do another little job.

# Chapter 17

*1430hrs – Wales*
THE BIOSCIENCE RESEARCH branch of the Defence Laboratories was located in a remote top-secret facility on the eastern edge of Wales. The super-modern offices were an impressive testament to their visionary architect. Built on three storeys, the building was a large curved metallic structure that looked much like a UFO when viewed from the air. The external walls around most of it were made from a triangular mesh of bomb-proof glass that ran from the ground floor up to the metallic roof. The complex was surrounded by thick woods and had a huge man-made lake at one end. Access to the building was via three carefully controlled entry-exit points that stood out at the edge of the car park like huge inverted glass bowls. Each access point had a spiral staircase that went down one floor underground where a long corridor extended into the main complex. One corridor was completely tiled in white from end to end, another was blue and the final one was red. The atmosphere inside the complex was carefully controlled to prevent anything nasty from leaking out by maintaining it at a slightly lower pressure than the outside world. At the end of each entry corridor there was a transparent tubular lift shaft which extended all the way up to the third floor.

The scientist who had been tasked with analysing the data sent from F-Branch walked at speed through the eerily quiet open plan office. His unbuttoned white coat fluttered behind him like a cape as he went. Clutching a red paper folder, he had a worried, distant look on his tired bespectacled face. But then Max Redwood had always been of a nervous disposition, he permanently looked to be on the verge of a heart attack. Dedicated to his work, he had worked through the night on the current puzzle.

'Hey, Maximus,' one of his colleagues shouted from behind a desk. But so lost in his thoughts was Max that he didn't hear him.

When the job first landed on his desk he was annoyed at the distraction. It took him away from his new and innovative top-secret project for the Army. But as he delved further into the gene sequences held within the data files, he realised something was wrong; very wrong. He had worked nonstop to figure it out. Even when he reached a conclusion he double checked it and triple checked it. There was no doubt that it was bad; very bad.

Short, thin and balding, Max was a career scientist at the Defence Labs and presently worked in the biological warfare division specialising in infectious diseases. A leading and respected expert with twenty years experience, he had seen some horrendous developments in his time. A frightening number of rogue states had tried to develop biological weapons of mass destruction with varying degrees of success. There was a regular influx of material to analyse, usually plans or samples stolen by the intelligence services. Although there was some nasty and worrying stuff out there, the trouble with bio-weapons was in their delivery. Conventional methods of launching a warhead just weren't effective when it came to bio-weapons. They tended to destroy the infectious agents before they could get to work, or they spread them in too small an area to do much damage. Max's biggest worry was terrorist groups. Terrorists could deliver bio-weapons simply by carrying them into a country. They could spread the agent slowly, city by city, town by town. They could infect the food chain, the water supplies, the transport systems. The Defence Labs had played out dozens of different scenarios in preparation for such attacks. And Max had always believed that it was only a matter of time before someone tried it for real. He feared that time had finally come.

Impatiently, Max waited at the entrance to the lift. He looked up at the glass shaft, the lift was coming down. When it stopped he quickly stepped in and pushed the button for the second floor. As it arrived at his floor he ran out so quickly that he tripped and dropped his papers. Unfazed by the onlookers, a couple of young administration girls who giggled to themselves, Max picked himself up, replaced his glasses and continued towards the office of the director. At the door of the clouded glass office, Max took a second or two to catch his breath and settle his nerves, then he knocked hard on the door before entering.

Colonel Vince Ackers was the new director of the Defence Labs. A former Army Colonel, he was a larger than life character with a booming voice and a very strong presence, if not a little over bearing for some. He had only been in the job a few months and still hadn't got used to working with civilians. And scientists, he felt, were even worse than civilians. Undisciplined and impossible to understand.

When Max walked in to the office, Col. Ackers was seated in a black leather chair by a glass table. Three other serious looking men dressed in dark suits were there too. They all stared up in wonder at the tired, unshaven mess that was Max Redwood. Struggling to get his words out, Max just stood at the door and stared back at his audience. His jaw moved up and down but the words failed to come out.

'Well, spit it out man,' Col. Ackers barked.

'Sir. This is, this, it's three,' Max stammered. 'You need to see this.'

'What are you blabbering on about? Can't you see I'm in a meeting?'

'It can't wait, sir,' Max said mustering as much confidence as he could. 'You need to see this now. It's scenario three. Immediate threat.'

# Chapter 18

*1430hrs – Cambridgeshire*

DURING THE DRIVE to the hotel that Sarah had booked for them, Ella had calmed down and explained everything from the beginning. Her father's untimely death, her unexpected inheritance, the odd letter with the cryptic instructions to spread his ashes. And then there was the painting. She told William that Darren had given her a copy, the real one was secured in the vaults of the museum.

Surreptitiously, William had left his phone on so that Sarah could listen in to the conversion from the office. It would save him having to update her later and she could get straight to work on her research.

'Maybe the painting really is worth something after all,' Ella said.

'Maybe,' William agreed. 'Until we work out what is going on you need to keep a low profile. You can't stay at home, you can't contact your friends.'

Ella was about to protest, but she thought better of it. Instead, she folded her arms and shook her head.

'You'll also need a temporary change of appearance, just in case.'

'How exactly?' she quizzed.

William smiled. 'What's your dress size?'

\*

The sat-nav directed William to the Hotel du Vin, a luxury boutique hotel in the centre of Cambridge. William rolled his eyes when he realised where he was. Coincidentally, the hotel was situated on Trumpington street on the other side from the Fitzwilliam Museum. Ella, however, who was desperate to see Darren, was over the moon.

'It's too dangerous to go there now,' William explained. 'Someone could be watching it, waiting for you to return. Even just calling Darren may put him in danger.'

'This is ridiculous,' Ella said. She sunk into her seat and sulked.

After parking up they checked in using the cover names. They walked up the stairs to Ella's room first, she was in the grand suite, the best room in the hotel. William was quietly impressed with Sarah's choice. Ella was less quiet about it. The room was spacious, stylish and beautifully presented. The interiors had an intriguing blend of modern vibrancy and period charms.

'Wow,' she said as she looked around it. 'There's two bathrooms!' There was also a lounge area with a large flatscreen TV and two sofa's. 'This is bigger than my entire flat.'

The trials of the day were quickly forgotten just as William had hoped they would be. After she had freshened up and eaten, William had no doubt that Ella would be ready to help him work out what was going on.

'Why don't you get yourself cleaned up, relax in the bath for a while, then meet me in the restaurant at seven prompt,' William said. He was looking forward to a taste of the fruits of the wine cellar. It had been a long day; they both deserved a little indulgence.

'But I've nothing to wear,' she said. 'And look at me.' She looked down at her filthy, ripped clothes.

'Oh, but you do,' he said. 'Have a look in the wardrobe. It's all yours, take your pick. And one other thing, there's some hair dyes and make-up in the bathroom. See what you can do with them. Just try to look . . . different.'

'Different?' she said with a frown, not sure what to make of the comment.

William shrugged. 'See you at seven. Prompt, okay,' he said and left the room.

When Ella looked in the wardrobe she was suitably impressed. It wasn't often that she had new clothes. In the bathroom she found plenty of make-up and two hair dyes, a red one and a blonde one. There was also a toilet bag with everything she needed. When she found a small travel bottle of Channel No.5 she laughed with joy. A small piece of card fell out from one of the bags. She picked it up and turned it over. There was a handwritten note on it, all it said was, "With compliments from Ajax Security".

After a long soak in the bath, Ella put on a white robe and jumped on the double bed. She snuggled up and rested her head on the large soft pillow, the Egyptian linen smelled fresh. Somehow the events of the day quickly faded to a distant memory.

*

The hotel restaurant was quiet, there were only a few other guests seated at the tables. The dimly lit room was small, but elaborately decorated. Murals of diners on the walls made it look busier than it really was. There was a welcoming, sophisticated atmosphere to the place. Calming classical music played quietly in the background, William recognised it as Brahms third symphony in F.

In his pocket his phone vibrated. He checked it, it was another email from Sarah, her end of day report detailing the latest findings. William read the details of the research into Ella's father. As he read he frowned at the text in disbelief and surprise.

Debating to himself whether he should tell Ella the odd details about her father, he looked at his watch and noted that she was late. Beginning to worry, he was just about to get up to check on her when an attractive, elegant young woman confidently strode into the restaurant. She immediately caught his, and most of the other men's, attention. Slim and well dressed in leather boots, tight blue jeans and a silky pastel top, the captivating young red-head walked confidently towards William's table. When she pulled out a chair and sat down opposite him, William was pleasantly surprised. The other men in the room reluctantly dragged their eyes away back to their own worlds.

'So, what do you think?' Ella said nonchalantly picking up a menu. 'Different enough?'

William's mouth hung open before he caught himself and straightened up. 'Wow. You look beautiful,' was all he could muster.

'I scrub up well,' Ella said and suppressed a grin. After much deliberation, she had decided to copy a glamorous look from one of the fashion magazines that was in her room. She'd made an excellent job of it and was relatively unrecognisable from a distance.

'But you know when going incognito you're supposed to blend in with the background. Be ordinary. Invisible,' William said with a smile. 'Not attractive and eye catching. We need to work on your undercover skills.'

Ella laughed and blushed. 'Thanks for the clothes. I've been in dire need of a new wardrobe for ages,' she said sheepishly. 'Everything fits perfectly. Who did the shopping?'

'A local retired operator did us a favour,' William said. 'Will they do?'

Ella frowned. 'Oh yes, they'll do all right. I take it I *can* keep them?'

'Of course. Compliments of the tax payer.'

'So what's Ajax Security then?' she said and showed him the business card.

'Ah,' William said looking awkward. 'Perhaps I should explain a few things. But first, let's order.'

William nodded to the waiter who trotted over with the French sommelier in tow. The menu was full of delicious, tempting dishes.

William settled on a foie gras and carpaccio starter followed by medallions of venison for his main. The sommelier, who was only just on the right side of condescending, picked out an award winning bottle of claret from Saint Emilion to go with his meal. When William agreed to go with his choice, the sommelier smiled smugly and nodded appreciatively. Ella opted for a blue cheese salad to start with and an exotic wild mushroom risotto for her main. She ignored the advice of the sommelier, much to his dismay, and opted instead for an Australian Viognier; her favourite grape.

After their drinks were brought out, William explained his role in Ajax Security while his dinner guest listened intently. He maintained much of the cover story, but still felt he had said more than he should have. But there was something about her, something trustworthy. And she was a good listener, which in William's experience was rare.

'I shouldn't be telling you this you know,' William admitted. He took another sip of the claret.

Ella smiled at him, she was hanging on his every word. William put it down to the quantity of wine that she was putting away.

'Don't worry, your secret is safe with me,' she said with a sparkle in her eyes. 'So you investigate national security issues?'

'Yes. They're usually brought to our attention through anonymous tip-offs, informants, but sometimes it's from things picked up by Echelon.' William noticed Ella's frown. 'There's nothing secret about Echelon any more. It's a colossal data processing project. Almost all UK based electronic communications, such as phone calls, emails and Internet traffic, are sniffed by the system's filters. Any patterns or key words of interest are flagged and sent to an analyst for research. If they have the time to bother looking at it that is. Then they send some of it to us to look into.'

Ella gasped. 'That really happens?' she said.

'Oh yes, and you should see what the American's have. But the problem is the sheer scale of the information. Not all of it can be analysed. Artificial intelligence helps, but there's nothing as good as the grey matter and gut instinct.'

'So what do you with these tip-offs?'

'We have a look at the people involved, see what they're up to, check their backgrounds and make an assessment.'

'So you're a secret soldier then . . . A spy.' She found herself grinning at him like a schoolgirl. She took a sip of her wine and tried to calm herself.

William laughed. 'After we've done our bit we pass the case on to another agency so they can find the all important evidence. We're just the dogsbody's.'

'*Another agency?* That sounds suitably vague. So you do all the hard work and then someone else gets all the glory?'

'That's a fair assessment. But I don't care for the glory.'

'So why do you do it?'

Why did he, he wondered. It certainly wasn't for the money. Deep down he knew the truthful answer, but no one would ever understand it.

'Believe it or not, I only joined the Army to appease my father,' he admitted. 'At school all I ever wanted to be was a skipper on my own charter yacht.'

Ella tried to stop herself from laughing but failed miserably. A dribble of wine escaped from her mouth, embarrassed she wiped her chin with a napkin.

'It's true. I come from a long line of military men. It would have brought shame on the family name if I'd done anything else. And I'd probably have been written out of the will.'

'A skipper?'

'Yeah. Fishing trips, charters for divers, private parties. Somewhere in the Caribbean would have been nice. Maybe Cuba.'

Ella cackled, but stopped when she thought he looked hurt.

'What's wrong with that?' he asked innocently.

'Nothing. Everyone needs a dream.' She smiled.

William raised his glass to her, Ella followed suit and they clinked together.

'To dreams of a better life,' he said.

The waiter arrived with their meals. Each was superbly presented. William and Ella wasted no time in tucking in and the conversion lulled while they ate. William noticed Ella's impeccable table manners, she even used the correct cutlery without question.

'So what do you do, Ella?' William enquired. 'When you're not embroiled in an international mystery, that is.'

'I'm a post graduate student,' she said looking less than impressed. 'Doing a PhD in Egyptology and ancient civilisations.'

'Impressive,' William remarked. 'You must be bright. Bright and good looking. A lucky girl.'

Unused to such flattery, Ella didn't know what to say. She ran her fingers through her hair. Then she remembered where she was and why she was there. Her smile faded.

'I don't feel lucky at the moment,' she said looking down.

'You're with us now,' William reassured. He placed his hand gently on hers. She looked up at him. 'We'll figure this out, then you can go back to being a post grad student. Everything will be fine. I promise.'

'Don't make promises you can't keep, William.'

After the meal they retired to the near empty hotel library and continued their analysis of the case. Not one to waste a good bottle of wine, William had taken the claret with him. Ella, taking full advantage of the situation, had moved on to a very decent glass of champagne. Ella sat down and laid the copy of the painting on the table. William sat opposite and read over the poem from her father.

'So your father's last request was for you to spread his ashes next to his mother's grave, which is in a church called St Mary the Virgin,' William surmised.

'It's in a village called Everton in Bedfordshire, apparently.'

'Then he mentions the Biblos Aletheia, whatever that is.'

'It's Greek, means the Book of Truth, or something like that. I Googled it and some weird Web site came up,' Ella said dismissively, she'd forgotten all about the odd site.

'A Web site?' William asked with a tone of concern.

'Yes. It was weird, there was just one sentence on the whole page and some kind of weird symbol.'

'A symbol? What, like the one in the portrait?' William moved across and sat next to Ella.

Together they examined the painting. Sitting only inches from her, William could smell her hair and perfume. Looking at her profile as she studied the works, he realised just how attractive she was. She turned to look at him, he felt his pulse quicken slightly, his breathing deepened.

'No, the Web site had a triangle with a pentagram and an eye in it. The triangle in the book in the painting just has numbers in it,' she said. Her eyes darted across William's face.

'Oh, wait,' she said and reached into her handbag. 'I forgot about this.' She pulled out the ring and showed it to William. 'It was stuck to the back of the painting. See the symbol on it? The Web site had the same symbol as this.'

William pulled Ella's soft hand closer and examined the ring. He looked up at her to say something, but when their eyes met he stopped. They looked at each other for a moment in silence. Her lips parted ever so slightly, her pupils widened.

'What did the text say?' William asked breaking the silence. He moved back to his seat. 'On the Web site.'

'It just said, "The Truth is Coming".'

'The truth?'

Ella nodded, she shrugged her shoulders.

'Let's take a closer look at that poem shall we,' William suggested. 'So your father tells you where to spread his ashes, mentions this Greek book, then asks that you undertake the task in secret. "*Forgive me my dear, All will soon become clear.*"'

'What are you thinking?' asked Ella.

'The poem must be the key,' he said.

'Why?'

Something troubled William, he stroked his chin thoughtfully before he replied. 'You're sure you've never seen or heard about any of this before your father died? The portrait or the Greek book?' he asked.

'I told you, I never knew him. He left years ago when I was a kid,' Ella explained. 'Mother has never said anything about him of any substance. She hates him, even now.'

'Do you know anything at all about him? Like what he did for a living?'

'No and I really don't care.' But her eyes gave her away.

William regarded her, then said, 'Look, Ella, there's something I need to tell you about your father.' He saw a worried look develop on her face. 'Our people have done some research on him and, believe it or not, he was sort of one of us.'

'What do mean, one of us?' she asked.

'He worked for MI6,' William said.

Ella's mouth and eyes opened wide. Never before had she even considered what he used to do. 'When? What years?' she asked trying to put the pieces together.

'He was recruited during his latter student years at Cambridge.'

'*He* went to *Cambridge*?' She was dumbfounded.

'Seems he took Russian which was a key skill back then.'

'Why didn't she tell me, she must have known,' Ella said angrily looking into space. 'My mother, she must have known.'

'Maybe, but maybe not. Don't beat her up about it. Even if she did know I can imagine it was tough on a family back then. The secrets, late nights, overseas postings. A lot of pressure during the cold war. He may have kept it from her, for her own safety.'

Unconvinced, Ella chewed her lip and shook her head.

'Look, whatever happened in the past, look back only long enough to learn. Then look forward,' William added.

'That's very philosophical, but how exactly does it help us now?' she snorted. She knocked back the rest of her champagne and waved the empty glass at a waiter who was clearing a table.

'Well, we now know that your father was exposed to the trade-craft of espionage. He knew how to keep secrets. And how to pass them on securely.'

'You mean codes?' Ella blurted out, suddenly interested. 'That's something I wondered about before. Look.' She ran her finger over the lines of the poem. 'See the smudges?'

'Do you think it's a sort of clue?' William was impressed with her thinking. He grabbed the hotel notepad and pen he'd placed on the table and wrote down all the smudged letters in the order he found them.

'Damn. It makes no sense,' he concluded.

'Maybe there's a special order they need to be in?' Ella suggested.

'Maybe. Or, instead of the letters, let's try the whole words first.'

'You've seen something haven't you?' Ella said smiling.

William copied down the whole word of anything that was smudged. The first three words were, *find*, and then *my*, followed by *mother's*. The next line of the poem had two smudges, *headstone*, then *trace*. When he wrote down the next two words, *her*, and *code*, he sat back and looked at Ella.

'*Find my mother's headstone trace her code*,' William said.

'Come on, do the rest,' Ella said excitedly. Butterflies fluttered in her stomach, she felt dizzy with anticipation. Or perhaps it was the wine and champagne.

Quickly scribbling down the rest of the words that contained smudges, William was oblivious to the way Ella was looking at him. When he finished he looked up at her.

'What does it say?' she asked.

'*Find my mother's headstone. Trace her code then find the Biblos Aletheia. It's yours. Follow this guide in secret.*'

# Chapter 19

*2130hrs – Cambridge*

IT WAS GETTING dark, the streets of Cambridge were quiet. Cossack ran down the white stairs of the Fitzwilliam Museum and crossed over the main road. He walked around the corner into a side street. His Range Rover was parked on the side of the road. On the window, held down by one of the wipers, was a yellow note. A parking ticket. He snarled, ripped it off the windscreen and threw it to the ground. He jumped in the driver's seat, took out his phone and made a call.

'It is not good news, boss,' he said through gritted teeth. 'The policeman failed to turn up at the rendezvous point. The girl and the painting are missing.' He knew he should have done the job himself, the policeman had always been a liability. A greedy, corrupt little man with only his own self interests at heart. Cossack had no idea why Hades had kept him as an asset for so long, his usefulness had long since expired.

'Find them!' Hades shouted down the phone, his face reddened. 'This is no time to fuck me around!'

'I'm not, boss. We need to contact Kerberos. I have nothing else to go on, I am in the dark.'

'He cannot be contacted, you know that, it is too dangerous. We cannot risk exposing him, especially now. I can assure you that he will alert me using the usual channels when it is safe for him to do so.' Hades paced over to the large window in his office and looked down onto the Tower of London.

'It may be too late by then,' Cossack said.

Hades took a deep breath and shut his eyes, he rubbed his forehead. All these problems were giving him a headache. 'What about the friend at the museum? The policeman said they stopped there to meet someone. Darren, I think.'

'He's not there and I do not have any more details about him. I could return to the girl's flat, but there was no one in when I walked past again earlier.'

'No, it may be being watched. But you have her laptop, yes?'

'Yes, boss.'

'Good. Find a decent hotel for the night, treat yourself. Search the laptop. Try the obvious keywords, it may reveal something useful. Hopefully tomorrow we will have more information from our assets.'

'There is a hotel around the corner, not far from the museum. I will get Nike to meet me there. Then together we will plan tomorrow's work.'

'Don't fail me, Cossack. Remember, your reward awaits you on the island.' Hades hung up and returned to his desk. He picked his glass of whisky up and sighed deeply. Feeling the tension build in his neck and shoulders he longed for Amber and her skills. But it was too late to call her in, he'd already sent her and her friends to the island. At least he had something to look forward to when it was all over.

The situation was getting out of hand, it worried him. They were so close to the end game, so close, yet it seemed so far away. He wished he could accelerate the plans and finish it once and for all. He downed the rest of the whisky.

'Why the hell not?' he said. Impulsively, he grabbed his phone and tapped on a Skype contact.

'Hephaestus, I'm ashamed to admit it, but I'm getting nervous,' he said. He sat down and rested his head on the back of the chair.

'You better not be having second thoughts,' Hephaestus queried.

Hades laughed. 'On the contrary, I want to bring your part of the plan forward. To Friday.'

'Friday? Not all our people will have left by then. Is there not a risk to them?'

'There is no risk. Our modelling shows there will be a short delay before it kicks in.'

'Then it will be done just as you wish, Hades.'

Relieved somewhat, Hades ended the call. He tapped to call Poseidon. 'Are things running to plan with you?' he asked.

'Yes, of course,' Poseidon said sounding tired. He had arrived at the island a few hours earlier to oversee the arrivals and had worked nonstop since. 'The last of the slave ships has arrived and they are being processed as we speak.'

The Brotherhood had identified the need for a number of sustainable labourers. While all the intellectual jobs like teaching, building, and managing the farms would be carried out by the *chosen*, a slave race was required to be at the beck and call of their masters. Their solution was to advertise for manual workers in third world countries. Candidates were lured on the promise of comparatively well paid work and housing in a modern location. Once on the island they would be assessed and selected into teams based on their sex and their strengths. Each of the teams would be informed of the duties expected from them and trained accordingly. In addition there would be a carefully managed breeding program to maintain an effective workforce that would meet the needs of the future generations. Everyone in their organisation had a purpose, the Brotherhood believed that people were happier with a direction in life, even if they hadn't chosen it themselves. Skills would be passed down father to son, mother to daughter. Jobs would be inherited and jobs would be for life.

'Good. Any trouble from the locals?' Hades asked feeling better for making the call.

'No, but we are fully prepared to deal with them if there is. As a precaution we have cut off all lines of communication to and from the island. Only the satellite phones work and our security team is monitoring for any unauthorised signals.'

'Sounds like you have everything in hand, well done. I will see you soon, my friend.' Hades pocketed his phone and strolled over to the window.

He gazed out over the vast city. The sun had set, a million street lights sparkled in the distance. Wisps of bright orange clouds hung low in the sky. He smiled to himself, the fate of the world was at his mercy. But there would be no mercy.

# Chapter 20

THE WAITER BROUGHT over another glass of champagne for Ella. He laid it down on the table and took the empty glasses away. William topped up his wine glass with the last of the claret. He swilled it around, raised it to his nose and smelled it deeply before taking a drink.

Ella drank from her champagne flute. 'You're not a wine snob, are you?' she asked.

'No. I like what I like,' he replied and put the glass down.

'Any women in your life? There must be a few, a handsome man like you. And don't tell me you don't have time for that sort of thing.'

It caught him by surprise, he hadn't expected that question. Ella saw something in his expression.

'Sorry,' she said. 'I didn't mean to pry.'

'You're not,' he said. It was the kind of question William would not normally allow himself to answer to anyone other than the psychologists he had been forced to confess to. Maybe it was the wine, maybe he was just fed up with holding it all in, but for some reason he felt comfortable talking to Ella about anything. 'I was in love, once. A girl I met in the Army, Emma. She was a linguist, an Arabic speaker. When we first met she worked in the Special Signals Group. She translated battlefield intercepts, a safe office based job. But, talented as she was, she was soon selected for work in the field. We were both deployed to Afghanistan at the same time, which we thought was a stroke of luck; we might not have seen each other for a year otherwise. We worked out of the same camp in Helmand even though we were in different units, so we got to see each other pretty often. We enjoyed the tour actually. We even got engaged while we were there. I asked her under the stars in the desert one night. You'd never believe how many stars there are when you are literally in the middle of nowhere. Anyway, we planned to marry the following summer. She started to plan it almost immediately, she wanted it done in a Scottish castle.' William laughed briefly. He finished his wine. 'But it wasn't to be. Fate had other plans.'

'So what happened?' she asked.

There was a distant look in William's eyes, he seemed to look straight through Ella. 'Her job was to debrief prisoners, villagers and anyone else who could provide information. I was part of a special forces unit, it was mostly surveillance but we had the occasional close protection job to do. One day there was a walk-in at the camp, a local who said some Talibs had gone to one of the villages looking for new recruits. Usually young boys taken against their will that they could brainwash. A rapid reaction force was quickly assembled to get to the village. I was on it as close protection, Emma was there as a translator. We left at dawn the next day.'

Ella sensed that William was holding the emotions back, his lips were taut and tense. His voice was different too, he seemed colder, distant, like he wasn't really with her.

'We set off in four snatch wagons, basically Land Rovers with light armour. Emma was in the second vehicle from the front, I was in the rear. Just before we set off she realised she forgot her ski goggles. They kept the sand out, so I gave her mine.' William smiled as he recalled the moment. 'When I hugged her she whispered something in my ear.' He swallowed hard and fought back the tears.

Ella listened with painful comprehension of how this was going to end. Tears formed in her eyes.

'She told me she was pregnant,' he whispered.

Ella took out a tissue and dabbed her eyes.

'We set off along the track roads to the target village, I'd done that kind of thing a dozen of times before, it was routine. But for some reason I knew it was wrong. She should never have been on the team. I had this horrible nagging doubt, but I ignored it. Maybe it was because of what she'd told me, maybe I . . . I don't know. Anyway, I told myself not to worry, we had aerial cover from Desert Hawk and there were half a dozen special forces troopers with us.

'A few miles before the village, the convoy slowed, there was a blockage on the road. We took the usual precautions and cleared the way safely. But then, a few metres further down the road, there was an explosion. A roadside bomb. They let the first vehicle past, then took out the second. Bastards.'

'Oh my God, I'm so sorry,' Ella said empathetically.

'I broke with protocol and rushed to the scene, no one could have held me back. But the wagon was just a twisted, burning mess. No one stood a chance. Shrapnel ripped through it like it was tin foil. At least it was quick. She never suffered.'

Ella didn't know what to say. Instead she reached out and held his hand. He was shaking slightly, she noticed.

'That was it for me with the Army, I'd had it. So I left and now I'm here.' He composed himself. 'Sorry.'

Ella smiled sympathetically and squeezed his hand. 'Don't apologise.'

William regarded Ella in the low light. Her face was kind, her eyes had a warmth to them. He wondered how she could have ended up in such a messy situation, she looked so innocent.

The waiter that had been tending to them sidled up to their table. 'Would you like another drink?'

Ella looked towards William for an answer. But the one he gave wasn't the one she had hoped for.

'I think we're done for the night.' William rose from his seat. 'We have an early start tomorrow.'

'All good things must come to an end,' she muttered under her breath.

While William gathered the notes and the painting, Ella walked ahead into the busy bar. She was slightly unsteady in her new boots, the champagne hadn't helped. She stumbled on a step between the two rooms and nearly fell over. Embarrassed, she turned see if William had seen. He hadn't. When she turned back towards the bar, she walked straight into someone.

'Careful little lady,' the man said as Ella bounced off his large chest. His accent was Russian.

She looked up at him. He had short blond hair. 'Oh my God, I'm so sorry,' she said and pushed herself away from him.

The man ignored her and continued on his way to the bar. Ella navigated her way out of the busy room and into the lobby.

'Ella,' William said as he caught up with her. 'Wait.'

She turned at the bottom of the stairs and smiled drunkenly at him. William took her by the arm and walked with her up the stairs.

'Can you do something important for me?' he asked when they reached her room.

'Of course. Anything for my handsome hero,' she replied, her words were slightly slurred.

'Call Darren, or text him,' he said. 'Tell him you'll meet him at the museum early tomorrow. Say it's important, but don't tell him anything about what's happened or where you are.'

'Why?' Ella asked. She repeatedly stabbed her key card at the slot in the door but missed each time.

'I need to speak to him,' William said. He took the key card from her and slid it in the slot in one go, there was click and he pushed the door open. 'Can you do that for me?'

'Only if you say the magic word,' she said teasingly with a wide grin. She leant on the door frame half in and half out of the room and waved her finger at him.

William rolled his eyes. 'Please.'

'Wrong. Try again.' Ella drifted closer to William. She had a hazy, unfocused look in her eyes.

William placed his arm behind her back. Ella's smile faded, she looked into his eyes encouragingly. With his other arm he reached down behind her legs and in one quick move he lifted her up into his arms. Ella yelped and laughed. He marched over to her bed and gently placed her down on it.

'Goodnight, Ella,' he said and walked back to the door. 'I'll see you for breakfast. I'll give you a wakeup call at seven. And remember to call Darren. Okay?'

'Got it, boss.' Ella saluted drunkenly from where she lay. When the door closed she sighed and stared up at the ceiling. The room began to spin.

# Thursday

*Hemera Dios* 'day of Zeus'

# Chapter 21

*0715hrs – Cambridge*
ELLA WAS ALREADY up, showered and was getting dressed when William phoned her room. They agreed to meet for breakfast in the hotel at seven prompt. William was sitting at the table reading a newspaper when Ella arrived, late.

'I'm so sorry for getting drunk last night,' she said. She sat down and picked up the breakfast menu.

William noticed that she wore much less make-up than the previous night. But she had still made an effort to disguise her appearance with her hair and clothes.

'You deserved to let your hair down after a day like that. Most people would have fallen apart,' he said. 'You did really well.'

Ella had a light continental breakfast, while William tucked in to a triple portion of black pudding with beans and fried eggs.

'Did you call Darren?' William asked.

Ella gasped, her eyes widened. She reached for her handbag. 'I'll do it now,' she said hurriedly. 'I doubt he'll be up yet anyway.'

'I'm going to pop over to the museum after this to check a few things.'

'Great,' Ella beamed.

'You, however, need to stay in the car,' William added. 'I don't want you anywhere near the place. Understand?'

Ella's face fell, but she nodded. 'And what are we doing after that?' she asked.

'We need to pick up your father's ashes, then we'll go to the graveyard. I'll have a look around while you can carry out his wishes. Is that okay with you?'

'Yes, sure.' She looked at him and frowned. 'You really think there's something there?'

'I'm counting on it.'

\*

After breakfast, they grabbed their things and met at reception.

William checked out while Ella used the hotel computer to locate the crematorium the lawyer had told her about.

'Did you find it?' William asked when he joined her in the small business centre.

Ella looked up from the desk. The printer in the corner noisily churned out some paper. 'Yes. I've printed a map of the church at Everton too. Have a look at this.' She waved William over to the computer.

Before he realised what she was doing it was too late. She had typed in the words *Biblos* and *Aletheia* into Google. William was about to reach out and stop her, but she quickly clicked on the one and only result. The web page loaded up. It was the same as before, just four words. Below the text was the symbol.

'"The Truth is Coming",' William read. He typed the web address into his phone and emailed it to Ollie. It worried him, for he knew of Web sites that were used to track people who visited it. Sting sites, an old trick for a modern world.

'Right, get your things. We're leaving right now,' William ordered.

Slightly taken aback by his urgent tone, Ella pouted but didn't say anything. She threw her rucksack over her shoulder and they slipped quietly out of the hotel into the cool morning air.

# Chapter 22

*0730hrs – Cambridge*

AT THE SMALL desk in his hotel room, Cossack sat with Ella's dismantled laptop and his portable forensic IT equipment. He had left the forensic software to analyse the 120GB hard drive over night. Now that he was alone, he was picking through the results.

From his window he could see the Fitzwilliam Museum, a few people were walking in the entrance already. He checked his watch; she would be there by now, waiting like a spider in its web, patient, but deadly. He looked over to the bed and smiled. He could still smell her perfume.

His mobile phone buzzed on the desk. 'Boss, good morning,' he said sounding unusually cheery.

'Have you found anything?' Hades demanded getting straight to the point.

'I have searched the girl's laptop using the keywords. After she searched the Internet for the Biblos Aletheia, she made another search. For a name.'

'A name? Who?'

'Francis Perryvall.'

Hades searched his mind. He knew he had heard of it before. But where? 'I know that name.'

'Is he one of the Brotherhood, boss?' Cossack enquired. Although he had discovered the real names of the current inner circle, he could never reveal that knowledge to Hades.

'No,' Hades said dismissively. Then it came to him: 'Ah, but he was, a long, long time ago.'

\*

William parked up on the street opposite the Fitzwilliam Museum and scanned the area using his mirrors before taking out his phone. Ella tried calling Darren once more from her own mobile. He hadn't answered any of her calls or texts all morning and she was getting worried. William, who had been furiously typing away an email, noticed her frustrations and looked up at her questioningly.

'Voicemail, again. Damn it, Darren, answer,' she shrieked.

'Right, you wait here and keep trying him.' William opened the door and made to leave the car. 'Do not leave under any circumstances, understand? Lock the doors and if there is a problem, sound the horn. One more thing, if you see a large man with short blond hair walking past, hide.'

'Hide? That's reassuring,' Ella snorted. 'What are you going to do?'

'Find out where the hell Darren is.'

From the car Ella watched as William ran across the busy road and disappeared up the stairs of the museum. 'Be careful,' she murmured as she tried Darren's number once more.

*

With his phone pressed to his ear, Cossack sat back and listened to the story. He watched the street below through the window. It was busy with the morning traffic.

'Francis Perryvall was the apprentice of Oswyn le Bone,' Hades went on. 'Oswyn is a direct ancestor of mine and he was also *Hades*. They both lived in Rockcliffe Castle in the early sixteenth-century, long before the hall was built. Francis was his man-servant, his right hand man, not one of the inner circle, but still a key and trusted member of the Brotherhood.'

It reminded Cossack of someone he cared dearly about.

'The story of what happened has been passed down the generations of our organisation,' Hades said.

While Hades talked, Cossack packed his rucksack. He glanced at his watch. It was nearly time for his next move.

'Almost five hundred years ago, the Catholic Church under the leadership of Pope Leo X, had somehow found out about the organisation and the book. There was probably a papal spy somewhere in our lower ranks. Anyway, they thought we were an offshoot of the Templars. An unholy secret society in any case. They commenced a secret offensive against our members. A merchant called Benedict de Quixlay, a Brother in the inner circle, was the first to be caught. Cardinal Scaramucci Medici, the Grand Inquisitor of the Inquisition, personally attended his interrogation. Benedict didn't survive it and soon afterwards a small army attacked Rockcliffe Castle.'

Cossack imagined what the fight must have been like. A religious army against a small rabble of heretics. They didn't stand a chance.

'All the males were killed on site, slaughtered. All except for one.'

'Francis Perryvall,' Cossack guessed.

'Yes. He disappeared and was never seen or heard of again. The book vanished at the same time. We always thought the Church took it, but we were wrong. They never found it. Perryvall must have taken it and hid it from them. It all makes sense now.'

*

The museum was busy despite the early hour. The air buzzed with the sound of excited children, school groups that were touring the exhibitions. Small huddles of tourists wandered around with their guides, explanations and stories were hailed out in German, French and Russian. William rushed past them and headed straight for the basement lab. He slipped through a fire exit into a dark stone stairwell, sped down one level and walked into the quiet corridor. A faulty strobe light flickered in the gloom.

Ella had told him that the lab was the fourth door along on the left. William approached it cautiously. He heard a muffled sound of voices. Then there was an odd sound, like a dog had tried to wail but had been cut off mid way. Gripping the handle of his pistol tightly, he carefully leaned in and peered through the glass panel on the door to the lab.

*

Cossack frowned and rubbed his temples, he paced around the room. Something didn't make sense. The organisation was still in existence, their history was intact, their secrets had been successfully passed down the generations. The Church failed to wipe them out.

'So how did the Brotherhood survive if they were all killed?' he asked.

Hades laughed. 'I said all the *men* were killed. The misogynistic Church never suspected that there were women involved too. Hestia, Hera, Athena, Aphrodite, and Artemis all survived untouched. They kept their heads down for a while, but with the reformation of Europe well under way the Roman Catholic Church had many other enemies to deal with. Lutherans, Calvinists and Humanists were challenging the very foundations of Christian society. Their attention turned to other battles and they lost interest in us. When it was safe to do so, the women recovered the books and artefacts that had eluded the papal thieves. They re-started the Brotherhood.'

Cossack looked at his watch. 'It is time, Hades. I must go.'

'Wait a minute,' Hades said. 'I have an incoming call from Calchas. I'll call you later. Good luck.'

After pocketing his phone, Cossack packed the rest of his things and was about to leave the room when his phone buzzed again.

'Cossack, I have some information that requires urgent action,' Hades said hurriedly. 'Calchas has just informed me that the Web site has been hit again.'

'But I have the girl's laptop here.'

'Listen. The site was accessed from a hotel in Cambridge. My asset informs me that it is the Hotel du Vin. You must get there immediately.'

'Boss, this is strange. I am here already. The same hotel.'

There was a pause on the line as Hades absorbed the information. 'Have you seen the girl?' he asked.

'No. But I will check with reception immediately. I will find her, boss.'

'Do it. Find the girl, whatever it takes.'

*

William could just about see the outline of someone. A woman. Tall and slim, she had light brown skin and long jet black hair. She wore a short grey skirt and black leggings which covered her long, slender legs. She was bent over someone who was sitting on a chair – tied to a chair, William realised. The man's black hands were bound with masking tape, as were his legs. From Ella's description, William guessed it was Darren.

There was something about the woman, something familiar. He searched his mind. Then it hit him; she was the Chinese waitress from the Wiener Staatsoper. He feared the worst for Darren. He pressed his face as close to the window as he could. The pair were talking, or arguing, but the words were too muffled to make out.

There was something else he noticed. On the floor, poking out from one of the desks, was a head. The eyes and mouth were open and there was a black hole in the temple.

The woman stuffed something into Darren's mouth and placed a piece of black over it. She took a step back from him and pointed a pistol at his leg. William heard the unmistakable cough of a silenced shot, it was followed by muffled screams from Darren who writhed in agony on the chair.

*

The hotel receptionist studied Cossack suspiciously, his eyes flicked down to the wad of cash that lay on the desk in front of him.

Nervously, he quickly glanced around the reception to check no one was watching, then he snatched away the cash. It was more than a full week's wages. He pocketed it and then turned his attention to the hotel computer. He clicked away until he found what he was looking for.

'They checked out together a half hour ago,' the receptionist said. He saw that the man was annoyed with this news and hoped he wouldn't ask for the money back.

'What else?' Cossack demanded coarsely.

The receptionist's eyes widened and he looked again at the screen. Guilt and fear were setting in, his hand began to shake. 'Booked by phone yesterday,' he said quickly. 'Two rooms. The booking was for a Mr Callan Blacklock.'

'And the girl's name?'

The receptionist looked up with a nervous smile. 'It doesn't say.' Beads of sweat collected on his forehead. 'But this morning the woman asked to use the Internet. She used the hotel computer and then they both left together.'

Cossack's eyes narrowed, he leaned in to the terrified young man. 'And where is this computer?'

\*

The woman ripped off the tape and removed the material from Darren's mouth. He was delirious, his head bobbed back and forth. She leaned in close to him and said something, but William couldn't make it out. Darren said something back and then the woman mercilessly struck him hard on the back of the head with her pistol. He slumped in his chair. The woman turned to leave.

William ran back up the corridor and hid inside the fire exit. He kept his eyes on the lab door. Moments later the woman came out. Furtively, she peered up and down the corridor then walked briskly in the opposite direction from William. He watched as she stopped at another door a few metres further down. Another quick glance over her shoulder, then she tapped on a keypad by the side of the door. She walked into the room.

William took out his phone and pressed down on the number five. It would send an alert to the operations room with his exact location. An armed response team and medical help was only minutes away. But he feared it was minutes he didn't have. He leapt out of the fire exit and down the corridor with his pistol outstretched.

Bursting into the lab with his pistol held tightly in both hands, he checked the room was clear. Darren's head hung down but he was breathing. His two colleagues, however, were on the floor dead, shot in their heads. A small syringe was stuck in Darren's neck, the needle was still in his vein. He pulled it out and threw it the floor. He suspected that it was nothing more than truth serum. Darren's right leg was gushing blood. William made a tourniquet from Darren's belt and tightened it around his thigh.

Cautiously, he edged back into the corridor. With his back up against the corridor wall, and his pistol held close to his chest, he crept towards the door the woman had vanished into.

When he reached it he saw that it was made of solid metal, the frame around it was a toughened security frame. The safe room, he guessed, probably where they stored the valuable art works. The door hadn't been closed properly; it was ever so slightly ajar. Very slowly, William pushed it open and peered through the gap.

The well lit room was medium in size. Narrow silver safes lined the walls all in a row. To the left of each safe was a placard with a serial number and a digital key pad. The woman was not in William's field of vision, but he noticed a shadow move on one side. Taking a step back, he took a deep breath and readied himself to yank the door open.

To his surprise the door was pushed outwards. The familiar girl looked up at him and they stared, unmoving, into each other's eyes for a nano-second, each frozen by confusion. Then the woman reacted instinctively and swiftly.

She dropped the painting she was holding, raised her pistol and began to squeeze the trigger. William flicked his arm out and deflected the weapon upwards. A silenced shot slammed harmlessly into the ceiling.

Keeping up the momentum, he lunged forward and grabbed the wrist of her pistol arm. He tried to bring his own pistol around to point at her, but she was lightening quick and nimble. Before he could twist her into submission she brought her foot up through the small gap between them and kicked his arm hard at a weak point. The heavy pistol was knocked from him, it clattered onto the floor.

Still holding her wrist with one hand, William battled to get control. He was heavier and stronger, but she was fast and supple. Her long legs and bony elbows pounded him repeatedly in the face, stomach and chest.

Gradually, he gained ground and pushed her into the safe room towards the rear wall. Violently he pulled her this way and that trying to shake the weapon from her. He threw her against the wall, her head hit the edge of a safe. She screamed at him hysterically.

Still grappling for control of the pistol, the woman tried a different tack: she lifted her legs up to her chest. Unbalanced, William couldn't hold her up, but wouldn't let go of her either. She fell backwards onto the floor and William landed on top of her.

For a moment the weapon vanished from William's view, but he still had a grip of her arm. His face was right up against the woman's. He could smell her perfume; it was Chanel if he wasn't mistaken. There was a strained expression on her otherwise pretty face. She struggled under him.

There was a brief cough sound and the smell of gunpowder. Something warm splattered onto William's face. The woman's eyes widened, she released her grip.

William pulled the weapon from her and pushed himself up. Blood began to pool around her waist. Clutching at her chest and unable to breathe, she looked at William with an expression of desperation and disbelief for a moment longer. Then she went limp. Her mouth hung open and her eyes gazed up vacantly at the ceiling. As quickly as it had started, the blood stopped flowing.

*

Back in the lab, William gently lifted Darren's head up by the chin. He tapped him on the cheek with his other hand. 'Darren,' he said. 'Darren, wake up.'

'Don't hurt me,' Darren murmured. His words were slurred, his eyes closed.

'Darren, open your eyes. Come on, you can do it.'

Slowly, Darren opened his eyes. When the dark cloak of his slumber lifted, he breathed in sharply. 'Who are you? Where am I?'

'I'm here to help; I'm a friend of Ella's.'

'My leg hurts,' he cried.

'You've lost a lot of blood,' William said. 'But you'll be okay. I've stemmed the flow, don't try to move.'

'Where's Ella?'

'She's safe. The Chinese woman, what did she want?' William asked.

'Ella's painting, the code to the safe,' Darren replied breathlessly. 'I gave it to her, I'm so sorry.'

'Don't be. Why did she want it?'

Darren shook his head and sniffed. 'I don't know.'

William kept Darren talking until the armed police unit arrived. He explained what had happened to the commander while several paramedics tended to Darren. William ordered the commander to provide armed protection to both the painting and to Darren until further notice. When he was done with the debrief, he left them to secure the crime scene.

*

Sat in the passenger seat of William's car, Ella watched as several police cars, sirens blaring, sped up to the museum and screeched to a halt outside it. An armoured police van had pulled up, several heavily armed officers clad in black protective clothing and helmets ran out, climbed the steps and disappeared into the museum. Moments later, two ambulances arrived. Paramedics dressed in green and white rushed out and followed the policemen into the building.

Ella's stomach clenched, the blood drained from her face, she felt cold. She pulled out her phone, her hand was shaking. She was about to dial Darren's number once more, but she saw something that curdled her blood. She dropped the phone and jumped out of the car.

Several paramedics cautiously carried a stretcher down the steps to the back of the ambulance. One of them held a bag of intravenous fluid above the young black man that lay on it. Unmistakably, the man was Darren.

There was no traffic on the road, the police cars had blocked it off. Ella ran towards the ambulance. 'Darren,' she screamed.

Just as she reached the ambulance, William sped down the white steps towards her. The police were evacuating the building, a long line of museum staff and tourists were guided away along the pavement.

'What's happened?' Ella asked William as they met, terrified of the answer.

The ambulance doors were slammed shut. Sirens blaring, it pulled out and sped off down Trumpington Street.

'Talk to me, William,' Ella demanded. 'What the hell is going on? Was that Darren in there?'

'Yes, but he'll be fine,' he assured. 'He was shot in the leg, it's not life threatening. He's in safe hands now. I'll explain it all in the car. We need to leave here. Right now.'

The spectacle had attracted dozens of onlookers. William guided Ella back across the street and into the car. He wasted no time in getting away from the scene and blended in with the busy morning traffic. Once they were on their way, he told Ella everything.

*

Recovering from the initial shock, but still fragile, Ella wiped the tears from her face with a tissue. They had driven to the Cambridge crematorium on the outskirts of the town. William drove down the long gravelled drive and stopped in front of the sombre building.

'Are you sure you're okay to do this?' William asked as he pulled on the handbrake.

'Let's just get it over with.' Ella blew noisily into a tissue.

When they entered the crematorium they were met by an elderly man dressed in a worn black suit with a white shirt and a thin black tie. He welcomed them and made a note of their names. He ran his shaky finger down a list on the desk until he found the record he was looking for.

'I'm very sorry for your loss, Miss Moore,' the old man croaked noticing Ella's red eyes. 'He is in a better place now.' The kindly man clasped his leathery hands together in prayer and smiled consolingly at her.

Ella and William followed their guide through the hallway at a snail's pace. Organ music played quietly in the background, Chopin's Piano Sonata, if William recalled correctly. At the end of the hall they reached a row of urns that were placed in neat crevices in the curved wall. The old man stopped and turned to face Ella.

'"Blessed are those who mourn, for they will be comforted",' he said. 'The Gospel of Matthew, Miss Moore. You will find all the comfort you need in the Good Book.'

Finding the correct number above one of the urns, the man held out his unsteady hand and took out a simple black porcelain urn. He passed it over to Ella.

'May God rest his soul.'

*

The pair set off from the crematorium and headed straight to the Church where Ella's father requested his ashes to be scattered. The quiet country roads took them through several picturesque villages west of Cambridgeshire then onto Bedfordshire. Ella held the black urn firmly in her lap. Lost in her own thoughts she hadn't spoken for the first half of the hour long trip. William respected her mood and followed the sat-nav directions in silence. He kept his anti-surveillance to a barely noticeable minimum.

'Do you believe in God, William?' Ella asked. The colour had returned to her face, but there was a sadness in her voice.

William thought carefully for a moment. 'I see the wonder of God in the trees and in the flowers,' he said. 'In the stars and in the harmony of nature.' Above the side of the road William noticed a Kestrel hovering effortlessly in the hot thermals. Its prey lurked unseen in the long grass somewhere far below.

'That's surprisingly profound,' Ella said and blew her nose.

'Do you?' he asked.

Thinking of the quote from the Bible that the man in Crematorium had made, Ella looked down at the urn in her lap. 'Did you know that the first New Testament was pieced together by Constantine I, a Roman emperor in the fourth-century AD?'

'No,' William admitted, wondering where she was going with this.

'He was a pagan like the Roman troops who served him. But after losing many battles against other Roman leaders, Constantine feared that his traditional Roman deities no longer answered his prayers for victory. So he opted to try out the new Christian God. The Romans often took on the gods from the peoples they had conquered, picking new gods to worship wasn't unusual back then. Many of the Roman deities were in fact just the ancient Greek ones with different names. But the Christians were different, they only had one God. All seeing and all knowing. At that time the Christian believers were the minority and were terribly persecuted for their belief in Christ. Constantine's decision was a big gamble, he could have been persecuted for it himself.'

'Forced to fight the gladiators or thrown to the lions to entertain the masses,' William said. He slowed to give way at a junction, in the rear view mirror he made a mental note of the cars that were behind him.

'Yes, they were particularly brutal to the Christians at the turn of the fourth-century. Initially Constantine had turned to their god out of desperation, but according to the legend he saw the light. Literally. It's recorded that he saw the shape of the Christian cross in the clouds, along with the words, "By this sign you will be victor". So he ordered his blacksmiths to fashion a gold cross on a staff with the letters Chi and Rho, the first two letters of Christ's name in Greek.'

'Greek? But he was Roman, didn't he speak Latin?'

Ella smiled and nodded. 'Yes, but Greek was the language of the philosophers and of the intellectuals. The four Gospels were all written in Greek. Anyway, for good measure, Constantine also had the Chi-Rho sign painted on all his troops' shields. Even though they were pagans themselves and did not believe for a moment in the Christian God.

'Then, in 311AD, he took his army to Rome to fight his old enemy, the tyrant Maxentius, emperor of Rome. Against all odds he beat the opposing armies. And Maxentius, during his retreat, fell from a bridge made of boats into the river Tiber and drowned.'

'Some people just have no luck.' William slowed to let the cars behind him overtake. In the mirror he took note of the two cars that were still directly behind him.

'Constantine entered Rome with his legions triumphant. Had the result of that battle been different, the world today would be a very, very different place. Constantine believed his victory was purely because the Christian God had favoured him. A divine victory. So to keep the god happy, and so he could remain favoured and successful, he ordered the persecution of the Christians to cease. The *Edict of Milan,* in 313AD, decreed that all men be free to worship whatever god they wanted.'

'Sounds like a good moral leader,' William said glancing in the rear view mirror. The driver behind him was getting impatient with his slow speed.

'You are joking,' Ella snorted. 'He was a misogynistic brute. Under Constantine's rule women who ran away with their lovers were burned alive. Even female rape victims were punished if they were deemed to be too far from home when it happened.'

'Okay, I take it back. He was a great leader,' he joked.

Ella slapped him on the knee. William slowed and pulled into a lay-by. The two cars that were behind him accelerated ahead leaving the road behind clear. He pulled out and continued in the same direction. Ella frowned, but opted to not say anything on the matter.

'But he did do some good,' she went on. 'He raised the profile of the Christians, restored their wealth and their land. He made the Catholic clergy salaried officials of the Roman government. And he commissioned fantastic temples for the people to worship the new Christian God. By 324AD, Constantine was the sole emperor of all that was Roman. He outlawed pagan sacrifices and rituals, prevented the Jews from keeping Christians as slaves, and brutally suppressed the ancient mystic ways. Including the ritual of bringing worshippers closer to the divine through *hieros gamos.*'

'Come again?'

'Sexual communion.'

William raised an eyebrow. 'I didn't know that worked,' he said. 'I'll need to keep it in mind. For the next time.' He smiled to himself and glanced at Ella from the side.

Ella smiled dryly. 'Constantine had the highly popular Temple of Aphrodite, a hive of sexual activity, raised to the ground. Eventually the Roman pagan celebrations and rituals, the acceptable ones at least, were morphed into Christian ones. He effectively forced the migration of ancient pagan beliefs to Christianity in only a few years.'

'Not an easy task I'd imagine, changing the entire religious beliefs of a civilisation,' William agreed. 'A whole way of life.'

'The ways of the mystic pagan religion were millennia old, their rituals were ingrained into their societies. So to make it more palatable the Christian and Roman festivals were blended together. December 25 was the Roman festival of the birth of the sun and the day of the winter solstice, so it made sense to pick it as the birth of the son of the one true God. Easter was originally the festival of the spring equinox and the beginning of a new year.'

'Clever,' William said. 'So he prevented a civil war by allowing the people to keep their key party dates.'

'Politics,' she affirmed. Ella was encouraged by William's interest, it pleased her to talk to someone with such keen ears. 'But it was no easy task. There were a few different versions of Christianity at that time, all based on different Gospels that existed. For years the early Christians fought between themselves over what the correct version was.'

'Sounds strangely familiar.'

'If Constantine was to succeed in gaining absolute rule of the Roman empire, he had to create a single Christian religion and prevent a religious war in Rome. The solution was a single doctrine, an official source of truth for the bishops to preach. So he initiated an investigation into the many Gospels and Christian scripts to find out which ones were genuine, or at least the most accurate.'

'Really?' William said, fascinated. 'My school teachers seemed to have failed to cover this part of history.'

'I wonder why,' Ella said cynically.

'So what happened?'

'A man called Eusebius, an early Christian scholar, had travelled around the region inspecting and analysing all the original versions of the Gospels and other Christian manuscripts. He looked at the language they were written in, who had supposedly written them and when. He even assessed the style of handwriting. After all, it was less than three-hundred years since the crucifixion in 30 AD.'

'So what did he find out?'

'He wrote in his epic *History of the Church*, that out of the many Gospels there were only two that had been written by people who actually knew Jesus. Matthew and John. They had been amongst the original band of disciples. The only two other Gospels that he considered authentic were those of Mark and Luke. Mark was the scribe, and some say the son of, Peter, another disciple. Luke was a colleague of Paul, the man attributed to being the founder of Christianity.'

'But I recall that Paul never met Jesus either?'

'True. Eusebius found that three decades after the crucifixion when Peter, the leader of the early Church, and James, the brother of Jesus were executed, the early Christian followers became worried that the word of the Christ would be lost forever. So many of his followers began to write down their stories. Some were written from accounts told by people who had directly heard the teachings of Jesus, but others were totally spurious, frauds and fakes.'

William frowned. 'But the bible has more than just the four Gospels in it,' he pointed out.

'Yes, twenty-seven writings. There were other scripts that had been assessed to be genuine, or were at least relatively undisputed. So they went in too. Constantine's army of bishops picked out what that they thought should be added based on what Eusebius and others had found. After the Council of Nicaea in 325 AD, the first New Testament canon was approved. It was this that was officially preached in the new Christian temples in Rome.'

'And the slaves became the masters, the oppressed became the oppressors,' William added cynically. He slowed down, a road sign informed him that he had entered the tiny village of Everton. The sat-nav showed that the Church of St Mary the Virgin was only a few hundred metres away.

'Christianity spread throughout Europe like a virus. They discredited and wiped out the remaining pagan mystical religions. The witch hunts, the burnings, the false confessions that were tortured out of anyone who disagreed with them. And the rest, as they say, is history,' Ella concluded.

They had arrived at the church. William parked up under a tree by the dry stone wall that surrounded the old building and turned the engine off.

'History? By that you mean humanity regressed several steps and that science and progress were suppressed for centuries?'

Ella looked at William and smiled. She felt relaxed and safe with him for some reason. 'It wasn't until the renaissance of the fifteenth-century that the western world re-emerged from the darkness and once again took to questioning the natural wonders of the world.' She looked out of the window to the church. Then she remembered herself and looked down at the urn in her lap.

'So, Ella. Do you believe in God?' William asked.

'Too many people have fought and died over them.'

'But millions have found comfort and hope in God.'

She shook her head. 'I'm not one of them,' she said.

But William wasn't so sure that he believed her.

'Right, let's do this,' she said. 'Then I want my life back.'

*

The Church of St Mary the Virgin was a typical village parish church. Situated in the thick of the beautiful Bedfordshire countryside, the atmosphere in the grassy churchyard was quiet and peaceful. Birds sang in the trees, a gentle warm breeze blew in from the west bringing with it a hint of lavender. Built during the Gothic Revival period in the eighteenth-century, the church had a brown stone end-tower with a clock, pointed windows and peaked doors. At the top of the castle-like tower sat four spiky pinnacles.

Walking past the gated entrance into the yard, William and Ella looked upon dozens of headstones that stuck out of the unkempt grass. Some seemed ancient, the inscriptions on the brown-grey stone had been all but worn away, only a few looked to be recent additions. Some were made from black marble, they twinkled like tiny stars in the sunlight, engraved white letters were easily read against the black of the stone.

William sighed, he felt like he was looking for a needle in a haystack. 'This could take a while,' he said.

'*Find my mother's headstone, trace her code then find the Biblos Aletheia,*' Ella said recalling the decoded poem. 'Simple.'

'Any ideas where to start?'

'None, I've never been here before. But her name was Elizabeth Davidson. She died in the sixties. Probably born sometime at the turn of the century. That's all I have.'

'Should be good enough. Well, there's only one way to find out. Let's start from that corner over there and we can work our way back.'

At the far corner of the churchyard overgrown shrubs and trees had claimed much of the land. A few of the older gravestones were hidden in the foliage. One by one, Ella and William read the engravings. Although the newer graves were neatly laid out in a straight line, the older ones were all over the place and their inscriptions were hard to read, in some cases worn away completely.

Frustrated, Ella sighed deeply. 'There's no logic to their order here. It could be anywhere,' she complained. 'Let's split up, we can cover twice the area. I'll start over there.' She pointed to the other end of the churchyard.

'We should stay together,' William protested as he squatted down to read another inscription.

'Please. I need a moment to go and find a nice private spot to spread his ashes. I won't be long,' she pleaded.

'Okay. But if you see the headstone, shout out. I'll see you soon.'

'In this world, or the next,' she said as she walked off.

Squinting in the sunlight, William watched her go. He admired her strength. In his experience people who found themselves in the face of hardship fell into two categories: victims and survivors. Victims went to pieces under the stress and often succumbed to their fate. But survivors fought on, whatever the risk, or cost. He knew which one Ella was. She reminded him of someone, someone he dearly missed. He smiled at the memories, and then went back to work.

*

Minutes later, after having inspected twenty or so headstones without success, William stood up and looked across the yard for Ella. She was nowhere to be seen.

'Ella!' he shouted. There was no response. Just as he was about to go and find her, he stopped, something caught his eye. He bounded over for a closer look.

By the wall on the very edge of the churchyard was a gloomy looking headstone made from some kind of dark granite. Grass and foliage had grown up around it and it was partially hidden from view. But something about it seemed unusual, different. In addition to the obscured inscription in the centre of the stone, there was an elaborate pattern around its edge. None of the other headstones had such a pattern. After ripping the foliage off, William read the inscription:

Here lies<br>Elizabeth Eleanor Davidson<br>Born February 14, 1918<br>Died December 25, 1969<br>RIP

# Chapter 23

*1410hrs – Bedfordshire*

THRILLED TO HAVE finally found the correct headstone, William looked out across the graveyard for Ella, but the bulk of the church blocked his view across the yard.

'Ella! I've found it,' he shouted. There was no response, he cursed under his breath. Using the camera on his phone he took several shots of the gravestone ensuring that the markings around its edge could be clearly made out. Inspecting the stone closely, he rubbed his fingers over the markings. To the untrained eye they looked like an elaborate pattern, merely artwork, or perhaps a strange, alien language. But William instantly recognised them for what they really were.

From the periphery of his vision, he noticed something move behind him. Thinking it was Ella, he rose and turned to face her.

The blow to his stomach caught him unawares. Winded he staggered back as another blow caught him on the chin. His eyes had barely focused on the blond man's face when another punch hit him hard on the side of the head. The world dimmed and William fell to his knees. He reached for the wall to steady himself. When he looked up, he saw a large black pistol pointed at his head. He recognised it instantly, it was a Glock 18C, military issue.

'Agent William Temple, I assume,' the man sneered with a heavy Russian accent. 'And the hunted becomes the hunter.' The sneer turned to a satisfied grin.

'Cossack,' William spat. 'How did you find us?'

Moving at lightning speed, Cossack smashed the butt of the Glock into the side of William's head. William fell to his knees, dazed, but conscious. The blow was hard, but clearly only intended as a warning.

'Get up,' Cossack ordered. 'Keep your hands where I can see them.'

Using the wall to steady himself, William stood up slowly. 'Did you follow us?' he pressed.

Cossack seemed to be amused by his persistence. 'If you must know, your stupid little bitch left a map on the hotel computer. Where is she?'

Disorientated from the pistol whip, William's vision was blurred and unfocused. His head throbbed. But he noticed something move, nothing more than a shadow, behind Cossack by the wall at the edge of the graveyard.

'What girl?' William said, he spat saliva and blood out onto the grass.

'Ha, very funny,' Cossack laughed. 'A tough guy.' The smile vanished, he narrowed his eyes. 'Don't try to be clever, or I will torture and kill you right here. Last chance, Temple. The girl who has the painting, Ella Moore, where is she?'

Behind Cossack the shadow moved again, it was no figment of his imagination, he realised what it was. William tried to keep the Russian's attention on him. 'What do you want from her? I can get you whatever you want. Let's negotiate.'

'Ha! Negotiate? I don't need to negotiate with anyone.'

Despite the pain, William tried to think clearly; then he had a thought: 'I don't have the Biblos Aletheia with me, but I know where it is.'

In a flash the expression on Cossack's face changed, he hadn't expected to hear those words. William watched him consider his response. As long as Cossack still thought he was in control, William knew he could manipulate him. Cossack opened his mouth to speak.

Two gun shots rang out from behind him, the blasts echoed off the church walls. Cossack flinched and instinctively looked over his shoulder.

In the split second of confusion, William lunged forward and grabbed Cossack's pistol arm at a pressure point. He snapped the arm back in a well practised move and pushed the Glock straight into the man's face.

Dazed, Cossack staggered backwards. William kept a hold of his arm and pulled it towards himself. He then slammed the pistol with such force into Cossack's face that the man's legs gave way instantly. Cossack slumped onto the grass unconscious. Blood poured out of his nose and over his cheeks.

Towering over the motionless body, William pulled the pistol from Cossack's limp hand and took aim at the man's head with it. He began to squeeze the trigger.

'No,' Ella screamed from a few metres away. 'What are you doing? He's unconscious.' She bounded over to him and placed her hand over the pistol. She frowned at William and shook her head.

Hesitant, William lowered his hand. 'Where the hell did you get that from?' he said pointing to the small smoking revolver in Ella's hand.

Looking down she seemed surprised to see that it was still there. 'It was the policeman's,' she admitted guiltily. 'I took it from the car after the crash and put it in my handbag. I don't know why. I'd forgotten about it, sorry.'

'Don't be,' William said taking the weapon from her shaking hand. 'You did well, I owe you one. Let's go before he wakes up.'

They ran to the car. Ella hesitated before she jumped in. 'Oh, wait. What about the headstone?'

'I found what we were looking for, jump in and I'll explain. But now we have a bigger problem.'

'What's that?'

'The Russian. Somehow he knew my name.'

# Chapter 24

*1630hrs – London*

AFTER CHECKING IN with the office, William had driven directly to central London. Pinkerton had insisted on an immediate face to face debrief and had signed off a special exception to allow Ella into the restricted F-Branch building. But to conceal the location, William was instructed to drive to the secure car park and take the underground tunnel into the building. From there it was virtually impossible to tell where the building actually was.

'What would you have done back there?' Ella asked as they drove along the Embankment next to the River Thames. 'If I hadn't stopped you.'

William narrowed his eyes and accelerated away from a set of traffic lights. He chose not to reply fearing she wouldn't understand his world. It was a simple equation and one he often went over in his mind: better to be tried by twelve than to be carried by six.

'You would have killed him, wouldn't you?' she persisted.

William turned and glared at Ella. She could feel his hard eyes burning into her. She looked away.

'We're not far now,' William said changing the subject. 'But I have something I need you to do. Remove the battery on your phone please.'

'No,' she said defiantly and folded her arms. 'How dare you.' The comment had brought back recent memories she would much rather forget.

'You can keep the phone. It's just a security precaution while we're in the building.' He could tell that Ella was fuming. 'They won't let you in with it. But you can call whoever you like from the office phones when we get there.'

Reluctantly, Ella complied.

William pulled into a side street and drove into the secure car park. The camera at the entrance read his number plate, verified him, and the barrier lifted. They parked up and walked through the long tunnel into the F-Branch offices. After signing Ella in at security, the two made their way to the *Greenfly* for a quick bite to eat before joining the rest of the team in the briefing room.

When William entered the room he found Pinkerton, Sarah and, to his horror, Paddy, already in the midst of a session. Papers and case files were untidily spread across the table. A laptop sat next to a laser projector at one end, its fan spun noisily.

'Agent Temple,' Pinkerton screamed enthusiastically. He shot up and strode across to shake William's hand. 'Great work, well done indeed.' He turned his attention to a bewildered Ella. 'And you must be Ms Moore. Very pleased to meet you. If there is anything you need from us, anything at all, just ask. You are in good hands now.' Pinkerton smiled as he guided her to a comfortable leather chair.

Flummoxed, William took a seat next to her and gave Sarah a questioning look. Sarah raised her eyebrows and mouthed the words, '*Well done.*' From the opposite side of the table, Paddy eyed Ella with interest. She had turned a few heads as they navigated through the quiet corridors of F-Branch. William noticed that Pinkerton had also kept staring at her. The team quietened when Pinkerton rose and walked to the front of the room.

'Our primary objective is the safety of Ms Moore,' he began. 'We need to protect her. But this is also a matter of national security, we must identify those who are behind it. We must find out what they are doing and disrupt their operations. Who are they, where are they? What are their objectives and motives? Unfortunately, we know so little. Except, of course, that it all seems to revolve around you, Ms Moore.'

Confused at what he was getting at, Ella was about to speak out when William jumped in. 'Ella is merely the heir to a painting,' he said. 'It's not about her. It's about the painting and something called the Biblos Aletheia. We can only assume they are valuable. Ella doesn't know the people behind this anymore than we do.'

Paddy flashed a look from Ella to William and winked. William fought the urge to lean across the table and punch him.

Pinkerton took his seat and put on his reading glasses. 'Of course, my point exactly,' he said. 'But the painting is safely locked away in the Fitzwilliam Museum. It's not going anywhere, that avenue of investigation is closed.'

'We've been working on a copy,' William added. 'But it's revealed nothing of significance so far.'

Sarah frowned and looked at William. His face told her not say anything. She bit her lip.

'Good, keep on it,' Pinkerton went on. 'As for Ms Moore, she is safe here with us for now, but we're not bodyguards. We need to discuss getting her into appropriate protective custody after her debrief.'

Ella opened her mouth and looked at William. He noticed that her cheeks were red.

'Sir, Ella has proved to be a lot tougher than she looks and is proving to be a very useful asset,' he explained. 'We still have a lot to work on. We need her help, she's all we have at the moment.'

'I'm not going anywhere until I find out what's going on,' Ella snapped. She folded her arms and glared at Pinkerton who removed his glasses and chewed on the end thoughtfully.

Sarah, who had been quiet so far, made a suggestion, 'Sir, perhaps I should show them what we've found about her father before we go any further?'

Nodding agreement, Pinkerton motioned for Sarah to go ahead. She took her place by the side of the projection screen and pressed the remote, the slides began. The first was a colour photograph that filled the screen. In it were two rows of men in smart suits, one row stood while the other was seated. All the faces except one were blurred out.

'This is the passing out photo of squad 154, MI6. And this is James Davidson,' Sarah directed the laser pointer to the man's face. 'A Russian speaker, for his first posting he was sent to the British Embassy in Moscow. He spent five years there before being sent back to base for further operational training.'

Sarah pressed the remote for the next slide. Another photograph, this time a close up of James transitioned into view. A few years older he was still youthful with handsome features and curly blond hair.

'This was taken just before an undercover assignment some years later,' Sarah continued. 'You would have been about six years old at the time, Ella.'

'Around the time he left us,' Ella said wondering if the two were linked somehow.

'Records show that his mission brief was to get close to a British businessman who was believed to be buying and selling Russian arms to rogue states,' Sarah explained. 'The job took him back to Russia, then onto the middle-east. He spent over a year on the case but never found anything conclusive. Soon after the mission ended he handed his notice in and left the service shortly after.'

Another click on the remote, another photograph of James, but this time he was much older. Unshaven and dishevelled, he held a placard with a number on it. It was a police mugshot. Pinkerton watched Ella's face for a reaction.

'Why doesn't that surprise me,' Ella snorted. For some reason she felt quite embarrassed.

'This was taken just three months ago by the police at Heathrow Airport. An allegation of theft had been made against him by a businessman in France. James was arrested as he came off the plane. The interview notes make for an interesting, if not bizarre, read.' Sarah picked up a manila folder from the table and slid it along to William. 'It's all in there, but the long and short of it is that he stole a five-hundred year old manuscript from a private collector. He tried to smuggle it back into the UK, but was caught red handed. The wealthy owner lives on a vineyard in France, where he keeps his private museum. When he was given his manuscript back, he dropped the charges. James was released. Two months later, James was dead.'

'Murdered,' William corrected.

Ella stood up and walked over to the screen for a better look of her father's mugshot. Paddy checked her out as she went; he looked back at William and showed his approval. William's blood boiled, he clenched his fist.

'See the ring on his finger?' Ella pointed to the gold band around her father's signet finger. 'Can you zoom in on it?'

Using the mouse, Sarah expanded the photo and zoomed in on the part of the hand that was exposed as James held up the arrest placard.

'It's the ring with the symbol, I'm sure of it,' Ella said.

'Pity the photo isn't clearer. But it looks like the right dimensions,' William concluded.

Ella returned to her seat, took out the gold ring from her handbag and slid it across the table to Pinkerton. After taking a good look at it, he nodded and passed it along for the rest to study.

'Was he wearing it in the passing-out photo too?' Ella asked.

Retrieving the photo, Sarah zoomed in. It was even less clear, but a gold band of some sort could be seen on the signet finger of his right hand. 'Interesting,' she remarked. 'Good spot, Ella. What does everyone think it means?'

'It could be the sign of a secret society, or it could be nothing. But the professor said they were, "a secret society so old and powerful that it defied belief,"' William recalled.

'What professor?' Ella asked, directing the question at William.

Regretting revealing more than he wanted to, William leaned over to Ella. 'I'll explain later,' he whispered. Then he took her hand and pushed the gold ring into place. He turned back to Sarah.

'Do you have the details of the burglary?' he asked.

'It was late at night. Entry was through the front door. The police assumed that either the lock was picked or the door was left open. James returned home from an evening out and disturbed the burglar. There was a brief struggle and he was stabbed in the heart. He died almost instantly. There were no witnesses.' Sarah's eyes flicked to Ella who appeared to be unfazed by the gory details.

'Any suspects?' William asked.

'None,' Sarah quickly replied. 'No forensics either. The weapon was left at the scene. There were no fingerprints and no DNA.'

'A little convenient for a common burglar, don't you think?' William pointed out cynically. 'Who was the investigating officer?'

Sarah picked up another folder from the table and took a moment to flick through it. She looked up: 'It was a Detective Constable Anthony Pepper.'

'Ha! Well, that stinks,' William exclaimed.

'Perhaps so,' Pinkerton agreed glancing at Ella who was aghast.

'You think this was a set-up?' Ella said, astonished. 'I mean deliberately killed? Assassinated, and the police covered it up?'

'It's a distinct possibility, I'm afraid,' Pinkerton conceded. 'And that is exactly why we must find out more about the manuscript he stole.'

Confused by Pinkerton's logic, William beheld him questioningly. 'Sorry sir, but I don't see the connection.'

Pinkerton sighed deeply and leaned forward. 'To understand our enemy, we must understand his victim. Just read the interview notes, you will understand what I mean. Tomorrow, I want you and Paddy to go to France and pay a visit to the owner of the manuscript. Find out everything you can about him and the document, then come straight back here for a debrief. Any questions?'

'What about Ella, sir?' William was quick to ask. 'Her knowledge of history may be of some use to us. There could be connections that we might miss.'

Pinkerton glared at William, he shook his head. 'Very caring of you, but don't worry, she will be in good hands at one of our safe houses.'

'No way, I'm not staying anywhere. I want to go with William,' Ella demanded looking directly at Pinkerton. Then she tried a different approach. 'Maybe the collector will be more willing to talk to me openly. I'll tell him I'm trying to understand my father better, understand why he behaved as he did.'

Exasperated, Pinkerton sighed and spread his hands out to Ella. 'I'm now responsible for you. I can't take any risks, you must understand.'

Paddy, who had been unusually silent throughout the briefing, piped up: 'Look sir, visiting some posh knob on a vineyard for a chinwag about some museum piece is hardly high risk, is it? Let William take the girl, at least she'll be out of harm's way. In the meantime I'll get to work on this Cossack geezer and anyone else the geeks find. They're making some good progress on that, sir, and they need someone to deal with the output.'

William frowned at Paddy, had he just done him a favour?

'Paddy's right, sir,' Sarah added. 'Technical Support have created a map of the communications links. The suspects all use the same encrypted Internet link to talk. Although we can't listen to the calls we can see who's contacting who and from where. It's an impressive lead, look, I've mapped what we have so far.'

Another picture opened up on the screen. It showed little icons of mobile phones with thin lines that connected them to the phones they had communicated with. The ends of the lines had little arrows which showed the direction of the calls, who called who.

'From this we have assessed that the contact known as Hades is at the highest command level. These here are his mid level lieutenants.' Sarah circled a handful of phones with her laser pen. 'These, in turn, command two or three foot soldiers each by the looks of it.'

The screen switched to a world map, icons of the phones were superimposed onto it. 'This shows the geographic locations of the phones we've traced so far. Most of the phones used have GPS modules in them, so some of these locations are down to the nearest ten metres.'

The phones were spread across the globe, William recognised most of the locations. There were icons over New York, London, Bordeaux, Shanghai and Sydney. Some locations were less obvious.

'Where's that one, the northernmost one that's in the middle of nowhere?' William asked.

'Glad you asked, it's a weird one. An Internet call was traced to a satellite phone,' Sarah admitted. 'The location had me baffled too, so I researched it. Turns out that the only thing there, other than ice and barren mountains, is NordGen.'

'And what's that exactly?' asked William.

'The Nordic Genetic Resource Centre. It's essentially a colossal seed bank, a library of living samples of almost every crop in every variety from all across the globe. If ever a crop species was to become extinct, NordGen could use their genetic library to reintroduce the plant back into the wild. They also hold genetic samples from all sorts of farm animals too. It's located in Svalbard, deep under a mountain.'

'A seed bank?' William frowned and looked questioningly at Pinkerton.

'Sounds like Noah's ark to me,' Paddy joked. But no one laughed. Slowly, and uncomfortably, the jigsaw pieces were assembling together in their minds.

'As for the other locations,' Sarah said, getting back on track, 'thanks to the accuracy of the GPS, we have even assessed where some of these people live. Research is being conducted on them as a matter of urgency. That's everything for now, sir.'

Pinkerton thanked Sarah and summed things up. 'So, we have our suspects. We don't know who they are or what they're planning, but we have to assume the worst. Thoughts?'

'Port cities,' William stated. 'Most of the locations are at or near coastal cities.' The team all looked at the map and nodded agreement with the connection. 'Sir, has this been passed to the other agencies yet?'

Pinkerton rubbed his tired face with his hands. 'It's in hand William, don't worry. You have your orders, I have mine.' He looked at his watch. 'In fact, I have a call with the Intelligence Committee now. Sarah, wrap up here. Paddy, liaise with Technical Support and get pro-active on these targets. Watch, but do not engage, got that?'

'Got it, sir.' Paddy raised his right hand to his head in a half hearted mock salute.

'And William,' Pinkerton glanced at Ella with a strange, disappointed look, 'go with Ms Moore to France, see what you can dig up with the collector.' He pushed his seat back and stood up. 'Good luck everyone. I will see you all here, same time tomorrow.'

\*

With Pinkerton gone, Sarah took a seat at the table and continued the briefing in a less formal manner. She clicked through the slides until she found the picture of Elisabeth Davidson's gravestone.

'When William sent in the photos of the gravestone we went straight to work on the research. I searched the military archives and it wasn't long before I found a hit. When the war began, Elizabeth Davidson initially served as a WREN in the Navy. But her talents in languages were quickly spotted, she was fluent in French and German. Turns out she became an SOE agent.'

Paddy raised his eyebrows and William nodded his approval.

Ella merely frowned. 'A what, sorry?' she asked.

'The Special Operations Executive. It was a highly covert military organisation formed during the Second World War,' Sarah explained. 'Their main role was to infiltrate occupied Europe, disrupt Nazi operations and assist, among others, the French resistance. They recruited and trained both male and female agents in the art of espionage and sabotage. Your grandmother was one such agent. By the spring of 1942 she was deep in occupied France working undercover with the Free French. She remained there for two years until she fell pregnant and was exfiltrated back to Britain.'

'She would have been highly trained in covert operations, codes and cyphers,' William added. 'Maybe she was the influence that encouraged your father to join the secret service.'

'Unbelievable,' Ella said shaking her head. 'I'd never have known this.'

'SOE agents were a very special breed,' Paddy explained. 'Real tough nuts, but bright with it and experts at keeping secrets. Few talked about their experiences after the war. Many took their stories to the grave.'

'After Elizabeth fell pregnant she was taken out of danger and spent the rest of the war working behind the scenes at one of the SOE bases in England,' Sarah concluded.

'My mother said my grandfather had been killed by the Nazis,' Ella said. 'Maybe he was SOE too?'

'Or could have been Free French,' Paddy added.

'Sorry, I haven't found anything about him,' Sarah said.

'Well, at least it may explain the code on Elizabeth's gravestone,' William said. The others looked at him with intrigue. 'I take it none of you noticed?'

'Noticed what?' said Paddy.

'Look at the headstone,' William prompted. 'Sarah, just flick through the rest of the pictures please.'

Sarah clicked through the images William had taken, but they were met with blank faces and frowns.

'The pattern around the rim?'

'What of it?' this was from Paddy.

William despaired. 'It's a code called pigpen, an old Masonic substitution code.' The blank faces remained. No one knew what he was talking about. He stood up and walked over to the projection and pointed to the symbols. 'These are symbols not pretty artwork. See the shapes? There's a square, there's a U, an L and a V-shape. See how they are repeated at various different ninety-degree angles? Some have dots next to them, some haven't.'

Paddy mumbled and nodded that he got it, but William knew he hadn't. Sarah and Ella frowned at him, unconvinced.

'Just trust me, it's a hidden message,' he shook his head and sat back in his seat.

'So what does it say?' asked Paddy.

'No idea, but I know just the man who can crack it.'

\*

At William's request, Sarah took Ella for a drink in the *Greenfly* while he and Paddy went to the lab and paid Ollie a visit. As well as having a crack at breaking the code, there was something more sensitive William wanted to air with the pair. Airing his concerns was a risk, but he saw no alternative.

The lab was quiet, most of the techies had left for the day; but fortunately Ollie was still at his desk glued to the four wide-screen computer monitors that surrounded him.

'William, great to see you,' Ollie said jumping up to greet him. He merely nodded his acknowledgement of Paddy. Paddy did likewise.

'I've been making good progress on the network of phones,' he announced. 'Conveniently for me, they communicate with an Internet phone application, Skype. I've followed every link and traced the IP addresses of the phones and computers that were used.'

'So I've heard, well done.' William slapped Ollie on the back. 'Great job.'

'Thanks,' Ollie beamed. 'I also looked into that Web site you mentioned, the one with the symbol. Unfortunately it has drawn a blank, anonymous hosting in China. But I can confirm that the code behind it is designed to track everyone who visits it. You were right. It logs the IP address, country, ISP and even the browser type. Essentially it creates a fingerprint of every visitor. It also drops a tracking Trojan onto unprotected PC's.'

'I have a couple of favours to ask,' William said. 'I need a ladies service watch, something in gold if you have it.'

'No problem,' replied Ollie. 'And the other?'

William produced a printed photo of the gravestone. 'What do you make of this?' he asked.

Ollie frowned as he scrutinised the photo. After a minute he nodded to himself, looked up and grinned. 'Pigpen! All around the rim. An old cypher often found on the graves of nineteenth-century Freemasons.'

'Well done. Can you crack it?'

'Of course,' Ollie chortled seemingly insulted by the question. 'It's only a substitution cypher. Kids play.'

From his printer, Ollie took a blank piece of paper and drew a large open ended grid on it with two horizontal and two vertical lines. The grid resembled a blank knots and crosses game. Next to the grid he drew a large X. Then, in each of the nine square sections of the noughts and crosses grid, he wrote two letters of the alphabet in sequence beginning with A and B. The last two letters in the grid, the seventeenth and eighteenth, were Q and R. The remaining eight letters of the alphabet were written into the large X in the same way, two per section. He then penned a dot above the second letter in each section of each grid. Paddy watched him work with interest.

'In Pigpen code each of those shapes represents a letter,' Ollie explained. 'But the letters can be placed on the grid in any order, literally millions of combinations. A keyword was often used to scramble the alphabet, although the word couldn't have any repeated letters in it. If the keyword was the word *happy*, it would be written H-A-P-Y in the grid. The rest of the alphabet would then follow in the normal sequence, but skipping the H, A, P, and Y, which had already been used.'

Paddy looked lost.

'But we don't know the key, assuming there is one,' William pointed out.

'Not a problem,' Ollie went on. 'Simple substitution cyphers are easily broken with frequency analysis.'

'And that is?' asked Paddy.

'In the English language the most common letter is E, followed by T then A,' Ollie explained. 'There are common letter pairs too or *bigrams* like ST, NG, TH, and QU. And there are even common words, like *the* and *and*. If the coded text is long enough these patterns will become apparent and the correct letters can be guessed.'

'How long will that take?' Paddy asked. The limit of his attention span had already been seriously breached.

'Not long. A while back I wrote a substitution cypher cracking program that will do it in seconds,' Ollie said looking sheepish. 'I was bored.'

Paddy and William exchanged a glance. Paddy rolled his eyes back and murmured something that sounded like 'geek'. Ollie ignored him and sat to down to work.

'First, I need to transcribe the code on the headstone into the corresponding letters using my grid,' Ollie said. He matched each symbol on the gravestone with the corresponding shape on his grid and wrote down the letter it was paired with. The resulting text was a nonsensical jumble of letters just as he had expected. Then on his computer he opened up the cypher cracking program and typed in the jumble of letters in the order he found them. He clicked on the mouse and started the program running.

'Where did you find the gravestone?' he asked.

'At a church in a village called Everton in Bedfordshire,' William replied.

Ollie frowned and looked up. 'That rings a bell for some reason. Got it! There was an SOE airbase there during the war.'

William and Paddy looked at each other, Ollie hadn't been updated on the SOE connection.

'The old runway is still there and the staging hut which is now a memorial to the SOE men and women who gave their lives,' he went on as he typed away on the keyboard. 'They're in the middle of a working farm. I visited it a few years ago, a colleague laid a wreath from GCHQ. There were some brave people in that outfit.'

'Elizabeth was one of them,' William said. 'She was Ella Moore's grandmother.'

'Bingo!' Ollie said. His program had stopped running and displayed a coloured graph on screen.

'It's cracked it already?' Paddy asked.

'Well, it's found the probability of what each letter might be,' Ollie corrected. Tapping away on the keyboard he tried out the different letter combinations that the program suggested. Within a couple of minutes he had found the right one. Quickly, he scribbled something down on the piece of paper he'd used to write the grids. He handed it to William and beamed.

'The key was *Francisperyvl*. Whatever that means. And the message, well, that really has me intrigued now. What's going on guys?'

William took the paper from Ollie and read the message out. '*He hid it from Medici in the crypt, this Atlantean treasure. Pascal Mark X.*'

*

Sitting happily at the bar in the *Greenfly*, Ella and Sarah had been getting to know one another over a drink. Similar in many ways, they had quickly formed a rapport. Sarah had shared a few of her experiences in F-Branch, some of which had left Ella agog. The two girls were laughing when William joined them with a large Scotch. They quietened down, Ella smiled at him warmly.

'I have a present for you,' William said to Ella. He took out the gold service watch Ollie had given him and held it out to her.

'Beware of Greeks bearing gifts,' she said.

William took her slim wrist and gently fastened the watch on it. Dainty and elegant, the watch suited her.

'Thanks,' she said with a frown. 'But why?'

'It's both an active and a passive radio tracking device. In case you get . . . lost.'

Ella's smile faded. 'You want to track me?'

'Only in an emergency,' William reassured. Gently, he took hold of her wrist again. 'If you're in trouble, just press firmly here.' He slid her finger to the winding dial. 'It will send an initial coded signal to a satellite and then one brief pulse every ten minutes for the first hour. After that it sends one signal roughly every hour or so. The time period is randomised to make it harder for anyone scanning the airwaves to detect. But as soon as it's activated we will come and find you.'

Ella was unsure how to respond. 'Very considerate of you,' was all she could muster.

'The battery lasts for several days once activated, but the tracking helicopter can scan for it even when it's not transmitting,' Sarah pointed out. 'That's the passive side. When it receives the correct search signal from the chopper we can then home in on it. It needs to be in range though, about a twenty mile radius from the air.'

'But don't worry, you won't need it,' William assured.

'Then why did you give it to me? Don't make promises you can't keep, William,' Ella said solemnly. 'Excuse me for a moment, nature calls.' Ella left her stool and headed for the ladies room.

'They've found a body,' Sarah explained quietly when Ella was out of earshot. 'A police dog located it under the floor boards of Ella's flat.'

'Have they ID'd it?' William asked.

'Tanya Collins, a student at Cambridge. One of Ella's friends I would guess.' Sarah's eyes narrowed. 'She'd been raped, beaten and strangled.'

'Bastard.' William closed his eyes and rubbed his temples, it had been a long day. 'Do me a favour and don't say anything to Ella. She's been through enough.'

'I won't.' Sarah looked into William's deep blue eyes. 'It's strange though, don't you think? Why would he do that?'

'Strange?' William shook his head. 'He's a killer, he likes it.'

'Exactly, but he's a professional killer. Yet he made no attempt to hide any of the evidence properly. He's taken a huge risk in doing what he did with that girl. Why?'

'Because he's evil.'

'There's something not right here, William. I can feel it.'

'You're telling me.'

'And the IMS still hasn't been updated. Albert said he wants something conclusive before we tell the world.'

William rolled his eyes.

'It's just not right, William. The IMS is there for a reason. Our friends and allies need to know about this, they may know something.'

'Do me favour, Sarah, talk to Paddy about your concerns tomorrow.'

Sarah nodded. They both stopped talking and turned to Ella when she returned.

'What are you two talking about?' she asked, suspicious of their sudden silence.

From his pocket, William took out a piece of paper and unfolded it on the bar. 'The transcription of your grandmother's code,' he explained. 'Our techies cracked it.'

'Atlantean treasure!' Ella's eyes lit up when she read the text.

'Do you think that's what the Biblos Aletheia is, an artefact from Atlantis?' William asked. 'That would explain why it's so valuable.'

'And why someone is willing to kill for it,' Sarah added. 'It must be priceless.'

Ella laughed and shook her head. 'I'm afraid Atlantis is only a myth,' she replied. 'It was a story invented by Plato to describe how wealthy societies that became corrupt, lose their way and are eventually punished by the gods. It's actually now thought that Plato's Atlantis story was influenced by the huge volcanic eruption that destroyed the Mediterranean island of Thera four-thousand years ago.'

'But is that a relatively recent theory?'

'Yes, fairly. Why?'

'Your grandmother wouldn't have been aware of it,' William said. He took a swig of his whisky. 'Anyway, what the hell has all this got to do with a virus? Are we missing something here, Sarah?'

Confused, Ella looked from William to Sarah and back again. 'What virus? And what was that about a professor?'

'Some of that information is classified, I'm afraid,' Sarah began.

William raised his hand and said, 'It's okay, Sarah. She deserves to know the full picture.'

Sarah shrugged her shoulders. 'On your head be it,' she said. She checked the time. 'Sorry, but I need to go home now.' She finished the remains of her drink and pushed the manila folder that was on the bar towards William. 'Read that before you call it a night, it might make things a little clearer.' She stood, said her goodbyes and left.

'So, what's the full picture then?' Ella said eagerly to William. There was a gleam in her eye, she realised that she was actually enjoying herself.

'A few days ago we were tipped off by a virology professor that a secret society was trying to create a virus as a weapon,' William explained. 'But he was killed by the same people who are after you. The same people who murdered your father.'

'Oh my God,' Ella gasped.

'But we've no idea who they are, or what they want. Other than that they want you, the painting and this book.'

'That's reassuring,' she said sarcastically.

William looked down at the manila folder. 'We should read this, then call it a night. One for the road?' he asked.

Ella nodded.

'Grab that table over there, I'll bring the drinks over,' he said and handed her the folder.

While William ordered, Ella took a seat at a table. Absentmindedly, she flicked open the front cover of the folder. A picture on the first page caught her by surprise; it was her father's mugshot. He looked tired and unhappy, defeated. Her first thoughts were that she could see herself in him, the eyes were familiar. But he had a beaten, disappointed look about him. Saddened, she peeled the pages over and began to skim-read the transcript of the police interview.

William placed the drinks on the table and sat down. 'Everything okay?' he asked when he saw an odd look on her face, a mixture of surprise and disbelief.

'Read this,' she said turning the folder around and sliding it to him. 'It's certainly . . . bizarre.'

After skimming through the transcript, William closed the folder and sat back. He picked up his glass and swirled the yellow liquid around before taking a drink. Ella watched him, trying to read his thoughts.

'Interesting,' he said coolly.

'*Interesting?*' she mocked and laughed humourlessly. 'Come on, it explains everything.' Her eyes were wide with excitement.

'Not quite everything.'

Ella was about to say more, but William raised his hand and stopped her. He took his phone out and dialled.

'Ollie,' he said. 'Are you still in the lab? Good. We're coming down.' He ended the call and downed the remains of his drink.

'And?' Ella said narrowing her eyes.

'Come on. We've work to do.'

\*

The lab was empty save for Ollie who was sitting at his desk glued to his screens. He slurped from a large paper coffee cup. When he heard the two enter he swivelled around in his chair.

'William,' he said. When he noticed Ella he stood up to greet her. 'And you must be Ella, I've heard so much about you.'

Pulling up two seats, William and Ella sat down at Ollie's desk. William passed the manila folder to him. Ollie took it and began to flick through it.

'It's the police interview with James Davidson immediately after his arrest,' William explained. 'He claimed that the manuscript he stole was written in 1517 by the Inquisition, the notes of an interrogation of a merchant who was suspected of belonging to a secret society: the Knights Templar.'

'The Templars?' Ollie's eyes lit up. The Knights of the Temple had long been a fascination of his. 'But the Church had wiped them out by 1517. Their brutal attack began on Friday, October 13, 1307. The original Friday the thirteenth.'

William nodded, he was familiar with the story. 'The notes reveal that, under merciless torture, their suspect informed them of another secret organisation. One so old that it went as far back as the time of ancient Egypt. A sacred artefact was mentioned, a book. He called it the Biblos Aletheia. The Inquisition set out to destroy both the book and the secret society.'

'But they failed?' Ollie enquired.

'Looks like it. A couple of months after that interview, James was murdered,' William added. 'And it looks like a policeman may have deliberately botched the investigation.'

Instantly Ollie's mind raced to find the connections and patterns. 'You think someone else read this report and went after James?' he said.

'Good man,' William said with a grin. 'You're keeping up.'

'Let me see what I can do,' Ollie said and turned to his computer. 'I think I know what you're after.'

Struggling to keep up, Ella leaned in to the computer screen for a better look. 'And what exactly *are* we after?' she said.

'Someone found out that your father knew about the book,' Ollie explained. 'The question is how? Well, the interview notes would have been put on the PNC, the Police National Computer. All police officers can access it and, more importantly, search it. Some specialist units can even set up automated keyword alerts so they can track things of interest as soon as they come up. A powerful intelligence tool.'

'And records of all the searches made and who made them are kept forever,' William added. 'Many bent officers who took money for information have been caught out this way. The watchers themselves are watched.'

Ollie tapped rapidly on the keyboard. He worked so quickly the program struggled to keep up with his commands. Windows opened and closed, databases were searched.

'Got it,' he said and pointed to the record on the screen. 'Look, there was an automated alert set up for the phrase "Biblos Aletheia".'

'Who was the user?' William asked, but he already knew answer.

'DC Anthony Pepper,' Ollie confirmed.

'Anyone else?'

'No, just him.'

'But how does this help?' Ella asked. 'We already knew he was one of them.'

Prepared for the question, Ollie navigated to the relevant part of the database. 'It's likely that they've been looking for the book for a long time. In fact that keyword search was added to the system over two years ago. They just didn't get a hit on it until recently. But they were looking for other keywords too and it's these that may be more helpful. What was their intelligence gathering tool is now ours.'

Whopping with delight, Ollie copied all the keywords that DC Pepper had set up into an off-line document. The team recognised many of them: Biblos Aletheia, Rockcliffe Hall, Arthur Tempest. And there were over a dozen other new names too.

'Holy mackerel,' Ollie exclaimed. 'It's a treasure trove. This is unbelievable. How could they have been so stupid?'

'They never planned on getting caught,' William answered. 'They never do.'

'Any of those mean anything to you?' Ollie asked.

'*Society of Eden*,' William murmured reading out one of the new names. 'Not come across that one before. Let's start there, see what you can find out.'

Ollie opened up his Internet browser and began with a Google search. There were dozens of hits. Methodically, he went through each one. The first was the official Web site of the Society. A volunteer organisation, it claimed to be a registered charity. The introduction said that it offered those who volunteered the opportunity to escape the stresses of modern life and retreat to an idyllic nature reserve. The gallery section showed images of impossibly happy and attractive young adults walking amongst colourful gardens and forests. Others showed the same people mountain climbing, fishing off a boat in the sea and working on a vineyard. One noticeable photo was that of a beautiful, angelic blonde girl in a black bikini who was sitting cross-legged on a white sandy beach looking out towards a deep blue sea.

'Looks like my kind of holiday resort,' Ella said.

There was no indication of where the offices or site locations were. Ollie made a note of the charity number and then navigated back to the other search hits. Most were of no interest, he scanned over them rapidly. Then one blog entry caught his eye. A young woman calling herself Lena Korol, wrote that she had been a Society volunteer. After an initial interview, which she described simply as odd, they took her to their island. She said she never knew where it was, no one would tell her, but she described that it was a warm, sunny and beautiful place. She felt that it was somewhere near Greece as the terrain looked similar. The Society staff at the island, she described, were cold, secretive and sexually nefarious. She ended her rant with a warning that the Society of Eden was nothing more than a sex cult that provided fresh meat for its perverted members.

'Strong words,' William said. 'Is there anything on her? She might be worth talking to.'

In no time Ollie had found a news report relating to a Lena Korol. 'Too late,' he said as read it. 'According to this she committed suicide a few months ago. After an overdose of pills and alcohol she took a bath and drowned.'

Ella felt a cold shiver crawl up her spine.

'A little too convenient,' William said. 'So who set this *charity* up then?'

'Just a moment,' Ollie said. He tapped on the keyboard and accessed a Government database, seconds later he had the answer. 'It was registered over twenty years ago, the founding benefactor was a Lord Tempest.'

'Let me guess,' William said. 'The father of Arthur?'

'Possibly, I'll have to do some more digging,' Ollie explained.

Time flew and they had spent over two hours researching the intelligence before calling it a night, by which time, Ollie had built up quite an intelligence picture. It had been a shocking eye opener for Ella, she had no idea the level of information that could be found so rapidly. The number and diversity of databases that could be tapped for information was staggering. Nothing, it seemed to her, was private.

The information was vast and complex, but one thing was apparent. Everywhere they looked, it all came back to one man. Sir Arthur Anthony Tempest.

# Friday

*Hemera Aphrodites* 'day of Aphrodite'

# Chapter 25

*0905hrs – New York*

JACK STARR SAT alone on a park bench at the southern end of Central Park, New York City. He slid his phone into the inside jacket pocket of his black pinstriped designer suit and smiled to himself. He put his head in his hands and rubbed his cheeks. Breathing deeply to calm himself, he shut his eyes and sucked in the warm air. He'd won the bid. The money had been transferred from his offshore account. The deal was done.

Slowly, Jack stood up, he stretched and ambled along the busy path that led out of the park. He felt giddy, both nervous and excited. Above him the morning sun shone brightly, the sky was blue and almost cloudless. Trees lined the park, there were a dozen shades of green. Dogs played excitedly on the expanse of grass with their masters. Joggers ran past him, sweaty and breathless. Mothers in tracksuits and trainers pushed their buggies speedily along, some chattered loudly on their phones as they went. A young woman in a tight, black jogging suit ran towards him. He admired her figure and smiled at her. She gave him the finger as she sped past him.

Jack's phone vibrated in his pocket. He looked at the caller name, it was his secretary. 'Hi Suzie,' he said.

'Jack, where are you? Ms Blackwood is here to see you, she finally managed to get her divorce papers signed.'

'Something's come up. I won't be in the office today.'

'So what shall I tell her?'

'I don't know. Just tell her I'm busy on an urgent case.'

'She won't be pleased that her hotshot lawyer has fobbed her off. I think she has a thing for you,' Suzie teased and giggled.

'Tough,' Jack said and hung up.

He exited the park and walked onto the busy streets of central New York. His instructions were clear, the pick-up would take place today. Remaining on foot, he headed southwards towards North Cove marina on the Hudson. Being a small marina, the boat he had to find, called the *Stravaiger*, a sleek 150 foot power yacht, would be easy to spot.

In no hurry, he took his time to get there and made several anti-surveillance stops in shops and cafés. Not that he was an expert in such manoeuvres, but he felt he had to take some precautions, just in case. Assessing he was clear of any unwanted interest, he confidently made his way across West Street, past the Irish Hunger Memorial and down onto the northern end of the marina.

Scanning his eyes across the small wharf he quickly spotted the distinctive long black shape that was his target on the southern end. It was moored up by the last pier at the far end of the marina. As he walked towards it he passed several vessels of unbelievable size. They were like mini cruise liners, easily big enough to sleep twenty. On one such beast, men in striped navy blue and white sailor uniforms cleaned the salt off its decks. The wealth required to own one was beyond Jack's imagination, yet here were six of them. Only a few blocks away were neighbourhoods where children sold drugs on the streets while their mothers sold themselves just to make ends meet. Jack shook his head. Despite modern advances, people still just did whatever was required to survive. Survival of the fittest, he thought.

On the jetty by the stern of the *Stravaiger,* Jack stood and peered into the cabin. The lower level was empty, there was no one to be seen. Above him, at the rear end of the upper level, was a balcony. An Isle of Man flag hung limp from a varnished wooden pole. Several small dark portholes ran along the sides of the boat on both levels. But there was no sign of life on the vessel.

'Hello, anyone there?' Jack shouted from the pier. There was no response. Squinting in the sunlight he looked over his shoulder, there were a few other people along the jetty. He walked up the metal gangplank onto the stern of the *Stravaiger.*

Jack whistled to himself when he took in his surroundings. Her designer had paid considerable attention to luxury. She was truly a millionaire's toy. From above he heard shuffling and banging. There were muffled voices too, then the sound of a door opening.

'Who's there?' someone shouted from one of the rooms on the upper level. His accent was unmistakably English.

'I'm here for the pick-up,' Jack shouted back. On the port side of the cabin was a wooden staircase. He climbed it.

'One moment please,' was the curt response.

At the top of the stairs to his right, Jack saw a set of wooden double doors. One was slightly ajar; opera music from Handel's Scipio quietly seeped out from the gap. He approached and cautiously surveyed the room through the narrow opening. Beyond was a lavishly furnished bedroom, the bed was unmade, clothes lay on the floor beside it. Jack's pulse surged momentarily when he saw a naked young woman rush past his field of view. She had long, bright blonde hair; it was almost white, and hung down to the middle of her back. Her tiny waste curved down to her shapely bottom. She stopped by the edge of the bed and bent down to pick some clothes up from the floor. Jack's wide eyes lingered on her slender figure before she moved away out of sight.

Grinning to himself, Jack turned and walked over to the gunwale. He rested his arms on it and looked out to sea. He breathed in the salty air deeply through his nose and slowly blew it out through his mouth.

'Can I help you?' the Englishman said from behind.

Jack turned around to face his contact. The fresh faced young man was barely over twenty. He had a tanned, handsome face and short black hair. The man was clearly from high calibre stock, thought Jack, aristocratic parents perhaps.

'I believe you have something for me?' Jack asked, but it was said more of an order, a demand.

A nod, a tight smile. Then: 'Follow me, please.'

Jack tailed the young man along the port side of the upper level towards the bow and into a small room. Two of the walls were covered with state-of-the-art navigation and communications equipment. From a desk in the corner the young man took out a small lined notepad, he handed it, and a Mont Blanc pen, over to Jack. His hand shook slightly as he did so; he tried to hide his nerves by placing his hands behind his back.

Using the wall by the door as a surface, Jack drew a large triangle on the pad. He handed the pen and pad back to the young man. Within the triangle the young man drew a pentagram and passed it back to Jack. Jack completed the sign by drawing an eye in the very centre of the pentagram. He handed the pad back to the contact, and pocketed the pen.

'Good,' the young man said visibly relieved. Beads of sweat had collected on his forehead.

'Now, where is my case?' Jack demanded brusquely.

The man moved over to one of the wooden panelled walls and pushed hard on it. A hidden door swung open, behind it was a large metal safe. He tapped in a code on the digital keypad and then pulled open the thick metal door. Inside was a black carry case, he lifted it out and dropped it on the floor.

Jack frowned. He took hold of the handle and lifted it. He strained, it was deceptively heavy. 'How am I going to carry this back?'

'The handle pulls up,' said the man helpfully. 'It has wheels too. You can just pull it along.'

Jack nodded. 'I need to check it first,' he said.

'Of course,' the man said, he shook his head and laughed nervously.

Crouching down, Jack turned the bevel of the combination lock to the arrangement he'd been sent earlier. The lock opened. He unzipped the case and slowly opened it up. Inside were dozens of clear plastic bags, each was filled with a pinkish powder. His heart skipped a beat when he realised how much of it there was. No wonder it was heavy. On top of the bags was a small electronic device, a single green LED flashed on and off letting Jack know that the case had not been opened since it began its journey, until now. Next to the device was a smaller blue bag, about a quarter of the size of the others. Jack took out the small blue bag, closed and locked the case, and stood up.

'This is for you,' he said proffering the bag.

The young man's eyes bulged. He accepted the bag and pocketed it. 'Thanks,' he said. 'Are we done now?' It was more of a wish than a question.

'Indeed, I think that concludes our business,' Jack replied coolly. 'I'll see myself out.' He grabbed the handle of the case and disembarked.

As he dragged the case along the jetty, Jack smiled to himself. Roughly he calculated that he had just paid less than a tenth of the market value for something he already had buyers lined up for. By the end of the day he would be a very wealthy man.

His phone buzzed in his pocket. He checked the number; it was the office again. He ignored it. Ms Blackwood could get lost. They could all get lost. For Jack was about to take early retirement.

\*

High above the city an unmanned plane circled in a wide figure of eight pattern like an eagle riding the thermal winds. A grey dome hung down from its fuselage like an eye. Inside it was a powerful camera that remained fixed on its distant target. It could read a car number plate from seven miles away. A thin beam of microwaves sent the live images up into space where a satellite transmitted the data back down to the command centre on Earth.

In the back of an unmarked van which was parked on a New York side street, Special Agent Brad Kozlowski watched his large flatscreen monitor. The black and white thermal image was presently fixed on a berthed yacht. The digital map on another screen told him he was looking directly at one corner of North Cove marina. Thermal imaging made for strange viewing, warm objects that emanated heat were dark, while cold objects were shades of grey and white. Eerie grey shadows were cast on the ground in areas shaded from the sun.

Kozlowski had programmed the camera to synchronise with the GPS data from the target's phone tracking. For the last hour it had automatically followed the target's phone, he had barely had to touch the joystick. He just sat back, watched the footage and enjoyed the remains of his pizza.

An overweight workaholic who was fuelled by a steady diet of junk food and caffeine, Kozlowski was just about the best surveillance commander the CIA had ever had. When he sunk his teeth into a target, he never let go.

'No change,' he said into his radio.

Gently, he tweaked the joystick and zoomed in on the target area. There was still no sight of the man who had boarded the yacht. But a translucent red circle that was superimposed on the screen showed him the position of the target phone. It was still over the yacht.

The circle moved, with it the camera followed. The dark figure of a man could be seen walking away from the boat on the jetty heading westwards towards the city. Kozlowski zoomed out.

'All call-signs, this is Alpha-one,' he said into the mic. 'Zulu has left the boat. Repeat, target has left the boat. Heading west, wait out.'

The crosshairs remained fixed on the target, the camera followed the shape of the man with impressive precision. But Kozlowski was poised ready to take the controls just in case the target disposed of his phone.

'Zulu appears to be pulling a suitcase behind him. Can anyone get eyes on?'

'Alpha-one, this is Tango-one. I have eyes on,' a voice crackled over the radio.

The agent on the ground, call-sign Tango-one, was dressed as a jogger. Pretending to stretch off the lactose in his legs he watched subtly through his designer sunglasses as the target walked straight past him. The target stopped by St Joseph's Church and waited, he held his free hand up to his face to shield his eyes from the bright sunlight.

'Alpha-one, this is Tango-one. Zulu is carrying a black suitcase . . . He's gone past Pumphouse Park onto South End Avenue. Approaching a cab.'

Alone in the half-light of the van, Kozlowski's eyes were fixed on the screen. A stone's throw from the target, across the other side of

West Street, was a stark reminder of why he loved what he did and why it was so important: it was Ground Zero, the site of the Twin Towers. 'Roger that. Charlie-one, are you in position?'

'Roger Alpha-one. We're ready.' Sat on his motorbike a block away from the target on South End Avenue, call-sign Alpha-one turned the ignition on and revved the engine. Another agent, call-sign Delta-one, climbed onto the back of the bike.

'This is Tango-one. Zulu is in the rear seat of a city cab with the suitcase.' He relayed the cab's number plate to the team. 'All call-signs, go, go, go.'

'Game on,' said Kozlowski. 'Get on the grid people, failure is not an option.'

The cab drove directly to the Waldorf Astoria hotel in Park Avenue. There were no anti-surveillance moves and no unexplained stops. Charlie-one led the chase most of the way, the weight of the traffic provided suitable natural cover. The rest of the team followed with textbook precision. At the hotel drop-off bay the target exited the cab with the suitcase and walked straight into the reception hall without as much as a glance behind him.

'Delta-one, he's all yours,' ordered Kozlowski.

Sliding off the back of the motorbike, Delta-one left her helmet with Alpha-one, shook her long dark hair out and strode confidently but briskly into the hotel.

In the busy hotel lobby she raised her mobile phone to her ear for cover and spoke quietly into her hidden mic. 'Alpha-one, this is Delta-one. Zulu is queuing at the reception desk,' she said. 'I'm going in close, wait out.'

Rushing past the pillars in the grand reception hall, Delta-one joined the line. Standing directly behind the target, she waited and pretended to read texts from her phone. A Japanese family and two uniformed airline staff queued beside her. At the front of the desk a bearded Asian businessman was given his room card, he picked his laptop case up and walked away. The target was next in line to be served. Delta-one moved in as close to him as she could and pressed the transmit button on her radio.

'Two nights please. No I don't have a reservation,' the target was heard saying to the receptionist. 'I don't have a credit card, is that a problem? I can pay in full now with cash if you like.'

From his pocket Delta-one saw him pull out a substantial wad of notes. The receptionist took the money, counted it and tapped away on her keyboard.

'Room number 1309. Have a nice stay,' said the receptionist cheerily as she handed over the keycard.

Delta-one released the send button on her radio. She moved forward to the desk and smiled at the receptionist.

'Delta-one this is Alpha-one. Do whatever it takes to book a room next to 1309.'

On the monitor the black and white image of the Waldorf spun around slowly as the drone circled it high above. The camera remained fixed on a window somewhere in the southwest corner of the hotel. Kozlowski took off his headset and picked up his mobile phone. He dialled the last used number, the odd international ring tone only rang twice before it was answered.

'Paddy, it's me,' Kozlowski said. 'We have him cornered. He can't take a piss without us knowing about it. When do you want us to lift the bastard?'

# Chapter 26

*0830hrs – London*

THE EARLY MORNING air at London City airport was cool and crisp. A light fog clung to the ground. On the grey runway a huge green and black Chinook started its engines. The rotors turned faster and faster until they were just a blur, the high pitched whine steadily increased until the noise was deafening.

'Put this on,' William shouted to Ella. He handed her a set of green military noise-cancelling ear defenders. When she put them on the whine of the engine all but disappeared. William fixed the throat microphone in place around her neck.

'Can you hear me?' he asked.

Ella nodded and said something, but William watched her lips move soundlessly. He reached for her hand and gently guided it up onto the side of her ear defenders placing her finger on the transmit switch.

'You need to slide that switch to speak. It will stay on until you switch it back, okay?'

'Got it,' Ella said coming through loud and clear.

'Good.' He nodded to the Chinook. 'Let's go.'

They crouched as they ran under the blur of the rotors towards the rear door. A soldier in a high visibility vest waved them up the ramp and into the empty fuselage. The seats were merely cushioned benches that ran along each side. They sat together and clipped in their seat belts. The soldier walked up the ramp into the fuselage and pulled a lever on a panel. The ramp closed and locked into place. Giving William the thumbs up, the soldier sat down opposite them and buckled up.

The pitch of the engines changed and the helicopter lurched forward along the runway. Moments later the power to the engines increased and it quickly rose into the air. Ella tensed and watched through the little side windows. Everything inside shook violently as the helicopter soared upwards. Ella felt herself being pushed into her seat. She watched wide eyed as the helicopter banked steeply several times over London before settling into its flight path.

She flicked the switch on her head set. 'How long will this take?' she asked.

'It's three hours to Bergerac.'

'Do we stop anywhere?'

'No. This thing has a range of a thousand miles and a speed of one-seventy miles per hour. I suggest you try to snooze. There's nothing else we can do.'

William released his seat belt and moved further along the bench, he curled up and shut his eyes. Ella sat rigid and stared out of the windows. The soldier smiled at her, then pulled out a newspaper and began to read. It was going to be a long, dull trip, she thought.

*

At the tiny Bergerac airport they made a smooth vertical descent onto the runway and touched down with only the slightest bounce. The soldier lowered the rear door and William and Ella made their way onto the tarmac. At the exit they were hit by a wall of heat, the dry air carried a strong scent of aviation fuel. Squinting, they shaded their eyes from the bright sunlight as they made their way across the tarmac into the terminal building.

William picked up the hire car, an unimpressive Citroen, and they drove off through the countryside to Château Monbazillac. After leaving the airport it wasn't long before they could see the Château in the distance, it stood prominently at the top of a hill surrounded by thousands of acres of vineyards and olive orchards.

Following the sat-nav directions, they soon reached the turn-off from the main road that led up to the building. They drove up a gentle hill on a long narrow gravelled private road until they eventually reached the car park in the grounds of the impressive Château. Built with large grey stones, there were four wide circular turrets at each corner of the square building. Atop of each turret was a pointed slated roof, each had a French flag at its peak. It resembled a medieval castle, thought William.

They parked the car and headed towards a set of studded wooden double doors. William pressed the buzzer and stood back, he noticed the discreet CCTV camera that was embedded in the panel.

'Bonjour? ' came the crackly voice from the speaker.

'We're here to see Thomas Connegan,' said William. 'He's expecting us.'

'Yes, of course. Inspector Temple we were expecting you, one moment please.'

Conscious that Ella was smiling quietly to herself, William turned to her. 'What's so funny?' he said quietly as they waited.

'You know you don't look or even sound at all like a copper,' she whispered.

William raised an eyebrow. 'Not my choice of legend,' he said apologetically. 'Look, I've been thinking, this guy doesn't know who you are. Let's just keep it that way. Just for now, okay?'

The huge doors shook, the locks clicked, then they swung outwards. Standing in the doorway was a tall and slender man in his mid fifties. He had a tanned, leathery face and short dark hair. Dressed in green tweed plus fours, the sleeves of his light blue checked shirt were rolled up to the elbows. William's first impression was that he looked like he was about to go out grouse shooting.

'Inspector, very pleased to meet you. I'm Thomas Connegan,' he said. His accent was English, notably upper class, but there was a hint of something else which William couldn't quite place.

'Pleased to meet you,' William replied, shaking his hand.

Connegan's attention shifted to Ella. 'Well hello. And you are?'

She hesitated and glanced at William who remained expressionless. 'Ella Moore,' she said. She took Connegan's soft, warm hand in hers.

'So, it's true what they say then. Police officers are getting younger.' Connegan laughed loudly. 'And prettier,' he added under his breath to William.

'May we come in?' William asked.

'Of course, I'm forgetting my manners. Please do, this way.'

They made their way into the small square room that was the main hall. The grey stone walls were bare save for a large painting on one side. The ancient old oak floor was dented and chipped in several places. The place looked neglected. William wondered if Connegan was one of those struggling aristocrats who had run out of the family money.

From the bright hall they followed Connegan through a creaky studded door into a dark, but large, well furnished room. Each wall was covered with a dark wood cladding. Dozens of paintings covered the walls like an art gallery. There were at least twenty framed pictures crammed onto each wall, they were arranged in no particular order or design. A small spotlight lit some of the larger and more impressive pieces. At the far end of the room was a gigantic stone fireplace. Opposite it, on the other wall, were floor to ceiling shelves that were stocked full of books. Above their heads the ceiling was blood red with three highly decorated white ceiling roses evenly spaced along it.

Small but elaborate chandeliers hung from each of them. William spotted the discreet infrared detectors in the top corners. There was a bare oak table in the centre of the room.

'This is the drawing room,' Connegan announced. 'It serves as my gallery and the library. It's the only room I really spend any time in these days.'

'It's a beautiful place,' William said.

'Big houses aren't really all they're cracked up to be you know,' he said modestly. 'Please take a seat. Can I get you a drink? Some wine perhaps? I have a bottle of our very own 1969 claret. It's quite sensational.'

'It would be rude not to,' William responded.

'When in Rome,' Ella added quietly shooting William a playful glance.

'Very good. I won't be a moment, please make yourself at home.' Connegan left them for the wine cellar.

Having a stroll around the room, William took the opportunity to admire the artwork on the walls. The paintings were an odd mixture of age and style. There were frescos and portraits, a few nudes and some highly detailed scenic pieces. Most of them were older looking traditional oil paintings, but there were one or two modern abstracts too. He came across a frame that held not a painting, but an old handwritten document that had yellowed with age. From its prominent central position on the wall it was clearly an important piece. William couldn't read the handwriting, but he picked out a couple of words, it looked like it was written in Latin.

The creaky door swung open, Connegan appeared with three burgundy glasses in one hand and a dusty bottle of wine in the other. He placed them on the oak table, popped the cork and poured a generous amount of red liquid into each of them.

'Fascinating works of art you have here, Mr Connegan,' William said.

'Call me Tom, please.' He swilled the blood-red liquid around in his glass, raised it to his nose and inhaled deeply. 'Ah, wonderful. Are you a wine man, Inspector?'

'Please, call me William,' he replied. Returning to his chair, he picked up his wine glass, swilled it, smelled it and drank. 'I know what I like, Tom. Hmm, and I love this little beauty.'

Connegan laughed. 'Thank you, always a pleasure to get good feedback.'

'Do you collect art, Tom?' William asked steering the conversion back to his objectives.

Holding his glass up to the light from a chandelier, Connegan thought for a second. 'You could say that. But I prefer the word *investor.*'

'You buy and sell?'

'If I see something I like, I buy it,' Connegan said. 'If it makes economic sense, then I'll sell it.' He pointed to the wall. 'You see that manuscript, the one you were looking at?'

'Yes, it's in Latin if I'm not mistaken.'

Connegan nodded and smiled. 'I bought it for two-thousand pounds many years ago from a small Spanish museum that was closing down. It's an original page from the notes taken during the Inquisition's torture of Jacques de Molay.'

Ella's eyes lit up. 'The very last Grand Master of the Knights Templar,' she pointed out.

Impressed, Connegan tipped his glass in salute to Ella. 'Yes, well done. And that piece of seven-hundred year old paper is now worth at least ten times what I paid for it, thanks to the explosion of interest in the Templars.' He grinned showing yellowed teeth. 'I used to do it for a living you know. I was an investment banker you see, in the city.'

'In London?' Ella asked.

'Yes. I worked for an alternative investments company. We invested in wine, art and collectables like stamps and antiques. I did rather well, seemed to have an eye for it. By the time I was thirty-five I had my own investment company. I was bought out nearly ten years ago for a very tidy sum, best thing that ever happened to me. I'm semi-retired now. This,' he gestured to the art around the room, 'is more of a hobby now. But I still dabble a little, it helps pay the bills.'

'And the vineyard?' William asked.

'An old mistress of mine, William, I love wine. And I love the south of France. When I saw this place up for sale a few years back, I jumped at the chance. The staff run the place, but I help out here and there. Doesn't make any money for me though, but thankfully I'm lucky enough not to need it. Not bad for the son of a milkman from Essex.'

That was it, William thought, the posh accent was fake, or at least developed, acquired. The man was a working-class Essex boy done good. He was no aristocrat and he was no collector. He was a wheeler-dealer turned treasure hunter.

'So how can I help you both? The officer who called me said you are investigating a murder,' Connegan said, getting down to business.

'How did you come to know James Davidson?' William asked.

The polite smile faded. 'Is he the victim or the suspect?'

'The victim, I'm afraid.'

Connegan's manner hardened. 'Look, I hope you're not suggesting I had anything to do with it,' he said sternly.

'No, of course we're not,' William assured. 'We just need to know how and when you met him and anything else you know about him that may help us find his killer.'

Stroking his chin, Connegan thought for a moment before speaking. 'About a year ago I was in Santa Barbara, California, at the Karpeles Manuscript Library Museum. It's the world's largest private holding of manuscripts and old documents. Like me, the owner is in the Manuscript Society. I went there looking for a new investment, specifically anything related to the Knights Templar. They are a fascination of mine. I was in luck; they had one thing that interested me, an original set of handwritten notes that mentioned the Templars. But strangely it was dated 1517.'

Ella was no poker player, her eyes widened and her cheeks flushed. She glanced at William briefly then picked up her glass and drank some more of the wine. Connegan appeared not to notice.

'It couldn't have been the real Knights Templar,' Connegan continued. 'You see they were officially dissolved in 1312.'

'By Pope Clement V,' Ella added.

'Yes. But I was intrigued all the same, so I made him an offer. He accepted and I brought the manuscript back here for translation.'

'What language was it in?' William asked.

'Latin. Not something I can read very well myself, so I put out an advert for a translator. On the advert I put a copy of part of the Latin text. Perhaps not the wisest thing in hindsight. Anyway, a few weeks later I received an email from a man called James Davidson, he said he would translate it all for free. Said it was a hobby of his and said he also shared an interest in the Templar Knights.'

'When did he come here?' William asked, he scribbled a few notes in his small leather notebook.

'About three months ago. He stayed here while he worked on the manuscript. I enjoyed his company, a very interesting man, knew his wine too. He was clearly well travelled, well cultured and very bright. He spoke several languages, including Latin.' Connegan picked up the old wine bottle in one hand, leaned over the table and topped up the near empty glasses. 'You can't imagine how so very disappointed I was when he vanished. A real breach of trust; I thought we'd become friends. I had given him a free run of the whole place, even my personal museum. Each evening over supper he would update me on his translations, and as time went on a truly fascinating story unfolded.' He looked down and seemed to drift off for a moment.

'How much did he translate?' asked William.

Connegan looked up. 'All of it, William, he didn't hide any of the story from me. But then he just ran off, and he took the whole manuscript and all the translations with him.'

'So what was the story?'

Leaning back in his seat, Connegan took a deep breath. 'It goes like this: In 1517, Cardinal Scaramucci Medici, who was the Grand Inquisitor of the Inquisition at that time, was sent from Rome to London on the orders of Pope Leo X. He had orders to personally interrogate a suspected heretic. They feared that a merchant called Benedict de Quixlay was a Knight of the Temple. A spy had seen him performing some strange rituals with a gold covered book that he kept hidden. He was reported for it.'

'But he wasn't one?' William quizzed. 'He wasn't a Templar?'

'No, of course he wasn't,' Connegan spat out and gave William an odd look. 'They were long gone by then, he was something else entirely. But it was a turbulent time for the Roman Catholic Church. The reformation of Europe had begun and they had many enemies. Christian doctrine was under attack from all sides, these were dangerous times. Anyone who challenged the official line of the Church was branded a heretic. Heretics were rounded up, confessions were tortured out of them. Often they were burned at the stake regardless.'

'Martin Luther would have only just published his Ninety-Five Theses then,' Ella added. 'His works challenged the very role of the pope and highlighted the corruption of the Church. He also wrote that everyone, including women, should be educated. Pope Leo X branded him a heretic. But many agreed with him, it started a religious revolution in Germany.'

'So what organisation was de Quixlay with?' William probed.

'Funny that, despite the pain they inflicted he never told them. He had been dragged away from a students' tavern in Cambridge, the White Horse I believe, and taken to an underground torture chamber in a nearby castle. They put him to the *Question*.'

Ella shuddered at the thought of the evils that were done by men in the name of their Lord. 'There's still a White Horse in Cambridge, I wonder if it's the same one.'

'I'm afraid not. This particular White Horse was a famous meeting place for Protestant reformers who used it to discuss their dangerous ideas in secret. It has long since been demolished.'

'So what happened to de Quixlay?' asked William.

'They broke him down to a quivering, bloody mess. He talked, but he never revealed the name of the organisation he belonged to.'

'Maybe there was no name to tell,' William proposed. 'A simple security measure.'

'Perhaps,' agreed Connegan. 'But they did appear to have a symbol, a secret sign known only to them. When de Quixlay was captured he had on his littler finger a simple gold signet ring. Cut into the gold surface were three symbols: a triangle, a pentagram and an all seeing eye.'

Ella coughed. She felt her heart beating so hard she feared Connegan would hear it. Connegan looked at her, she was sure he was studying her face, trying to read her mind. She felt the need to say something, anything.

'To medieval Christians the pentagram symbolised the five wounds of Christ,' Ella blurted out. 'But for at least three-thousand years before Christ it was a Greek symbol that represented mathematical perfection.'

'Greek?' Connegan observed. 'I never knew that, very interesting. Anyway, de Quixlay told them all about the book he was seen with. He called it the Biblos Aletheia. It's Greek too, it means Book of Truths.'

Bursting with questions, Ella looked to William. But he shook his head ever so slightly and she remained silent.

'De Quixlay described it as a powerful and ancient book that had been around since the dawn of mankind,' Connegan continued. 'But it was clear he knew nothing about what the book was actually about. He simply said that he had transported the sacred object from Alexandria to England for his master.'

'Who was his master?'

'An Englishman called Oswyn le Bone. Strangely there are no records of such a man as far as I can determine from public records.'

'Where did he take the book to?'

'Rockcliffe Castle. It still exists today, at least its remains do anyway. It's in the grounds of Rockcliffe Hall in Bedfordshire. I looked it up on the Internet.' Connegan smiled.

William stopped with his wine glass midway to his mouth. His eyes narrowed. 'So what happened next?'

Connegan looked at William oddly, then he turned to Ella and studied her face. 'Not surprisingly de Quixlay died from his ordeal. The manuscript doesn't say what happened after that.'

'But it's a good bet that the Church went after the book and Oswyn le Bone.'

'Yes, probably. But I haven't found anything further about that either. And believe me, I've tried all the tricks.'

'Can we see the manuscript?'

Connegan laughed. 'I thought you'd ask that. I'm afraid I sold it. Not long after it was returned to me by the police I was contacted out of the blue and was made an outrageous offer.'

'Who by?'

'A private collector. What was his name? Oh yes that's it, Arthur Tempest.'

William and Ella exchanged a look. Connegan folded his arms and viewed the pair through narrowed eyes.

'Now then,' he said. 'I've answered your questions, so why don't you do me a favour and tell me who you really are and why you're really here.'

*

Perhaps it was the wine, perhaps it was something about Connegan himself, but William felt there was no reason to deceive the man completely. After all, he could still be useful. William explained the story of James Davidson's dying wish, the coded poem and the gravestone. But he left out all of the more classified details, and maintained the ruse that he was a detective investigating a suspicious death. Ella kept quiet, keen not to reveal herself.

William passed the note of the decoded message over to Connegan. He scanned over the text, when he looked up his eyes were as wide as saucers. '"*He hid it from Medici in the crypt, this Atlantean treasure*". Well, well. Medici must be Cardinal Scaramucci Medici. And an Atlantean treasure? *Pascal Mark X.* So who is, or was, Pascal Mark the tenth?'

'We've no idea,' William conceded. 'Our research has drawn a blank.' He eyed Connegan carefully for a moment. 'Let me show you something else, I'd like your opinion on it.' He reached into his rucksack and pulled out the copy of the painting. Unrolling it flat on the table, he used the wine glasses to hold the ends down. 'This should be right up your street.'

With professional interest, Connegan cast his now serious eyes over the composition. 'Such detail,' he opined sounding a little surprised. 'My first impression is that it's not unlike an Edmund Blair Leighton. Pity there's no signature.'

'The original has a brass plaque on its frame that reads Francis

188

Perryvall, 1517,' William added.

'The same year de Quixlay was interrogated,' Connegan realised. He looked questioningly at Ella who blushed and looked away. 'But the painting is obviously not as old as that.'

'It's not much older than a century according to a friend of mine,' Ella said.

Connegan pointed to the gold book that the man in the painting held. 'Is that supposed to be the book, the Biblos Aletheia?'

'Possibly. We assume so,' this was from William. He studied Connegan's facial expressions as the man thought through this new information.

Hovering his face inches from the surface of the painting, Connegan studied the gold book. He shot back up, and said, 'One moment please, let me get something.' Briskly, he walked out of the room.

'I don't like this,' William whispered to Ella when Connegan was gone. 'I've told him too much. See the way he reacted over the message on the gravestone? He thinks there's treasure to be found.'

'And there is,' Ella pointed out.

Moments later, Connegan returned holding a large Sherlock Holmes-like magnifying glass, a wad of loose printer paper and a pen. He poured over the painting once more, only this time he used the magnifying glass and scrutinised every inch of its surface. Again he lingered over the image of the gold book. William raised an eyebrow at Ella, she shrugged her shoulders.

'Found something?' William asked.

'As a matter of fact I have,' Connegan said with a satisfied grin. He sat back down and placed the magnifying glass flat on the table. 'I thought I recognised it when I first saw it.'

'Recognised what?'

'Pascal's triangle. It's on the cover of the book.' Connegan could tell by their blank looks that it required further explanation. 'Pascal was a seventeenth-century mathematician. His triangle is a mathematical arrangement of numbers. At the very top of the triangle we start with a one. Then directly underneath we put two other number one's to make a small triangle. To make the triangle bigger we follow a simple mathematical rule: each new number is the sum of the numbers directly above it.'

'You've lost me,' William said frowning. 'Come again?'

Connegan grabbed the pen and paper. 'Simpler if I draw it. Firstly, row zero consists of a single number one. Row one below it is merely two number ones together. Like so . . .

1
1 1

'For every new row, each new number is the sum of the numbers above it to the left and to the right. The first and last number of each new row only has one number above it, always a one, so those values are also always a one. The middle number has two one's above it. One plus one, so it's a number two, thus . . .

1 2 1

'Row three starts with a one, then a three, a three again, then a one.'

1 3 3 1

William nodded his recognition of the pattern. 'So the fourth line begins with a one. Then one plus three which is four. Then three plus three: six. Then four then one?'

'Correct.' Connegan drew out the next three lines of the pattern.

1 4 6 4 1
1 5 10 10 5 1
1 6 15 20 15 6 1

'This pattern continues for infinity, the triangle just gets bigger and bigger, but the pattern remains the same. The amazing thing is that we find all sorts of mathematical patterns in it. Fractals, natural numbers, prime numbers, Fibonacci, magic elevens, all sorts.'

'Amazing,' William said, barely holding back the sarcasm. 'But I don't see the relevance.'

'I do,' Ella jumped in; she had been studying the painting with the magnifying glass while the other two had been doing their maths. 'Some of the numbers are wrong.' She looked up at William with a gleam in her eyes.

'Let me see,' Connegan said taking hold of the magnifying glass. 'Hmm, you're right. Well, maybe it's not Pascal's triangle after all. Wait a minute, it's hard to see, but I'm sure some of the numbers are in a slightly different style. Pity you don't have the original, I'd be able to tell from the brush strokes.'

Ella snapped her fingers. 'It's another coded message,' she interrupted. '*Pascal Mark X*. We thought it was a name, we were wrong.'

'X marks the spot?' said William.

Ella nodded vigorously.

'Pascal's numbers mark the spot?' Connegan frowned.

'Yes. Well, the wrong numbers do,' William concluded. 'The one's added later, if you're right, Ella.'

To compare the numbers they copied down the series from the

painting, there were seven rows of numbers in total. Connegan completed seven rows on his own, correct, triangle. After doing a spot-the-difference they found six double digit numbers that did not correspond.

'How can twelve numbers mark the spot?' Ella asked.

But William knew the answer; it had been drilled into him during Army basic training. 'They're coordinates. Northings and eastings. It's a map reference.'

'So how do we find where it is?' Connegan said impatiently.

'Simple. Do you have access to the Internet?'

*

The three of them crowded around Connegan's laptop in his office. The small room was cluttered with books and papers. The state-of-the-art, stylish Mac was seated upon an antique walnut desk. Firstly, William Googled for a UK mapping tool. Quickly he found one and clicked on the link. On the webpage he typed in the first six numbers into the X axis box, then the remaining six into Y axis box.

'Here we go,' he said and stabbed down on the return button.

The web page took a second to react, then a satellite map showing the whole of the UK opened up. A virtual red pin dropped onto an area of the country like an arrow. It landed in the countryside, somewhere northwest of London. William span the wheel of the mouse and zoomed in. When he was close enough in to recognise the landscape he laughed.

'Would you believe it!' he said.

'Where is it?' asked Ella.

'The hornet's nest,' whispered William.

# Chapter 27

*1627hrs – Wales*

IN THE MAIN conference room at the Defence Laboratories, Max Redwood and three of his junior staff laid out small, wafer thin, tablet computers for each of the delegates around the long smoked glass table. The rectangular room itself was minimalist, a dozen comfortable black leather chairs were positioned around the table. Panoramic false-colour pictures of various viruses and bacteria hung on the longer wall. Opposite it were floor to ceiling windows with a spectacular view over the grounds.

When the door swung open the scientists stood up and greeted the National Emergency Committee members, a collection of politicians, security service staff and senior civil servants. The delegates were quick to notice the strained smiles and the bags under the eyes of the scientists, they looked like they hadn't slept in days. Their creased lab coats were in stark contrast to the sharp suits worn by the delegates. Col. Ackers was the last to enter along with his secretary, a stern looking older woman with short grey hair and angular features. She sat at the far end of the table and opened up a large silver laptop in front of her.

'I know it's been a long few days people,' Col. Ackers said to the scientists. 'But please hang in there, this is of the utmost importance to national security. Your work is crucial.'

Max nodded. 'We're ready, sir,' he said and sat down next to his team at the top of the table.

Col. Ackers motioned to his secretary, who began to type the minutes. 'There's no need for introductions, let's get straight to the point,' he said loudly, casting his eyes over the delegates. 'Since our last update we have received unconfirmed intelligence that the suspect agent may be released in the next few days. We don't know where, or how.' He paused for a moment to let the information sink in. 'Max, I want your full assessment of the threat.'

'If you'd all kindly look at your screens, I'll begin,' Max said. Remaining seated, he tapped on the screen of his own tablet computer and opened his presentation. 'What we have discovered is an engineered virus, something totally new. No one on the planet will have any antibodies for it, no resistance, no immediate immunity.' Using the touch screen controls he flicked through his slides and animations. 'The virus itself is a coiled, circular strand of RNA, much like a plasmid. And it's all tightly encapsulated in a phospholipid cell.'

'Keep the technical terms to a minimum,' Col. Ackers warned without even looking up from his screen.

Max grimaced and tapped the screen to play a 3D animation of the molecular structure. The delegates' eyes remained glued to their screens. Some picked them up for a closer look, while others had them propped up on the table at an angle using the lever on the back.

'It's a very simple biological structure and similar to Influenza,' Max explained. 'And thus, it needs a living host to grow and multiply.'

'Is it zoonotic?' one of the more technically minded members asked. A female civil servant in her mid-thirties.

Col. Ackers screwed up his face but said nothing. He looked to Max for the answer.

Suppressing a smile, Max adjusted his glasses. 'Can it be passed between vertebrate species? Yes,' he said. 'Mammals and birds according to our experiments so far. Obviously we have not risked testing it on a human subject.' Although he had thought of a few people he'd like to try it on. 'Once the host is infected, our studies show that the virus multiplies exponentially. Its lifecycle involves three distinct phases.' With a gentle tap on the screen, Max started the video footage of the research. Caged animals could be seen in various stages of infection, two scientists dressed in yellow biohazard suits tended to them. In one scene a young rhesus monkey coughed and sneezed. Childlike, it looked innocently into the camera with wide brown eyes.

'Firstly, the virus replicates in the respiratory system causing cold and flu like symptoms,' Max described. 'It is highly contagious during this stage, but not lethal. The second phase is the clever part, but let me explain why. Every time DNA or RNA is replicated there are random errors. With DNA the errors are very rare, only one in a billion after biological proof reading, but they do occur and it is perfectly natural. In fact, evolution depends upon it. However, during RNA replication there is no proof reading process, this increases the chance that any particular nucleotide will be copied erroneously to one in one-hundred-thousand. Replication mistakes in RNA are therefore very common. It's pretty much how the flu virus changes and evades our immune system ever year.'

'Fascinating, but what's the relevance?' Col. Ackers snapped.

Feeling the heat from the blood that rushed to his cheeks, Max turned to the old soldier. 'The second phase of the lifecycle is what's relevant. You see this clever and clearly carefully engineered virus relies on a random replication mutation to alter two specific nucleotide bases of its RNA. When a G in one specific part of the sequence is accidentally copied as an A, and simultaneously at another spot a U is copied as a C, it creates an active gene out of what was originally meaningless genetic code.' He sat back in his seat and eyed his captive, if somewhat confused, audience.

'And then?' Col. Ackers said with a frown.

'And then boom!' Max clapped his hands together, some of the delegates jumped. 'It codes for another virus entirely. One that we have no vaccine for and one that's deadly.'

'Which one?' Col. Ackers probed.

Max tapped on his screen again, another video flashed up on the presentation. It showed the same cute rhesus monkey as before, but this time the sad beast was dying. Painfully. Writhing on the floor of its cage, it was covered in blood.

'The Zaire Ebola virus,' Max said solemnly.

There were gasps of shock from the more knowledgeable delegates, while others frowned and looked desperately around the table. The cacophony of a dozen whispers and murmurs filled the room.

'Please explain the significance of this, we're not all virologists,' one of the delegates said loudly, a middle-aged woman with short dark hair and red glasses. The room quietened down, all eyes were on Max.

Max cleared his throat. 'My apologies. The first recorded outbreak of Ebolavirus was late last century near the Ebola River Valley in what was then called Zaire.'

'The Congo,' Col. Ackers added to no one in particular.

'The virus invades the endothelial cells that line the interior surface of blood vessels and causes severe haemorrhagic fever.' Amongst the worried faces, Max detected a few blank expressions, something he was getting used to. 'Victims essentially bleed to death from the inside as their organs turn to mush.'

'I take it that's the final and fatal phase?' asked Col. Ackers.

'It is,' Max agreed. 'Ebola has a very high fatality rate, about ninety-percent. But it only kills monkeys and humans.'

'And as such it is classified as a Category A biological weapon,' Col. Ackers explained sternly. 'The Aum Shinrikyo doomsday cult tried to develop it as one, they went to the Congo to find a sample. Thankfully, they failed.'

'I thought you said it was zoonotic?' one of the delegates said, the same female as before.

'I did, and it is,' Max confirmed. 'But only the flu phase of the virus. The Ebola phase, however, only affects monkeys and humans.'

'So what you're saying is that almost everything on the planet can spread this disease, but it will only kill us humans and monkeys?' This was from another delegate, one of the politicians. Her mouth hung open and she held her hands out in disbelief. 'My God, this is no mere terrorist threat, this is a goddamned extermination.'

'Hold on, hold on,' Col. Ackers said loudly to break through the cacophony of voices that had filled the air. 'Let's not get ahead of ourselves. Please let Max finish.' He nodded to Max as the room quietened.

'Ebola's effectiveness as a biological weapon on its own is very limited,' Max explained. 'It kills its victims too quickly which prevents it from spreading it too widely. And in any case, it's hard to pass on. Very close contact with a victim is required.'

'So the threat is low then?' This was from a bald black man in his early sixties, a delegate from the security service. 'Isolated cases, but not a national problem?'

Max sighed and shook his head. 'Ebola on its own would be just as you described, but this engineered virus has a solution to the transmission problem. Before the Ebola is coded for in the host, it needs the mutation to occur. This could take days to happen, weeks even, or conversely it could happen within hours of the original infection. It's totally random. And while it waits to pounce the victims walk around spreading what they think is a cold, the flu part of the package. Then bam! All of a sudden they develop haemorrhagic fever and die in agony drowning in their own blood.'

The secretary stopped typing and looked up. An eerie silence fell upon the room. All that could be heard was the tick-ticking of the clock on the wall. Even that seemed to stop for a moment.

It was Col. Ackers who eventually broke the silence. 'So the flu-like virus is the delivery method and the Ebola is the warhead,' he said. 'Very clever. Very, very clever indeed.' Unusually, he seemed lost for words.

'Precisely,' Max agreed solemnly. On his presentation he navigated back to the 3D animation of the virus and played it. 'What both amazes and frightens me is how simple it is. In fact, it is so simple it can be easily synthesised in the lab from scratch. That's how we made it. Mass production would be easy. But it does have a weakness.'

Col. Ackers' eyes lit up. 'Explain.'

'The initial flu-like virus can survive in the open atmosphere. But only for a very short period of time.'

'How short?'

'A minute or two.'

'Which means?'

'Which means,' an exasperated Max said, 'that it needs the initial victims to become infected in the first place, not an easy task. But the virus is hard to store in its native form, it needs to be kept away from oxygen and other reactive agents or it dies.'

'So it's difficult to weaponise?' Col. Ackers said, ever hopeful.

'Yes and no,' replied Max. He removed his glasses and rubbed his face.

'Come on, Max,' Col. Ackers said shaking his head. 'We've no room for ambiguity here.'

'Look,' Max continued. 'Can you stuff it into the end of a missile and launch it towards London? Yes, but it wouldn't be very effective, most of the agent would be destroyed. Can you explode a bag of it on the underground? Yes, but again, the explosion would damage the agent and you'd only infect a small number of people who would, in no doubt, be rushed to isolation rooms. Better to just use the explosives with a few nails in it if you want to make the headlines. You can't paint it on door handles or on fruit in a shop like you can with ricin. I suppose you could go around infecting people one by one with a syringe, but it wouldn't be long before you were caught.'

'So, pray tell, how would *you* deploy it?' Col. Ackers challenged.

Max looked to the ceiling and thought for a moment before he answered. 'I would infect as many hosts as I could in the shortest possible time, *covertly*. Animal or human, but humans would be more effective, they travel quicker and further. Then I'd let the hosts pass it on to everyone they came in contact with in complete ignorance. I'd target travellers. Trains and planes.'

Col. Ackers rolled his eyes. 'Yes, but *how*? A spray? A liquid? We need to know if BioNet will detect it.' BioNet was an early warning system for chemical and biological attacks. Special detectors were permanently placed in all ports, airports, major rail stations and tube stations across the country.

'I really don't know,' Max sighed. 'Putting it in water denatures it quickly. We injected it into fruit, again it killed it. Oil didn't work, nor plastics. I seriously doubt BioNet will work with this one.'

'Damn it!' Col. Ackers slammed his fist on the table. 'Don't tell me what won't work, tell me what will.'

Max glared at his director, he couldn't bear the bullish military types. He chose his words carefully and delivered his reply slowly. 'It would take a network of people. They would have to be highly organised, dedicated. The agent would need to be sealed somehow, maybe in tiny soluble capsules of some sort. Then it would need to be distributed to large numbers of people over a large area and quickly.'

'The food chain?' Col. Ackers proposed.

'A distinct possibility,' Max conceded. 'But however it is delivered there is a serious problem for the terrorists. And this is the real key to the problem.'

The team looked at Max expectantly.

'The terrorists would all need to be immunised,' he said. 'The risk of exposure would be huge. And deadly.'

'So there must be a vaccine?' Col. Ackers probed.

Max chuckled. 'Oh yes, there is a vaccine. A complimentary RNA blocking sequence. It was encoded in the files we were sent along with the viral gene sequence.'

A wave of confusion washed over the delegates. Max was in danger of losing his credibility.

Col. Ackers threw his hands in the air. 'So what the hell is the problem then?'

All eyes were on Max.

'It doesn't work. The protection is only temporary, it soon wears off.'

# Chapter 28

*1745hrs – The Dorchester Hotel, London*

STAGE-FRIGHT WAS an all too common experience even among professionals. To stand in front of a thousand people, all expectant and eager to be entertained, was a daunting task for even the strongest of characters. Some made it look easy, made it look natural, just like talking to a room full of friends. But it was far from easy.

Terry Malone had been asked to host the dinner event at very short notice. Despite feeling under the weather, he jumped at the chance. Their first choice, a big shot presenter who had enviably chiselled features and a perfect smile, had let them down. Terry wasn't sure how many others they asked before him, but he didn't care. A minor celebrity and DJ from a London radio station, he was also a second rate comedian. Used to small live audiences, his often drunk crowd were easy to please. This event was something else entirely. A thousand famous faces right in front of him and the public watching at home in their millions. This was his big moment, it could make or break him. He was nervous as hell.

Fortunately, he had some medicine for that particular ailment. He usually took a line or two of coke before live performances. It gave him the confidence he had always lacked in normal life. "Such a quiet boy", his school teachers had always said. But the medicine brought him out of his shell. It enhanced his talent, sharpened his mind and his wit. He never performed without it. It had helped him through the previous night and it would help him through this one.

Left alone in his dressing room, he took a moment to study his reflection in the large mirror. Impressed with what the make-up artist had achieved, he straightened his bow-tie and resisted the temptation to touch his immaculately styled hair. Annoyingly, a bead of sweat collected on his forehead. He had felt hot all day and was convinced it was getting worse. Maybe it was just the make-up, he wondered; it was probably the nerves, he conceded. Careful not to remove the make-up, he dabbed his damp forehead with a tissue.

Noting the time, he locked the door and took out his antique snuff box. Relieved that there was more than enough powder left, using a razor blade he laid out two neat lines on the desk. His dealer had called it 'pink' due to its colour and had said it was a new blend he'd just got in. He said it would give a better and longer lasting hit, but when Terry used it the night before he hadn't noticed anything different. No matter, it still did the job, and it was cheaper than his usual blend.

There was a loud knock at the door.

'Just a moment,' Terry shouted. Using a rolled up banknote he leaned over the desk and snorted the lines. He felt the blood rush to his head, his weight seemed to lighten, his face tingled. He sat back in his chair, breathed out and grinned.

He coughed; a deep, throaty cough that took him by surprise. Spots of pink coloured phlegm were scattered on the mirror. He wiped his mouth with a tissue, there was a light red coloration left on it. He frowned and studied his face in the mirror. It must have been from the pink dye in the coke, he concluded. He collected some more tissues, pocketed them, and made his way over to the stage.

Behind the curtain the floor manager checked and positioned him while the warm-up comic finished off his gags. Terry was beginning to feel rather hot under the collar, even more so than before. His hands were clammy, his shirt felt damp on his back. The floor manager began the silent count down with his fingers. This was it, Terry thought, his big chance at real fame.

Three, two, one. Terry made his way onto the stage and up to the podium.

The excitable crowd had been worked up into a frenzy by the warm-up comedian and their applause, whistles and cheers were deafening. Smiling and nodding confidently, Terry assumed his position at the podium and tried to focus on the words that were projected onto the glass auto-cue. The crowd quietened. Words began to roll up the screen. He squinted at them, they were all jumbled up, he opened his mouth to say something but he couldn't formulate the words. His mind raced, the silence became deafening, all of a sudden he felt dizzy.

He coughed chestily. Then again, and again. He wheezed noisily and struggled to draw breath. The crowd watched in stunned silence. With his eyes bulging, Terry took out a tissue and wiped the saliva from his mouth. The tissue turned bright red. For a moment he stared at it, confused. Then he began to cough uncontrollably. Blood exploded out of his mouth onto the auto-cue and podium. He couldn't breathe in. Someone in the audience screamed. The crew panicked and people started to run around waving orders frantically.

Staggering across the stage, Terry dropped to his knees. Time slowed, the world closed in. He felt cold. All of a sudden a single thought hit him like a hammer blow: he was going to die. He collapsed backwards onto the floor and looked up at the blinding lights. He barely noticed the terrified faces that appeared over him. They were shaking him, but he couldn't feel it; they were shouting at him, but he couldn't hear them. He felt like he was falling. Everything looked distant, detached. He felt peaceful.

Then the darkness closed in.

# Chapter 29

SEVERAL PRINT-OUTS were spread across the table in the drawing room at Château Monbazillac. Ella, William and Connegan had each been studying them intensely. Using the seemingly unlimited resources of the Internet they had printed off road maps and satellite images of the target area at varying scales. Some covered a wide area and showed the local towns, others zoomed in close showing the ground in great detail. A deciduous forest surrounded the large cross that they had drawn to mark the centre of the coordinates. Farms surrounded the forest and a small river ran through the area.

'I'm sure that's a small bridge that's bang on the coordinates,' Connegan explained looking up from one of the satellite images. 'There's a river, or a stream more like, and a farm track that crosses it.'

'There's a river and a bridge in the painting,' Ella pointed out. 'Unlikely to be a coincidence. Maybe it's a clue.'

'How far is the bridge from the old Rockcliffe Castle?' asked William.

Shifting the papers around, Connegan scoured over the maps with the magnifying glass. 'It's hard to tell where it is, the forest canopy makes it hard to see the ground. But it looks like there's some kind of rubble around here.' He tapped his finger on the image. 'It could be big enough to be an old castle. I guess it's about two-hundred metres from the bridge.'

'Let me see,' William said, he leaned over and looked for himself. 'That must be it. The bridge is our next target.'

Connegan gave William an odd look. Then he smiled to himself, shook his head and went back to examining the print-offs.

'So what now?' asked Ella.

'We'll have to go there, take a quiet look around,' William stated. 'I'll make the necessary arrangements for early next week.'

'All of us?' Ella said with a quizzical look, she glanced briefly at Connegan.

Connegan looked up expectantly. 'Well, you can't close me out now,' he chortled. 'It's just got interesting.'

'You've been a great help, Tom,' William said. 'But I'm sorry, there's no way I can allow it. This is a police investigation. There may be evidence there, any search needs to be handled properly and carefully. We'll need to plan the next move back at the station.'

Connegan chuckled briefly and shook his head. 'Come on, pull the other one,' he said. 'You're no copper. Who are you? What's this really about?'

Deadpan, William regarded the old banker. 'Thanks for your hospitality, Mr Connegan. But we really need to be going now.' He turned to Ella. 'Ready?'

With a nod, Connegan accepted that he'd get no further and backed down. 'Okay, I understand. But it's been a pleasure. Perhaps you'll call me after you find the book? Put me out my misery. Please?'

'I think we can manage that,' William replied.

Connegan gave them a warm smile. 'He was a good man at heart, James. I suspect that there was more to his actions than met the eye. He was no thief, no criminal. I'm just sorry he couldn't have been honest with me. I'd have given him the manuscript if it was that important.'

After saying their goodbyes, Connegan stood by the front entrance of the Château and waved as Ella and William drove off. When the car had gone he slid back indoors and returned to his office. After a quick look out of the window, he sat down in front of his laptop. He rubbed his eyes and stretched his arms; it had been a long day. He put on his headset, took hold of the mouse and double clicked on the Skype application. He selected a contact and made the call.

'It's me,' Connegan said when the call was answered.

'Dionysus,' was the stern reply. 'Is there a problem?'

'No. They've just left. But I think we've finally found it.'

'Tell me more,' the tone had lightened.

'You're simply not going to believe where it is.'

*

'What a charming man,' Ella announced as they sped along the country road back to Bergerac airport. 'Don't you think?'

'You're too trusting,' William chided. 'He knew more than he was letting on. And he knows our main suspect, which worries me.'

'God, you're so cynical,' Ella shot back. 'Not everyone is a threat you know.'

William rolled his eyes. 'It pays me to be cautious. That's all.'

'It must be a lonely life,' Ella mumbled. Resting her head on the passenger window, she stared out at the countryside. They passed by several farmhouses and acres upon acres of vineyards. Bunches of dark purple grapes hung off the vines in their billions. Above the lush green of the land the dark blue sky was dotted with a scattering of small clouds that began to glow orange as the sun set.

With his phone pressed to his ear, William went through his voice mail. The first message was from Sarah. The good news was that the research was going well, they had identified a couple of the suspects and had placed surveillance assets on them. The bad news was a warning that Pinkerton was on the warpath, something about disobeying orders. The next message he listened to was from Pinkerton himself. He chastised William for missing the evening briefing, berated him for being unprofessional and demanded that he return to the office immediately. William rolled his eyes and shook his head. The third message was again from Sarah, but this time she sounded panicky, rushed. There had been a very public death of a comedian, and speculative diagnoses by the media had been swift. The Home Office were unofficially linking it with the research from the Defence Labs. William winced when he heard her mention the word Ebola. Things had escalated, William decided on his next course of action and made a call.

'Paddy, it's me,' he said. 'I won't be home tonight, but keep it to yourself.'

'Be gentle with her,' Paddy joked.

'Look, that thing we talked about, keep a close eye on it. Something's happening, I'm sure of it.'

'I'll keep my ear to the ground.'

'Did you know he wants me off the case?'

'I heard.'

'There's too much at stake to waste time now.'

'Just do what you need to do,' Paddy said. 'I'll look after everything at this end.'

William turned his phone off and pocketed it. He could feel Ella's eyes on him. 'Get some rest. It's going to be a long a night,' he said.

'What do you mean?' Ella eyed him suspiciously.

'We're going to pay a little visit to that bridge.'

'But you said . . .' she began, but stopped and smiled. 'You played him, didn't you? Just in case.'

'I take it you *do* want to come?' he said with a wry grin.

'Of course,' she said brightly.

'Good. We'll get about three hours sleep during the journey there. We'll be dropped off a mile or so from the bridge.'

'How will we find it?' Ella quizzed. 'It'll be pitch black!'

William smiled. 'Ever used the latest in military night-vision before?'

Ella raised an eyebrow. She pushed her seat back and shut her eyes. Exhausted, she quickly drifted off to sleep. But her pleasant dreams were short lived.

# Chapter 30

ALONE IN HIS library at Rockcliffe Hall, Hades sat in front of his computer and adjusted the webcam. He put on his headset and made the video call. The encrypted Internet traffic had been routed through anonymising proxies in three different countries. If anyone was monitoring the traffic it would look as if he was contacting a server in China. It wasn't impossible to trace the traffic to its real destination, but it would take days, if not weeks. Time that Hades knew the authorities didn't have.

The picture on the large flatscreen TV came on, it showed a long black table with the remaining eleven of the inner circle sat patiently around it. The walls of the large room were made of an uneven brown rock, it looked like they were in a cavern. Hanging down from the three visible walls were six large red flags, two on each wall. Printed on the flags in black was their symbol.

Each person at the table was dressed in an immaculate white uniform. The men wore a thick gold chain around their necks which had a thick gold pendant in the shape of a triangle. Each of the women wore an elaborate gold tiara which sported a bright red oval jewel in the very centre.

At one end of the table was a large TV screen with a high definition webcam on the top. Their heads turned towards it when the connection was made.

'I'm so pleased to see you all,' Hades began. The latency was slight, but noticeable, the picture occasionally froze and pixelated. 'I take it everything is going to plan?'

The one known as Zeus stood up and answered. 'Yes, of course, Hades. Everyone is here now. We have assembled our security force and the island has been secured, no one comes or goes without authorisation. The *chosen* have taken their places and are running things as directed. All the slave ships have arrived, the workforce is healthy and all were processed without hitch. Most seem to have accepted their new roles with remarkable enthusiasm. The rest will fall into place soon enough.'

'They will quickly realise we offer them a better life than the ones they left behind,' Hades stated arrogantly. 'And together we will build an impressive, peaceful civilisation for the future generations.'

'We did have one small incident,' Hephaestus added giving Zeus a quick side glance. 'One of the skippers of a transport ship wanted to leave with some of his crew. They became quite violent when we tried to stop them, so our troops took immediate and deadly action. It was witnessed by dozens of the slaves who were still disembarking.'

'Good, now they will all know how serious we are,' Hades replied. 'Word will spread, they will fear us and be more cautious in future. No harm done.'

'We saw something of concern on the news, it appears that the weapon has been released early,' Artemis said with a stern tone. Some of the others shook their heads at her, but she ignored them and ploughed on. 'It would be disastrous if the problem was to be identified too soon by the World Health Organisation, would it not?'

'An isolated incident,' Hades replied shrugging off the risk. 'A dealer jumped the gun by one day. There is nothing to be concerned about. By the time they figure out what is going on it will be too late. Kerberos is looking after things for us.'

'Strange how it took effect so soon,' Artemis continued, oblivious to the sighs from the table. 'There would have been no time for the agent to spread. What good is that?'

A bearded Asian man, the one known as Ares, threw his arms in the air. 'We've been through this before, Artemis. Don't you ever listen? Our live tests showed that it takes anything between one and seven days to contract the full disease,' he lectured. 'The timing is wholly random and unpredictable. That is why it is the ideal weapon for us. It was just unlucky that it took effect so quickly with this first victim.'

Artemis opened her mouth to snap a response back, but, after a look of warning from Zeus, she thought better of it. She folded her arms and sat back in her chair. The conversation moved on and in turn they updated Hades on their progress on various tasks. Eventually, after Hades had been assured that everything was running as it should be, he congratulated them all on a job well done.

'I have some crucial business to attend to now,' he said. 'But whatever happens, I, Cossack and Kerberos will be joining you by Ekranoplan on Sunday.'

In preparation for the journey, Hades had commissioned a Russian maritime engineering company to design and build him an

Ekranoplan. Using the ground effect, a slippery cushion of air created between specially shaped wings and the surface of the sea, the craft, which was a cross between and plane and a boat, could reach speeds of four-hundred knots. It was highly fuel efficient and because it flew just a few metres above the sea it was invisible to radar. It was the perfect getaway vehicle.

'Do not let your lust for the book blind you, Hades,' Artemis warned. 'We do not want to lose you at this crucial stage.'

Forcing a smile, Hades looked into the camera. 'Thank you for your concern,' he said. 'But I have everything perfectly under control, the book will be in our hands soon. And don't underestimate its importance, with it back we will decipher our past and use it to mould our future. And it will be a glorious future. For too long we have suffered the mongrels who have abused this planet for their own corrupt ends. When they are gone we will reset the balance with nature and our planet will heal. From the gardens of our Eden we will emerge into a fresh new world. Our world!'

# Saturday

*Hemera Khronu* 'day of Cronus'

# Chapter 31

*0345 hrs – Bedfordshire*

DROPPING LIKE A huge dark rock from the clouds, the Chinook skimmed low over the drop zone in the pitch black of the night. With stomach churning G-force it banked steeply several times until it finally straightened up and rapidly slowed to a hover over the middle of a field. The rear door was already fully open. Two figures dressed in black jumpsuits waited, crouched by the exit. Slowly the craft lowered, when the ramp touched the ground the figures in black both walked briskly down it onto the soft grass. They ran forward in a crouched position and, when they were clear of the rotors, dived down onto the damp ground and waited. Blowing loose grass and water into the air, the Chinook rose and lurched forward. It circled once more around another field before it finally rose up into the clouds and disappeared.

When the silence returned to the field one of the dark figures sat up and scanned the area with thermal imaging binoculars.

'It's clear,' William whispered. He put the binoculars back into his heavy, packed rucksack and slung it over his shoulder. He put his night-vision goggles back on and stood up. 'Let's go.'

When Ella took a step forward she immediately lost her balance and held out her arms to steady herself. William grabbed her and steadied her. She adjusted the night-vision goggles that were strapped tightly to her head.

'Takes a bit of getting used to,' he said helping her.

'I feel nauseous,' Ella admitted. 'There's no depth to my vision.'

The green-black image of the landscape was almost as clear as daylight. Rocks and farm equipment, trees and fences could all be easily made out. But it was all two-dimensional, distance was hard to judge.

'It will pass quickly. Stay close to me.'

Using the visual directions from the satellite navigation system that integrated into the night-vision goggles, William led the way across the terrain. The display told him that as the crow flew they were just over two kilometres from the target. It was going to be a long and difficult walk across such uneven ground. Ella stumbled a few times before she worked out that she had to adjust her gait to account for the lack of perspective. Despite the cold air, she quickly developed a sweat.

'How far now,' Ella panted as they entered a thick forest.

'A couple of minutes more,' William said. He put his hand on her shoulder. 'Just wait here a moment.'

The night-vision was less effective in the wood, its thick canopy blocked most of the ambient light that the device relied on. William switched on the infrared torches that were embedded into the top of their goggles. The infrared light was invisible to the naked eye, but with their goggles on the path ahead was lit up with an eerie green glow. They continued at a reduced pace through the wood.

They heard the stream before they saw it. The peaceful sound of gently running water was strangely calming. No more than three metres wide, the stream looked pretty shallow. The raised banks on each side were less than a metre above the water's surface. They walked along the bank and followed its winding path hoping that it would lead to them straight to the bridge.

Misjudging a fallen tree that crossed her path, Ella lost her footing and tripped. She tumbled over the edge of the bank and hit the water with a splash. Although it was shallow, she ended up on her back partially submerged in the freezing water. The black jumpsuit was coated with waterproofing, but she gasped when some of the icy liquid seeped down the back of her neck.

'Are you okay?' William asked leaping down to help her.

'Oh, I'm fine,' she said sarcastically pushing herself up. 'Cold, tired and now wet through. It's the best Friday night out I've ever had. I should come out with you more often.'

'Come on.' William took her hand and helped her up the muddy river bank. 'It's not far now. Stay close to me.'

'I'm really cold,' Ella complained.

Taking her by surprise, William pulled her close into his chest and vigorously rubbed her back. He gripped her tightly and held her against him. Feeling his warmth she put her arms around him and pulled him in. She felt her pulse rise as they stood together.

'Better?' he asked when he finally let her go.

'Better,' she said with a slightly embarrassed smile. They continued on their way following the winding river at a safe distance from the edge of the bank.

'So what would you rather be doing then?' William asked. 'Out being wild instead of being out in the wild?'

'Oh, let me see. Normally I'm out all night getting drunk and sleeping with random men,' she said sarcastically. 'It's what you're supposed to do on a Friday. Didn't you know that it was the day of Aphrodite? The Greek goddess of love and beauty, the one the Romans called Venus.'

'It's Saturday now in case you hadn't noticed,' William teased.

'Ah, the day of Cronus.'

'Who was he then?'

'A Titan, the god of happiness, the Romans called him Saturn. He was the supreme ruler of all the gods until his son, Zeus the god of the sky, led a war against him and the rest of the Titan's. He won and claimed the throne for himself.'

'So Fridays are attributed to the sexy god and Saturdays to the happy one? I like the Greek way of thinking,' William said.

Ella gently nudged him in the ribs with her elbow. 'Don't mock them, they were a great race. Their philosophers, astronomers and mathematicians were centuries ahead of everyone else at the time. They knew that the sun was at the centre of our solar system. They even worked out the circumference of earth to the nearest few miles. They invented maps and numerous other things that advanced mankind. But they did have some strange ways.'

'Like sacrificing animals to their gods,' William added, 'and reading the bloody entrails to divine the future.'

'That and the occasional human child for good measure. But at a time in human history when many tribes were behaving like herd animals, the Greeks had an advanced and vast civilisation. And they could write in great detail, an amazing feat that ensured that the records of their endeavours and beliefs were preserved, unaltered, for the future generations to study. Where would we be without them?'

William reached his hand out to Ella and they both stopped. A few dozen metres ahead they could make out the hazy shape of a bridge.

'We're here,' William said quietly. He crouched down, took off his night-vision goggles and scanned the area with the thermal imager. 'No signs of life. It's clear.'

They continued along the river bank until they reached the bridge. Smaller than they had imagined it from the satellite images, it arched low over the river. Built with uneven rounded stones it was covered in moss and ivy. At the far side of it, on the other side of the river, the narrow track road that went over the bridge disappeared up the hill further into the forest.

'What do you think we should look for?' Ella asked as they waded through the shallow stream under the arch. It was only just high enough to walk under, William had to duck slightly.

'I don't know. Markings, I guess. A plaque, a symbol, or maybe a door of some sort,' he said. But the underside of the arch was featureless. Just damp, moss covered stone.

They walked around to the other side and inspected the other surfaces. They too were featureless, there was nothing of interest, nothing that could be a message or a clue.

Ella sighed and rested her back against the wall. 'You sure this is the right spot?'

'We're dead on the coordinates,' William replied after double checking the sat-nav. 'Come on, let's see what's up top.'

They clambered up the steep bank onto the top of the bridge. William was up first and held out his hand for Ella, she took it to steady herself. The single-track farm road that stretched across the bridge was covered with hundreds of tall foxgloves and a carpet of long, wild grasses. William could smell the sweetness of the flowers in the still air, but couldn't make out their magnificent colours. It was all a mix of green and black to him. On the ground there were no obvious vehicle tracks, it seemed the road hadn't been used in a long time.

'Great,' Ella said downheartedly. 'What now?' She sat on the low wall and hugged herself to keep warm.

Scrutinising the ground as he went, William wandered across to the other end. When he reached the other side he noticed one small area to the left by the wall that seemed to be lacking in any overgrowth. He went over to it and crouched down for a closer look.

'Found something?' asked Ella looking over.

'Just an old piece of mangy carpet,' he said. But as it was out of place he studied the tatty sodden material, then pulled it away. Underneath was a rusty circular manhole cover. 'Well, look here.'

'That must be it,' Ella said as she crouched down next to him.

'Only one way to find out,' he said and smiled.

From a hidden ankle sheath, William pulled out his lethal looking service dagger. He dug the long, blackened titanium blade into the side of the metal cover and levered it up until he could get his fingers under it. Made from solid iron, it was heavy. He heaved it out and leaned it against the wall. Underneath was a man sized hole that led down into the darkness. William peered down the shaft and focused the infrared torch down it. Metal hand rails led the way to the bottom a few metres below.

'Ladies first,' William said with a boyish grin.

'Ha. I think not,' Ella replied. 'Age before beauty.'

Holstering the blade, William climbed into the manhole and made his way down the ladder. After a short descent he jumped onto the damp cobbled floor, lost his footing and fell over. When he picked himself up he saw that the square room he was in was tiny. The four walls were bare stone. He scanned the bleak surroundings. On one wall there was a small hatch, it was locked shut with a chunky heavy duty padlock. A shiny new one, he noted.

'There's something down here,' he shouted up the shaft to Ella. 'Coming?'

Alone in the cold, Ella didn't need to be told twice. She clambered down into the bridge's secret interior. When she was down, William took off their night-vision goggles and switched on a large Maglite torch. When their eyes adjusted to the bright white light they saw that the walls were featureless, there were no markings or writings on them. But the hatch had a symbol scratched onto its surface – *the* symbol.

Ella looked questioningly at William. 'So what now?' she asked. 'Do you have a hacksaw?'

'I don't need one.'

Eagerly, he grabbed the padlock and went to work on it with a lock-pick tool he had taken out of his rucksack. Within a minute he had cracked it, there was a faint click and the lock opened. He pulled it off and discarded it. The hinges creaked as he swung the heavy iron hatch open. Behind it was a long horizontal shaft. He shone his torch down it, it was only just wide enough to crawl through. And it wasn't for the claustrophobic.

'You think we'll fit in there?' Ella asked as she peered into the tunnel.

'Only one way to find out,' William said. 'Wait here, I'll shout when I get to the other end.' He grabbed his rucksack and hauled himself in.

A cloak of darkness closed in on Ella as she watched William drag himself slowly down the tunnel. After about ten metres he reached the end, he dropped into the adjoining chamber and shone the torch back up towards Ella.

'It's not far,' he shouted, his voice echoed eerily in the small chamber. 'Your turn.'

Lying flat against the cold stone, Ella pulled herself along the shaft towards William's torchlight. There wasn't much room for movement, she struggled to haul herself forward. A wave of panic surged through her, she feared she might get stuck. William shouted words of encouragement and guidance and she settled into a worm-like rhythm. When she reached the end, William helped her out.

'I'm not doing that again in a hurry,' she complained as she dusted herself off.

They found themselves in an old narrow tunnel that had been cut into the rock. William had to crouch to keep his head off the uneven ceiling. Water dripped continuously from the damp ceiling onto small pools that collected on the ground. The air was bitterly cold and had an odd stale odour to it. The meandering tunnel led downwards at a gentle angle into the darkness where the torchlight couldn't penetrate. They followed the path at a cautious pace. At one point the tunnel was so narrow they had to squeeze through one at a time.

'What do you think this was?' Ella asked.

'Could be an old mine shaft.'

'Or a medieval escape tunnel from the castle,' Ella suggested. 'We're on the right side of the river and I'm certain it's angled in the right direction.'

'Could well be,' William agreed.

The ground eventually levelled out, a few metres ahead of them the tunnel curved to the left. On turning the corner they were confronted with a wall made from small stones. William shone the torch over it. Bare rock merged with the stone wall around the edges. At its centre was a steel door. There were two large black metal handles on one side of the door. Next to the handles was the round dial of a combination lock. William pulled on the cold handles, but it didn't move as much as a millimetre. The door was locked firm.

'It's a Manifoil Mark IV combination lock,' he said. 'Strong and unpickable, not with the tools I have with me anyway. It uses three sets of double digit numbers, a six-digit code. Any thoughts?'

'Another code,' Ella sighed, she shook her head and looked around the chamber. 'There must be a clue to it somewhere, my father's style. He's got us this far.'

Inspecting the surfaces, William shone the torch over the door and walls. But there was no writings, no symbols, nothing.

'What about the painting, or the poem?' Ella suggested.

'There was nothing that indicated a combination lock code,' he said. 'Wait a minute.' He smiled and set to work turning the dial. Holding the torch over the lock, he spun the dial anti-clockwise and clockwise stopping at numbers seemingly at random. Ella frowned as he worked. Slowly, he twisted it one final time. Nothing happened.

'Damn it,' he said looking up the ceiling. Refusing to be beaten he spun the dial to reset the lock and immediately tried another combination. Again, he twisted the dial anti-clockwise and clockwise.

On the last spin there was a click. He looked at Ella and grinned.

Ella gasped. 'How did you do that?' she asked.

He winked at her. 'A lucky guess. I tried your father's birthdate,' he said.

'That was it?' she said, incredulous.

'Actually, no. It was yours.'

Ella raised her eyebrows and smiled.

Heaving on the weighty door, William slid it to one side and shone the torch into the dark room beyond. Ella peered in; her eyes widened and her jaw dropped when she saw what lay behind.

'Oh my God,' she said as she cautiously entered the room.

*

Leading the way into the room, William took out his pistol and scanned the area with both his weapon and the torch outstretched together. Cautiously, Ella followed behind.

The first thing they noticed were the rifles, there were dozens of them. Shelves and racks were stacked with various types aligned vertically in neat rows. They looked old, the kind used in the Second World War. William easily recognised the Bren guns, the long Lee-Enfield 303's and the silenced Sten submachine guns. Another shelf housed a long row of black Browning pistols and several military grade Smith & Wesson Victory Models. William swept the torch around the rest of the room. There was a shelf full of dusty hand grenades, rows of brown ammunition boxes were stacked floor to ceiling and there were even a few gas masks. On one shelf in the corner there were a dozen small boxes with the word "explosives" written on them in bold letters.

'What is this place?' Ella gasped taking it all in.

There were two car batteries on the floor by the wall, William bent down for a closer look. A modern light switch was attached to a wire that disappeared into the plastered wall. He flicked it on and the lights in the ceiling lit the room up with an artificial yellow ambience.

'It's one of Winston Churchill's secret bunkers,' William explained. 'There were hundreds of them built during the war. It was a backup plan, in case Britain was successfully invaded by Nazi ground troops.'

'Oh my God,' Ella whispered. She hovered by one of the shelves and ran her fingers over a dusty grenade. It was surprisingly heavy when she picked it up.

'I wouldn't do that,' William warned. 'It's a Gammon bomb. The RDX explosives in it might be a little unstable after all these years.'

With theatrical care, and holding her breath, Ella gently placed the grenade back on the shelf and took a step back. As he watched, William suppressed a smile.

'Were there many of these bunkers then?' asked Ella.

'They were all around the country. A number of carefully selected people were made aware of the location of their local bunker only. They were usually former military personnel, many were trained SOE agents.'

'Like my grandmother.'

'Yes, but others were ordinary civilians or Home Guard. Bank managers, butchers, builders.'

'Tinkers and tailors?' Ella smiled.

'Any patriot who could keep a secret.' William wandered over to a shelf and picked up a 303 rifle. 'They created a secret army and trained them in guerrilla warfare tactics. If the worst happened and Britain fell to the forces of evil, then these people were to recruit a trusted band of rebels and attack the invaders in whichever way they saw fit. They were independent of any central command.' With a struggle he managed to cock the old weapon and inspected the mechanism. It was full of dirt and rust, it had probably never been used, and never would be.

'You mean they were to operate like terrorist cells?' Ella asked sounding astonished.

'Freedom fighters,' William corrected. 'It's all a point of view, you see.' He put the 303 back and picked up a Browning pistol.

'It always is,' she mumbled.

William noticed something at the end of the room, it looked like a door handle. He squinted in the low light and realised that there was another door, it blended in with the wall and was hard to make out. He motioned for Ella to keep silent and drew his pistol. The silver door handle was clean from the dust that coated the shelves and weapons. William pulled on it and the door freely opened outwards. He thrust his pistol forward and scanned the room beyond. It was half the size of the adjoining one and was lit up by a small lamp on a desk by the wall on the right hand side. The air was warmer inside it for some reason and it smelled fresher too. There were no weapons in it, just a single bed on the left hand side that was pushed up against the wall. At the far end of the room was a closed grey metal cabinet two metres high. Covering the wall by the bed were several maps, photos and newspaper cuttings.

'Your father's very private study, I imagine,' William said. He holstered his pistol and placed his rucksack on the floor by the end of the bed.

'Oh my God,' Ella said when she studied what was on the wall. 'Look at these.'

Stuck to the wall were what looked like surveillance photos of various people. Names were written on them in black marker pen at the bottom. Below each person's name was the name of a different Greek god. In one black and white shot a smartly dressed man was helping an attractive young woman out of a luxury sports car. Taken from some distance away, the handsome man was looking almost directly into the camera. On the bottom of the photo was written "Arthur Tempest", and below that was another name that William recognised.

'Hades,' he exclaimed.

'And he's named the rest of the gang too by the looks of it,' Ella added. She recognised most of the names from the research that Ollie had done.

'I need to report all this back to base.' William checked his phone, but there was no signal. Using the torch to improve the lighting he held his phone up to the wall and photographed everything.

'Why was my father tracking these people?' Ella asked as she scanned over the photos. 'I thought they had been trying to find him, not the other way round.'

At the cabinet at the end of the room, William used his lock picks to attack the simple lock. Within ten seconds he had opened it. Inside he found shelves stacked full of thick A4 sized binders and books. Flicking through one of them at random he could see that it contained detailed notes of a very complex investigation. He flicked through another file, it was the same. And another.

'This goes back to long before you were born,' he said. 'Your father has been obsessed with this for years.'

He passed one of the older binders over to Ella. She sat on the bed and began to flick through the pages. She frowned and shook her head as she read through them.

'Oh my God,' she gasped. 'Listen to this, "*There are twelve people, both men and women, in the very inner circle of the so called Brotherhood. Each position is codenamed after a Greek god. First-borns from those in the inner circle are groomed for their role from birth, eventually inheriting their place amongst the brethren. But others are recruited into their ranks too, I estimate that they have around three hundred followers. Many are recruited from the* Society of Eden, *a quasi-religious cult run by them and used as a façade for their operations. But only a select few ever know what they are really following, these they call the* chosen. *The inner circle also runs a network of human intelligence sources that they manipulate for their own ends. Such agents are recruited with impressive precision from all walks of society, whatever is of use to them. They have penetrated global banks, the media and even various intelligence and security agencies. I have no doubt that they have politicians in their pockets too.'"*

'This is no terrorist group,' William said. 'They sound more like the Illuminati.'

Fascinated, Ella scanned through the pages while William continued to search the cabinet. 'This is strange,' she said. 'It says here, *"I have lost my only source within them. He has failed to contact me for some months now. Perhaps they have found him out, or perhaps my Russian asset has finally been converted himself."'*

'Cossack?' William wondered.

Ella looked up at him and frowned. 'Why do you think that?'

'Your father worked a lot in Russia,' he explained. 'Maybe he met him there and recruited him as his own spy.'

'It doesn't say here, but there's bound to be useful information in all of this.' Ella fanned through the pages and shook her head. 'There's so much, it will take days to go through.'

'We don't have days,' William said sternly. He took a couple of binders from the cabinet and threw them on to the bed. 'Scan through as much as you can. Try to get the general gist of it. I'll see what else is in here.'

He returned his attention back to the cabinet. He ran his fingers along the underside of the shelves looking for anything hidden, but there was nothing. In the far corner of the bottom shelf, he saw a silver tin box, it was about the size of a biscuit tin. When he took hold of it to lift it out he was shocked by its heaviness, it was like a lead weight. He took it over to the small desk and sat down. There was no lock on the box, he eased off the lid. On the inside, on top of piece of brown leather, was a letter. Two words were written on it in blue ink, "To Ella".

'William,' Ella said excitedly. 'There's a section in here that mentions the painting. It says it was commissioned in 1901 and *was* painted by Edmund Blair Leighton. It must be worth something after all.' She beamed, finally lady luck had wandered her way.

'Ella,' William said calmly, looking over his shoulder. 'I've found something here too.' He swivelled around to face her and held out the letter. 'This is for you.'

When she took the envelope her heart raced, she threw William a worried look. Quickly and carelessly she ripped open the envelope and unfolded the letter within. After reading the first line a lump caught in her throat. She swallowed and coughed.

'Everything okay?' William asked seeing a tear well up in her eye. It ran down her cheek.

'Yes,' she said forcing a smile and holding back the emotion. 'It's from my dad. He's apologising for leaving us. Said he had no choice, said his quest for the truth was putting us in danger. So he let us go to protect us.' She held back the tears, then shook her head and laughed. 'Sorry, I'm just tired and emotional.'

'No need to apologise.'

'He also mentions the Biblos Aletheia, said it's written in a strange language. He says that the book is supposed to contain an ancient story of a journey from an unknown civilisation.'

As Ella read over the letter, William carefully lifted out the heavy leather wrapped object from the box. He laid it flat on the desk and carefully peeled back the brown leather cover. His eyes lit up when he saw what it revealed. Now he understood why people were willing to kill for it. Glancing over his shoulder to the bed he saw that Ella was still engrossed by the letter. Her soft hair hung over her face covering one eye. He noticed the gentle curves of her high cheek bones.

'I have something else for you,' he said as he sat down next to her on the bed.

She looked into his eyes and held his gaze. Her pupils were wide black holes in the low light; they narrowed briefly as they focused on him and then relaxed again. She smiled a gentle warm smile. In his lap, William slowly peeled back the leather covering from the object. Ella looked down at it in amazement as the contents were revealed. The smooth gold surface gleamed in the half-light.

'And here it is, the Biblos Aletheia,' William said.

The solid gold surface was covered in dozens of small symbols, they were all aligned to make the shape of a large triangle. Some of the symbols were repeated, like the ones around the top edges. It didn't take much for them both to work out what they were. They had seen the pattern before.

'Pascal's triangle?' Ella guessed.

'Yes, the symbols must be numbers. Arranged in Pascal's triangle to make it easy to decode,' William said. 'For any advanced civilisation that understands maths, that is.'

'And written in gold to stand the test of time. I've never seen anything like it before,' Ella gasped. She ran her fingers over the raised symbols. 'This is nothing like ancient Greek or Egyptian.'

When she lifted the object out of William's lap her face lit up with pleasant disbelief. 'Wow, it's really heavy,' she said.

'Probably solid gold.'

'It must be worth a fortune.' Ella almost laughed, she put her free hand to her mouth.

'We need to keep it safe. And you too,' William said. He looked into her eyes, they seemed to sparkle in the light. 'It's a precious and beautiful thing.'

Ella smiled back at him warmly. But as quickly as it came, the smile vanished. She replaced it with an eager, hungry look, her eyes flirted over his face.

William felt his stomach somersault, his pulse surged. Cautiously, he placed his hand on the small of her back.

Slowly, Ella leaned in closer to him. Her heart raced, she feared he would move away, but he didn't. Together they moved closer still. Their lips met.

There was a dull thud. Both William and Ella shot a look to the floor by the bed. Ella released herself from William and peered over. The Biblos Aletheia had fallen onto the floor. Strangely, it had opened.

'Look,' Ella said with astonishment. 'It has *pages*.'

Each pure gold page was only a couple of millimetres thick, there were dozens of them. Both sides of each page were covered in strange symbols that were etched into the gold. They looked different from those on the front cover. When Ella closed the book up, the pages fitted together so tightly that it looked like it was one solid gold object.

'Amazing,' she whispered as she ran her fingers over its surface. She put the book down by her side and leaned into William. 'Now, where were we?'

She smiled and bit him gently, teasingly, on the chin. Slowly she moved over to his lips and explored his mouth with her tongue. William unzipped her jumpsuit halfway down her chest and slid his warm hands behind her back, gently brushing past her ample breasts. Ella breathed in sharply and pulled him closer.

Without warning the door to the room was pulled open sharply. A man dressed all in black rushed in. William made to move, but the man swiftly pointed his weapon and pulled the trigger. There was a bang and two darts shot out from the end of the gun and hit William square in the chest. A huge electric current surged through him. Ella watched in horror as his rigid body shook violently for a moment, then he collapsed on the bed unconscious.

Graham J Thomson

# Chapter 32

*0703hrs – Bedfordshire*

WILLIAM OPENED his eyes. He was lying face down on the bed. His hands had been bound tightly behind his back. They felt like plasticuffs, he had had some experience with them during a training exercise some years before and knew there was no chance of him breaking free in any hurry. His chest burned where the powerful current had passed into him. He became aware of voices and realised that he wasn't alone. Mustering up some power, he rolled over onto his back and sat up.

A large clenched fist slammed hard into his face. He fell back against the wall. Quickly, he sat up again and glared at his tormentor in defiance. Cossack took a step back and pointed the Taser at his victim. He smiled at William and winked.

'Agent Temple, so glad you could join us,' said Hades from across the room. Perched on the end of the desk he held the Biblos Aletheia firmly in his hands. 'We've been having a lovely chat with your pretty little friend here. It seems you have had quite an adventure. Well done to you both.'

Sat on the chair next to the desk was Ella. Her hair was a mess, it hung down half covering her face. The top of her jumpsuit was still unzipped, the top of her bra was exposed. Her hands were bound behind her back, the thin plastic dug into her wrist just below her watch. Tears ran down her frightened face. She lowered her head and sniffed occasionally.

'If you dare touch her . . .' William began until another punch to the face stopped him.

Cossack grabbed William by the head and shouted into his ear, 'Shut up!' He threw him back against the wall.

Glaring up at the Russian, William refused to be intimidated. Breathing rapidly through his nose he stared up into Cossack's eyes and held his gaze. A trickle of blood ran out from the corner of his mouth.

'Enough!' Hades barked at the two men.

'Take what you came for and get lost,' William commanded. 'The rest of my team will be here soon. And they're not too worried about the rules of engagement.'

'I already have what I want,' Hades said as a matter of fact, he held out the Biblos Aletheia and raised his eyebrows. 'And it's all thanks to you. Oh, and I know you are here alone, I'm afraid there's no one coming for you.'

Ella flashed a worried look at William. William's face remained unreadable.

'I've been searching for this most of my life,' Hades went on. 'And you found it in less than a week! And it was right under my very nose all this time. Ha!' He sighed deeply and stroked the surface of the gold book, he seemed mesmerised by it, lost in his own thoughts. 'It belonged to my ancestors you see. But it was stolen from them by one of *your* ancestors, Ms Moore.'

Looking up at Hades, Ella frowned. 'I don't understand,' she snivelled nervously. She used her shoulder to wipe the tears from her cheek.

'It's true. Francis Perryvall was one of your ancestors. And he was one of us too.' Hades held his free hand to his chest in a salute of sorts. 'He was the apprentice of Oswyn le Bone, a direct ancestor of mine from the early sixteenth-century. At that time, Oswyn carried the burden of leading the Brotherhood. But somehow the Catholic Church found out about us and launched a brutal attack at this very location. My people didn't stand a chance; most of them were slaughtered that very same night.

'But some survived and out of the ashes they rebuilt the organisation. This time they ensured that secrecy was paramount, it was drilled into every member upon pain of death. They recovered as much of our hidden treasures as they could, ancient and valuable artefacts and manuscripts that had been collected over the centuries. But our most valued and most sacred item of all was missing. Forged from solid gold and written in a long forgotten language, the Biblos Aletheia, our book of truths. I can only presume that Francis fled with it during the battle and hid. Perhaps he even escaped using this tunnel.' Hades gestured around the room.

William's eyes narrowed, he scanned the small room scrutinising every wall and corner. When he looked back at Cossack he saw that he was watching him. William smiled and winked. Cossack curled up his lip and drew his finger slowly across his throat.

'I just can't understand why he hid himself away forever though. But he did, he was never heard of again,' Hades went on. 'And ever since my people have searched every corner of the planet for this book.' He closed his eyes and kissed the gold surface. 'No matter now. It's back in the hands of those who rightfully own it.'

'Who made it?' asked Ella.

Hades smiled at her like a proud father. 'I'm glad you asked. Some say they came from Atlantis, others refer to it as Eden; there have been many names. But the true name for their homeland no longer exists, so ancient and forgotten are they.'

Ella and William looked at each other.

'But surely that's just myth,' Ella protested.

'It's no myth, I can assure you,' Hades said. 'This book was crafted eleven-thousand years ago by the very first advanced human civilisation. For fifty-thousand years they lived on a fertile and stable landmass. Ten kings ruled their land, tribal leaders who were considered to be living gods, deities who had been reincarnate as human. They used astronomical events to identify their kings and the chosen ones were brought up destined to lead and teach the rest. But when the ice melted at the end of the last ice age, their perfect, tranquil world was ripped apart. Their homeland was ravished by floods and the entire society fled across the Atlantic in great ships, or arks, in hope of finding new and safer pastures. Their land died and was lost forever.' Hades looked down at the book and opened it up. He ran his fingers over the text and smiled to himself. His eyes defocused as if he was looking far beyond the book into another world.

'However, while their land is truly lost, their stories, their beliefs and their skills are not,' he said. 'After their escape, the survivors landed on new shores and formed new settlements. Eventually they traded and mingled with the primitive local tribes. They taught them their ways, their traditions and their skills: building and farming techniques, the art of writing and teaching. Most important of all, they taught them the wonders of maths and astronomy. These teachings and their stories were absorbed by the local tribes across the planet and subsequently passed down through the generations. But of course meanings and stories changed, as they do, over time. Nowadays their stories are mere whispers of what once was. Fossils buried in the sands of time. Or as you say, myths.'

'But how could such a successful civilisation be wiped from history completely?' Ella asked. 'There's always a trace, one way or another.'

Hades smiled and nodded. 'You're right, my girl. But the evidence *is* there. It's just so old and warped that it's hard to make it out from the rest of the noise.' He shifted on the desk and leaned down towards

Ella. 'On every continent that they landed on there is evidence of their existence; evidence in the archaeology, and in the mythology of that race. But because their ways were copied and amended so long ago, the full picture has been blurred beyond recognition.'

Ella frowned, but something stopped her from probing further. Hades looked down at her and tilted his head to one side as if in pity. His eyes wandered over her body. She looked away, disgusted, violated.

'Many geographically separate civilisations and religions have stories of global floods and of lands that fell to the sea, yes?' he prompted.

Ella nodded.

'Like the Greek story of the great flood that Zeus sent to purge the world of evil,' he continued. 'In that myth only two people survived, and they did so by building an ark. Sound familiar? And there are many other similar stories of Eden, versions of creation and myths of the gods, are there not?'

Still looking away, Ella nodded.

'It was them,' Hades whispered. 'They started it all. The intellectual revolution that changed the world.'

'So where exactly does your little band of murderers fit in to this? Don't tell me you think you're their distant descendants,' William mocked.

Hades face fell and he grimaced. 'No, we don't.' He slid off the desk and approached William. He loomed over him and shook his head in disgust at the sight before him.

'Four hundred years before the Christ was born, the world's first ever historian, a Greek called Herodotus of Halicarnassus, travelled to Egypt to study the tribes and cultures. In an area close to the pyramids of Giza, he met a tribe who claimed to have lived there for over nine-thousand years.'

'Three-hundred and forty-one generations,' Ella recalled.

Hades turned to her raised his eyebrows. 'Yes, my girl,' he said with a smile. 'Well done. So you've read *The Histories?*'

Regretting her words, Ella reluctantly nodded. She made a mental note to learn to hold her tongue.

'Herodotus followed and studied this Egyptian tribe for some months, eventually he gained their trust. They shared with him their stories and beliefs and they showed him their most sacred object. An ancient book made from pure gold.'

'That wasn't in *The Histories,*' Ella snapped, ignoring her own promise. 'He mentioned something about the *Atlantis* sea being beyond the Pillars of Heracles, but is assumed to be an error and that he really meant the *Atlantic* sea. After all it was years before Plato first ever mentioned the word.'

Striding back to the desk, Hades smiled and nodded vigorously at Ella. 'It's a subtle clue, my girl. You see, Herodotus was part of a small secret society of scientists and philosophers. They were known as The Secret Brotherhood of Olympus.'

'*The Olympians?*' William mocked, he laughed loudly and deliberately.

Hades' eyes narrowed, his face reddened. 'Don't underestimate them, they were a powerful group,' he went on. 'The Brotherhood recognised that knowledge was power and they recruited like minded people to forge that power. Together they used it to become rich and influential. In secret, their skills were passed down the generations.'

Subtly, William observed the room as Hades turned his attention back to Ella. Cossack still had the Taser in his hand, but he had lowered his arm and was listening with interest to the story.

'When Herodotus returned to Athens he told his brethren about the sacred book that he had discovered,' Hades said, recalling the story he had learned from his father as a young teenager. 'He knew it was like nothing that had ever been seen before in the known world. They all agreed that it was wasted in the possession of a primitive Egyptian desert tribe. So they embarked on a mission to steal it from them. A band of mercenaries were hired and they travelled to Egypt. They raided the tribe in a precision planned dawn attack. Once the Brotherhood had found the book they slaughtered the entire tribe to ensure that word of what happened never got out. When it was all over they held a private celebration in Alexandria for the hired troops. But the wine was poisoned, the Brotherhood killed all the outsiders.'

While the two men were engrossed in the story, William tried to get Ella's attention. He twitched and winked at her several times, but was careful to not let the others see what he was doing.

'The Brotherhood then spent years trying to decode the book. They made little progress until a chance find some two-hundred years later. A strange clay tablet full of unknown symbols had been found by a Greek philosopher. He took it to the museums in Alexandria for further study. Soon after, one of the brethren came across it and instantly realised its importance. For it contained within it not only the very same symbols that decorated the sacred book, but also Cuneiform – the earliest Sumerian script. Naturally the Brotherhood took the tablet, not by murder and deceit this time, but with a large amount of gold.' Hades laughed heartily. 'With that crucial find they were able to start deciphering the secrets that had been held for so long.'

'So what is it then, a shopping list?' William chided, deliberately trying to keep Hades off balance.

Hades tried to ignore him and remained focused on Ella. As he spoke she glanced occasionally over to William who was still mouthing something to her.

'Amongst all the stories that it told, there were dozens of mathematical and technological revelations,' Hades said. 'Each new translation was a wonder, and often a truth so strange, so frightening, that the Brotherhood knew it would never be accepted by the religious and political zealots of their time. So they vowed to keep it secret, to document their work and record everything for the future generations, for a time when it would be accepted. And, being scientists, historians and philosophers, they recorded more than just their research on the book.' Hades raised his eyebrows and grinned knowingly.

Ella tried to work out what William was signalling her. Her mind raced. Then, in a flash, it all became clear. Her pulse raced, her face flushed red. She feared Hades would notice, but he was too engrossed in his own moment.

'You see,' Hades continued, 'Herodotus is my ancestor.'

Gently, Hades placed the book down and slid off the desk. He approached Ella and extended his fist out to her face. Her eyes widened, she pushed her head back. William made to stand up, but Cossack moved swiftly over and pushed him down.

'Do you recognise that?' Hades asked her. He held out his signet ring in front of her face. She nodded. The gold ring had a symbol on it. A symbol that she had seen many times before.

'I know you are wearing an identical ring,' he said quietly. 'They were forged from Egyptian gold in Alexandria over two-thousand years ago.'

Blood rushed to Ella's head, her stomach somersaulted. She felt dizzy as the realisation ran through her. When she looked at William he once again mouthed the same words. Her eyes narrowed. There was so much she wanted to ask, so much she wanted to know. The ridiculousness of her predicament almost made her laugh.

'These are just minor relics of the treasures that the Brotherhood has passed down through the generations,' Hades continued. '*Our* ancestors, Ella. Like *The Histories*, they kept detailed records of many historical events as they occurred. The *real* histories of the ancient world, untainted and unaltered by religion or politics. The *truth*.'

'Then why not publish it,' William said. 'Set it free. Let the world benefit from it.'

Hades laughed. 'And let the mongrels twist it, spin it, or brand it all as lies and heresy? No, that time has passed. *Their* time has passed. The time of popular ignorance, selfish capitalism and religious corruption will be gone forever.' He held out his palms. 'The new era has already begun. Surely you know that much, don't you, Agent Temple?'

William frowned, the pieces began to fall into place. 'Surely you can't be serious,' he said.

Ardent, Hades' eyes narrowed. 'It is the natural order of things.'

'How?'

'A plaque of Thebes,' he stated. 'I will simply take advantage of their own sins, their own greed. *"For it is because of these things that the wrath of God will come upon the children of disobedience"*.'

'You're insane.'

'No, the world is insane. But not for much longer. Our vision is pure, what we must do is clear. From our Eden the new world shall emerge. With better people, a better way of life, a world free from the constraints of the medieval religions that have corrupted the progression of humanity.'

'Eden two-point-zero? Ha!' William mocked. 'You're fascists. Mad and twisted. In other words, scum.'

Hades' blood boiled. He grimaced and nodded a silent order to Cossack. At the same moment William looked directly at Ella and mouthed the word, *"Now"*.

Reacting instantly, Ella stood up. 'If I really am one of you,' she said innocently with the slightest pout. 'Then take me with you. I want to know more.' It was all she could think of to grab their attention.

But it worked.

Having already readied himself, and with a face full of rage and passion, William leapt up from the bed and kicked Cossack squarely in the face. The Taser flew out of his hand and clattered along the floor. William kicked Cossack in the stomach and brought his foot down on his knee. Cossack stumbled backwards and fell to the floor clutching his bleeding face.

With only his legs as a weapon, William continued his attack. Focused on his next target, he jumped towards Hades. Ducking low, he kicked out in a low sweeping movement so sure and so swift that Hades' legs were swept from under him. Shocked by William's speed, Hades watched in awe as William jumped into the air and swiftly slid his arms under his bottom and thighs. He landed in an awkward crouched position, but quickly stepped out of his bound hands one leg at a time. He righted himself, stretched his clasped hands out in front of his chest and prepared himself for the next move.

Cossack recovered and lurched for the Taser. William took a two handed swing at Cossack's head and knocked him over onto his back. With maximum aggression, Cossack kicked out at William's stomach. The force pushed William backwards towards the bed. Cossack righted himself while William struggled with his balance. Cossack smiled an evil grin and threw himself at William, he was enjoying this. The pair collapsed onto the bed and grappled at each other.

Despite having his hands tightly bound, William managed to get a few blows in with his elbows. But Cossack had the advantage. He grabbed the plasticuffs and pushed William's arms up over his head. With all his might William struggled, but a firm and well aimed punch to the solar plexus winded him and dampened his energy. Cossack heaved William off the bed and threw him across the room. William crashed into the wall on the other side and fell to the floor. He pushed himself up once more.

'Now boss,' Cossack shouted. 'SHOOT HIM!'

In an instant Hades aimed the weapon at William's chest and pulled the trigger. There was a flash and a loud crack. For a nano-second William stared in disbelief as the darts hit him once more. Instantly he collapsed in agony as the electric shockwaves surged through him. Gritting his teeth, Hades continued to squeeze the trigger and delivered an agonising electric charge for several seconds.

The last thing William saw was Ella cowering wide eyed on the floor by the cabinet. Feeling cold and numb, he reached out to her. Then he passed out.

# Chapter 33

*0745 hrs – Bedfordshire*

WHEN ELLA HAD emerged from the tunnel and climbed back up onto the bridge with Hades, she was shocked to see that it was daylight. The still morning air was cold and smelled of the forest. A thin layer of mist clung to the ground. The foliage was wet with dew. Hades escorted Ella along the track road to one of two quad-bikes. For some reason, Cossack had stayed behind.

Cold and tired, Ella perched on the back of the quad-bike. She no longer feared for her life, Hades' intentions with her were clear. But she feared for her future, she feared for William's fate and for the fate of everyone she knew and cared about. Still cuffed behind her back, she gripped the rear bar of the bike tightly. Inches in front of her, Hades drove, he raced along the farm track through the forest towards Rockcliffe Hall.

They sped along the bumpy forest track, up the hill and past the ruins of the old Rockcliffe Castle. There was hardly anything left of it. All that stood were the remains of three high stone walls, the rest was a pile of rubble strewn over the forest floor and covered in wild plants. Before they had gone far, Ella saw Cossack following close behind on the other quad bike. She feared what he might have done with William.

Past the castle ruins they sped and continued over the brow of the hill. Beyond, Ella could see Rockcliffe Hall. There was a white commercial helicopter in the grounds. Ella's stomach clenched, she had a horrible feeling about it. They drove straight up to the helicopter, stopped and dismounted. The pilot was already in the cockpit waiting. He nodded when he saw Hades.

'There's no time to waste,' Hades said to Cossack. 'We have everything we need.' He took Ella firmly by the arm and helped her off the bike. Then, without a further word, he frogmarched her to the door of the helicopter.

'I'm not going,' she shouted. She shook away from him and refused to move any further.

'It's where you belong,' Hades snapped and tightened his grip. 'You are one of us whether you like it or not. Get in or you will perish here like everyone else. Or perhaps you would prefer to spend your last moments with Cossack?'

Reluctantly, Ella stepped into the helicopter and sat down. The small cabin was closed off from the cockpit. It was furnished with oak surfaces and soft light-brown leather seats. Ironically it was the first piece of comfort she had felt in a long time. Hades fastened her seatbelt for her. She avoided his gaze. The cabin was warm, as she settled into the seat she felt a wave of tiredness wash over her. She'd forgotten that she hadn't slept properly in days.

'You'll like it, the place where we are going,' he said as he sat down opposite her and fastened his seatbelt. 'I call it New Eden.'

Ignoring him, Ella stared out of the window at the mansion.

'You'll get used to us,' he said shaking his head. 'If you know what's good for you that is.'

The engines began to whine, the rotors gained speed and were soon a blur. From the arm of his seat, Hades pulled out a folding tray, he took a small thin laptop out from his briefcase and placed it on the tray in front of him. Ella looked out of the window, she winced when she saw Cossack leave the house with a large black bag and head for the helicopter. But after he stowed the bag in an external side hatch he climbed into the cockpit with the pilot.

Slowly and steadily the helicopter rose into the air. It turned around, angled forwards and flew over the grounds of Rockcliffe Hall gaining speed as it went. Ella noticed how quiet it was in the cabin compared to the hold of the Chinook. When they passed over the old castle, Ella leaned into the window for a better look. She saw the bridge, there was black smoke billowing out from it. A thin column had risen high into the still morning air.

Then, a few metres along from the bridge, there was an explosion. Soil and debris erupted upwards in a thick cloud of black and grey smoke. The cloud twisted and mushroomed as it rose, below it a fire raged. Ella watched in shock as several mini explosions continued after the main explosion. Thin trails of black smoke shot out of the blazing fire as the rest of the old ammunition succumbed to the intense heat.

She shut her eyes and prayed. 'I will see you again, William Temple,' she said quietly under her breath. 'In this world, or the next.'

The helicopter banked steeply and headed away from the castle. Ella slumped back in her seat. As the tears welled in her eyes she looked over at Hades with a consuming mix of hate and disgust. He didn't even look up from his laptop. She thought of William, she thought of

Paddy and Sarah. She feared she would now never be rescued. All was lost.

Then she remembered something; her eyes widened. How could she have forgotten, she cursed inwardly. Watching Hades carefully, she twisted her wrists and ran her fingers over the service watch. The plasticuffs dug into her skin. With some difficulty she felt her way along the side of the watch and pressed the winding dial in. Relief washed over her when she felt it click silently into place.

Hades looked up at her and eyed her suspiciously. She held his gaze nervously, then she sneered at him and shook her head in disgust. He looked back down at his screen and ignored her.

Ella relaxed a little and looked of the window; there was still hope.

# Chapter 34

*0751hrs – London*

DRESSED CASUALLY and pulling a black suitcase behind him, Albert Pinkerton pushed his way through the revolving doors and strode into F-Branch. As he swiped through the security turnstile he nodded a hello to the security guard as he went. Nonchalantly, the guard looked up from his desk and nodded back, he eyed the suitcase as Pinkerton made his way into an empty lift. When the lift doors closed, Pinkerton turned and examined himself in the mirror. Beads of sweat collected on his forehead, he wiped them off with a white handkerchief and adjusted his collar unnecessarily.

He had passed the retinal scan to his office floor a thousand times before. But, for some reason, this time he was worried it wouldn't work. Relief washed over him when the green light flashed on and he pushed the door open. As he'd hoped, the place was empty. There was always a duty operator in the office as a minimum, but Pinkerton knew that they spent most of their time either asleep in the ops room, or watching films in the lab. He sped past the blank computer screens, the tidied desks, and the empty meeting rooms, and headed straight to his own private office.

At his desk he sat down and switched his computer on. Something dug into the small of his back, he reached down and pulled out his silenced SIG-Sauer P230. He placed the weapon on the desk. The PC prompted him to authenticate, he typed in his fifteen character complex password and pushed his ID card into the thin slot of the attached card reader. The PC continued its boot up sequence.

Out of habit while he waited, he closed the blinds and then switched the wall mounted TV on. The muted news channel flashed up with a picture of an attractive, world famous super-model. Pinkerton recognised the young socialite, she was the daughter of an ageing rock star he had once met at an awards function in Buckingham Palace. The picture briefly switched to the teary eyed face of someone the caption described as a close friend of the model, then the story moved on to a scene outside a luxury hotel in Monaco. The hotel was familiar too,

Pinkerton was sure he had stayed at it once. He recalled the memory; the lavish hotel was part-owned by a former F1 racing driver. The camera switched from the hotel and focused on a blonde female reporter, the very kind that annoyed Pinkerton. She was all hair, teeth and make-up. Easy on the eye, but shamelessly one dimensional and hopeless at interviewing. In the scene behind the reporter were medical crews dressed in biohazard suits. When Pinkerton saw the words, "4th Victim dies: Ebola crisis worsens", scroll across the bottom of the screen, he turned the volume up.

'*It is believed the model died on the floor of the hotel bar in the early hours of this morning. She had flown in from London late the previous night. As you can see, the place is crawling with military CBRN crews and armed guards,*' the blonde said, trying to sound overly worried. Her accent was American, Californian most likely. '*The hotel has now been evacuated and the area has been secured. We can't get any closer than this. Earlier we saw hotel guests and staff being taken away in ambulances by the military. According to a source they have been taken to a secure isolation facility as a precaution where they will be closely monitored for any signs of infection.*'

The screen switched back to the news room. A free-phone number was displayed on the screen below the white haired anchorman. The stone faced anchor looked up and began to read from the auto-cue.

'*Anyone who has been in close contact with any of the victims over the last two days is advised to call the emergency helpline,*' he read. He turned to his right and switched his attention to the news room guest, a professional expert on medical matters who was regularly wheeled out for comment.

'*What's the risk of infection, Carol? Should we all be worried? What can we do to stay safe?*' he said in an affable tone.

'*Firstly, it's only a suspected case of Ebola at this stage,*' Carole the expert explained with a smug, know-it-all smile. '*But if it does turn out to be Ebola, as the case has been with the previous three victims, then as the virus is transmitted via bodily fluids, only those who have had close physical contact with the victim at the final stages of her infection should be concerned. Perhaps the hotel staff and the guests who tried to help her when she collapsed, certainly any sexual partners who were with her in the last few days.*'

'*But it does beg the question, how could she, or the other three victims, have contracted Ebolavirus?*' asked the anchor with a degree of exaggerated incredulity. '*Are they all linked in some way? Will we see more cases emerge?*'

On cue, the expert's facial expression changed. '*The police and the World Health Organisation are urgently looking into all the possibilities,*' she said nodding solemnly. '*But we do know that three of the victims worked in the entertainment industry. A model, a presenter and a comedian. From the press reports we know that at least two of them knew each other socially. But oddly, the fourth victim, a city lawyer, had been overseas on business until last Wednesday. The only obvious connection is that all four lived in London. What we don't know is if they had all met each other in the last few days, maybe at a party, a meal or an industry event.'*

'*Of course there is the possibility that this was a deliberate and targeted attack, perhaps by anarchists, or terrorists,*' the anchor proposed with raised eyebrows. Using leading questions aimed at creating a stir was a particular favourite of his.

The expert frowned and tilted her head slightly, unsure of how to respond at first. '*It is a possibility,*' she eventually conceded with a nod.

Pointing the remote control at the screen, Pinkerton switched the TV off. From the depths of his wallet he took out a tiny USB stick and plugged it in to his PC. He opened the only file stored on it, highlighted the text from the document and copied it. Then he double clicked on the icon for the Intelligence Management System. As he waited for the application to open he looked towards the door nervously; he was sure he had heard something outside. He jumped up and walked over to the door, stuck his head out and scanned the office. It was still empty. When he returned to his seat the IMS was ready, a list of the latest intelligence headlines from around the world was listed on the front page like a news reel. He grabbed the mouse and clicked on the tab to create a new report. Once the blank document was open he pasted the text he had copied into it. He clicked to save the file, it prompted him for a name, he typed *FB-9005 Ebolavirus Source* and classified it as *Top Secret: Echelon*. Once he had quickly reviewed the text, he clicked on the *publish* button. A moment later it was live on the network, the entire intelligence community would be crawling over it within minutes.

Reaching for his desk phone, he put the handset to his ear and pressed a pre-set number. 'I'm ready for my car now,' was all he said before replacing the handset.

He walked over to the wooden cabinet by the wall and opened the smoked glass doors. Inside was his prize bottle of Louis XIII Cognac. The crystal carafe, with its intricate artwork and solid gold collar, was simply exquisite. For years he had been saving it for a very special occasion. It was still cradled in the velvet lined case it had come in all those years ago. Carefully, he took the bottle out and placed it on his desk next to his pistol. He returned to the cabinet and picked up his medals, there were four of them in a black frame. Smiling at the memories of the postings, he put them back down and closed the cabinet door. He had no need of such things; they would only remind him of the life he had left behind.

There was a definite noise from outside his office. Pinkerton's head snapped around towards the door and he drew a sharp breath. He froze on the spot and listened carefully. There were footsteps. They stopped. Then his office door flew open.

'Oh! Sorry, sir,' Sarah said, her eyes were wide and her eyebrows were raised high. For a moment she was lost for words. Half in and half out of the room, she held onto the door handle as if it were a walking aide.

'I . . . I didn't know you were here,' she stammered, forcing a smile. On the floor she noticed the black suitcase, then she saw the Cognac and the gun on the desk. Confused, she looked back over to Pinkerton with a frown.

'Are you off somewhere?' she asked, instantly regretting the question.

For a moment Pinkerton didn't know what to say. His mouth hung open. 'What are you doing bursting in here?' he barked. 'Who else is in the office?'

Sarah was taken aback by his tone. 'I had to finish some research off. It's just me, I think,' she said hurriedly. She felt awkward and a little frightened. 'I'll leave you to it. See you on Monday, sir.'

'Wait,' he said. He paused, unsure of what he was going to say next. 'I need to speak to you. It's about Agent Temple.'

'Oh,' Sarah said, she relaxed a little but stayed by the door.

Pinkerton waved her in and, despite her instincts telling her otherwise, she found herself naturally obeying the order. At the desk the silenced pistol caught her attention once more. Pinkerton followed her worried gaze.

'My P230,' he announced, 'fitted with a custom made silencer.' He picked the weapon up and turned it over in his hands. 'An excellent assassin's tool, don't you think?'

Sarah frowned. Her instincts were on full alert, but her legs were rooted to the floor. 'I really need to be getting back to things,' she said awkwardly.

'Of course you do,' Pinkerton said. 'But there's just one thing I need you to do.'

Tilting her head slightly to the side, Sarah regarded Pinkerton quizzically.

In one swift move, Pinkerton raised the weapon towards her and pulled the trigger twice. At point-blank range, the two bullets were coughed out directly onto their target. In an instant Sarah's legs gave way and her body collapsed to the ground. On the way down her head smashed onto the desk with a loud gut wrenching crunch. A thin cloud of blood and saliva exploded out of her mouth and splattered onto Pinkerton's face and shirt. Pinkerton stood motionless with the weapon outstretched and stared, wide eyed, as Sarah's dying body twitched on the floor of his office. Wisps of white smoke oozed out of the end of the silencer. He looked at the weapon, his hand began to shake. Sliding his personal phone out of his pocket, he tapped on the Skype application and selected a contact.

'It's me, Kerberos,' he said quietly, almost whispering. 'It's done. I'm on my way now. I'll see you at the Ekranoplan.'

Working fast, Pinkerton wiped the blood off his face with a handkerchief and pushed the pistol into his waist line at the small of his back. He stowed the Cognac in a side pocket of his suitcase and, after a quick glance around his office, he grabbed the suitcase and left.

The lift took what seemed like an age to arrive at his floor, he fidgeted nervously and kept looking over his shoulders. When the lift finally came it was empty. He walked in, his legs felt like jelly, he cursed at himself for being so pathetic. He pressed for the ground floor and the lift descended. In the mirror he looked himself up and down. There were tiny spots of dark red blood on the collar of his shirt, he flicked his blazer collar up to try to hide it. At ground level the doors opened and he strode out towards the exit. The grey haired security guard eyed him as he swiped through the turnstile. Pinkerton ignored the guard and dragged his suitcase speedily to the revolving doors.

Ear piercing alarms went off. Pinkerton recognised the tone instantly: it was a lockdown, an invacuation. All the external doors of the building would lock automatically, the lifts would ground. No one would be allowed in or out of the building until the all clear was given. He feared someone had found Sarah. Feigning ignorance he continued towards the exit.

'Sorry, sir. They're all locked,' the guard shouted over the noise of the alarm. 'We need to go to the invac room downstairs. Armed police will be here in three minutes to check the place.'

'Do you know who I am,' Pinkerton barked desperately. 'I need to leave right now for a Cabinet Office meeting.'

The guard frowned and hesitated, but this old soldier was no fool. 'No one leaves, sir,' he said firmly. 'This way please.'

Pinkerton ignored him and pushed the revolving door. But it stood firm. Enraged, the guard paced over to Pinkerton. Putting his arm behind his back, Pinkerton turned to face the guard.

'I won't ask again, sir,' the guard began as he approached.

Pinkerton swung his arm around to his front and grabbed the pistol with both hands. Taking a brief moment to aim, he fired off a single shot. The guard never saw it coming. He clutched his chest and fell to his knees in silent agony. Pinkerton carefully aimed the weapon and finished the job with a single shot to the dying man's head. He turned to the glass panels of the revolving door and fired into it three times. The glass shattered.

'Don't move or I'll shoot,' someone shouted from behind Pinkerton.

Squinting over his shoulder, Pinkerton saw Paddy crouched in a firing position by the lifts. After slowly raising both his hands up above his head, Pinkerton cautiously turned to face the exit.

'Don't shoot,' Pinkerton shouted back. 'I'm going to drop the weapon now. Just take it easy, whatever you saw, I will explain.'

The pistol fell from Pinkerton's hand and clattered on the floor. A nano-second later, Pinkerton jumped forward and curled into a ball. He crashed through the remains of the glass panel and rolled along the pavement outside.

Paddy cursed and surged towards the exit with his pistol outstretched.

Despite leaving his suitcase and pistol behind, Pinkerton picked himself up and took off down the quiet street as fast as his legs would carry him.

'Stop or I'll shoot,' Paddy shouted after him. He squinted in the bright sunlight and took aim. But Pinkerton was fast; he was out of range. Paddy cursed and charged after him.

Although Pinkerton was initially fast, he had no stamina and his age was against him. Quickly, he drained of energy and his sprint slowed to a fast jog. Paddy was no runner, but he knew no pain and soon caught up.

'Stop,' Paddy shouted breathlessly when he was only a few metres behind. 'It's over.'

Passers by moved onto the road to avoid the pair, while onlookers stared in awe at the spectacle. The sounds of police sirens could be heard in the distance. Out of energy and knowing Paddy wasn't going to give up, Pinkerton slowed to a walk. He raised his hands in the air.

'Why did you have to kill her?' Paddy asked pointing his pistol at Pinkerton. 'Why?'

Pinkerton stopped and turned to face Paddy. His blotchy red face was dripping with sweat. 'I didn't mean to,' he said shaking his head. He sounded almost apologetic. 'It wasn't supposed to happen like this.'

Breathing rapidly, Pinkerton strained to keep his arms above his head. Paddy noticed that his left fist was clenched, while his right was open.

'It's too late you know,' Pinkerton said.

'Too late for what?'

'For everyone. You're all dead now. Everyone is.'

'What are you talking about?' Paddy noticed that slowly Pinkerton's arms were lowering, they were now level with the tops of his shoulders. Paddy kept the pistol pointed at his chest.

'We put it into the drugs you see,' Pinkerton laughed. 'Who would ever find it in there? An unregulated substance taken by huge numbers of people without question as to what it's made up of. They insist on having labels on everything these days, but not on their drugs. No one cares what they mix with that.'

'You put what in the drugs?' Paddy asked, he quickly wiped the sweat from his eyes with his sleeve.

Pinkerton shook his head, he looked Paddy in the eye. 'The virus,' he hissed. 'Our virus. The one that will wipe the Earth clean.'

'Put your hands on your head and get on your knees,' Paddy ordered loudly. He'd had enough of this rambling madman.

Pinkerton smiled a sickly smile and looked to the sky. 'No, my dear boy, it's far too late for that,' he said. Closing his eyes tightly he quickly moved his left hand to his mouth and threw something in it. He bit down hard and swallowed.

'No,' Paddy shouted, he surged forward and grabbed Pinkerton by the arm. But there was nothing he could do other than watch. White froth instantly bubbled out of Pinkerton's mouth and ran down his chin. Within seconds his head fell back, his legs gave way and he collapsed backwards onto the ground. He lay motionless on the pavement. When his bowels gave way, Paddy knew he was gone.

# Chapter 35

*0759hrs – Bedfordshire*

WILLIAM AWOKE and opened his eyes. He saw nothing but pitch black. He could feel that he was lying face down on the floor. His hands were still bound in front of him. As his eyes adjusted, he realised there was a quivering orange glow coming from under the door. He became conscious of a strong smell of smoke.

Ignoring the searing pain in his chest, he pushed himself up and perched on his knees. Instantly his lungs filled with an acrid substance which made him cough. Unable to breathe the thick smoke, he ducked back down onto the floor and tried to draw in some cleaner air. Hoping his rucksack was still where he left it, he crawled under the bed and blindly reached out for it. When his fingers found the material he dragged the bag in to himself. From it he took out the night-vision goggles and strapped them on over his head. There was a bright flash of green in his eyes before the image settled down, then he scanned his surroundings. The room was empty, thick smoke poured in from the gaps in the only door and moved like a river across the ceiling to the back of the room. William held his breath and reached for the door handle. As soon as he touched it he withdrew his hand. It was red hot.

There was a loud bang from the other room, a moment later another, and another as the ammunition succumbed to the intense heat. When the image of the boxes of explosives flashed into his mind his heart jumped into his mouth. Time was running out and he was trapped with a ticking bomb.

Lying close to the floor, he took several deep breaths and held it. He grabbed the rucksack and rose up slightly. The heat was intense on his head and back. Noticing the way the smoke moved, he followed it towards the opposite end of the room until he reached the cabinet. It was hard to make out, but he was sure that the smoke was being sucked down behind it. As he moved in closer it became clearer. Thick wisps of smoke drifted down from the ceiling, along the back wall and went behind the cabinet where it seemed to vanish.

William wasted no time. Gritting his teeth and bearing the heat, he grabbed the back of the cabinet and heaved it over. Binders, books and folders scattered onto the floor. Much to his satisfaction there was a small round hole in the wall behind. After throwing the rucksack ahead of him, he squeezed through and clambered into the next room.

It was cold and pitch black, but at least the air was breathable. His night-vision goggles struggled to find any photons to enhance, he switched the infrared torch on. Through the hazy cloud of smoke that had permeated into the chamber he could see that he was not in a room, but in a narrow manmade tunnel. The old cobbled walls were uneven, the wooden supports looked rotten, some were broken. The old escape tunnel from the castle, William presumed. He took out his dagger and sawed furiously at his bindings. He was soon free of his bondage.

There was a loud explosion from where he had just come from, quickly followed by the sound of falling debris. A thick nauseous smoke billowed into the tunnel. He recognised the burning smell; one of the grenades must have exploded. It was followed by several loud cracks as more ammunition went off.

Spurred into action, William took off down the rickety tunnel at speed. A few metres down he passed under a narrow shaft that was cut into the ceiling. All the smoke was sucked up into it where it disappeared. Beyond the shaft, the cool, crisp, clean air was pleasantly welcoming. William jogged up the slight incline for about one-hundred metres before he finally reached the end: a dead end. He found a set of stone stairs that rose only a couple of metres until they stopped at the roof of the tunnel. William climbed them and examined the ceiling with his night-vision. There was a flat stone slab above the very top of the stairs, it seemed to be the only obvious exit point. He placed his back under it and pushed as hard as he could. Nothing moved. With the blade of his dagger he stabbed into the edge of it and sawed along the sides. Loose soil fell out from the gaps. He dug the blade in as deep as he could and removed as much loose dirt and stones as was possible. Positioning himself once more under the slab, his calves burned as he pushed up with all his might.

This time something gave way. The slab moved upwards an inch and then stopped. After a moment of rest to catch his breath, he removed the night-vision goggles, wiped the sweat from his eyes and tried again. He heaved. This time the slab began to move higher, bit by bit, inch by inch. A thin beam of sunlight sliced through the dusty air into the tunnel. Through the thin gap he could see grass and sky, he could smell fresh air, it was filled with the sweet fragrance of the summer forest. He pushed the slab until the gap was big enough to climb through. After throwing his rucksack through to the surface he hoisted himself up.

The bright sunlight caused him to squint. When his eyes adjusted he found himself surrounded by shrubs in the quiet forest at the edge of the old castle ruins. The stone slab was covered in soil and foliage. He'd been lucky to have moved it all, the area was covered with huge stones that had been part of the old castle wall. If any had fallen on the slab, he would have been trapped. He spotted the farm track by the side of the old castle and began to walk towards it.

The silence was broken by the racket of a helicopter, it shot past above the tree tops. William watched it bank over the trees and climb upwards. He had no doubt as to who was in it, but there was nothing he could do to stop them.

There was a loud explosion from the direction of the bridge. A huge fire ball rose into the still morning air. A series of smaller explosions continued afterwards as the rest of the ammunition released their fury. Watching the pillar of smoke rise, William took out his phone and called Sarah's mobile. There was no answer. He threw his rucksack over his shoulder and followed the track all the way to the mansion. When he arrived at the deserted house, he called the office once more.

'Sarah,' he said quickly when the call was finally answered, 'it's me. I need you to organise a lift, urgently.'

'William, it's Paddy. I've got some bad news.'

# Chapter 36

*1135hrs – Bedfordshire*

FROM THE GROUNDS of Rockcliffe Hall, William watched as the Chinook approached from the distance. Its familiar sound was comforting. As it approached he saw the large dome on one side of the fuselage, it was a powerful camera designed for long distance surveillance and target acquisition.

When the huge helicopter landed on the grass by the front of the house, the rear door opened, but the engines remained on full power. An armed soldier dressed in full combat gear appeared from the ramp and waved William in.

As William boarded he saw several people sat on the benches along the narrow fuselage. He recognised Paddy, but there was a bespectacled, balding civilian that he didn't recognise and five anti-terrorist troopers dressed in black combat gear.

Nodding a hello to Paddy, William took his place on a seat opposite. He eyed the various weapons that the troopers clutched. There were black KAC PDWs – short but highly accurate assault rifles that fired six-millimetre armour piecing rounds – a couple of Heckler & Koch MP7 sub-machine-guns fitted with hefty silencers, and a Heckler & Koch G36k that had a grenade launcher attached. Several hand grenades and smoke grenades were fastened to their bullet-proof vests. Large combat rucksacks, or Bergens as they were known, were tucked under their seats. This was a unit prepared for some serious close combat.

William turned his gaze to the bespectacled stranger who forced a smile at him. He couldn't help thinking how out of place the worried looking little man was.

'You're a site for sore eyes,' Paddy shouted. He handed William a set of ear defenders.

As he put them on, William turned to look outside and caught his reflection in the small window. His face was blackened by soot and soil, there were spots of dried blood on his cheeks and chin. Paddy raised his hand to his throat mic and spoke an order to the pilot. A moment later the helicopter lurched into the air, banked at an acute angle and accelerated southwards.

'We've got some catching up to do,' Paddy said to William once he had switched his headset on.

'Tell me about Sarah first,' William demanded.

'Our suspicions about Pinkerton were right. But I was too late.' Paddy looked down and shook his head. 'Sarah walked into his office just when he was clearing out, permanently. He'd gone in to submit a false report on the IMS – his last act of betrayal. The bastard has been running circles around us.' Paddy's hardened face then softened for a moment, he knew how well William and Sarah had got on. 'He shot her at point blank range. She died instantly – no pain.'

Expressionless, William stared out of the window at nothing in particular. Wisps of cloud shot past the window, far below was a sea of greenery, the land a patchwork of farms. 'Another waste of a good life,' he murmured.

'He tried to escape on foot, but I caught up with him,' Paddy explained. 'The traitor topped himself with a cyanide pill before I could do anything.'

'Coward.'

Paddy nodded. His steely gaze remained fixed on William.

'What was in the IMS report?'

'Ollie picked up on it immediately,' Paddy said. 'It was misdirection on the virus case – more bullshit designed to delay our work. We've pulled it now and sent out an alert to the community with the real threat assessment and all the intelligence we have.'

'Which is?'

Paddy took a deep breath and sat back. 'Ollie tracked one of the target phones to New York – he'd hacked into it and scooped the GPS data. From that he worked out where the suspect lived, and then from that found out who he was. I put a friend from the Company on the case without Pinkerton's knowledge.' Paddy grinned at William. 'Call it an independent review. Pinkerton's resistance to sharing didn't sit well with me either.'

'So what happened? They play ball?'

'Oh yeah. My guy there loves it, any excuse and he's out there. The CIA team followed the target to a city marina. He picked something up from a boat and went straight on to a posh hotel. Five people visited his room soon after. Each was picked up when they left and taken in for a rapid debrief.'

'Did they talk?'

Paddy laughed and grinned. 'I think the threat of a little waterboarding had them chatting away pretty quickly.'

'So who were they?'

'Three lowlife drug dealers from different city gangs and two chinless wonders who said they regularly bought from the target. Turned out they supplied to the high and mighty. Lawyers, bankers, zed-list actors – you know the type.'

'And who was the target?'

Paddy leaned forward as if it somehow enhanced his voice. 'Get this – a city lawyer with a clean record. A nobody. No links to terrorism. Nothing. They raided the hotel room in the night and picked him up with the rest of the gear. All two-million dollars worth, so they reckon.'

William's whistle was drowned out by the noise of the engines. 'So how does it link to our case? Don't tell me this is a drug war?'

Paddy shook his head and narrowed his eyes. 'Oh no, it's much, much worse than that.' He tilted his head to the man sitting next to him. 'This is Max Redwood, a scientist from the Defence Labs. I'd better let him explain the rest of it. Word of warning – it gets a little complicated.'

Hesitantly, Max pressed the transmit switch on his headset. His eyes darted furtively from Paddy to William. 'I analysed the data files your office sent over, the ones from the virologist. They contained the genetic code for a deadly genetically engineered virus.'

'So we heard,' said William. 'What's new?'

Max went on to describe the two phases of the virus, how it spread from victim to victim and how it gruesomely finished off its quarry.

'Nice,' William said looking at Paddy who was unusually silent. An uneasy feeling was brewing in his stomach as he pieced the information together.

'There are victims already, William,' Paddy added solemnly. 'Just a few – but in several countries. It's started already. We're too late. All thanks to that traitorous bastard.'

'There are only a dozen or so victims, but the CDC is on full alert for a pandemic of catastrophic proportions,' Max added. 'It's what we call *scenario three* – a global outbreak of a lethal virus with no known vaccine.'

William looked from Max to Paddy. 'They're using the drugs to spread it, aren't they?' he quizzed.

'Yes, it was found in the cocaine from the New York job. But I'll bet my left bollock that wasn't the only batch around.'

'The virus was contained in microscopic dissolvable capsules,' Max explained. 'It turns the drug pink.'

'Which is what they're calling it on the streets all across the uncivilised world,' Paddy added sarcastically. 'There are hundreds of police reports about it. It's the latest recreational phenomenon.'

'The perfect bio-weapon,' William stated coldly, but sounding oddly impressed. 'Illegal but widely used. No one asks what's in it, it's not regulated or checked. And there are countless volunteers from all walks of life willing to distribute it to the masses. Genius.'

'And many won't even admit that they use it,' Max added. 'Which makes awareness and deterrence programmes pretty useless.'

'So the wealthy, high flying, chinless idiots will spread the infection across the globe like wildfire,' Paddy concluded.

Something occurred to William. 'Hades said something to me in the bunker, *"For it is because of these things that the wrath of God will come upon the children of disobedience."*'

'The Epistle to the Colossians,' Max recalled. 'It's a quote from the bible.'

William nodded, he'd thought as much. 'I think he sees himself as a saviour. He's justified his actions and believes that he's acting for the greater good – his greater good.'

'What, the extermination of our race?' Paddy snorted.

The team felt their stomachs rise as the helicopter rapidly lost altitude. The G-force increased for a moment as the Chinook banked and rose again. Max turned even paler and placed his hand over his mouth. Paddy glanced at Max from the side and suppressed a smile.

'So what's the plan?' William asked. 'How do we stop this?'

'Global vaccination,' Max stated, his voice was shaky. He removed his glasses and dabbed at his watery eyes with a folded white handkerchief. 'It's the only way. The CDC and the WHO have extensive plans for this kind of scenario, both overt and covert. The ball is already rolling. Vaccine factories and emergency medical centres are being set up the world over.'

'But there's a problem,' Paddy added. He grimaced and sucked his teeth.

'Let me guess,' William said with a sour smile. 'There's no vaccine?'

'Not entirely true.' Max cleaned the sweat off the rest of his face, refolded his handkerchief and put it away. 'We have half of one,' he added. 'We think the professor cobbled something together at the last minute.'

'We think?' William said incredulously.

'It's a form of RNA that binds to the engineered virus and slows its growth. Actually, all it does is slow the flu-like virus from mutating into its deadly phase. It only gives a temporary protection and will never eradicate the virus.' From his jacket pocket Max pulled out a small black plastic case. Inside was a syringe, some fresh needles and several small vials of a yellowy liquid. He pushed a fresh needle into the end of the syringe and used it to withdraw some of the contents of a vial.

'This will protect you until we find the proper vaccine,' he said. He undid his safety strap and moved across to sit next to William.

William threw Max a deterring glance. With his eyebrows raised, Max looked to Paddy for help.

'We've all had one,' Paddy assured. He tapped his own arm and pointed to the troopers.

Reluctantly, William rolled up his sleeve. Max injected the liquid into his arm then returned to his seat and put the medical kit away.

'So where is the proper vaccine?' William asked. 'I take it there is one?'

'We hope so. Theoretically it will be at the enemy's headquarters,' Max explained.

'*We hope so? Theoretically?*' William snorted. 'Come on.'

'They must have one,' Max pleaded. 'It's the only logical thing to do.'

'Logical?' William laughed. 'You think these idiots are logical?'

Sheepishly, Max opened his mouth to defend himself, but he closed it again without a word. He sat back, shrugged his shoulders and shook his head.

William threw his hands in the air. 'I'm used to winging it but this is ridiculous,' he said to Paddy.

'It's far from over, William. We've been given the authority to acquire any resources we need to get the job done,' Paddy explained proudly. 'Air, sea or land. Anything from any NATO force. All we need to do is give the operational codeword.' It was the most power Paddy had ever had the luxury to wield. And he planned to use it to the full.

'Which is?'

Paddy grinned. 'Operation Intrepid-Eagle.'

William grimaced and rolled his eyes. 'And the boys in black?' he said nodding to the troopers.

'Let me introduce you the Marines,' Paddy replied. 'The troop commander is Rupert.' He half smiled at William when he said it, then he turned to the commander and gave him the thumbs-up.

Rupert looked no older than twenty-five. He had short blond hair that was longer at the front than it was at the back. He acknowledged William by raising his hand to his head in a brief half-salute.

'The rest of the lads are Dipper, Fitz, Thembe, and Ish.'

In turn each of them nodded to William. Dipper had a pale, unshaven face, with piercing blue eyes. Fitz was a stocky white man in his early thirties. He had a shaved head and a black moustache that curled down beyond his lips. Thembe was a black man in his mid twenties. He had wide trusting eyes and a soft, gentle face. Ish looked to be the oldest of them all – an Algerian man, he had strong angular features and short jet black hair.

'Our special attachment troop,' Paddy concluded.

William tipped his head to the troopers, then turned back to Paddy and asked, 'So what's the intelligence? Where do we start?'

'As it stands we don't know where their HQ is or even where it might be,' Paddy revealed. 'None of the intelligence points to it. They've been very careful.'

'So where are we going? You must have something to go on.'

Nodding, Paddy raised his eyebrows and smiled. 'Your girl sent the alarm signal,' he said.

'Ella? She activated the service watch?' William was elated, proud even. He sat back and looked up smiling.

'Yes, a couple of hours ago. It couldn't have been long after they took her. Ollie is tracking it from the office. The first signal was located at the mansion, then the satellite tracked her at various different points moving south at over one-hundred miles-an-hour.'

'I saw a chopper leave the house,' William recalled.

'They won't go far in it, we'll find them. The Chinook is fitted with the local receiver. As soon as we're in range we'll know exactly where she is.' Paddy tapped his hand on the green, heavy duty case that was by his side.

William seemed to consider something. He looked up at Paddy through narrowed eyes. 'He's mine, understand? When we get there, he's mine.'

Paddy frowned raised his eyebrows. 'Who?'

William took out his phone and opened one of the photos he took of the chamber wall. He zoomed in on a face. 'The Russian, Cossack. Got it?'

'You're the man,' said Paddy. His hand wandered to his ear and he looked up at nothing in particular. 'That was Ollie. He's had another trace on the signal. That's two at the same place. They must have stopped.'

'Where are they?'

'Littlehampton marina, it's on the coast of West Sussex,' Paddy replied. 'It's a small private marina according to Ollie. We'll be there in twenty minutes.'

'Okay everyone, listen up,' William said to the team. 'Here's what we're going to do . . .'

# Chapter 37

*1321hrs – West Sussex*

THE CHINOOK HOVERED low over a hill seven miles north of the target area. Paddy had a heavy duty green briefcase open on his lap, inside were two LCD screens, two flat dials, a keyboard and a joystick. William was seated next to him, and together they studied the images.

One of the small screens showed the live, colour video stream from the camera, at its centre was a thin black crosshair. The camera was zoomed in on the small marina. The other screen showed a digital map of the area, on it a translucent red circle with a red dot in the middle pinpointed the exact position of the service watch. Paddy's briefcase had a tracking device in it that pinged the watch every thirty seconds and could locate it to within one square metre. Currently, it was a little over seven miles away and was shown to be stationary. Superimposed on the map was a black cross that showed where on the ground the centre of the camera was pointed.

Paddy nudged the joystick until the black cross of the camera was on top of the red circle. Turning the dial delicately he zoomed in further.

'That looks like the chopper I saw leaving the house,' William said pointing to the side of the screen. 'Can you zoom in anymore?'

Paddy twisted one of the dials. From the high quality, highly stabilised image, they could see that the helicopter was empty.

'Yes, that's definitely it,' William confirmed. 'Move back to where the signal is coming from.'

On the map, Paddy carefully moved the cross back onto the red circle. The image focused on a small grey hangar next to the chopper. He zoomed out a little to assess the wider ground. Positioned close to the water's edge, the hangar was separated from the rest of the busy marina by a long, gravelled, single-track road.

'They must be in there,' Paddy said pointing to the hangar. 'We need a better angle.' All they could see was the featureless rear wall. There were no doors or windows, and no cars or people outside it.

'Ask the pilot to move further south to the coastline, keeping a five mile stand-off from the marina,' William commanded.

Paddy nodded and relayed the order over the radio. Immediately, the chopper angled forward and accelerated. He and William watched the little screens as the Chinook skirted around the target area. The image of the hangar slowly spun until it was side on. The Chinook slowed and hovered over the new observation point. The large doors of the front of the hangar were clearly open but, as they were still relatively perpendicular to it, they couldn't see in. A concrete jetty led from the hangar down into the sea.

'Do you think they have a boat?' Paddy asked. 'Or a seaplane?'

'I hope so,' William said. 'Either way, they'll lead us to the their base. Let's not show our hand too early.'

When two people emerged from the hangar and walked onto the jetty, William's heart skipped a beat. His eyes focused on the screen. Paddy zoomed in until he could see their faces. The picture was surprisingly clear, if a little hazy from the rising warm air.

'The one on the right is the Russian, Cossack,' William pointed out. 'I don't recognise the other man, but by the way he's dressed I'd say he's the helicopter pilot.' Strangely, he felt relieved.

The pilot seemed to back away from Cossack. Menacingly, Cossack fronted the man and pushed him hard on the shoulder. The man staggered back, then he turned and started to run towards the helicopter. Without warning, Cossack withdrew his pistol and shot the man in the back. Immediately he fell to the ground. Desperately he crawled towards the helicopter. Cossack approached him. He loomed over the helpless victim and fired off another two shots. The pilot collapsed, a pool of black blood ran out from under him. Casually, Cossack holstered the weapon and returned to the hangar.

'He doesn't mess around,' remarked Paddy.

'That man is evil,' said William. 'There's no other word for it.'

'Hold on. The signal is moving again.'

Slowly, something large began to emerge from the hangar. Initially its silver nose looked just like that of an aeroplane, but as it inched out it began to resemble a speed boat. Once it was a few metres from the hangar doors it became apparent that it was neither a boat nor a plane, but something in-between.

'What the hell is that?' asked Paddy.

William studied the picture on the screen. He shook his head. 'No idea.'

'I know what it is,' Max said from behind them. 'It's an Ekranoplan.'

The craft was fully out now, it was being pushed down the jetty on a trailer of some sort by a green Land Rover.

'A what?' this was from Paddy.

'It's a plane that flies just above the surface of the water,' Max explained. 'It's like a hovercraft, but much, much faster.'

'How fast?' asked William.

'Depends on the build, but it could be as a fast as an aeroplane. Maybe two or three-hundred knots. Maybe more in calm conditions.'

Paddy and William looked at each other.

'We're in trouble,' Paddy said what they were both thinking. 'We can't keep up with that. We have to attack them right now while we have the element of surprise.' He raised his hand to the transmitter switch.

'No, wait,' William commanded, he grabbed Paddy's arm. 'Get on to Ollie, tell him to scramble a Phantom Eye. We'll follow the signal as close as we can for as long as we can, then the spooks in the sky can take over. We'll need to make some other arrangements to catch up. '

Paddy frowned. 'But we can take them now,' he insisted. 'They're sitting ducks. It might be our only chance.'

William eyed the old soldier and shook his head. 'We need to find their base, Paddy, whatever the risks are. Without that vaccine we're all screwed.'

Reluctantly, Paddy nodded his agreement. He made the call to Ollie. They both watched as the craft was lowered down the jetty into the sea. Cossack jumped out of the Land Rover and clambered into the Ekranoplan. There was no sign of Ella or Hades. William assumed they were already in the craft. The signal from the watch still emanated from it.

Just as William had feared, the Ekranoplan didn't hang around for long. They watched the screen as the craft ploughed gently through the water. Gradually it picked up speed. Initially it was easy for them to follow, it left a white trail in the sea. But as soon as it reached international waters it accelerated to almost three-hundred knots and headed southwards. It hovered just a few metres above the surface of the ocean and left no trail as it went. William's stomach tightened as he watched the craft disappear over the horizon and out of sight.

He feared he would never see her again.

Her fate, and everyone else's, now lay with the spies in the sky.

# Chapter 38

*1356hrs – Africa*

HIDDEN DEEP in the hostile desert of an African ally, the sandy camouflaged doors of a bomb proof hangar opened. A British Army logistics vehicle emerged, it pulled a small, sleek, triangular aircraft behind it. There were no windows on the craft and no markings, its smooth black surface reflected little light. When it was in position on the deserted runway, the logistics vehicle detached and returned to the hangar.

The air burned as the craft's liquid hydrogen propulsion engine powered up. Two concentrated cones of intense light-blue flames shot out from the rear of the craft. It began to taxi down the short, dusty runway. Within moments, and at neck braking G-force, the craft shot forward. Seconds later it pulled up and rose steeply into the sky. More like a missile than an aircraft, the unmanned High-Altitude-Long-Endurance stealth spy plane climbed to sixty-five-thousand feet and shot towards its target at a dizzying velocity of five times that of sound. The Phantom Eye took mere minutes to reach the target area.

Over a thousand miles away, in a secret UK base, the pilot – a young female Corporal from the Army Air Corps – sat in a dark bunker surrounded by LCD screens and numerous controls. Screens buzzed with information and flight data, while dozens of lights flashed on and off on the complex control panel.

'This is Phantom-one. We're in position,' she said over the radio link. 'I'm scanning the area now. Wait out.'

The pilot used the craft's radio imaging sensors to scour the vast target area for any large moving objects. It would easily detect every manmade object on the ocean surface. The small team of image intelligence analysts would then work on the data and use the array of powerful thermal imaging cameras to identify the correct target. The Ekranoplan would show up clearly as a single black object against a sheet of grey sea.

Once the target was acquired, the pilot would select it on one of the touch sensitive screens and leave the software to keep the Phantom

Eye in place high above. She would barely have to touch the controls, and the craft would fly like an invisible eagle with perfect eyesight.

*

'Roger that, Phantom-one,' Paddy replied from the Chinook. 'Good work.'

After receiving word from his CIA contact, Paddy had issued a new destination to the Chinook pilot. They were headed for the USS *George H W Bush*, an enormous Nimitz-class nuclear powered aircraft carrier. Presently it was located one-hundred miles from the island of Madeira in the Atlantic Ocean and was sailing towards the north-western coast of Africa.

Paddy shook William's arm, he had dozed off on the long bench. 'They have eyes on,' he said when William opened his eyes. 'The spies in the sky, they've found them.'

William stretched his arms and rubbed his face. 'They've found them? Are they sure it's them?' he said feeling like lead weights were pulling on his eyelids.

'It's them. They're heading east through the Mediterranean Sea, still in international waters, east of Gibraltar.'

'Great work. And there's no escape from the Phantoms.' Despite the wave of relief, he knew it was far from over. The mission was still uncertain, it all depended on where the Ekranoplan was headed. 'We can't allow it to berth in a hostile country.'

Paddy nodded solemnly. 'We'll keep a close eye on its direction. If it looks like it's heading that way then we'll just have to stop it at sea and get the water-boards and thumb screws out.'

*

The sea was calm and blue, the sun blazed in the cloudless sky. From the windows of the Chinook the team could see the long white wake created by the huge fast moving aircraft carrier. As they approached it they saw the rows of fighter jets and helicopters that neatly lined the long runway of the USS *George H W Bush*. From the stern the Chinook approached the vessel, it descended gently onto one of its landing pads. The whine of the engines gradually reduced to nothing and the passengers disembarked.

The first thing William noticed was the heat. It radiated from all angles. Up off the sea, off the deck and down from the sky. When he sucked in a deep breath of the fresh sea air, it was spoiled by the strong scent of high octane fuel and oil. He looked at his immediate surroundings and raised his eyebrows, the huge craft he found himself on was nothing short of a floating airport. On one side of the ship in its centre was the Island, the command centre that loomed several storeys above the deck. Away from the ship on all sides there was nothing but a great expanse of ocean as far as the eye could see. In places it sparkled from a billion reflections of the sunlight. It was like being centre stage at a stadium with a million camera flashes going off randomly.

'Welcome to the Avenger, men,' said a man with a deep American accent. The officer was dressed in an immaculate, khaki Navy uniform, a short-sleeved shirt and trousers. Above the left breast pocket was a mass of coloured campaign ribbons. His name tag was emblazoned above the right side pocket. On his head he wore a khaki garrison cap. He did away with the salute and threw his hand out to William whilst grinning widely and confidently. 'Captain Godlasky. But everyone just calls me God,' he said, and laughed loudly.

William took the Captain's hand – the man's grip was firm, his shake confident. 'Pleased to meet you, Captain,' he said. 'Let me introduce you to the team. This is Max Redwood from the Defence Laboratories.'

The Captain frowned at the sight of Max. He was about to say something but decided against it. Max smiled nervously and shook the Captain's proffered hand.

'Paddy Howard from F-Branch.' Another handshake. 'And Rupert, the commander of the troop.'

'It's an honour to have all you on-board,' Captain Godlasky said. 'I don't know what you guys are up to, I don't need to know either. But you have the full support of the US Navy. I've been told by the highest command that Operation Intrepid-Eagle gets whatever it needs. We have just about everything here. Planes, choppers, tanks, and more weapons than you can shake a long shitty stick at. All you need to do is ask. And there are plenty of bars and restaurants. We have a bowling alley and three cinemas. Make yourselves at home.'

'Thank you, but I doubt we'll be here long enough to appreciate the place,' William said. 'What we do need though, is a briefing room with access to maps and secure comms. And plenty of strong coffee.'

The Captain smiled and placed his hand on William's shoulder. 'You got it, sir.'

The team grabbed their bags and equipment from the Chinook and assembled on the deck. The troopers had all donned matching sunglasses.

'These are yours by the way,' Paddy said to William. He handed him a huge green Bergen and a KAC PDW rifle. 'I hope the clothes fit, but I doubt it.' He grinned.

'One size – fits nobody,' William said with a laugh.

When the team was ready they followed the Captain past the rows of aircraft towards the Island. Max struggled to carry his chunky, heavy duty briefcase. He kept stopping and switching hands, his face was covered in sweat. Paddy, William and the troopers each had a Bergen on their backs, and their weapons slung over their chests. Despite the weight, they made it look effortless.

Paddy grinned as he looked over an F-22 stealth fighter. 'I love this,' he shouted to William over the noise. 'This is what it's all about.' He slapped his rifle like it was an old friend he hadn't seen for a while.

It was refreshingly cool inside the ship's command centre. Compared to the relentless racket of the deck it was quiet too. In the background the air conditioning hummed continuously. Captain Godlasky guided them through the narrow grey corridors to their designated, temporary command room. It was small but had everything they required for their short stay. Heavy duty computers, monitors and communications equipment lined one side of the room, while portholes on the other side looked out to sea. There was a long white table at the centre surrounded by flimsy metal chairs that were painted pale blue.

'It's yours for as long as you need it,' the Captain said. 'Call me if you want anything.' He walked to the door and paused. Then he turned and threw up a sharp salute. 'Good luck men.'

*

It took Paddy little more than a few minutes to set up his field laptop and establish a secure communications link back to both the Phantom mission control room and F-Branch. Real-time video footage from the spy plane was streamed into their makeshift operations room. The spy craft's powerful camera had locked onto its target and it followed the Ekranoplan effortlessly as it sped over the ocean oblivious to its watcher.

'Where is it now?' William asked. He had changed into a set of green and black combat clothes. On the table he unrolled a large map of the Mediterranean and sat down next to Paddy and Rupert.

'They're just between Sardinia and Tunisia, still heading east,' Paddy said. 'But they're slowing down. Speed is now one-hundred knots.'

'Heading for Sicily?' William said pouring over the map. He picked up the handheld satellite phone and called the office.

'Ollie, we need to know what naval ships are near Sicily and Malta,' he commanded. 'Find something that can provide us with air transport and fire support. Put them on standby for immediate action.'

Max had made himself useful, he returned to the room with a tray full of coffee, bottles of water and a stack of sandwiches and chocolate bars. The men needed no invitation to tuck in. The food didn't last long.

Taking regular location updates from the live tracking, William had plotted the path of the Ekranoplan on the map. With the remains of a sandwich in one hand and a coffee mug in the other, Max leaned over the table and glanced at the map. The path of the Ekranoplan was angled towards the northern end of Sicily.

'They could be heading for the Aeolian Islands,' said Max with his mouth full. He slurped some coffee down.

William and Paddy looked at each other then at Max.

'Why do you say that?' William asked.

Max shrugged and swallowed the rest of his sandwich. 'Seems logical to me that the ideal place to both hide from scrutiny and protect yourself from an impending global catastrophe, is on a remote island,' he said. 'It would need to be small enough to easily secure, but large enough to sustain the survivors for at least a few months. That path you've drawn is pointing directly to the Aeolian Islands, a volcanic archipelago just north of Sicily. I went there some years ago, just a day trip during a cruise. Their mythical founder is the Greek god Aeolus, the god of the winds. It's one of the stories in Homer's epic poem.'

'I have a feeling about this,' William said to Paddy. He wasted no time and picked up the phone again. 'Ollie, I need some real-time satellite images of the Aeolian Islands. Email them through to Paddy. And Ollie, I need them ten minutes ago.'

*

By the time the satellite photos came through, it was clear that the Ekranoplan was heading for somewhere along the northern coast of Sicily, the Aeolian Islands were looking a likely possibility.

'I think we've found it,' William said looking around from one of the computer screens. 'One of the islands is surrounded by sea planes and large ships.'

'That's not unusual for a tropical island, William,' Paddy said.

'But there is no one at all on the beaches. And look, there's another craft that looks much like the Ekranoplan.' William zoomed in on the strange vessel, it had been moored like a boat to an orange buoy. 'There can't be too many of those around.'

'That must be it,' Paddy said brightening up.

'How far is the target from that location?

'Thirty minutes, tops, at its current speed.'

The satellite phone rang, William answered it. He listened for a moment then shouldered it keeping the line open. 'Ollie has found a naval support ship just north of Malta, the RFA *Largs Bay*,' he said to Paddy and Rupert. 'She's heading to an exercise near Cyprus and they have a fully armed Merlin helicopter on deck.'

'That'll come in handy,' said Rupert.

'Right. Decision made,' William said. He passed some orders to Ollie. After he hung up, he stood up and addressed the men.

'Listen in everyone. Be ready to move in ten minutes. We still need to keep operational security, so no one but us gets to know the actual target location. No one but us, got it? Paddy, contact Phantom-one, tell them to keep their eyes on the target and get them to send all their data directly to Ollie, we'll be out of touch for a while. We'll need Ollie to guide us in when we reach the island. Rupert, make sure your men have everything they need.' He walked to the door.

'Where are you going?' Paddy asked.

'To see God. We need to borrow a plane. And we could do with a miracle or two.'

# Chapter 39

*1710hrs – the Aeolian Islands*

A WARM TEMPERATE breeze blew in from the sea and washed over the volcanic island. The air, heavy with moisture, flowed over the white sandy beaches and seeped up through the sub-tropical forest. Wet foliage glimmered in the shafts of bright sunlight that broke through the occasional gaps in the clouds. The wind took the air further inland towards the centre where it was pushed higher and higher by the rising land. At the peak of the rocky volcanic mountain, white wisps of mist licked at the dormant beast.

Back by the shore, three male members of the Society of Eden watched in silence from the wooden pier as the Ekranoplan ploughed gently through the calm waters into the island's only port. Each of the watchers was dressed in an identical dark red uniform with a black leather belt and a holstered pistol on the right hand side. All three had short black hair and wore sunglasses. Epaulettes on their shoulders had numerous gold triangles on them that displayed their rank. Above the left breast of their uniforms was a black badge with their symbol emblazoned on it.

Together they secured the Ekranoplan to the pier's bollards and pushed the gangplank to the craft's cabin door. When the hatch opened the elite security team stood to attention and simultaneously saluted. Their salute was a rapid, rigid movement of the right arm, fist clenched, across the chest. The arm was held so that the fist covered their badge.

Cossack emerged from the Ekranoplan first, he held Ella firmly by the arm. He dragged her behind him down the gangplank onto the pier. When he reached *terra firma* he nodded to the men and they sharply lowered their arms and stood easy.

Ella squinted in the bright sunlight. The heat of sun was intense on her face. The wooden pier was built into the black and grey rocks of the coast. On each side the water was crystal clear, she could see dozens of tropical fish swimming through it. Beyond the pier was a concrete path which led into a dense forest. The tree line hugged the coast as far in each direction. To her right, further along, was a narrow sandy beach. It was deserted. The sea lapped calmly at the shore.

'Take her to the medical centre, she needs to be vaccinated,' Cossack ordered to the men. 'Then have her cleaned up and prepared. Get her a uniform. Hades will collect her later from a temporary secure room. She must be watched and escorted at all times.'

'What rank and division will she be in, sir?' asked the leader of the security team.

Cossack looked Ella up and down and sneered. 'She is one of the *chosen*,' he spat. 'She is to serve in the history section of the education division.'

'What?' Ella cried. Confused and frightened, she tried to speak, she had a million questions to ask all at once. But the words failed to form quickly enough.

The team leader nodded his understanding and saluted once more. The two other security men grabbed Ella by each arm. She struggled and shouted protestations, but they only increased their grip on her. She was led away up the path and into the forest.

\*

After a short journey on foot through the forest, Ella and the security team came to a large entrance that was cut into the side of a rocky cliff. Huge elaborate marble pillars flanked the open entrance, above them was a triangular gable. Ella didn't have time to make out the complex artistry that decorated the structure before they walked her under it and into the underground complex. Just inside, guarding the entrance, were two armed soldiers dressed in green combat uniforms. They saw them in with a nod to the security team leader.

The large entrance hall was grand to say the least. The floor was made from large black and white tiles. Huge, complex mosaics decorated the white walls. Here and there along the walls were larger than life white marble statues of various Greek gods. Most looked brand new, but a couple were worn, grey and clearly ancient.

'What is this place?' Ella demanded. Hot and flustered, sweat dripped off her forehead, she shook her arms away from the men and wiped her face with her sleeve.

The team leader frowned at her. 'Don't you know? This is the home of the Society of Eden,' he said proudly. 'It's the closest thing to paradise on this Earth.'

Ella noticed his manic grin; she'd seen the likes of it before. One day at the university, whilst sheltering from the rain in the cloisters at

Neville's Court, Trinity, she was accosted by a religious cult member on a recruitment drive. As she lent harmlessly on one of the Doric columns, he preached relentlessly to her. Despite her obvious disinterest, he tried to persuade her to join their ranks – she was a sinner, she was lost, they would help her find her way. As he spoke he had, she observed, the demented and joyless smile of the brainwashed.

With the security escort never more than a few feet away, Ella was taken through the wide and brightly lit stone corridors of the complex. The tunnels were cut deep into the mountain. For the most part the surfaces were smooth, but in places rough bare rock was exposed. The air was cool, she could hear the low hum of the air conditioning system in the background. Draped down from the tunnel walls every now and again were red flags that had their symbol emblazoned on them.

They passed several other people on their way. The strangers paid no particular attention to her. Each person, she noticed, was dressed in a uniform that was similar in style to the security team, but in two different colours: pure white, and dull dark grey. She observed that there were more greys than whites, and that the greys were mainly of east Asian appearance, while those in white were from a mix of the world's races. Another thing she noted was that the women in white were, on the whole, what she considered to be young, slim and attractive.

They passed more armed soldiers who saluted the team leader with the same strange salute as they went. Rapidly, Ella began to work out the hierarchy. The fact that there was one worried her.

The door to the medical centre was open when they arrived. One of the security minions knocked loudly three times and walked in. The room was impressive; no expense had been spared on its construction. Within the large, well lit chamber was a small fortune in state-of-the-art medical equipment. The white, tiled room was spotless. Dozens of stainless steel cabinets and shelves were filled with books, bottles and small boxes. There were several of other rooms which led off from the main chamber. Ella thought that it would have been the envy of any hospital in any country.

A doctor appeared and approached the security team. 'Can I help you?' he said with a welcoming smile. Dressed in a traditional white doctor's coat, Ella noticed that he wore the white uniform under it. He looked no older than twenty-five, he was well tanned and spoke with a European accent. He looked at Ella and smiled. His strong, handsome features put her at ease.

'A new recruit. One of Hades' girls,' explained the security team leader. 'She needs vaccinated.'

The doctor nodded and turned to Ella. His eyes were pale blue, his face was kind. He reminded her of someone.

'Please follow me,' the doctor said softly. 'This won't take a moment, but it's important, for it will save your life.'

Ella followed him over to a silver cabinet. Behind the glass doors were silver trays that held hundreds of tiny glass vials, each were full of a clear liquid. The doctor tapped a four digit code into the keypad on the side of the door. The panel beeped twice, the doctor cursed under his breath. He tried it again, much slower this time. A different tone sounded and the cabinet opened. He reached in and grabbed a vial and then attached it to chrome device that looked much like a toy gun.

'This won't hurt,' he reassured her. 'It uses a pad with thousands of microscopic needles to deliver the serum into the skin. You won't feel a thing. I promise.'

When he moved towards Ella with the gun, she flinched and backed away. She glanced nervously at the security team who were watching her.

'It's okay, don't be nervous,' the doctor said. 'You are one of us. We will not harm you. Please, allow me.'

Ella acquiesced and stepped forward. Firmly, the doctor pushed the end of the gun to the side of Ella's neck and squeezed the trigger. She tensed from a natural reflex, but she didn't feel any pain. The sensation was odd, her skin tingled. She looked into the doctor's eyes as he worked, he smiled at her again. She wondered how such a pleasant, bright man could end up a member of the Society, hidden away on a secret island. It was madness, she thought, she couldn't figure it out.

'All done,' he said brightly as if she were a child. 'If you need anything, anything at all, you know where to find me.' He winked at her and walked away.

*

Once more Ella found herself being led briskly through the tunnels by the security team. But she walked with them now, as opposed to being dragged. She strode alongside the team leader. A cold and unfriendly man, he hadn't said anything more than a few barked orders to her along the way. The two others followed close behind in complete silence.

They took her into a storeroom where she was measured up by a young Chinese girl who was dressed in the grey version of the uniform. Once done, the girl scurried away into the back of the store. Moments later, she returned with an armful of new clothes. Ella took them in both arms. They looked like the white uniforms she had seen some of the others wear.

'Thank you,' Ella said to the girl. 'What's your name?'

'No talking,' barked the security lead.

The Chinese girl lowered her head, her eyes fixed to the floor.

'Come. We're done here. This way.' The leader beckoned to her.

At the door, Ella glanced back. Keeping her head down, the girl slowly raised her sad eyes up towards Ella. A chill ran up Ella's spine.

*

After another silent journey through the maze of tunnels, Ella was shown to her room. She was told again that it was only temporary. Seeing as she was a newcomer, her proper living quarters were still being prepared. She was instructed to freshen up, change into the uniform and wait until someone came for her.

When the security team left they shut the door behind them. Ella heard the click of a lock. She raced over to it but there wasn't even a handle. She banged on it and shouted, but there was no answer.

Still holding the clothes in her arms, she leaned with her back to the door and looked around her prison. She wanted the tears to come, but they failed to materialise. Mentally she kicked herself. Instead of wallowing in her self-pity, she told herself to study her new surroundings and look for another way out. She threw the clothes onto the bed and wandered around the place.

The basic room was small and narrow, there were no windows. At the far end was a door that led into a modest ensuite bathroom. The solid stone walls were bare save for a full length mirror on one side and one of their obligatory red flags on the other. Pushed against one wall was a small wooden dressing table with a few drawers on each side. In one corner of the room there was a single bed, which had been neatly made up with white sheets and two pillows. For some reason Ella thought of the Egyptian linen and the beautifully soft pillows from the hotel she'd stayed in with William. She drifted off for a moment to a better time. It seemed like a million years ago now.

Snapping out of it, she walked into the bathroom. It was equally basic. There was a toilet, a sink and a small shower. No windows, no doors – no way out.

Defeated, she sat down on the bed and put her head in her hands.

She wanted to cry, but the anger and frustration still prevented her from doing so.

Looking down, she noticed her watch. It was dainty and stylish. Small and unnoticeable. Innocent. She had no idea if it was working or not, it read the time okay, but she had to believe that it was doing the job it was really designed for. It was her only hope of salvation.

She undressed and showered, but it did little to refresh her. She put on the white uniform, it was surprisingly comfortable. Exhausted, she lay down on the bed. With nothing to do but wait, she removed one of the pillows and used it as something to hug. She curled up and closed her eyes. Within moments she was fast asleep.

*

Vaguely aware of a loud banging on the door, Ella opened her weary eyes. For a tranquil moment of ignorant bliss she forgot where she was. She sat up and looked around at her drab surroundings with an element of confusion. Then, in a terrible single moment, it all came back to her. Her stomach leapt into the air, she felt dizzy and nauseous.

The lock turned. The mechanism in the door clicked and it slowly began to open.

'I'm so sorry to lock you up like this,' Hades said apologetically as he edged cautiously into the room. 'I hope you will forgive me.'

Ella remained silent. She sat up on the bed and tucked her legs into her arms. Still a little bewildered, she looked him up and down as he stood in the doorway.

He was dressed in a pure white uniform that consisted of plain linen trousers and a robe-like long jacket that had a high, rounded collar. A thick gold pendant hung around his neck, on its end was a large gold triangle. On his feet, he wore brown leather sandals. Ella thought he looked like a new-age druid. In other circumstances she would have laughed at the sight.

'Good, I see you have changed into your uniform,' Hades said, seemingly pleased with her. He spent a moment admiring her, then he clasped his hands together and smiled. 'Wonderful, you look stunning in it. I knew it would suit you.'

The tight fitting white uniform left little to the imagination. Ella felt somewhat exposed; it made her feel even more vulnerable than she already was. The fact that the soft, brushed cotton was actually very warm and comfortable was of little consolation to her at that moment. She noticed Hades' eyes linger on her. It repulsed her; she looked away and pulled her legs in tighter to her chest.

'What is this place?' she snapped. 'Who are those people dressed in grey?'

Hades smiled and nodded. 'You really are a feisty one, aren't you? All in good time, my girl,' he replied. 'All in good time. You have much to learn about us.' He held his hand out to her. 'Come, there is something I must show you.' He beckoned to her. 'I think you will be very interested in this. I have a proposition for you. A most unique opportunity.'

Reluctantly, Ella slipped off the bed. When she left her prison she noticed that there was no security detail this time waiting outside. Hades led her through the vast underground tunnels alone. They curved and twisted through the mountain, the featureless walls made it impossible to tell one corridor from another. Only the occasional signs on the walls and doors indicated a reference to where they were. Ella noticed that the doors that led off from the tunnels each had a letter and a number on them at the top. She recalled that the medical centre had been marked M-101. Her prison had been S-276. The letters and numbers began to make sense to her. It was a grid system. They passed a room marked as E-534, and at the next junction they turned left. Ella guessed what the next room would be marked as. When they passed it, she smiled. She had cracked it and began to build a picture of the place in her head. It was vast, and she felt sure that she hadn't seen the half of it.

Hades explained that many of the rooms were living quarters, while others that they passed were libraries, kitchens and training centres. 'A little more than five-hundred of us live and work here,' he proudly told her. 'We have teachers and farmers, horticulturists and builders, scientists and medics. You name it, every skill that a functioning society requires, we have it. Everyone here has a purpose, their skills are essential for our survival and for the future progression of humanity.'

A man dressed in grey approached, he was pushing a trolley full of gardening equipment. When Hades and Ella walked past him, he stopped and bowed. His eyes were lowered to the floor, he held his right arm across his chest. Ella guessed that the thin, nervous looking man was of Vietnamese decent. Hades completely ignored him and walked past.

'And the third class citizens, are they essential too?' Ella sneered. She knew she was pushing her luck but didn't care. She had seen enough.

Hades turned and took a firm hold of her by the arm. 'Listen here young lady. They have a significantly better life with us than the one they left,' he snapped, his face had reddened. 'And they left it voluntarily, for your information. Do you really think we are all born equal? Do you think life is fair and just?'

Ella knew the truthful answer, but said nothing. She just looked up at him and narrowed her eyes.

'Equality and fairness are only words, concepts invented by humans to comfort themselves from the harsh realities of the cruel natural world. They are looked after here,' he said. 'Everyone is. And just like us, they work for their living. But there is a rank system. It is a requirement of every functioning society, nothing more. Tell me of a society where everyone is equal, where there are no divides, no classes, where the idle are rewarded as much as the productive. Tell me.'

'But that's no reason to treat people like slaves,' she retorted. Hades' arrogance was infuriating her; she pulled her arm away from his grip. 'History teaches us what happens when people are held captive. They rebel eventually. The tides turn, and the slaves become the masters.'

Hades laughed heartily. He shook his head. 'If only it was that simple, my girl,' he said. He waved her on. 'Please, we must continue.'

They went on their way down the corridor side by side in an uncomfortable silence. Hades seemed troubled by something. Ella cared not.

'You will understand soon,' Hades said breaking the sullenness. 'You are one of us after all, whether you believe it or not, and whether you like it or not. Eventually you will see what this is all about and then you will understand why all of this is so important.'

'So you say. But you're wrong. This never works, there is no such thing as a perfect society and there is no master race. We are all the same whether *you* like it or not. And people are flawed, imperfect, it's what we are. No one can change that.'

'No, we are not all the same. It's survival of the fittest and our survival over all these millennia proves our place at the top of the evolutionary tree.' He sighed deeply. 'I do hope I'm not wrong about you, I really do. It would be very unfortunate if I was.'

Ella logged the vague warning in the front of her mind. She was under no illusion just how precarious her situation was. She had to watch her tongue in future. But Hades was right, she was one of them. She always had been. And as he had said, it was survival of the fittest. She had no intention of not surviving.

Eventually they came to a metal security door set into the rock along a long tunnel. Hades stopped and turned to face it. Carefully, he entered a four digit code into the keypad on its side, each number made a different sound as he typed. The door unlocked with a buzz and a click. Ella eyed the keypad, Hades had concealed the numbers, but she heard the tune. She sang it in her head, over and over. Hades pulled the heavy, thick door open and together they entered the room. When they were both inside, Hades pulled the door closed behind him.

The high-roofed, circular chamber was vast and dark, it took a moment for Ella's eyes to adjust. The floor was made up of large black and white tiles arranged in a circular pattern. Dozens of long red flags covered the walls all the way around the room. Running down each flag were a series of black triangles, pentagrams and Eyes of Horus. Only a few of the flags had the three combined to form the symbol that Ella had seen so many times. At the very centre of the chamber was a carved stone altar. Strange symbols were cut into the light brown stone. On top of it, sat on a wooden lectern, was a gold object the size of book. A spotlight somewhere high above illuminated it splendidly, it seemed to radiate with brilliance in the otherwise gloomy chamber. Ella recognised it instantly.

Hades walked over to the altar and gazed in wonder at the Biblos Aletheia. 'What I'm about to show you, Ella, is the world's most sacred knowledge,' he said. 'Since its discovery over two-millennia ago, we have gradually deciphered its secrets. Only a select few have ever had the privilege to be enlightened by its knowledge. And even now we are on a road to discovery, since its safe return to us. All thanks to you, Ella, and of course to your father and to his ancestors who protected it for us.'

A wave of anger washed through her veins. Her face reddened. 'How dare you suggest he did it for you,' she snapped. 'You had him killed, you bastards.'

Slightly taken aback, Hades was momentarily lost for words. He frowned and shook his head. 'No, no, no,' he pleaded. 'We tried to reason with your father. He was one of us, we would never harm our own. We wanted him to join us. There was a misunderstanding.'

'A misunderstanding? You're a liar and a murderer,' she shouted. She lunged towards Hades, arms flailing, and hit him several times on the chest. Hades grabbed her arms and gripped her. She burst into tears and fell to her knees sobbing.

'I'm sorry for what happened to your father, Ella. Really, I am. But there is nothing that can be done now.' He knelt by Ella's side, his voice softened. 'But I can make up for it. I've saved you, saved you from the wrath that will cleanse the old world. I wanted to save you, Ella, ever since I learned of you. You are beautiful and intelligent. You are truly one of us. If only we had discovered you sooner.' Hades placed his hand gently on Ella's shoulder. Strangely, she didn't shake him off. She sniffed and wiped her face on her arm. Her breathing calmed and slowed.

'I brought you here for a very special purpose,' Hades continued. 'When the dust finally settles in the old world, maybe in a year or so's time, I want you to lead a very special mission.'

The sobs and sniffs had gone. Ella focused on calming herself.

'I want you to study the Biblos Aletheia and uncover more of its secrets.' Slowly, Hades stood up. Gently, he helped Ella up and guided her towards the altar. He reached out and stroked the surface of the gold book.

'You see, Ella, this is more than just a book.' There was a gleam in his eye. 'It's also a map.'

'A map?' Ella whispered, she gazed upon the gold object. Almost solid gold. She remembered how heavy it was.

'Our ancestors knew the clues were in there, but they couldn't decipher them, not all of them anyway.'

There were sliding doors on one side of the altar, Hades bent down and slid one open. Inside were shelves stacked with dozens of books and papers. He pulled out a thick, leather covered book and placed it on the altar. The hefty thing looked ancient.

'My ancestors discovered that the Biblos Aletheia describes how three guiding stars lead the way to its old homeland.'

'To Atlantis?'

Hades nodded and smiled. 'We think that somehow it has something to do with the pyramids of Giza.'

'Orion,' Ella whispered, her eyes widened. She looked at the gold book again.

There was recognition in Hades' face, he grinned proudly. 'As you can see we have worked extensively on it over the centuries.' He tapped the old leathery book. 'But it was impossible to do much more after the Biblos Aletheia was lost. For the last five-hundred years all we have had to work on was an incomplete copy of the text. But now that we have it back, we can complete the work.'

'To translate it?' Ella asked.

Pleased by her interest, Hades nodded. 'As I said, we have our very own Rosetta Stone – the Cuneiform tablet.' The smile turned to a more serious look; he moved closer to Ella and put his hand on her shoulder.

'What I'm saying, Ella,' he said softly, 'is that I want you to complete the work our ancestors began. Re-translate the Biblos Aletheia, decode its secrets, and find their lost homeland. If you want to, that is.'

She stood firm and let him touch her. 'Where is it?' she asked looking into his hungry eyes. 'This tablet, do you have it here?'

Briefly, he glanced at the open cupboard door. It was only a fleeting glance, a split-second look, but Ella saw it.

Gazing back into Ella's eyes he smiled at her. Slowly, he brushed his hand over her back down to her hip. He pulled her towards him. His breathing deepened and his lips parted, he gazed further into her eyes. She held his gaze, he pulled her closer. He leaned in to kiss her. She tilted her head back, and their lips touched.

'I do want to,' she said softly. She pulled back slightly and turned her head towards the Biblos Aletheia. 'There is nothing more I want than to find the truth.'

Hades put his hand on the side of her face and moved in to kiss her again. Ella felt his interest growing against her thigh. She kissed him briefly, and then bit him teasingly on the lip before pulling away once more.

'It's too much, too soon,' she said quietly, turning to the side. 'Right now, all I want is to know more about this.' She turned and reached for the Biblos Aletheia. It was heavier than she remembered. She held it tightly in both hands.

Hades grinned at her and shook his head. 'My girl, there is so much more to show you, so much to—' he began to say, but didn't get to finish the sentence.

In a firm and swift move, Ella smashed the Biblos Aletheia hard against the side of his head. Hades stumbled backwards. He lost his balance and fell to the ground. Instantly, she realised that it hadn't been hard enough.

'You bitch,' he shouted from the floor. Blood began to pour out of his nose. He clutched the side of his face and made to stand up. 'You stupid, soon to be dead, bitch!'

Fire burned in her eyes. Ella raised the Biblos Aletheia high above her and lunged towards Hades. He looked up in disbelief and raised his hand to protect himself. But his defences were useless. She brought the object crashing down on the top of his head with all her might. There was a loud crack. Hades' face dropped and he began to fall forwards. Ella swung the object again, this time hitting him square in the face. There was a sickening crunch of bone and gristle. Blood splattered everywhere. Hades slumped backwards onto the floor. The blood flowed out rapidly from his nose and mouth over his face. Spluttering, he arched his back and kicked his legs.

Ella staggered backwards and stared in shock at what she had done. For a moment she froze and watched.

Hades arched his back once more. There was no sound now, no breathing. Finally, he collapsed and lay still. The blood flow stopped.

Ella looked down and saw the blood on her hands. She seemed surprised to find that she was still holding the improvised weapon. She placed the blood covered Biblos Aletheia on the altar and ran over to one of the walls. After ripping down one of the flags, she used it as a cloth to wipe as much of the blood off herself as she could. It did little to remove the stains from her white uniform.

She turned back to where Hades' body lay. She knew he was dead. A pool of blackened blood surrounded his head. Feeling no remorse, she threw the soiled flag over the body to cover it.

At the altar she picked up the Biblos Aletheia and the old book. Together they were heavy. She looked around for something to carry them in, but there was nothing. She ran to one of the walls again and ripped another flag down and used it to wrap the books up.

After taking a moment to compose herself and catch her breath, she approached the exit. Purposefully, she avoided looking back at the corpse, but it seemed to pull her eyes like a magnet. She fought it until she reached the door.

She pushed it, but it was locked. There was another keypad on the wall to the left. Ella stared at it and tried to conjure up the tune. As she had no idea which numbers made which tones, she pressed on number one, then two. There was some logic to the order. She hummed the tone out loud and tried to work out the code. Believing she had it, she pressed on four digits. There was a low buzzing sound, a red light flashed on the panel, the door remained closed. Fingers shaking, she tried another series. Again, the low pitched buzz sounded. She took a deep breath and recalled the tune. She sang it in her head over and over. Then, once more, she typed in four digits. It sounded right this time. There was a different buzzing noise, the door opened. Without so much as a glance back, she exited the chamber.

\*

Ever conscious of her heart pumping hard in her chest, Ella concentrated on trying to walk calmly through the corridors. Every bone in her body told her to run, to sprint out of the place as fast as she could, but she told herself to remain calm, cool. No one knew anything; no one knew who she was, or what she was doing. No one knew what she had done. She was one of them, she wore their uniform; just another mad face in this mad underworld. All she had to do was find an exit and walk out. She could vanish into the forest, find help. As she walked through the complex, the flag-wrapped books were held so tightly to her chest that it hurt her arms.

Within moments she came to a junction in the tunnel and stopped. Something nagged at her mind. Then it came to her: the Cuneiform tablet! She cursed herself; she had to go back for it. She turned around and briskly began to walk back, but after a few steps she heard faint voices from up ahead.

'Damn it,' she cursed under her breath. It was too risky. She about-turned and accelerated off in the opposite direction.

At another junction she stopped and tried to remember which way to go. Her mind had gone blank. No matter how hard she tried she couldn't retrace her steps, her thoughts were clouded by fear. At random she turned left and began to walk. Things looked more familiar, she was sure she had seen the room numbers before. Her mind cleared, she assembled the image of the grid system in her mind and quickened her pace.

After turning the next corner, she froze. Her heart skipped a beat, she drew air sharply. The same Vietnamese man from earlier was walking towards her with his now empty trolley. He bowed his head as he passed her but he didn't stop this time, there was no salute. Ella nervously glanced behind her. Hesitantly, she approached him.

'Can you help me, please?' she said a little too quickly. 'I'm lost.' She strained a smile. The little man looked up at her blankly and frowned. He shook his head and mumbled something in a language she didn't understand.

'The exit,' Ella emphasised. 'Way out?' There were signs of vague recognition in the man's weary face. He said something but Ella still couldn't understand him.

'Out?' she said, vigorously pointing upwards. The little man nodded and waved for her to follow him. He pushed his trolley up against the wall and headed off down the corridor. Despite her concerns, Ella knew she had little option. She followed.

Two soldiers appeared, coming her way from around a corner. They walked quickly and with purpose, almost a jog. Each of them held a short sub-machine gun held tightly in both hands. Ella's stomach somersaulted, the blood drained from her face. As they approached she drew breath and held it. They were almost upon her. Her chest tightened, she felt her legs weaken. But the soldiers ignored her and shot past without as much as a second glance.

She followed the little man until he stopped at a door, it was marked S-21. He opened it and went in, Ella followed.

Ella found herself in what she thought looked much like a changing room. It was full of metal cabinets and wooden benches. Each cabinet was marked with a four digit number. Grey uniforms and black boots were scattered untidily along the benches. From an adjoining room came the sound of a running shower.

She had an idea. She looked around the place for something. Quickly, she rifled through some of the unlocked cabinets. Frustrated and confused, the little man waved frantically at her from a door at the back of the room. But Ella was too busy to notice. Finally she spotted what she was looking for and reached for it: a black rucksack. She emptied its contents onto the floor, and clumsily, tried to stuff the flag-wrapped bundle into it. The Biblos Aletheia slid out and fell to the floor. There was still some wet blood on its surface. Quickly, she picked it up and stuffed it into the bag along with the book and the blood-soiled flag. The rucksack was heavy, she slung it over her shoulder and caught up with the little man. He frowned deeply at her.

She smiled nervously. 'Exit?' she prompted.

The man pointed down a dank, narrow tunnel. 'Up,' he said waving his hand for emphasis. 'Up.'

At the end of the narrow, dimly lit tunnel, Ella could just make out a spiral, metal staircase. It rose up into the cut bare rock. 'Thank you,' she said, and left him at the door as she walked away. She didn't dare look back, but she could feel his worried little eyes on her. Her legs felt like they were about to fail her, she forced herself forwards. When she reached the stairs she braved a glance back. The little man had gone. Despite the weight of the rucksack, she bounded up the steel steps as fast as she could.

*

The stairs rose up through the damp rock for at least fifty metres. Ella went around and around, up and up. She had to stop several times to catch her breath. When she finally reached the top she was exhausted. Sweat poured off her forehead, her heart pounded her chest. She squatted on the cold metal floor and scanned her surroundings.

Cut into the stone was a single door with a small light above it. The door looked much like a fire exit; there was a metal push-bar across it at waist level. Screwed to the wall was a sign that read "South Wing Emergency Exit", and it had a basic map of the complex that showed where the exit was located. Barely visible, high up on the ceiling, was a CCTV camera.

Ella forced herself to her feet and approached the exit. She pushed on the bar. It didn't budge. She pushed harder. But still no movement. She stood back and kicked it. The door burst open, bright light poured into the chamber. She raised her hand to her eyes and squinted.

As she exited she noticed that a red light above the door had started to flash on and off. An alarm, she feared. She cursed under her breath. There was no hiding from them now. At the exit she clung to the door and waited until her eyes adjusted to the light.

Squinting, she took in her new surroundings. To her relief she was outside by the side of the mountain, about one-hundred metres up from its base. There was nothing other than the wilderness for as far as she could see. Up ahead was the dense forest. Above her, a storm was brewing.

She looked down at her watch and ran her fingers over it. The dial was still pressed in. There was still hope that help would be on its way. A lump caught in her throat. She thought of William and smiled to herself. Somehow she knew she would see him again.

A sudden noise from behind caught her attention. Nervously, she peered back into the vast underground complex and listened carefully. She could just about make out the faint sound of jackboots on metal stairs. They became louder with every step. Time was running out. Time to move.

Above her, the sky was at war. White, grey and black clouds battled for supremacy. The land that lay before her darkened. From somewhere far off came the low rumble of thunder. She settled her eyes on the way forward; the forest beckoned her.

High above the tree tops at the forest's edge, a gap formed in the grey canvas. Squinting, Ella watched as the gap morphed into an unmistakable shape: a cross. The familiar shape conjured a voice from the past; the words echoed in her mind. *By this sign you will be victor.* Bright yellow sunlight spewed through it and the warmth radiated onto her pale face. For some reason the tension in her chest momentarily disappeared, a brief wave of confidence cleansed her of the negative thoughts. She shut her eyes and smiled. But as quickly as it came, the gap closed and the ray of warm light vanished.

Finally, the tension in the air was released. A bright bolt of blue-white lightening burned through the air. Sharp forks of intense energy arced across the sky over the forest. The clouds lit up, once, twice, then again in the space of a second. A moment later the ensuing thunderclaps were deafening, they echoed across the island. It began to rain.

Feeling a surge of energy and drive, Ella launched herself into the unknown. She ran for her life.

As she ran straight towards the forest, the rain quickly soaked her. The ground was a slimy, sodden sludge. Her feet sank into the mud as she sprinted, it rapidly drained her of her strength; her legs became dead weights. She gritted her teeth and battled on. Intuitively she used the rocks as stepping stones wherever she could find them.

Hearing voices, she glanced back towards the mountain and scanned the scene. Her heart skipped a beat when her eyes focused on the figures that pursued her. Two, no three, soldiers were gaining on her. Determined to escape them, she faced forward and gave it everything she had. Dropping the rucksack would give her an advantage, she knew, but its contents were priceless. She had to keep it with her at all costs.

On reaching the forest, the ground became firmer and her pace quickened to a sprint. The wind whistled in her ears as she disappeared under the thick canopy.

An exposed tree root caught her foot. She tripped and tumbled in the detritus, the heavy rucksack dragged her down. Immediately, she picked herself up, wiped the mud off her face and spat out the filth. She looked around desperately and tried to get her bearings. Her eyes widened, she had no idea where she had come from or where she had been heading. It all looked the same.

Strange whizzing sounds shot past her, they were followed almost instantly by loud thunder claps. Instinctively she ducked. Coming from somewhere behind her, two of the rounds hit the sides of a nearby tree. Wet bark and wood exploded into a shower of splinters and steam. There was only one direction to run in.

Ella sprinted from her pursuers deeper into the forest. As she went she prayed that her path would lead, somehow, to safety. Hope spurred her on, fear and adrenaline provided a boost of energy that she never knew she had. She zigzagged from tree to tree, leaped over fallen trunks, and tried to stay out of sight. But in her white suit she stuck out like a beacon in the dark forest.

Several more shots were fired. Orange tracer rounds whizzed past her barely metres away. The ground burned and hissed where they landed. But still she sprinted onwards.

Up ahead, she saw what looked like a clearing. Soft light penetrated through the canvas of trees. A road, she hoped, she prayed. Relief washed over her, the options played out in her mind. She could flag a driver down, call the police. Spirited with fresh hope, she gritted her teeth and gave it everything she had for the final few hundred metres. Her muscles burned and her lungs and throat felt like sandpaper; the contents of her stomach petitioned her to stop.

As she approached the clearing she saw the crisp bright light of the sky that bit through the trees. There was a swishing noise too, louder and louder it became as she neared. Eagerly she raced towards the light. When she reached the edge of the forest she stopped. Her breathing was short and rapid. She gripped the rough trunk of an old pine tree. Her legs were unsteady and shaky, her heart pounded. Ella stared wide eyed at the sight before her in utter horror. Then she doubled over, vomited and fell to her knees.

Ahead of her the forest floor disappeared down a cliff and into a ravine. At the bottom was a fast flowing river. Angry rapids, white and frothing, crashed noisily against the black rocks.

There was no road, no traffic. No way out.

'No,' Ella screamed hysterically into the valley, all her hopes finally and cruelly crushed. 'Please help me, someone,' she screeched between short, shaky breaths. 'Please.'

Cautiously, the three soldiers approached the clearing; their weapons held tightly. Streaks of black and green camouflage cream covered their sweaty faces. Each wore a combat uniform with an armoured chest-plate, webbing and pouches. High on their left arms was a square patch that had the red triangle, the pentagram and the eye.

Ella turned on her knees to face her tormentors. She clasped her hands together. Tears ran down her petrified face. She pleaded for mercy as the soldiers crept closer. Her eyes focussed on one of the weapons. It was a flame thrower. A bright blue flame burned furiously at the end of the long black shaft.

A strong gust of wind blew around her. Trees were violently blown back and forth. Loose leaves and rainwater took to the air and danced around the soldiers obscuring their vision.

There was a deafening noise and, frozen by fear, Ella could only watch in awe as a huge red and orange fireball expanded towards her.

# Chapter 40

*1912hrs – Mediterranean sea, north of Malta*

THE ROYAL FLEET AUXILIARY vessel, *Largs Bay*, was a Bay-class landing ship which supported the Royal Navy with an advanced amphibious capability. The huge grey vessel could transport hundreds of troops, dozens of tanks and tons of military equipment. The large bay doors on its bow were designed to deliver its payload directly to enemy shores.

Through the ocean she ploughed at full speed ahead. The sea was rough. Tide and wind clashed furiously which produced a huge swell. Angry waves peaked at ten metres high. The vessel's bay doors mercilessly crashed through them and threw up a gush of water fifty metres into the air, which then crashed down over the deck. As she sailed ever closer to the Italian coast the sky darkened. They were headed into a storm.

From the ship's stern, a V-22 Osprey transport jet slowly approached. A cross between a Chinook and a transport plane, it had wings fitted with large rotors, a twin tail fin and a grey, bulbous, glass nose. The rotors moved to the horizontal position and the plane transformed into a helicopter. Once it was directly over the ship's deck it hovered thirty metres above. Below it, on deck, a sailor with a high visibility vest battled with the wind and waved two batons that glowed bright orange. The Osprey pilot fought with the controls to keep the craft level with the ship, while one by one the team fast-roped down. Their heavy Bergens dangled on a bungee two metres below them as they went. The wind, laden with seawater, clawed at them as they descended to the deck. Paddy gave Max a quick two-minute education on fast-roping before the terrified little man descended to what he feared would be his death. When he made it down safely he wiped his brow and grinned nervously up at the craft. Paddy followed him out.

William was the last to exit. He pulled on a pair of black gloves, pushed his Bergen off the ramp and held onto the thick fast-rope. When Paddy had safely made it, William threw himself out. When he was halfway down the Osprey dropped several metres and lurched to the side. He held on tightly and wrapped his legs around the rope as he swung from side to side. Beneath him, the sea boiled. The water rushed up towards him, he braced himself for impact, but it never came. He felt the strain of acceleration, and the Osprey moved back into position. Below him the sailor waved his batons frantically. William relaxed his grip and slid down the rope. When he reached the deck another sailor rushed over and helped him to his feet. The Osprey rose vertically and flew off to the side, its rotors moved to the forward position and the aircraft vanished into the clouds.

'Welcome aboard, sir,' said the sailor shouting to be heard over the wind and rain. 'Follow me.'

William slung his Bergen over his shoulder and followed his guide into the safety of the ship's inners. He was taken straight to the officers' briefing room. The rest of the team were assembled there and were already preparing for the next phase of the mission. Paddy sat with his laptop out on a table, a satellite phone was pressed to his ear. Max made himself useful by linking the laptop up to a laser projector. The four troopers were stood huddled around a map of the area that was pinned to one of the bulkheads, while Rupert briefed them from it.

'And you must be Agent Temple,' said a short man whose tanned but serious face was covered by a thick, black beard. Dressed in a navy blue uniform, he had black epaulettes on his shoulders with several thick gold lines that showed his rank. 'I'm Captain Hilary. I received your orders some time ago, but I'm afraid she's not built for speed. We're twenty miles off the Italian coast.'

'Is the helicopter ready?' William asked. He laid his Bergen on the floor next to the rest of them.

'Yes, the Merlin is on deck, fully fuelled and ready to go. But let's hope this storm doesn't get any worse.'

'Postponing this mission is not an option,' William stated firmly. 'Any armaments?'

'Fitted with an M134 Gatling mini-gun.'

With a boyish gleam in his eye, Paddy turned to William. 'It's a six barrelled, electrically driven machine gun,' he said like Christmas had come early. 'Fires seven-point-six-two millimetre at a rate of three-thousand rounds per minute. The best fire suppressant a soldier can ask for.'

The Captain nodded. 'We were going to test it during the exercise,' he added. 'The operator is a gunner from the Royal Marines. Do you need him too?'

'Please,' William said. 'We'll be leaving as soon as we have confirmation of the target.'

When the Captain left the room, William joined Paddy at the table. His laptop was open and he was reading through the data Ollie had emailed him.

'So what's the update?' William asked.

'Ollie picked up another signal from Ella's watch. At the time it was located at a point at sea not far from the Aeolian Islands. But he's had nothing since, no signal, nothing. It's gone quiet.'

'And the eye in the sky?'

Paddy turned back to the laptop, the screen was projected onto a whiteboard mounted on the bulkhead. He opened one of the video files and pressed play, it was a section of colour footage from the Phantom Eye. The Ekranoplan could be seen pulling up to a pier by an empty white beach. A series of numbers on the bottom corner of the screen showed the date, time, longitude and latitude.

'Where exactly is that?' William asked.

Minimising the video window, Paddy opened another file, a satellite image of the whole island. 'Right here, where the red circle is,' he said.

Paddy switched back to the video footage and they all watched as the Ekranoplan pulled up to the pier and docked. Three people dressed in red uniforms could be seen attending to the craft. The camera zoomed in, it showed the scene in incredible detail. The hatch to the Ekranoplan opened and a man emerged.

'Cossack,' William spat. His heart jumped when he saw Ella being dragged behind him. 'Bastards.' He watched her as she was dragged by the men into the forest. If William hadn't been so engrossed with the footage he would have noticed that the room had fallen silent. When the four figures disappeared under the forest canopy the colour camera was useless; the image flickered, the colours vanished and were replaced by an odd mix of black and white. It took a moment for the team to adjust to what they were seeing.

'Thermal imaging,' Paddy announced. 'Warm is black, cold is white.'

Four black figures were easily made out walking under the cloud-like white and grey canopy that was the forest. The camera followed them along a winding path until they stopped. It was clear from the camera angle that there was a wide entrance cut into the mountainside. The figures walked into it and disappeared. The camera zoomed out and systematically scanned the surrounding area.

'The image analysts from the Phantom team have studied the footage,' Paddy went on. 'They reckon there is an extensive underground complex under the old volcano.'

With an extendible pointer in one hand, William took up a position by the side of the map on the bulkhead. The whole extended team gathered around him.

'Our mission is to locate and recover the vaccine. Our mission is to locate and recover the vaccine,' he repeated loudly and clearly as protocol dictated. 'We'll be dropped off here,' he tapped the pointer on the map, 'and will tab towards the entrance to the underground complex located here,' another tap. 'For the entire operation we'll have aerial support from a Phantom Eye. Fire support will be from the Merlin and, if necessary, we can call in a missile strike from the supporting frigates that are in range. Once we are in the complex we will have to find the vaccine by whatever means necessary.'

'That means we need the occupants alive. Don't kill anyone unless they pose an immediate threat,' Paddy added. 'Naval war ships are racing to the area loaded with Marines. They will mop up and secure the island once we've gone in.'

'And what of the hostage?' asked Rupert.

William looked at the deck and drew breath. 'Let's just hope we find her before it's too late,' he said.

*

There was little room left in the Merlin once the team had boarded. The gunner was the last man in, he assumed his position behind the powerful mini-gun. William regarded the young Marine, he barely looked twenty years old. He had a serious, professional look about him, clearly unfazed by the impromptu mission. William had seen the look before, many times. A face that had seen war.

While the pilot started the engines, Paddy checked that everyone's radio was working. Each of them wore a state-of-the-art headset with a throat mic. Their transmissions were digitally enhanced, filtered to reduce noise, and encrypted for security. The helicopter also acted as a rebroadcasting station, it beamed their transmissions up to a military satellite so they could keep in touch with Ollie. Paddy gave the thumbs up to William when he was confident that everything was working.

Over the radio William told the pilot they were good to go and moments later the engines roared. The helicopter lifted into the air. Pummelled relentlessly by the wind, the Merlin rose above the ship, banked to one side and then accelerated on its way.

Their journey was a bumpy one. To remain under radar the pilot flew as low as he could. This meant riding the storm. The Merlin shook vigorously, the engines moaned and whined. Occasionally the craft dropped out of the sky and plummeted towards the sea before being pulled back up again. To make matters worse, the cabin door had to be left open to give the gunner the best view of any threats. He took hold of the Gatling gun and stared down its long barrel out over the rough seas. Max was sick several times into a paper bag, when he was done he was encouraged to throw it out into the sea.

After receiving word from the pilot, William held up all ten fingers to the team. 'We're ten minutes from the target,' he announced.

Paddy opened the green briefcase on his lap and powered the tracking equipment up. The Merlin wasn't fitted with the camera module so only one of the screens worked, the geo-mapping. The internal GPS module in the briefcase would pinpoint where they currently were, and if it found the signal from Ella's watch, it would show where she was too. Once the equipment had booted up, Paddy checked in with Ollie, who would be their third eye.

'Anything to report?' Paddy asked Ollie.

'Nothing significant,' Ollie replied. He was at his desk in the lab, the live footage from the Phantom Eye was displayed on a high definition screen in front of him. 'There have been no further arrivals at the island, and no departures either. The place is pretty quiet.'

'Are there any security patrols or obvious defences?'

'Nothing more than two guards at the entrance to the complex. Occasionally one of them walks a few metres into the forest and then back again. Random timings.'

'What weapons do they have?'

'The highly distinctive FN P90 rifle,' Ollie said. 'These guys must have some serious money and resources.'

Paddy's screen flashed. A red circle appeared over a small area near the centre of the island. 'Ollie, I'm getting a reading from the service watch. It's within range.'

'Send me the coordinates and I'll put the camera on it.'

Paddy read out the grid reference, Ollie immediately relayed it to the Phantom Eye pilot. Within moments he could see the camera panning around on his screen. When it settled on the coordinates it zoomed in on the target.

'There's an exit by the side of the mountain,' Ollie said. 'The door is open. Someone is standing by the door, it looks like a woman. She's dressed in a white uniform. Hold on, they are zooming in further. Yes, it's Ella. It's definitely Ella.'

'William, we've found her,' Paddy said.

William's eyes widened. He felt a huge weight lift from his shoulders, but he remained straight-faced.

'She's running now,' Ollie added. 'She keeps looking back. I think she's trying to escape.'

'Escape?' William said, incredulous. 'What's our ETA to her location?'

Paddy studied the map on his little screen. 'Three minutes tops. I'll contact the pilot.'

'Listen up everyone,' William said addressing the team. 'We've found the hostage. We will track and extract, then tab on to the primary objective.'

'We need to keep the element of surprise,' Paddy warned.

He nodded. 'We'll pick her up when she's a safe distance from the complex.'

'She's being pursued,' Ollie reported, speaking quickly. 'Three soldiers are chasing her. They're firing at her, small arms.'

'We're tracking,' Paddy replied. 'One minute to intercept.'

'They're under the canopy of the forest,' Ollie went on with his commentary. 'Switching to thermal.'

Quickly, Paddy assessed the map. The red circle moved steadily through the forest. 'There's nowhere to land,' he said to William.

'We'll fast-rope it,' William replied. 'Just find somewhere to hover.'

Predicting Ella's most likely route, Paddy picked out a spot. Making clear the urgency of the situation, he relayed the orders to the pilot.

The Merlin sped to the drop zone. It banked this way and that over the terrain. Max shut his eyes; his knuckles white as he gripped his seat. William moved forward to the cabin door and took up a position next to the gunner.

'Five-hundred metres,' Paddy announced.

Over a forested hill they flew. Just beyond was a narrow ravine with steep, rocky sides. Up ahead, at the edge of the forest above the ravine, William could just make out the figure of a woman dressed all in white.

'I have visual. It's her,' William shouted. 'Get there now!'

The Merlin angled towards the lonely figure, the pilot reduced altitude but not speed. Within seconds they had reached the drop zone. Banking steeply the pilot slowed the craft to a hover.

Ella had dropped to her knees on the forest floor. William saw three soldiers approach, one of them had a flame thrower and was pointing it at Ella.

'Shoot them!' he ordered to the gunner. 'Now!'

Head down in concentration, the gunner narrowed his eyes and took aim. When he squeezed the trigger, the Gatling gun barrel spun around and spat out an almost solid beam of red hot rounds. A nano-second later there was an explosion on the ground where the soldier with the flame thrower had stood. An orange and black fireball billowed upwards and scorched the trees as it rose. The two other soldiers had been thrown to the side, they rolled around on the forest floor trying to douse the flames that engulfed them. The gunner showed no mercy, he squeezed the trigger once again and brought the focused beam of hot metal onto each target.

With the three soldiers eliminated, William fast-roped down onto the ground. Small fires were scattered across the forest floor where he landed. An acrid smell of burnt fuel and smoke filled the air. He ran towards the white figure that was lying face down on the ground.

'Ella,' he shouted as he approached. She didn't move. He crouched down by her, placed his fingers on her carotid vein and was relieved to find a strong pulse. She had passed out.

'Ella,' he repeated. 'Wake up. It's me, William.' He shook her shoulders gently and swept her hair from her face.

When she opened her eyes she initially recoiled at the sight of another armed soldier. But when she focused on his face, she relaxed, brightened, and smiled. 'William, thank God.' Tears welled in her eyes.

'In *this* world,' he said softly, 'definitely in this world.'

She laughed and made to stand up. William took her hand and helped her up. Holding her by her shoulders, he leaned in and gazed into her eyes. She gazed back and they both smiled.

'I'm okay,' Ella mouthed quietly. 'Thanks to my hero.'

Then they hugged one another tightly.

*

'Sorry to break up the party,' Paddy shouted as he approached, the Merlin hovered noisily above him. 'But this isn't a rescue mission. We need to find that vaccine before it's too late.'

Behind Paddy, the troopers fast-roped down and took up defensive positions across the forest floor. Max hit the ground heavily, but he picked himself up, put his glasses back on, and dusted himself off. After Rupert landed he helped Max carry his equipment.

Once the team was down, the Merlin hovered as a harness was winched down for Ella. The gunner gripped the Gatling gun and scanned the area for any threats.

'You've come for the vaccine?' Ella asked. She shot a quizzical look at William.

Despite her slightly hurt appearance there was no time for lengthy explanations. 'Things have gotten worse,' he said. 'Much worse. We need to search the complex for their vaccine. Assuming they have one, that is.'

'They do,' Ella said brightly. 'And I know exactly where it is. It's in the medical centre. Room M-101.'

Paddy and William exchanged glances, and then looked back to Ella. She picked up her rucksack and strapped it tightly to her back.

'No way,' William said, shaking his head. 'No way. You're leaving right now.' He took her by the arm and guided her towards Rupert who was holding the harness under the Merlin.

'Yes way,' she said defiantly, and shook away from his grip. 'I'm coming with you. Don't you dare leave me again.'

'It's too dangerous,' William pleaded. He took the harness from Rupert and held it out to Ella. 'You are leaving. Right now.'

Defiant, Ella stood with her arms folded and refused to move. Her hair blew around in the downdraft. 'I can help you. I know my way around. You don't. With me you'll get there quicker.'

'We don't have time to waste,' this was from Rupert who glared at William.

William looked from Rupert to Ella, then to Paddy. He shook his head. Paddy seemed to shrug. William shut his eyes and sighed knowing there was no arguing with her. 'Okay, okay. It looks like we're all going. Let's not waste any more time, we've probably already lost the element of surprise.' He let go of the harness and waved up to the pilot.

It was Paddy's turn to shake his head. He turned to the rest of the team and said, 'Right troops. You heard the boss, let's do this. Move out.'

*

The Merlin backed off out of sight, but remained close enough in case called upon for fire support or extraction. The team made off in the direction of the complex. The light was failing quickly; it would soon be pitch black. But by using the thermal imaging intelligence from the Phantom Eye – which was relayed to them over the radio from Ollie – they were never blind. With the troopers leading the way, the team swiftly navigated through the forest until they were only a few hundred metres from the main entrance to the underground complex. Paddy stayed close to Max, while William walked with Ella. They met no resistance.

The island, it seemed, was deserted.

\*

'This makes me nervous as hell,' Paddy whispered to William as they lay down in a dense wooded area close to the base of the volcano. 'It's been too quiet. Where are they all? They must have more defences than this.'

Night had fallen, the air was still and quiet. The storm had passed and the clouds had all but vanished. The sky above the forest canopy was full of stars. The crescent moon had been their only light source. It lit their path through the forest with a silvery half-light.

A few metres from where the team lay was the path that led from the port, through the forest and up to the entrance. Bright halogen spot lights attached to the cliff-face lit up the perimeter.

Paddy scanned the entrance through the telescopic sight on his PDW. Just as the Phantom Eye had reported, there were two armed guards stood just inside on each side. Next to Paddy, William rested his cheek on the butt of his weapon and studied the scene through the telescopic sight.

'They're all inside, Paddy,' he said. 'And they're not an army, they're a cult.'

'Even worse,' Paddy retorted. 'Nutters.'

'We can't wait for the guards to patrol. We need to draw them out.'

William crawled ahead to where Rupert was and whispered to him that it was time to make a move. Rupert nodded and flicked his hand at two of his men. He then spoke into his radio and ordered the Merlin pilot to stand by.

Using the trees for cover, Dipper and Fitz cautiously approached the entrance. They crawled as close as they could get to the forest edge. Dipper, lying on the ground, moved his silenced HK53 into position. Carefully controlling his breathing, he closed one eye and settled the crosshairs onto the head of his stationary target. Gently, he squeezed off a single shot. The sub-sonic round barely made a sound as it was coughed out of the weapon and hit the target.

At the entrance the soldier slumped to the floor. The other soldier on the opposite side of the entrance took a second to realise what had happened. It was a second too late. Before he could react another silenced shot was fired. The second soldier fell to the floor, dead.

Fitz knelt by the side of a tree and gave cover with his silenced MP7 while Dipper made a dash for the side of the entrance.

But before he reached it all hell broke loose.

A blaze of gunfire emanated from somewhere inside the entrance. Dipper went down instantly. A moment later there was a flash of light and a loud explosion from close to where Dipper lay fighting for his life. The grenade blast ripped through him.

Fitz shouted back to his commander and fired several shots into the entrance. He couldn't see the soldiers but saw the flashes from their weapons as they fired indiscriminately into the forest. Fitz retreated backwards for cover and waved frantically to his commander.

'Contact, contact at the entrance. Fire support required, now!' Rupert commanded to the Merlin pilot.

While they waited for Merlin the entire team fired suppressing shots into the entrance. Thick metal doors began to slide shut.

'Ollie, we're taking fire. Has anyone appeared on the outside,' Paddy shouted over the radio.

From his screen, Ollie could see the action in full thermal high definition. The Phantom Eye software had marked each person on the ground with a numbered yellow box. If any other heat signatures appeared, they would be marked and highlighted. 'No one has left the complex,' he replied. 'I'll let you know if they do.'

'They're locking themselves in,' Rupert shouted.

Ish fired a grenade from his H&K G36k. It hit the side of one the doors and barely made a dent in it. The shots emanating from the entrance reduced, and when the doors closed it stopped.

'Ceasefire!' Rupert shouted. 'Is everyone okay?'

In turn everyone shouted out 'okay', except for Dipper.

'Do we have any charges?' William asked.

Paddy smiled, and said, 'We've got better than that.'

A second later they heard the Merlin approach from overhead. Before it was even in position the gunner released the fury of the M134 Gatling gun. An intense beam of bright orange tracer rounds rained down on the entrance. Stone, metal and brick exploded into a cloud of dust, sparks of molten metal and debris. It made quick work of the doors, which were reduced to a mangled mess in seconds.

'Ceasefire,' Paddy ordered to the Merlin pilot.

The short burst had devastated the entrance. Smoke billowed out of it, small fires burned inside. Paddy nodded to the troop commander.

'Prepare to move. Move!' Rupert ordered to his remaining men.

All four troopers immediately ran towards the entrance in a well practised fire-manoeuvre. As they approached they fired covering shots into the smoke filled hole. Their fire was not returned. When they reached the side of the entrance, one of the men threw a grenade in. After it exploded they stormed the entrance. Several shots were fired.

'Clear,' one of the troopers shouted when it went quiet.

'Entrance clear!' Rupert said into the radio for the benefit of the rest of the team.

William and Paddy took Ella and Max and headed towards the entrance. They passed the shredded body that was Dipper. Ella tried not to look. Max's eyes were wide open. He nearly tripped and fell as he was ushered past. Rupert waved them into the entrance. Inside, an alarm was sounding. A thick cloud of dust and bitter smoke filled the air. Small fires burned all around. The troopers took up defensive positions on all sides.

'How far is the medical room?' William asked Ella.

Speechless and eyes wide open, Ella looked in awe at the carnage that lay before her. Amongst the rubble were several mangled bodies – or at least what was left of them. She saw at least ten Society members that were dressed in the green combat uniform she had seen earlier. Four bodies were dressed all in red.

'Ella!' William prompted. 'Look at me.'

She shook out of it. 'Not far. Maybe fifty metres down the corridor. It's built on a grid system, letters for the horizontal row, numbers for the vertical. But they're not particularly straight lines.'

Paddy raised his hand. He listened to something with his headset, and then said, 'Ollie said that dozens of people are exiting the complex on the other side of the mountain.'

'The emergency exits. Good,' said William. 'Let's hope the place is empty.'

After William spoke to the troop commander, he quickly walked around and checked the faces of the dead enemy soldiers. When he finished he looked up at Paddy and shook his head.

Ella watched William and frowned at him.

'Let's move,' William said to Rupert.

Rupert nodded to Ish, who was standing by the tunnel that led further into the complex. Ish took out a grenade, threw it down the tunnel into the darkness, and shouted, 'Fire in the hole.'

'Cover your ears,' William said quickly to Ella and Max.

There was a loud bang. Instantly Ish and Fitz ran down the corridor with weapons drawn. Several shots rang out rapidly.

'Clear,' one of them shouted back after a moment.

The rest of the team followed them in. William and Paddy were last in line and covered the rear. They passed two dead soldiers whose bodies lay on the floor of the corridor. Max stared at them as he passed. William ushered him along, then bent down and checked their faces.

'There's something I need to tell you,' Ella said quietly to William as they continued along the tunnel. 'I killed Hades.' Her eyes were cold and sincere.

'Good,' said William without breaking pace. 'And Cossack?'

She shook her head. 'I don't know, I guess he's still alive. I haven't seen him since I was taken here.'

The lights flickered for a second and then went out all at once. The team stopped. For a moment it was pitch black, a deep blackness that sucked the air from Ella's lungs. The hum of the air conditioning wound down until it stopped. Ella gasped and grabbed William's arm. The troopers froze and listened. Seconds later the emergency lighting kicked in and the corridor was lit up again. It was significantly dimmer than before and the air conditioning remained off. From the walls up ahead the reflection of an orange light flashed on and off.

'Fire in the hole,' Ish shouted again.

There was another loud crack from further down the tunnel. Faint screams could be heard too, raised voices and rapid footsteps echoed in the distance. More shots were fired by the troopers, but only as a warning to clear the way. With no further resistance they continued along the corridor until they reached the room marked M-101.

'Is this it?' William asked Ella.

In the half-light she studied the markings on the side of the door, nodded, and said, 'Yes, definitely.'

'It's locked,' Fitz said after heaving himself against the door.

'Blow it open,' Rupert immediately replied. He waved everyone back to a safe distance, while Fitz took out a door charge from his Bergen and secured it to the door.

'Firing,' Fitz shouted as he ran towards them.

Seconds later there was a loud bang, dust and debris filled the air. Fitz and Thembe ran forward, Fitz kicked the remainder of the door in, and Thembe stormed into the room.

'Clear!' he shouted. The rest of the team followed him in.

The room was much darker than when Ella was last there. It took her a moment to orientate herself. She remembered the layout and ran over to the cabinet where the doctor had taken the vaccine from.

'This is it,' she said. 'But it needs a code to open it.'

'No, it doesn't,' Fitz said confidently. He took out a short, black crowbar from the side of his Bergen and went to work on the cabinet.

Max cleared a space on a table and set his equipment up. From the silver case he had been hauling around, he pulled out a laptop and an array of other, less recognisable items.

Fitz wrenched open the cabinet. Inside were the trays with the little vials.

Ella picked one up. 'This is the vaccine,' she said.

William grabbed a handful of vials and gave them to Max.

'How long will it take to do whatever you're doing?' he asked.

Max screwed his sweaty face up. 'An hour, maybe longer,' he said reluctantly.

Paddy cursed and shook his head.

Max turned back to his instruments. He broke open a vial and poured the liquid onto a small black tray that was connected to the laptop. Max could feel everyone's eyes on him, but tried to ignore it.

Paddy turned to Rupert and said, 'We're going to be here a while.'

'Secure the exit,' Rupert ordered to his men. Ish and Thembe instantly headed to the door.

As Max opened more vials and poured their contents into various parts of his equipment, William joined him at the table.

'It's a state-of-the-art lab-on-a-chip, used for bio-molecular analysis,' Max said without looking up. 'A series of microarrays for DNA fingerprinting and liquid chromatography. It will analyse the chemical make-up of the vaccine and send the results back to the lab.'

'Once we're topside and it can see the satellite, that is,' William added.

'Yes,' agreed Max.

'We're sitting ducks,' Paddy snapped, he paced around the room clutching his rifle. 'Can't we just take the vaccine and go?'

'The place is empty, Paddy,' William reassured. 'They've all fled.'

'I wouldn't be so sure of that.'

'We can't leave until I am one-hundred percent sure that I have the right material,' Max piped up. 'It would be disastrous for us all to get it wrong at this stage. Just give me some space, some time.'

Paddy glared at him; Max snapped his head back to his laptop screen.

Ella fidgeted with one of the vials. She put it down and looked to William. She bit her lip and narrowed her eyes. She opened her mouth to say something, but stopped, and walked away.

William noticed her reaction and approached her. 'Don't worry about what you did,' he said sympathetically. 'You did what you had to do.'

She looked into his eyes and nodded. 'There's something else,' she said quietly.

'What is it?' William asked, concerned now seeing the turmoil in her face.

'There's something I need to get,' she said and bit her lip. 'But it's in another room.' She winced and looked down when she said it.

'It's far too dangerous,' William said shaking his head.

'It's really important. Look.' She slid the rucksack from her shoulder and opened it just enough to show William the Biblos Aletheia.

He looked up at her, smiled wryly, and shook his head.

'Hades told me that there's something that they use to translate it,' she pressed on with an unmistakable eagerness in her voice. 'A kind of Rosetta Stone. It's not far from here; I know exactly where it is.' Her eyes pleaded with William. 'Please. We'll probably never get another chance.'

Glancing from Max to the troopers, William thought for a moment then turned back to Ella. 'Okay,' he said. 'But just us.' He tightened the straps on his Bergen, pulled out his SIG-Sauer P229 and offered it, butt first, to Ella. 'For your safety, I know you know how to use one of these. It's made-ready, thirteen rounds in, and no safety catch. Got that?'

She slung her rucksack back over her shoulders, fastened the buckles under her chest and took the proffered pistol from William. 'Ready when you are,' she said brightly.

Paddy looked up from a conversation with Rupert. 'What's up, William? Where are you two going?' he asked.

'There's something else we need to get before we leave. Ella knows where it is, I'll look after her,' William said. 'Once Max is done, take him topside and send the data. We'll meet you out there. . . And one other thing, Paddy.'

'Yes?'

'If we're not out in time, leave without us. Do not come looking for us, do not jeopardise the mission. Understand? We can look after ourselves.'

Paddy disapproved, but he knew William had made his mind up. 'Whatever you say,' he said.

Cautiously, and clutching his PDW, William peered out from the exit and looked up and down the dark tunnel. It was vacant. 'Which way?' he asked Ella.

'Left,' she said confidently, and they set off together.

*

The tunnels were empty and cold. The alarm continued to sound. Ella and William weaved their way through the complex with their weapons raised.

'Not so fast, Ella,' William whispered. 'Stay by my side.'

'It's just up here,' Ella said, eager.

They turned a corner and came to another junction. Ella checked the markings on the doors. She turned left, and said, 'This way . . .'

She stopped dead in her tracks. The pistol held out in front of her.

Just ahead was a woman dressed in the white suit. She also stopped when she saw Ella. She was about to say something when she noticed William, she gasped and made to run.

William raised his weapon and shouted, 'Don't move! Put your hands on your head.'

The woman did as ordered. 'Please don't shoot,' she said desperately, her accent was soft and weak with Russian tones. She had a slender figure and an attractive, Slavic face. Atop of her long blonde hair she wore a gold tiara which had a bright red oval jewel in the centre. 'I'm not one of them, they held me here against my will.'

'Bullshit!' William spat.

'Please don't hurt me,' she pleaded. 'I'm unarmed.'

'Where is Cossack?' William demanded.

The woman's expression changed, she frowned and hesitated. 'I don't know. He's probably gone already.'

William thought for a moment. The woman looked Ella from foot to face and gave her a disappointed look.

'Just get out,' William barked. 'Run, get out, now.'

The woman needed no prompting. She nervously stepped past them in the narrow tunnel and then ran around the corner and out of sight.

'Let's go,' William said to Ella.

After another fifty metres they rounded a bend.

'It's just around here,' Ella said.

'So you keep saying,' William murmured.

When they turned the bend they saw the metal door. There was a soldier standing by it with his back to them, a short rifle held tightly in his hands.

Ella froze.

William immediately raised his PDW towards his target. The soldier turned, but he barely had time to show his surprise when William pulled the trigger. Rapidly, several rounds were fired off. The bullet proof vest the soldier was wearing offered little protection. Blood exploded from the man's chest onto the tunnel walls. The soldier fell back and slumped onto the ground. Approaching cautiously, William checked the soldier. He was dead.

'Is this it?' he asked, nodding to the metal door.

'Yes,' Ella said.

'It's locked, electromagnetically sealed.' William observed. 'Damn it! I don't have any charges to blow it open.'

'I know the code,' Ella said reaching for the panel. She tapped in a four digit number, there was a buzz, and she pulled the door open. 'Voila!'

William raised his finger to his mouth and then indicated for her to stay put. Cautiously, he poked his weapon through the door and slowly edged into the darkness.

The first thing he noticed was the smell. It was an acrid, heavy stench that filled his nostrils. Then, when his eyes adjusted to the gloom, he saw what was causing it.

Bodies. Dozens of them.

Every one, as far as William could make out, was dressed in a white uniform. The uniforms were stained with blood. He turned to stop Ella from entering, but it was too late. She pushed her way in.

'Oh my God,' she gasped and put her free hand to her mouth. 'What happened?'

'They were all shot, by the looks of it, executed.'

'There must a hundred in here at least.'

'It's a blood bath. See how most of them are slumped up against the walls. It looks like some of them tried to run away before they were cut down. A clean up job, silence the witnesses.'

'But Hades said there were five-hundred people down here.'

'Most will have fled, and I doubt we'll find the leaders in here either. This lot probably just knew too much.'

They walked towards the centre of the room. When Ella's eyes focussed she realised what was lying on top of the Altar. She gagged and nearly threw up.

'You okay?' asked William, he placed his hand on her back.

'Let's just do this and get out.'

They approached the altar, careful to step around the bodies as they went. There were pools of dark sticky liquid on the floor, Ella had no doubt to what it was, but tried not to think about it. She covered her mouth and nose with her sleeve.

'Is that Hades?' William asked.

The body was laid out on top of the altar. The face was black with blood and bruising; the white clothing was soaked in blood.

'Yes,' Ella whispered, she tried not to look at it. She moved around to the back where the cupboards were, leaned down and slid the door open. She put the pistol on the floor and began to search through the books and manuscripts.

'Do you know what are you looking for?' William asked, there was tone of impatience in his voice. The smell was overwhelming. He looked across the floor at the faces of the corpses. They all looked relatively young, he thought. He shook his head at the waste.

'No, don't rush me, I'm stressed enough,' Ella snapped, feeling the pressure. 'I'm just checking each one, but I'm hoping it will be obvious though when I see it.'

'Is it a book or a stone tablet?'

'A clay tablet . . . I think . . . I don't know!' She sighed deeply. 'I'm sorry, I just don't know. It could be a book, an annotated copy of the original tablet.'

As she picked each book off the shelf she glanced at its cover, flicked through it quickly, and threw it to the floor. Most of the books were published works, she quickly discarded them. Some were merely a collection of handwritten notes, they were interesting, but not what she was looking for. She worked as quickly as she could, but there was so many to go through.

'Ella, come on, we really don't have all day.'

'I'm doing my best,' she pleaded. A lump caught her in throat. She felt the tears well up, the reality of the situation was getting to her. Forcing herself on, she reached for the next book. It felt different. It was made of wood. She pulled it out and saw that it was actually a box. It was heavier than she had expected. When she opened it, she knew she had found what she was looking for. Inside were three paper notebooks, and under them, wrapped in a leather sleeve, was a clay tablet.

'Got it,' she said, she sighed with relief. She closed the wooden box and stowed it in her rucksack. Grabbing the pistol, she stood up. Her eyes were drawn to the corpse on the altar, she stared wide eyed and swallowed hard.

'Let's get out of here,' William commanded.

Needing no encouragement, Ella turned and headed for the exit. William was about to follow her out but he noticed something else inside the altar. He bent down and reached for it. It was a bottle of whisky, half full, next to it was a single crystal glass. He took out the bottle and read the label, he raised his eyebrows and whistled. He stowed the bottle in the inside of his flak jacket.

'Ella, wait,' he said as he took off again.

But Ella had run ahead and was now close to the exit. The atmosphere of what had become a colossal crypt was too much for her. She felt sick.

William sprinted to catch up. His foot hit something slippery. Laden with his Bergen and his PDW, he lost his balance and fell over onto a body. His weight pushed in the lungs of the victim, and air was expelled through its mouth. For a moment it looked like the cadaver had come alive. He pushed himself off the body, stood up, and ran.

When Ella exited into the corridor she stopped, bent over, and vomited. William watched her as he approached the exit, he was still several metres away. She pushed herself up, but before she was fully erect, a shot rang out. The bang echoed around the chamber. Ella's back arched, her legs gave way. And she fell forward onto the floor.

William raised his weapon and accelerated. But before he reached the exit someone appeared at the door, just a brief shadow, it seemed to throw something, and then the door slammed shut.

'No!' William shouted.

Silence and darkness fell upon the chamber.

Instinctively, William dived to the floor and buried his head in his arms. As he did so the entire room lit up brightly for a brief second, with it there was a huge, deafening blast.

# Sunday

*Hemera Heliou* 'day of the sun'

# Chapter 41

*0002hrs – Hades' Eden*

ELLA OPENED her eyes. She found herself lying face down on the cold corridor floor. There was a searing pain in her left shoulder and a strange taste of metal in her mouth. She started to crawl forward.

'Look what we have here,' someone said from close by. The thick, gruff accent was unmistakably Russian.

Ella froze. From the corner of her eye she could see the man standing by the access control panel at the security door. He tapped rapidly on the keypad, the eerie tones rang out.

'How could someone so small, cause so much damage?' he said. 'You caused all this, didn't you? You killed Hades?'

Ella remained silent.

'Didn't you?' he shouted.

She turned her head to look at him, a sharp pain shot through her shoulder, she winced. He was dressed in an all red uniform with a black belt and black jackboots.

The control panel beeped a solid tone for a second and then went silent. Satisfied that he had changed the access code, Cossack turned and approached Ella. There was a pistol in his hand, he raised it and pointed it at her head. 'You killed him, didn't you? Answer me!' he demanded.

'Yes, I killed that perverted, twisted, bastard,' she said. 'And in a moment I will kill you too.'

Cossack threw his head back and laughed loudly, then leapt down onto Ella and pressed his knee into the small of her back. He grabbed her by the hair, pulled her head back and pushed the end of his pistol into her face. Ella yelped from the shooting pains in her shoulder.

Cossack leaned down and whispered into her ear. 'I'm going to teach you a little lesson. A lesson in the delightful art of pain. Like father, like daughter.'

'You bastard,' she screamed.

Cossack grabbed her face firmly; his hand covered her mouth and nose. He pushed his face against hers, cheek to cheek. He licked her ear and then bit down on it, hard. Ella tried to scream; she writhed and struggled under him.

All the lights went out. This time they stayed out. The alarm stopped ringing. Complete darkness descended on the tunnel. Black and silent.

'Damn it,' Cossack cursed, his words echoed in the gloom.

He released his grip on Ella and sat up straddling her just below her rucksack. He kept one hand on the back of her neck to pin her down.

Ella breathed short, rapid breaths. She struggled and twisted under his weight.

With one hand, Cossack took out his Zippo lighter from his suit. In one swift move he flicked it open and pulled down on the metal wheel. The flint sparked and the flame came to life. A soft, orange glow lit the immediate vicinity.

Cossack frowned. Something didn't make sense. He found himself staring down the barrel of a SIG-Sauer P229. At the end of the weapon was Ella, her head twisted around in an awkward position. Her mouth was screwed up in concentration, her eyes burned with fury.

Cossack flicked the Zippo closed and darkness fell once more.

There was a bright flash and a loud bang that echoed down the tunnels for what seemed like an eternity.

Then there was silence.

Ella felt the pressure on her release. She heard Cossack fall to the floor, but couldn't see him. There was a strange gurgling noise; she pointed the gun in the direction of it. Something hit her arm, hard, and the gun fell out of her hand and scattered on the floor. Frantically, Ella kicked her legs along the ground and pushed herself back towards the wall. Something grunted and scuffled close to her, it sounded like a wounded animal.

From the side was a creaking sound and a thud. A brilliant bright white light exploded into the corridor. A dark figure stood behind it. Like a searchlight the circular beam swept along the floor until it found Ella. She squinted, the light remained on her for a moment, and then it swept the area again. It stopped when it lit up the man on the floor. Cossack was clutching his neck with one bloody hand, a thick stream of blood was jettisoning out from between his fingers. The floor around him was covered in the sticky substance. Cossack, pale faced, lifted his head and looked into the light. His eyes were wide, he mouthed some words but no sound came out. He reached out with his other hand.

A brief but intense blast of bright yellow flame exploded out from the muzzle of the PDW. Then another. And another.

Cossack slumped where he lay, his head fell back, his eyes and mouth open. The blood from his neck stopped jettisoning out. A final slow hiss of breath escaped from his bloodied mouth. And then there was silence.

William rushed over to Ella. 'Are you okay?' he asked. He detached the torch from the rifle and used it to check over her. 'You've been hit. We need to get you out of here.'

'William,' she said looking up at him with watery eyes. 'Calm down. It hurts, but I'm okay.' She reached her good arm up to his cheek and smiled against the pain.

William slid his Bergen off and discarded it. Carefully, he took off Ella's rucksack and threw it over his shoulder. He reattached the torch to the PDW and held out his hand to Ella. She took it and he gently pulled her up. A sharp pain shot through her shoulder, she winced and groaned, but stood.

'Come on, let's go,' he said.

With the torch illuminating their way, they walked slowly through the dark, silent, complex to the main exit.

*

When William and Ella emerged from the shadowy tunnel into the entrance area, they were momentarily blinded by half a dozen torch lights. Paddy and the troopers had been waiting for them. Max sat in an open area outside with his equipment and uploaded the data to the satellite. The place was crawling with Marines who had followed them in by sea and air and taken up defensive positions all around the island. Prisoners were being dealt with. Anyone who tried to escape by boat was quickly intercepted.

'I need medical help here,' William shouted. Ella had her arm loosely around William's neck. Pale and delirious, she could barely keep her head up. Her once white suit was covered in blood.

Paddy and Rupert rushed over with a medical kit. They sat her down against a wall and tended to her. She screamed in pain and drifted in and out of consciousness.

'Stay awake, Ella,' William prompted. 'Stay with us.'

Rupert turned away and spoke into his radio. 'Requesting an immediate med-evac at my location,' he said.

Paddy gave her a shot of morphine. He took out a marker pen and wrote a large M on her forehead, next to it he wrote the time.

'I'm scared,' Ella whispered, her voice was weak and shaky. 'It's cold.'

'You're in good hands. It's going to be okay, trust me.' William

297

smiled to reassure her, but he knew the injury was serious.

While William put pressure on the wound to stop the blood flow, Rupert pulled out a bag of blood substitute solution and pushed the needle into her arm. Gently, he squeezed all of the liquid into her.

Ella moaned, but gradually the morphine kicked in and she settled down. Once the wound was dressed, William fed her some water from his flask. She gulped it down. Tenderly, he cleaned some of the blood off her face and neck with a rolled up bandage.

'It's all over now,' he said calmly to her. 'You made it. You're going to be okay.'

Ella looked up at him with a hazy, drunken grin. She raised her hand to his face. 'No. It's not over,' she said softly.

William frowned.

She glanced briefly at the rucksack on William's back, and then smiled up at him through watery eyes. 'It's only just begun.'

# Epilogue

The moment the Defence Laboratories had received the crucial data from Max, they went to work synthesising the vaccine in mass quantities. Instructions were issued to every factory in every country capable of doing the same synthesis, and thus began the biggest global vaccination programme since the eradication of smallpox in 1979. Concurrently, governments around the globe activated their well practised pandemic emergency plans – vaccination centres sprung up in cities and towns the world over.

The WHO made the prudent decision to be open and honest with the public from the outset. The truth about the infection, and particularly its source, was released to the global media. Within minutes the entire world learned how close they had come to virtual destruction. However, acting under the influence of western governments, the WHO did make one little white lie: they reported that any hard narcotic could have been infected with the virus, not just cocaine. Every drug user was encouraged to hand their hoard in for incineration and proceed immediately to their local vaccination centre.

Drug users and anyone showing the symptoms of a cold or flu were given priority for vaccination. Within a few days enough of the population had been protected to stem the spread of the disease. Having been successfully contained, it was only a matter of time before it was eradicated completely.

Later, it was calculated that the virus had claimed more than five-million souls. Most of the casualties were from the developed nations, a high concentration were from the cities, the economic hubs. The initial victims were the users of the doctored cocaine, then their family, their friends and close colleagues. From there the virus spread like wildfire across the planet.

Once confirmed that the pandemic threat had been eliminated, the world returned to normal. It was business as usual – well, almost. There were some surprising, and notable, absences from the world stage. The entertainment industry had been hit particularly hard, as had many blue chip organisations. City banks and law firms lost swathes of their best and brightest. Inevitably, a global recession ensued. The recovery was slow and had its own casualties.

There was, however, one positive outcome reported by all law enforcement agencies: the global market for hard drugs collapsed virtually overnight. Subsequently, crime rates fell dramatically in every country.

Despite their hard work, F-Branch was never mentioned in any public material relating to the incident. Full credit for the discovery of the virus, and its vaccine, was given to the Defence Laboratories. Colonel Ackers was knighted. Max was promoted.

After a month in hospital, Darren made a full recovery. His knee was rebuilt, but he would never play rugby again.

The truth of what had happened was soon lost amongst the ubiquitous conspiracy theories. Some said that it was a deliberate act by a western government to collapse the drugs trade. Others claimed it was a plague sent by God to punish a corrupted world that had forgotten its place. But others knew better. A few knew the truth.

*

*Six months later – Central London*
SAT BY THE WINDOW of his new office, William turned and gazed out onto the snow covered road beyond. A haze of brilliant white snowflakes, illuminated by the street lights, danced randomly in the wind as they fell.

He glanced at his watch; it was getting late. Ever since Ella had gone he had stayed later and later at work each night. There was little else for him to do, and it took his mind off things. He opened his drawer and took out a quarter-full bottle of whisky and a small glass. Gently, he worked the cork out and poured a modest amount of the yellow liquid. He swilled the glass around and brought the rare malt to his nose. Inhaling deeply, he shut his eyes and enjoyed the sweet aroma.

'To life and love,' he said, and took a sip. He let the liquid settle in his mouth, allowing him to enjoy the multitude of flavours and sensations before he swallowed it down.

Getting back to work, he took out his tablet computer from his drawer, and opened the IMS secure document store. There was a case file named *Operation Greek Fire*, he pressed on the icon and the document opened. Emblazoned in large red letters on the first page were the words "Top Secret – Orion". He flicked through the pages until he found the small photographs. There were eleven people that he had come to recognise like old friends – faces that he had first seen on the walls of Ella's father's study all those months ago. Just as he had thought, none of the cult leaders, other than Hades, had perished on the island. They had vanished as if they had never existed at all. He zoomed in on one image and smiled. He knew he'd met the attractive woman face to face in the tunnel all those months ago. A lifetime ago, it seemed. He looked up from the screen and contemplated the memories.

His mobile phone rang; he looked at the caller name and answered. 'Hello gorgeous,' he said with a smile. 'Nice of you to keep in touch.'

'William, I've found it,' Ella said excitedly. 'I really think I've found it this time.'

'Calm down. Where are you? You sound distant.'

'I'm in Baghdad. You need to come, there's no time to waste.'

'Baghdad? What the hell are you doing there? I thought you were in Cairo?'

'I was, but I've found something. William, it's amazing. It's wonderful.'

'What is it?'

'The first marker – the first clue on the road that leads to Atlantis.'

William winced when she spoke that word. 'Ella,' he said calmly, 'be careful of what you say. Remember what we talked about?'

'Trust me, I've been very careful,' she assured. 'No one knows why I'm here or what I'm really looking for.'

William wasn't so sure, but he held his tongue.

'Please come,' she asked desperately. 'I need you here.'

Taking a deep breath, William spun his chair around and looked out of the window. He rolled his head back, shut his eyes and breathed out slowly.

'William?' Ella prompted. 'Please, for me?'

'Okay, okay,' he said, shaking his head. 'I'll come.'

'Yes,' Ella squealed. 'I love you.'

'Love you too,' he said gently.

He finished the glass of whisky, put his coat on, and walked out into the cold.

## The End
\* \* \*

9084354R00181

Printed in Great Britain
by Amazon.co.uk, Ltd.,
Marston Gate.